"EA Luetkemeyer has accomplished in a single novel what most authors would need volumes to articulate. *Inside the Mind of Martin Mueller* is a trip worth the psychological toll to pass through the misadventures of the mind.

—Zach Hudson, *How Dare You Zine*

"a first rate literary novel...the prose is exquisitely good...*Inside the Mind of Martin Mueller* entertains enormously."

—*Reader's Favorite*, 5-star review

"A short wild ride of a novella...it is impossible not to liken this tale to a modern-day *Siddhartha*."

—Sage Kalmus, *Free Will Flux*

"a darkly, well written tale...at the end you are left still wondering where the truth really lies."

—Arthur W. Scholbe, *Uncle Strangely Presents*

"a mind-bending novella...A brilliantly conceived journey into the darkest corners of the human mind...a luminous, far-fetched, existential mind-trip with a freaky twist ending"

—*Online Book Club*

I0588990

PRAISE FOR *PENITENTIARY TALES: A LOVE STORY*

"an insightful and at times darkly disturbing glimpse into an institution rarely entered by most readers...compelling and realistic...filled with vivid character descriptions...[*Penitentiary Tales: a Love Story*] is a fictionalized account of a pivotal period in the life of the author... through his wit, insight, athletic prowess, bravado, and luck, [protagonist Dean Davis] is able to navigate successfully between racial gangs, the administration, the guards, and otherwise dangerous individuals in order to survive and to thrive...Much like Erving Goffman's portrayal of total institutions...[Luetkemeyer] reveals a common theme among inmates, and one that I discovered in my own prison research: all incarcerated individuals (and perhaps all of us) operate behind...protective masks, preserving a part of one's self-identity only for one's closest intimates"

—Dr. John M. Coggeshall, Clemson University

"Bold prison tales...from the perspective of a white drug dealer serving time in a state penitentiary...with an emphasis on the eccentricities of other inmates...[Luetkemeyer's] self-assured visceral approach...is unflinchingly abrasive when capturing the realities of prison...readers will appreciate the testosterone-fueled language"

—*Kirkus Reviews*

"a work of literary fiction...set in an Illinois prison filled with... [racially diverse] inmates from the difficult and dangerous streets of Chicago...an intriguing and committed character study which effectively explores the social and political consciousness of the current class and racial divides in modern-day America...nuanced and personal...contains graphic depictions of violence, sex, and distressing situations, and...explicit language appropriate to its context... the scenes we move through...stick in the mind and the social conscience of the reader long after the scene is through...a well written and poignant dramatic novel which comes highly recommended."

—K.C. Finn, *Fallow Heart*

"Dean Davis...came from an affluent family and had his life under control...[until] he is sentenced to prison in Illinois [and] will now have to fight every day of his sentence...packed with emotions, drama and the struggle of a man who...learned about life in the hardest way possible...the reader [will] experience what Dean was going through...an amazing job at writing an impactful story."

—*Readers' Favorite*, 5-Star Review

"*Penitentiary Tales: a Love Story*...is a cross-examination of social inequalities in race and gender...Dean Davis, an educated white male [is] doing time for dealing marijuana...How a highly literate convict manages to survive makes for a brilliant depiction of how the human spirit can triumph under the most adverse conditions...Luetkemeyer [demonstrates] that love can spring forth...in a setting that hardens criminals but softens our hearts to miracles."

—Vincent Dublado, *The Weed and the Rose*

PRAISE FOR *INSIDE THE MIND OF MARTIN MUELLER*

"EA Luetkemeyer has created a fascinating conceptual novel which has to be read to be believed. Martin is an intriguing example of how the human mind works under incredible conditions of stress, pressure and personal demons, and the results of his 'work' are truly astounding."   —K.C. Finn, *Fallow Heart*

"a very detailed, intricate and erudite piece of writing...recommended for those who love a challenge when they read and who enjoy a puzzle...a literary Rubik's cube for enquiring minds."

—Viga Boland, *No Tears For My Father*

"Luetkemeyer's dreamlike tale follows a prison inmate as he thoroughly examines the nature of existence...[He] packs an impressive amount of content in a concise narrative...An eccentric but extraordinary story...a sense of surreality reigns"

—*Kirkus Reviews*

Penitentiary
Tales

Also by EA Luetkemeyer

Inside the Mind of Martin Mueller
A Novel

The Book of Chuck
A Memoir

Penitentiary Tales

A Love Story

EA Luetkemeyer

Laughing Buddha Books
Jacksonville, Oregon

Illustrations and cover art by the author

Published by Laughing Buddha Books
Jacksonville, Oregon
www.ealuetkemeyer.com

ISBN: 978-0-578-58122-4

Book designed and produced by
Lucky Valley Press
Jacksonville, Oregon
www.luckyvalleypress.com

Printed in the United States of America on acid-free paper that meets the Sustainable Forestry Initiative® Chain-of-Custody Standards.
www.sfiprogram.org

To my loving wife, Leslie, who did her time on the other side, and to Omar, Alias Abdul, who will get it the most.

A SHOUT OUT TO THE MANY good people without whose contribution *Penitentiary Tales: A Love Story* would not have come to light. It is a long list. If your name is not on it, it is written in my heart: Laurie Foos for her incisive editorial comments. Tony Eprile, Rachel Kadish, A.J. Verdelle and Laurie Foos of Lesley University for their uncompromising instruction in the art and craft of writing. Michael Lowenthal, and Anthropologist John M. Coggeshall of Clemson University, for their scrutiny of *The Gump Report*. Doug Hobbie, whose enthusiasm for fiction long ago kindled my own. Art Scholbe, Harry Loy, Leroi Moodey, Joanna Grabarek, Stephanie Triller Fry, Sarah Kilgallon, and Jennifer Top of Tulip Tree Press, for their early reading of the manuscript. The late actor, Michael Clarke Duncan, for the influence his warm and generous personality had on the characterization of Mother Goose. Malcolm X and Minister Louis Farrakhan for the role their fiery rhetoric played in the creation of the White Devil Speech. Omar, alias Abdul, whose world view influenced my own, and whose work inspired *Nation of the Damned*. Bill Broda for the special effects and the VHS. Warden Allan Wisely, for his earnestness and good intentions. Ginna and David Gordon of Lucky Valley Press for their encouragement, kind words, boundless creativity, and for assembling *a beautiful book!* And, as always, eternal gratitude to my children and their children for being in my life. High fives and knuckle bumps all around.

~ EA Luetkemeyer

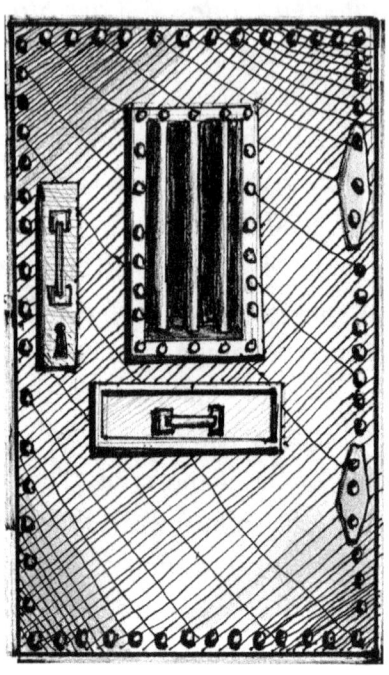

All my major works have been written in prison. I would recommend prison not only to aspiring writers but to aspiring politicians, too.

~ Jawaharlal Nehru

BOOK I

DESCENT

One mustn't look at the abyss, because there is at the bottom an inexpressible charm which attracts us.

~ Gustave Flaubert

LA PETITE MAISON

COMPLICATIONS

IN THE EVENING of the last day my name was Danté Allegro, I watched my wife Lucy pace the floor of the cozy cottage we rented in the upscale community of Sausalito, California. She stepped over a stack of framed pictures yet to be wrapped in newspaper, around boxes yet to be filled, and kicked a wide roll of packing tape across the polished hardwood floor of the living room, where it careened off a box, bounced off the stone fireplace and bumped against the carved dark teakwood bar where I sat with a snifter of brandy in my hand.

I hate this, she said. I don't know what I'm doing. Why am I doing this?

Yes, why are you? I said. The movers will finish the job.

It's my stuff, she said. Our stuff. I won't see it for five years. I want to see it one last time.

She looked around the room.

I like this house, she said wistfully. I wish it was ours.

It's been a good house, I agreed.

I dreamt last night that we had another baby, a boy named Bertrand.

Bertrand! Where did that come from?

It was a dream. We called him Bertie. We lived here, you and I and Lola and Bertie. Lola said to me, Mommy, why do you call my baby brother a birdie? I said, Because, honey, one day he'll have wings and be able to fly. And Lola said, Mommy, will I have wings, too?

That's a nice dream, Lucy, I said. We'll make it come true. There'll be another house one day. And another baby, too. Together they'll soar to the sky.

With my free hand, I fluttered my fingers like a pair of birds aloft.

Lucy shouted, I'll be too old for another baby!

Thirty five is not too old, I said.

It's old! she exclaimed. Her lower lip quivered.

Relax, Lucy, I said. Roll yourself a joint.

Relax? How can I relax? Are you relaxed?

Getting there, I said, refilling my snifter from the bottle on the bar. I sensed the anger and frustration in her voice, that she wanted to blame me for the turn her life was taking, but could only blame herself. I hadn't misled her. I had told her what to expect.

Please don't get wasted tonight, Dean, she said. I'm going to need you.

I'll go slow, I said. I'll be fine.

He's having a mid-life crisis.

He's sixty. He's having a three-quarter life crisis.

Jesus! Sports cars! Weekends in Vegas! Betting on horses! He shouldn't have retired. He has too much time on his hands. He's going to go broke.

He'll be all right, I said.

I didn't share Lucy's misgivings about her father's radical makeover. When you reach a point in life where you realize you can no longer be who you are, you find another someone to be. I was flattered Wally admired what he thought of as my freewheeling entrepreneurial style. He'd come out of the now-defunct Sacramento College of Pharmacology thirty five years ago and opened Fuller Pharmacy here in Sausalito and had done well for himself until it went belly up a few years back, unable to compete with the big chains moving in. He retired and not a day too soon. He'd become a parody of himself: predictable and unimaginative. Now he was free to grow out of his old inflexible shell and spread his wings. No more Wally the Wallflower for me! he'd confided once. Now I can be like Danté!

He would soon learn that being like Danté came with a price.

I popped a cassette into the player on the mantel above the fireplace. Soon my head bobbed to the beat of Sinatra's *My Kind of Town*. Lucy sat on the black leather couch opposite the bar, opened the silver box on the coffee table and pulled out a bag of pot and a pack of rolling papers.

And don't let him get too drunk, either, she said. He won't remember what we've told him.

I thought it ironic that Lucy would not want Wally to get too drunk, considering we were presenting him with a bottle of fifty-year-old scotch this night as a farewell present. But I chose not to contradict her because she loved her father and he loved his scotch and they would be apart for a long, long time.

It's not something he's liable to forget, I said.

He won't believe it, she said, rolling the joint neat and tight between thumbs and fingertips. He loves saying, Yo, Danté! He'll never get used to saying, Yo, Dean!

He can still call me Danté if he wants.

He's going to be crushed. We're all he has since mom died. She was a pain-in-the-ass drunk but he loved her.

You sure you don't want me to be the one to tell him?

I'm his daughter.

And I'm the asshole who's taking you away.

This is fucked! If only we could …

Her voice trailed away. There was nothing else to be done. We had considered all options. Taking her and Lola to Mexico would have made a bad thing worse. I'd have been there already, drinking tequila and planning my next move, but they deserved a better life. Lucy's walk on the wild side, and the romance of being the outlaw's wife, had run its course. And now there was Lola. Surrendering was the only way, and it would be hard. Harder on her than on me. I was less anxious about the next five years of my life than the years after them, when I risked becoming what I had successfully avoided being all my life: a tax-paying Citizen of the Empire; a pigeon, a patsy, a fool. The five years ahead loomed as a perilous adventure, an extension of my outlaw days. When I pondered the years to follow, I saw a grey mist.

I watched the tip of her tongue trace a line of wetness down the rolling paper's gummed edge. She pinched the ends of the joint and put it between her lips and struck a match. I loved those lips, the fine line of them, pink and soft as the petals of a rose. I watched her inhale. She wore an embroidered cotton peasant blouse with puffed sleeves and a plunging neckline. It was winter and she had carried Lola through the summer and gotten no sun and her flesh showed white against the deep magenta of her blouse. She took another hit. I watched her bosom heave. I put down my snifter and left my stool and walked behind her. The back of the couch pressed against my thighs. I leaned over and slid my hands down the front of her blouse. I cupped her breasts, felt the warmth and the weight of them.

Let me tell him, I said. It's my story to tell.

All right, she said. You're the storyteller in the family.

She directed the joint up and over her shoulder to my lips. I inhaled and held the smoke and while she took another toke I squeezed gently.

She closed her eyes and her breath quickened. I exhaled. The smoke curled between strands of her hair. I touched my lips to her ear and whispered: We'll be all right.

Her shoulders quaked.

Lucy, I said, are you crying?

She pushed my hands away. She dabbed at her eyes and examined the trace of mascara on her fingertips.

I have to clean up, she said. I can't let him see me like this.

She stood abruptly, crossed the living room and bounded up the stairs.

I returned to the bar and my brandy. Sinatra declared: That's life and I can't deny it. I was thinking there was nothing left to do but let events run their course when I heard the crash and the racket out back. I got up to investigate. I passed through the kitchen to the back door, grabbing a knife off the counter on the way to the deck outside. I turned on the porch light and opened the door slowly and took a peek. On the far side of the deck the trash container had been upended. Snuffling through its strewn contents was a family of raccoons, oblivious to the light and my presence. I stomped on the deck.

Yo! Rocky! I shouted. Hit the road and take your wife and kid with you!

The larger of the raccoons turned its head and regarded me with a baleful stare. It uttered a grunt which seemed to be a command because the other two turned and in unison all three rose up on their hindquarters and stood shoulder to shoulder, a small dark mountain of teeth and claws and fur, and hissed deep in their throats.

Never mind, guys, I said. Just kidding. Enjoy. Can I get you something to drink?

I stepped backwards into the kitchen. The raccoons resumed their picnic on the porch, and I resumed my perch at the bar.

WALLY SAT AT THE BAR NEXT TO ME with a drink in his hand. Lucy returned with a fresh new face.

Don't get up, Dad, she said as she crossed the room, but he did get up and put his hands on her shoulders and kissed her on the cheek. They were of the same height, she a little taller than average, he a little shorter. She stepped back and looked him over.

Wow, Dad, what is this?

What is what? he asked.

Your outfit, she said, indicating his attire with a sweep of her hand.

He looked down at his ensemble: a three-piece camel-colored suit with padded shoulders; a pale blue cotton shirt with white collar; a yellow silk, brown-dotted tie and a scarlet handkerchief protruding from his breast pocket.

I mean, Dad, you look … you look—

Like what? he said.

I know, I said, snapping my fingers. Like Gay Talese on the boardwalk in Ocean City, New Jersey.

The name sounds familiar, Wally said.

Honor Thy Father. Thy Neighbor's Wife. I was on the boardwalk in Ocean City one day and I saw this dapper little man, salt and pepper hair parted on the side like yours, combed across his head, a tight-lipped smile. He's wearing the very outfit you're wearing now, Wally, down to the handkerchief in the pocket, and he's having his picture taken with a big camera on a tripod and a reflective umbrella to the side. I remember thinking, This guy is somebody. Then one day I'm leafing through Esquire and I'll be dammed, there's the picture I saw being taken, and an interview with Gay Talese.

Well, Wally said, I could do worse than look like a famous writer.

Have you been getting ideas from Esquire, Wally?

No, but he obviously has a good taste in clothes.

It's not you, Dad, Lucy said. Your style is more, you know—

What? Dreary? Uninspired?

Well ... conservative.

That was the old Wally. This is the new—move over Gay Talese!

My dad! Lucy said. What's next? A love shack where he takes young girls?

Who told you about my love shack, Lucy?

Dirty old man, she said.

She kissed her father quickly on the cheek. She was being gay, effusive, but I noticed the anxiety in her voice, and had Wally's perception not been muted by a double scotch, he might have noticed, too.

I'm starving, Lucy said. Let's get this show on the road.

Aren't we taking Lola?

We have a sitter.

I want to see her before we go. I want to see her face.

She's sleeping, Dad. You can see her tonight.

LA PETITE MAISON SAT ON A QUIET STREET in Tiburon, a few miles from Sausalito, where the commercial district met the residential. A house in the colonial style, painted white with black trim, only the side lawn converted into parking spaces and the slim sign hanging beneath the gas-light on the walk suggested it was anything more than a residence.

The dining area was three small rooms of exposed brick and beam. Old china lined the rafters. The carpeting was a delicate floral pattern in warm hues of lilac, peach and magenta. White linen draped the tables. In the center of each, a single rose in a slender crystal vase. The lighting was soft. An Edith Piaf melody wafted from hidden speakers.

We were shown to the smallest of the rooms. Old books, spines peeling, lined rough-hewn dark wooden shelves. A fireplace crackled and popped.

It's so cozy, Lucy said

French Provincial, Wally said. He looked at me.

It's nice, I said. It has an Old Country feel.

The owner, André, was the maître d' at Alouette's in Sonoma, Wally said. His father knew my father. If I didn't know André from way back we wouldn't have gotten a table on such short notice.

And why have you never brought me here, Dad?

I have, we have, your mother and I, when you were young. The waiter brought you crayons and paper and you drew barnyard animals: cows and chickens and pigs.

Our waiter came round and introduced himself. A slim, smiling mustachioed man in short waistcoat, Michael's speech was pleasant and vaguely accented. He gave the wine list to Wally, passed out menus, and informed us that the *plat du jour* was ragout of sweetbreads with baby vegetables, and the *spécialité de la maison* was poached chicken breast Alouette with tarragon and dill. Or he could recommend the braised rabbit with honey and mustard, thyme and bacon. But no, no, there was nothing he could not recommend; all would delight; nothing would disappoint! But do take your time, he said. At La Petite Maison we live in the moment. We savor and enjoy!

I felt for Lucy. Her time had run out. She would freeze it if she could, to savor and enjoy the moment forever. As though reading my mind, she looked at me and said, You look nice tonight.

I had put myself together this evening a little more carefully than usual. I wore my favorite faded levis and my Tony Lama boots, and a beige sport coat over a pale blue cotton shirt with pink mother of pearl buttons. I had even switched out my gold hoop earring for the filigreed silver one I'd found at a Tibetan curio shop on Telegraph Avenue in Berkeley. It matched the turquoise and silver Zuni belt buckle I'd salvaged from my failed Native American Jewelry shop in Santa Fe, New Mexico. My moustache was trimmed and my hair was shiny. I wanted her to remember me at my best.

Thanks, Lucy, I said.

She looked from me to Wally.

My two boys, she said.

Her smile was brave.

Michael took our drink orders: scotch on the rocks for Wally, a dry white Dubonnet for me.

I'll wait for wine, Lucy said.

Wally handed me the wine list. I put it down.

We should know what we're eating first, I said.

I picked up my menu. Lucy glanced at hers.

The specialty sounds good to me, she said with feigned enthusiasm.

I think that will pair nicely with a white burgundy, I said. And I'll have the turbot. Wally, what looks good to you?

I think I'll have French Onion soup and Dover Sole, he said.

He put his menu down. Lucy shook her head in dismay.

Dad, you order Dover Sole everywhere you go. How boring. I thought you were stepping out. Try something adventurous.

Such as?

The Ragout Of Sweetbreads.

Sweetbreads! Aren't those like pig nuts or something?

You're thinking of Rocky Mountain Oysters, I said. Sweetbreads are the meat of the thymus gland or the pancreas.

Oh, that's appetizing. What are you having, Danté? Turbot? I'll have turbot, too. I'll save adventure for my love shack.

Funny, Dad, Lucy said.

I read from the wine list: Crue Vineyard Montrachet. The Stradivarius of white burgundy, selected personally by owner Andre Arseneau, cousin to fabled vigneron Pierre Ramonet. Full-bodied and scented, dry yet succulent, its opulent bouquet suggestive of peaches, apple blossoms, cinnamon, greengages, nuts, and yellow roses.

What do you think, Wally? I said.

You decide, Danté. You're the connoisseur.

I closed the wine list.

No, Wally, I fake it, I said with a faint sigh. I'm a phony connoisseur and a phony entrepreneur, too.

Lucy gave me a look that said: Not now, Dean. Let's enjoy our supper. Let's tell him after. At home. Please.

Why do you say that, Danté? Wally said. You seem to have done all right for yourself.

I smiled thinly.

I suppose I have, Wally. Sure I have.

Wally frowned.

You seemed troubled, you two, he said. Is there something I should know about other than this bonehead move to Chicago?

Lucy and I gave each other a glance.

Just the usual stress over a move, Wally, I said. Everything's fine.

Well, it's not fine by me—

Michael came and took our order. He complimented our choices and went away.

Danté, maybe it's none of my business, Wally said, but a blues club in Chicago? Why not open a blues club in San Francisco?

Does San Francisco need another blues club? I said.

Does Chicago?

It's not just another blues club, Wally. It's a landmark and I love it. BB King has played there. And Bobby Blue Bland. And Muddy Waters. But there's a cash flow problem. I think my partner is cooking the books. I have to watch him and I can't do that part-time and long-distance.

Sounds dangerous, Wally started, then trailed off, catching one's partner cooking the books at a blues club in Chicago being outside his realm of experience. As it was outside of mine. I shook my head and laughed as though at a private joke.

Why are you laughing, Danté?

It's complicated, Wally.

Make it simple. Sell the club. I'm sure Bobby and BB and Muddy Blue Waters can manage without you. Settle here. It's sunny. Do you really want to raise your baby in Chicago?

It was good enough for me.

Sausalito is a great place to raise a kid.

I like the bright lights of the big city.

We have San Francisco across the Bay.

It's not the same.

Buy the cottage, Danté. Lucy loves it.

Too late for that, Wally, I said. The cottage has been sold. We move out. They move in.

Buy another one, then, dammit! I want to watch Lola grow into a beautiful young lady. Why can't I have that?

I was moved by Wally's appeal. Lucy looked at me as though it was possible to comply.

Don't think I haven't considered it, Wally, I said, but as I say, there are complications.

Complications! Tell me about it. I've dealt with my share of complications.

I looked at Lucy. Her eyes said, Please wait.

I can appreciate that, Wally, I said. You've got a few decades on me. I'll tell you what—let's enjoy our dinner and make small talk and save the serious conversation for later. Back at the house we'll have another drink and I'll share some information with you that will make it all make sense.

Wally looked at me for a long moment.

Fair enough, Danté, he said. I await your revelation.

Michael brought the wine and filled our glasses. We held them aloft.

To complications! Wally said.

To revelations! I said.

There followed a pleasant meal laced with light-hearted banter facilitated by a second bottle of Burgundy, and tales of my youth on the mean streets of Chicago, where I had never been. Even Lucy seemed to enjoy them, though she knew better. Sometimes all you can do is be here now.

DANTÉ'S INFERNO

BACK AT THE COTTAGE I BUILT A FIRE. The sitter had taken her leave, followed out the door by the appraising gaze of Wally, to whom Lucy had presented his gift bottle of fifty-year-old scotch in a purple velvet drawstring pouch with a gold label reading Chivas Regal. He drank from a tumbler of it now as he slouched on the couch nearing three sheets to the wind, awaiting the information that would make it all make sense. Lucy sat at the other end of the couch, Lola on her lap, babbling and cooing. I sat at the bar sipping brandy, wondering where to begin. I took a deep breath.

Wally, I said brightly, I want you to meet my wife: Mrs. Dean Davis.

I looked to Lucy for approval. She shrugged as if to say, You have to begin somewhere. She looked at Wally, who frowned and looked at me.

But you're married to my daughter, he said. To Lucy.

Yes, I said. Lucy Davis. My wife.

Wally shook his head.

I don't understand, Danté.

The name's not Danté, Wally. It's Dean. Dean Davis. Danté is dead. He died shortly after he was born. I took his name.

Wally looked confused. I realized the unfairness of being obtuse. I had to play it straight. I came down off my stool and sat in the armchair near the couch, which put me on the same level as Wally. I leaned forward with my elbows on my knees and looked him in the eyes.

Here's the story, Wally. I wasn't born in Chicago. I was born in Oakland. We moved to Marin County when I was six years old. I've been here ever since. I went to San Francisco State. I dealt marijuana up and down the coast. I made a lot of money. I opened a market in the Midwest and made even more, but I was busted. I fought my case for as long as I could, but I lost, and was given ten years in an Illinois State Prison. While out on appeal I created an alias, Danté Allegro. I married Lucy. I created an alias for her, too, Mrs. Danté Allegro. The plan was, if I lost my appeal we'd go to Mexico, but we had Lola and changed our minds. I lost the appeal and was given two weeks to get my affairs in order. In thirty-six hours, Wally, in the company of my attorney, I surrender to a County Sheriff in Southern Illinois and my new landlord will be the Department of Corrections.

I leaned back in my chair and looked at Lucy. She pursed her lips. The truth was on the table. She looked at her father, who blinked like a flash of light had gone off in his face.

You ... you're going to prison?

Yes.

For ten years?

Five with good time.

For marijuana?

It was a lot of marijuana. The Judge thought so, anyway.

Wally frowned.

How could I have not suspected something? he said.

I'm pretty good at being someone other than who I really am, I said.

He looked at Lucy.

Did you know?

He told me shortly after we met.

And you stayed with him?

I love him.

Why didn't you tell me? Wally said, a trace of pique but no accusation in his voice.

How could I, Dad?

He leaned forward and filled his glass from the bottle on the table and drank half of it down.

Well, he said, that's ... one hell of a complication.

He stared at his drink. I steeled myself against the expected recriminations and accusations of betrayal, but Wally only said, So ... you're not Italian?

No, I said. English, Irish, German and whatever else. Some Gypsy maybe.

And you're not from Chicago?

Never been there.

And there is no blues club? No partner cooking the books?

No.

And you didn't have a gallery in Greenwich Village and a turquoise business in Santa Fe?

I did, but I only ever made any money dealing dope.

What about your family? Are they here?

My father died a few years ago. I have a brother, Brodie. He teaches poetry at San Francisco State. He and Lucy are friends. My mother is … is in a facility for the chronically confused.

I don't know what that is, Wally said.

A private hospital in Napa, I said, touching my fingertip to my temple.

I see, Wally said. Well, I don't.

She thinks she's a Gypsy, I said.

Wally became quiet. He seemed to be searching inward for the best next question.

Where will Lucy stay? he said.

We have a furnished rental near the County Jail, I said. When I'm permanently assigned, I'll call and tell her where I am. She'll move to the nearest town. She'll visit once a week and I'll watch Lola grow up in one-hour increments.

Wally sighed.

This is horrible, he said.

There are worse fates, I said.

You seem resigned, he said.

Resigned and resolute, I said, but I knew I was only speaking for myself, that Lucy remained apprehensive—about my safety, my state of mind, our future together.

I suppose it's the only way to be, Wally said. What will you do when you get out—assuming you make it out?

Don't be bleak, Dad! Lucy said. Of course he'll make it out.

I don't know, I said. I'll have plenty of time to think about it.

This is all too much to bear, Wally said.

He looked away. His lips moved silently. He looked at me and raised his glass and smiled a wry smile.

To a fellow drug dealer! he said.

How's that, Wally?

Fuller Pharmacy!

Right, I said.

I clicked his glass with mine, pleased at his brave attempt at levity.

Do you have any here now? he said.

Any what, Wally?

Marijuana.

I hesitated. I looked at Lucy.

I want to smoke some, Wally said with a petulant air. I want to get high!

Jesus, Dad, Lucy said. You're three sheets to the wind already.

Well, I wanna be four sheets. Wanna be Wasted Wally! No more Fuddy Duddy Fuller for me!

She rolled her eyes. She carried Lola upstairs and put her in her crib and returned and rolled a joint. Soon, Wally's head listed to one side. His eyes were at half-mast.

You kids are doing the right thing, he said with a voice thick with sentiment and booze. Getting your life right. I should do the shame. Shtop drinking. She drank her shelf to deaf ...

He looked from Lucy to me.

I'll try to shtay alive until you kids come home, he said.

Dad, you'll be alive in five years! Lucy said. Don't say things like that!

Wally patted me on the shoulder. His chin puckered.

You're a good boy, Danté! And a good father and hushband.

Yes, he's good, Dad, Lucy said. But he's Dean now. There is no more Danté.

Wally cupped a hand to the side of his mouth. He yelled across the room.

Yo! Dean!

He shook his head.

It's not the same, he said.

I stood suddenly.

Let's have a ceremony! I said.

I bounded up the stairs and returned with a manila envelope. I sat on the hearth and put another log on the fire.

Sit here, I said. We'll have an execution. Danté will die again. We'll burn him alive.

Lucy removed the afghan from the back of the couch and put it on the floor in front of the fire. She and Wally sat. I opened the manila envelope and pulled out three passports and handed them to Wally. He opened them one by one and looked at the photos of Mr. and Mrs. Danté Allegro and daughter, Lola.

Throw them on the fire, Wally, I said.

Wally hesitated. He tossed the documents into the fire. We watched the faces of Danté and Lucy and Lola bubble and crack and burst into blue flame. I felt an unexpected sadness at this fiery annihilation of my alter ego. I'd grown fond of Danté. We'd had some fine times together. Perhaps I'd find an occasion to resurrect him one day. I didn't imagine that Lucy felt the same; the demise of Danté meant the resurrection of Dean. Wally hunched over and sobbed. Lucy rubbed his back.

They're not real people, she said.

You're all I have, he said. Wum I shuppose a do now? I'm jush a shad shack of a oh man. Jush a oh fuddy duddy.

He slumped forward and became still.

Help me get him to the couch, Lucy said.

We each took an arm and hoisted him up. He remained bent over like a child hugging a beach ball. We walked him to the couch, where he collapsed and folded up like a fetus. Lucy covered him with the afghan. I propped his head on a couch pillow. We stood over him and listened to his gentle snore. With his tuft of wispy hair, and his thin lips open slightly and extended like a beak, he looked like a baby bird just fallen from a tree. I put my arm around Lucy. She put her arm around my waist.

Are you thinking what I'm thinking? she said.

I'm thinking he needs you more than I do, I said.

Yes, Lucy said.

Come to Illinois till I'm permanently assigned, I said. Visit once, then go home.

Home? The cottage is sold.

Stay with Brodie till you find a place. Take care of your poppa. Take care of Lola. Fly out twice a year. I'll be fine.

I'll come out more often.

Save your money, I said. You'll need it.

She wiped away a tear.

Alright, she said.

Dance with me, Lucy, I said.

I put a tape in the player. Johnny Mathis promised that someday there'd be a time for us. When chains were torn by courage, born of a love that's free. I took her in my arms. She put her head on my shoulder. We moved slowly in the glow of the fire.

Thanks for not getting too wasted tonight, she said.

I wanted to, I said.

Don't let prison change you, she said. Be the same Dean when you come home that you are right now. The man I know and love.

I'll be a ship in the night, I said. Just passing through. When I walk out those gates in five years it will be as though I had never been there.

I spoke these words with all the assuredness I could muster, but I doubted they were true. I kissed her on the lips.

Take me to bed, she said.

I led her upstairs. We stood over Lola's crib.

Take good care of our little girl, I said.

Whatever Lola wants, Lola gets.

You don't want to spoil her.

Yes, I do, she said.

All right, I said.

We made love tenderly. She fell asleep. I went downstairs and filled my snifter and rolled a joint and went out to the deck. Overhead, dark clouds scurried past a full yellow moon. I took another toke off the joint. A space opened in my head. The clouds shaped themselves into a perfect eye, the moon its mystic iris. The eye of God, I thought. The Universe watches and waits.

I know you're up there, Miranda, I said. I'll see you when I see you.

She would make her appearance when it pleased her. She was that kind of muse: arbitrary and capricious.

I stepped to the edge of the deck and relieved myself into the bushes. I liked to piss outside, the old penis pent up in the pants all day. It felt like freedom. I didn't imagine I'd have the opportunity to piss outside for a while.

I went inside and turned off the lights. The dying embers in the fireplace cast a soft orange glow about the room. It's been a good house, I thought. A very good house. I finished my drink, savoring the last drop, and went to bed.

COUNTY JAIL

A BOGIE FAREWELL

WE BADE OUR TEARFUL GOODBYES in the snow-packed parking lot of my attorney's office in the Mississippi River town of Alton, Illinois. More precisely, she bade a tearful goodbye. Mine was more the cavalier Humphrey Bogart, Here's looking at you, kid, variety of farewell. What purpose would be served burdening Lucy with my apprehensions? She'd have hardship enough making a life for herself and the baby without me. It was going to be a long five years and I had to walk through those big iron gates alone, dry-eyed and determined.

We're doing the right thing, I assured her. Your father needs you. And you've got to have a life. You wouldn't have one in this burg and the winters are a bitch.

I can't stand thinking of you all alone.

I put my hand over my heart.

I won't be alone, I said. You'll be right here.

Lola will be almost six, she said. She won't know you.

She'll know me. Keep saying, Daddy loves you, Lola. Daddy loves you.

I will.

Let me hold her, I said.

She handed me the baby, bundled against the biting cold. Her cheeks and the tip of her nose were red, but her eyes were round and bright and looked into mine.

Daddy loves you, Lola, I said.

I kissed her on the nose and the forehead and the lips and handed the bundle back. I felt torn between two worlds. I wanted this moment to be over. I wanted the next phase of my life to begin. I looked over my shoulder at the door to my lawyer's office.

I've got to go, I said.

Lucy caught her breath. I put my hands on her shoulders.

One of us has to turn around and walk away, I said.

I don't want to watch you walk away, she said. I'll go first.

I don't want to watch you walk away, either, I said. Let's turn around and walk away at the same time.

Alright, she said, and don't look back.

I won't, I said. Ok, on three: one … two …

Wait, she said, one more kiss!

We kissed and I held her and Lola.

Please don't let it change you, Dean.

I'll be the invisible man, I said. Out of sight, out of mind. Now turn around, walk away, and don't look back.

We each turned around. I walked twenty feet and up three steps to the threshold of my attorney's office.

I put my hand on the doorknob.

I turned around.

She had turned around, too. The hell with Humphrey Bogart! I thought. I ran down the steps to Lucy and Lola and she ran to meet me and we embraced for the last time in a very long time.

BLACKENED CATFISH

THE OFFICES OF WEINSTEIN, SCHORR and McDonald hadn't changed since I had last been in them, two years ago, when the appeal process began and I disappeared to create a new identity. She was new, though, the fine young receptionist in the short tight skirt and shiny silk blouse who announced with a sugary lilt: Mr. McDonald will see you now. May I show you to his office?

Yes, please, I said.

It gave me the opportunity to walk behind her and appreciate the slope and sway of her hips.

Fat Mac McDonald sat like a toad behind the sprawling antique mahogany library table that served for a desk. Not bad for a poor Mick from Chicago, he had said the first time he sat me down three years ago in the plush green leather armchair across from him. He had surveyed the room for my benefit: the view of the barge and tugboat traffic on the Muddy Mississippi; the broad-leafed potted plants; the signed prints on the paneled walls; the Rodin replicas on plaster pedestals; the gilt-edged, leather-bound books in their glass-doored cases. His eyes had rested on the framed diploma from Loyola University School of Law, no doubt because he wanted me to acknowledge the Magna Cum Laude beneath his name, but I hadn't given him the satisfaction. I'd been there to save my own ass, not to kiss Fat Mac's.

How's your golf game, Mac? I said now. Not that I gave a damn.

Down to a twelve handicap! he said. And I hit a hole-in-one at the Cave Creek Course in Phoenix! Can you believe it?

He jumped up and grabbed a plaque off the wall attesting to his deed, then told me about his luxury condo in Scottsdale to which he would retire soon; about how his twin boys Aden and Arthur were in college in Cambridge; about how his wife Alicia hadn't had a drink in a month and was taking Pilates mat classes at the new studio in town.

But I wasn't interested in Fat Mac's exploits on the back nine, or the glowing prospects of his precocious progeny, or the tenuous sobriety of his skinny wife. I was here on a grim mission.

C'mon, Mac, I said, let's get this over with.

Dean, relax! You're in a hurry to get locked up? The sheriff can wait. I have a meeting in an hour with a very important client. Can you come back at one o'clock?

Are you kidding me? I came two thousand miles to turn myself in.

Go have lunch, Mac said with a wave of his hand. Have you been to Tony's on Piasa Street? Five stars! Try their blackened catfish. It's to die for! And not too pricey. But maybe you're tapped. Do you need a few bucks?

I wanted to get up and strangle the man, but knew I'd never get my hands around his fat neck. I wasn't interested in another five-star restaurant. I'd had my final, farewell gourmet repast at La Petite Maison two nights before and that's how I preferred to remember what I'd be deprived of. But a drink—now that was another matter! There must be a bar in this burg open at ten a.m. somewhere, I thought, and if there were, I'd find it!

No, I got a few bucks, Mac, I said. I'll see you at one.

OH HENRY

BUT I DIDN'T SEE MAC AT ONE. I never saw him again. The next morning I woke up wondering why someone somewhere had put sand behind my eyelids and planted a howling demon in the center of my brain that kept me from remembering who and where I was.

I pressed my fingertips to my temples and strained to remember. I saw a long bar, old and funky and dark; a stuffed wild boar with buttons for eyes; old rusted farm implements hung from the ceiling by wire; a Pabst Blue Ribbon Beer sign; a Jack Daniels whiskey sign. I smelled stale beer and peanuts, sawdust, cigar smoke, hard-boiled eggs and pickled pigs feet. Weathered old men in denim dungarees sat on stools, hunched over shots of liquor and bottles of beer. The old man on the stool next to mine, between interludes of sliding his chewing tobacco from side to side, told me that it takes a hundred and two days to grow a crop of corn on bottomland and you can grow two crops a year. He'd grown a hundred crops in his lifetime and he figured he'd grow a few more. And I thought I remembered telling the man how long it takes to grow a crop of sinsemilla, seedless marijuana, in the hills of Humboldt County, California.

Then I remembered the barge, tethered to a dock, the ice-chunked Muddy Mississippi lapping its hull, and the little shack that served as a business office for the barge company. And did I ask the man in the office if they needed a deckhand? Yeah, he might have said. Matter a fact, buddy, we're a hand short, and we're shipping out bright and early. You can sleep off your drunk in a bunk below deck and do the paperwork first thing in the morning.

Where you going? I might have said. And he might have replied: New Orleans by way of Memphis.

That's down the river, isn't it?

That's right, buddy, it's down the river.

And I might have quipped: That's too bad because I'm going up the river.

But if I did, he didn't get the joke.

The last thing I remembered for sure was the Sheriff saying, Davis, you're late! And you're drunk! Where's your attorney?

And me saying, We don't need no fucking attorney!

And then I opened my eyes. I was lying on my back. Overhead was a water-stained grey concrete ceiling crossed with pipes and wires. I struggled up and looked around. I was in one of several individual cells with bars from floor to ceiling, around a common area furnished with a Formica-topped table littered with old newspapers and several plastic chairs. Two bare bulbs lit the room. In the far corner, water dripped from the ceiling into a pan on the floor. Next to the pan, a single white, brown-streaked toilet was attached to the wall. The air was sour. From two cells down I heard television voices and saw flickering silvery television light. I stood, unsteady on my feet, and went to investigate. The barred walls of the cell were draped in coarse blue blankets. I parted the blankets and stuck my head inside. Dense smoke wafted in the foul air. Crumpled fast-food wrappers littered the floor. A burly, bearded black man sat on his bunk leaning against the wall, a blanket draped over his head and wrapped around his torso. Only his face was visible. A long-suffering, sorrowful face. He smoked a hand-rolled cigarette, fat in the middle like an anaconda that had just eaten a pig. A green pouch of Bugler tobacco and a pack of rolling papers were at his side, a Folgers Coffee can half filled with butts on the floor at the foot of his bunk. He looked away from the flickering television screen and his gaze met mine.

Mornin, Mr. Davis, he said. How y'all feelin?

His voice was a rumbling baritone, his accent deeply Southern.

Like a million bucks, I said. Why do you know my name and I don't know yours?

We met last night.

I don't remember.

I'm not surprised. You here for murderin folks, Mr. Davis?

No. Why do you ask?

I always do, so I can sleep at night when a new man comes in. Don't want to be murdered in my sleep. Prefer to be murdered with my eyes open. I'd of asked last night but you passed out before I could.

He held out his hand.

Folks know me as Oh Henry, he said, but call me just plain Henry to my face.

I took his hand. It was warm and thick and scratchy dry.

Pleased to meet you, Henry, I said.

I wished I didn't feel like I'd fallen off a cliff and was waiting to hit the ground. I'd have liked to be more receptive to my first encounter with a denizen of the deep hole I'd dug for himself.

Pull up a chair, Mr. Davis, Oh Henry said.

I got a chair from around the table in the common area and put it in Oh Henry's cell and sat down. I looked at the black and white television propped on a chair at the end of his bunk. On the flickering screen, Fred Sanford berated his son.

You watch TV? Oh Henry said.

Not much, I said.

I watch all day ever day till way past midnight, Oh Henry said. Then I sleep with it on. TV my only friend. I play Checkers, too. Play against myself. One of me always wins.

Oh Henry chuckled with the air of one accustomed to being alone with himself for a long time.

You play Checkers, Mr. Davis? he said.

Not lately, I said. And you can call me Dean.

There's a board on the table outside, Mr. Dean, Oh Henry said, with a predatory gleam in his eyes.

I retrieved the board. Henry set it up on his bunk. I slid my chair over and we got acquainted while we played.

Oh Henry told how he came to be called Oh Henry on account of the candy bar of the same name.

My momma took me to the general store to get some flour for biscuits, and a tin of lard, and some chewing tobacco for my daddy. She
had one of my hands in one of hers, and her little purse in the other,
and while she told the man behind the counter about her groceries,
I looked at the candy bars on the candy bar shelf. I could read just
good enough to read my own name. Momma bought me one, and I
told ever body who would listen: Lookee here, they name a candy bar
after me! Folks been calling me Oh Henry ever since.

He added with a wink and a grin: And when I came of age, all the
pretty ladies started calling me the Candy Man!

He told me how he was born and raised on a dirt farm in the bayous
of Alabama. They planted peanuts and soy beans and sweet potatoes,
and had a few laying hens, and they did alright for dirt farmers, till
the big city grocery store come to town and took away their business.
His momma and daddy up and died and are buried in that dirt today,
his brothers and sisters drifted away, and he had a wife and three babies to raise up and not enough food to feed them. One day he'd gotten drunk and stole a car and set out for Chicago to find work, and
when he would find it, the plan was, he'd send for his wife and babies.
Only he'd strayed from the plan, he didn't recollect just how, probably the liquor, it'll knock the recollection right out of a man, and he
found himself walking on a two-lane blacktop through a small town
in this rural county, a long way from Interstate 55 North, and was ar-
rested for breaking into a payphone's coin box. He wasn't sure if the
charges against him were theft, damage to property, drunk and dis-
orderly, resisting arrest, or all of the above. He was sure, though, that
he wasn't trying to rob no coin box, no sir, he only wanted to make a
collect call back home. His bail was set at $1,000.00 cash, which he
didn't have the first dollar of, and he'd been here in the County Jail,
holed up in his makeshift cave, for seven months.

Seven months! I said. You don't have an attorney?

Got the Government man.

The Public Defender? What'd he say?

Say if I make a deal, I'll do six months on a work farm. If I don't,
they find me guilty, don't know for what, and I'll do two, maybe

three years in a penitentiary.

Why don't you make that deal?

I ain't did nothin.

What the hell, Henry, you've been here seven months to avoid doing a six-month sentence. I'll bet they'd give you credit for time served and cut you loose tomorrow!

Done tol' you I ain't did nothin.

All right, I said. I admire your integrity, but don't you have family or friends who can scrape your bail together? Pay it and hop on a Greyhound bus going south and don't look back. I doubt if they'd come after you. Probably happy to see your sorry ass gone.

Henry scoffed.

Ha! Thousand dollars! All my people in the world between em ain't got two dimes to rub together.

Well, you're between a rock and a hard place, Henry, I said.

Worse places to be, I suppose, cept maybe here in the bullpen on a Saturday night.

Why, what happens on Saturday night?

That's when all hell break loose. When the bullpen get used for a drunk tank. When the knucklehead cracker ass farm boys get liquored up and want to fight The Negro. But I ain't complainin. Goin upside the head of a drunk ass peckerwood on a Saturday night is the only fun I have, cept TV and Checkers.

You look like you can take care of yourself.

I gets my licks in, but sometimes there's two a them corn-fed crackers and they get their licks in, too. You gonna be round for the show, Mr. Dean?

What's today?

Thursday.

I don't know. I'm waiting for a ride to the penitentiary.

Goin to the Big House! You must be a bad man, Mr. Davis.

Dean.

You don't look like a bad man to me, Mr. Dean.

Just dope, I said. Marijuana.

Marijuana! They sendin you to the Big House for a little reefer?

It was a whole lot of a little reefer, Henry.

For how long they lockin you up for a whole lot of a little reefer?

Ten years. Five if I mind my manners.

Sweet Jesus, Brother Dean, that's a whole mess of years for reefer, I don't care how much or how little!

Well, they want to give you a whole mess of years for stealing from a pay phone, Henry. What's worse?

A DEPUTY BROUGHT BREAKFAST: a cold ham, egg and cheese sandwich and cold coffee from Burger King. I kept the coffee and gave the breakfast sandwich to Henry. I couldn't have kept it down. We played Checkers till noon, Oh Henry absently winning every game while rolling and smoking and telling tall tales about growing up in the bayous of Alabama: how he'd met his wife at a jook joint on a full moon night, took her from another man, had to stick a knife in the ol boy's belly to get his point across; how he had an abandoned shack on stilts in the swamp where he could get away for a spell to drink his liquor and make love to his pretty women—black, brown, white, Cajun, don't make him no never mind! He'd once had him a Creek, a Choctaw and a Cherokee woman on the same night! All the pretty women stuck on the candy man's stick! The rich ones, too! Why, if he'd of charged them a dollar apiece, he'd have money in the bank, would never of stole that automobile and come up north and got put in the white man's jail!

And so forth. When I got up to take a leak and left Oh Henry talking, and came back and sat, it was as though he hadn't known I was gone; he'd blathered on without missing a beat. Lord, God Almighty, he said, it's good to have someone to talk to ... not that I don't talk to myself, but having someone to listen make it twice as nice!

A DEPUTY BROUGHT LUNCH: a slice of bologna and mayonnaise on white bread, a green apple and a carton of milk. I gave the sandwich and apple to Henry and drank the milk. I lurched to the toilet and lost the milk and whatever else I had eaten at the bar in town the day before. I took a nap. The mattress smelled like piss. Mid-afternoon I awoke and remembered all over again where I was.

Despite the uncertainty ahead, I was glad that my days of debauchery were behind me. I looked forward to never feeling like this again.

A DEPUTY BROUGHT DINNER: a cheeseburger and fries and coke from Burger King. I guessed they didn't have a kitchen in the County jail. I gave my burger and fries to Henry and drank the coke. Oh Henry told more tales while he took me to Checkers School. I supposed that a big heart was a prerequisite for dominance in the game because when the long day was over, and I said goodnight and shuffled wearily back to my bunk, the score was Oh Henry fourteen, Dean Davis zip.

THE NEXT MORNING AT BREAKFAST—a cold ham, egg and cheese sandwich and cold coffee from Burger King—the Deputy said I'd be happy to know the Sheriff was driving me today to Arcadia State Penitentiary, an intake facility for the Department of Corrections. The good news, he said, was that I wouldn't have to find out what Saturday night in the County Jail was like.

When the time came, Oh Henry and I shook hands.

You're a better listener than you are a Checkers player, Mr. Davis, he said, and don't you take no shit from nobody in the Big House!

I told Oh Henry he'd better get out of this hole before he died here, of lung cancer from too much Bugler, or brain cancer from too much television. I wondered had I still been there on Saturday night when all hell broke loose, and Oh Henry was called upon to go upside the head of some peckerwood drunk ass farm boy, if I'd have been by his side getting my licks in, too. I liked to think so but I'd never know. I doubted our paths would cross again, but was sure there'd be more characters like Oh Henry in the days to come and I looked forward to meeting them.

ARCADIA

SEISMIC ACTIVITY

I STARED AT THE PHONE ON THE WALL. The word incongru-
ous came to mind. Earlier that day I'd been checked into Arcadia
Correctional Center, an intake facility for the Illinois Department
of Corrections. I'd been stripped and searched and straddle-walked
butt-naked over the delousing spray pipe on the floor. I could still
smell the pungent disinfectant wafting up from my groin. I was issued white cotton underwear, blue bib overalls, long-john tops and
bottoms, scuffed leather work boots, toiletries, and a padlock and
key on a string. I was escorted to the holding cell for new arrivals
and assigned a bunk—the top bunk—and a wooden trunk where I
stowed my toiletries and the books and yellow legal pads and pens I'd
brought in with me. I sat now pretending to write while casting cautious glances at a scene worthy of Hieronymus Bosch: eighty bunks
in a cracker box of green concrete walls and steel mesh a hundred
feet long by thirty wide, forty bunks on each side, twenty up, twenty
down; outside, frigid Midwest winds frosting the fallow fields, but
inside, hot air blasting from vents on all sides, causing the green walls
to perspire and glisten like the entrails of a slaughtered beast; overhead lighting so bright it lit the scene in stark relief; four television
sets, mounted high on opposite walls, cranked to the max so you had
to yell to be heard—but no one seemed to mind, least of all the eighty
men clad in bib over-alls, or in white cotton boxer shorts, or in white
towels tied at the hip, who lounged on their bunks reading girlie magazines or playing card games, yelling trump *that*, motherfucker, or
loitered in the narrow aisle between the rows of bunks, posturing,
posing, pontificating, greeting partners from the street, catching up

on what was happening in the hood.

At the far end of the room was a wooden platform beneath two showerheads, in front of which a line of men, towel-wrapped or in the raw, awaited their turn, and to the left of the platform, on the wall, a telephone. I watched a short, slouching white inmate shuffle to the phone, pick up the receiver and speak—he seemed to be cursing—then slam it down and walk away. I leaned over from my bunk and addressed the two black inmates who loitered beside it.

Excuse me, I said.

The taller of the two glared at me.

Choo wan, motherfucker? he snapped.

I wasn't sure I'd heard the man right. Was he telling me to chew on something, motherfucker? More likely he'd said, What do you want, motherfucker? I would have to fine tune my ear to the local dialect.

On the wall there, I said with a civil tone. Is that a phone?

You been locked up a long time, you don't know what a phone is, fool!

I know what it is but who can use it?

Anybody who want.

Really! Who can you call?

Call your momma. Call your bitch. Call anybody anytime, they got the dime, motherfucker!

You mean you've got to call collect?

The fuck you think I mean?

When can you call out?

All day ever day, sucker!

Thanks, I said.

I leaned back on my bunk. I found the presence of the phone disturbing. I had expected to be able to make calls eventually, but figured I'd have to jump through hoops: fill out a form, make an appointment, go to a special room, be timed for ten minutes, but not all day ever day anybody anytime they got the dime, motherfucker! As easy as standing in a phone booth outside a bar I could call Lucy, but I resisted. Our parting had been painful. I turned my attention to the world around me.

In the center aisle, a large, muscular middle-aged African American regaled a group of youths.

When you young bloods get up to Statesville or down to Menard, he said, y'all better pucker up them butt-holes real tight cause some crazy-ass nigger doin life gone tear off that booty in a minute! Better bring you some diapers, cause y'all's ass-hole grippers gone be so worn out, shit be runnin down your legs! Thas right! Better call home now, tell your mommas send you some plastic pants. Stan the Man ain't lyin, young bloods. You goin to the Big House, now!

Stan the Man's listeners looked worried, but one said with disdain, Old man, you is too lyin! I got plenty partners in the penitentiary, they ain't had they booties tore off!

Thas what they be tellin you, son, but you find out. Booty bandits see your pretty face in the fish line, you be some gangster Chief's kid in a minute.

Sheeit. I ain't nobody's kid. Gone be me an my partners doin the tearin off!

You a bad man, son, I can see that, but it don't make no difference how bad you is, them big black booty bandits gonna have their way. Ain't gonna come at you one at a time, two at a time. Gonna be three deep, four deep, six deep, a dozen, a whole mess a motherfuckin gang bangers fightin to get they swipes up your pretty little booty—and you be the first! Thas right! Better call you momma now, son, get you some diapers sent in you don't want shit runnin down your leg! Better get a big box for all your little partners!

There was something merry about the big man. He was trying not to smile. He caught me looking.

And you young pretty white boys specially better run and hide!

I discounted the warning. I was neither small nor young nor especially pretty, and there were half a dozen scared and skinny white kids in the cell ten or fifteen years younger than I was who were more likely to get their booties tore off, but I appreciated the compliment. And I felt that in the fleeting moment my gaze had met that of Stan the Man, a bridge had been crossed, that I had made an unlikely connection with another human being very unlike myself. Or maybe not.

Maybe I was deluding himself. Maybe come booty tearing-off time, Stan the Man would be the first in line. But I didn't think so.

At ten o'clock the televisions went off. A guard entered the pen and walked down the aisle between the rows of bunks.

Lights out in five minutes, he yelled. Time for bed, boys and girls.

Fuck you, screw!

Kiss my ass, peanut-butter-neck motherfucker!

There's room on the floor of the hole if you'd rather sleep there, said the screw.

Inmates drifted to their bunks. The bright lights went off and three small dull orange bulbs in wire cages came on, casting the long room in a hellish glow. A few men carried on loud conversations, like children at a pajama party. Others shouted, Shut the fuck up! The guard patrolled the aisle every few minutes. Soon the conversations ceased and the guard came less often. Then, the scurrying began, inmates to the bunks of others, shadows flitting back and forth in the murky orange glow. There came the sound of flesh whacking flesh, of fist on face, of the squeaking of springs, of grunting and moaning and an insistent voice cooing, Come here, you pretty pig!

Peace descended. Cigarette tips glowed in the dark, arcing from lip to butt-can like silent wayward meteorites. I propped myself on an elbow and looked out the window in the wall behind my bunk: flakes of snow drifted in the glow of lights on poles, a soundless dream-like scene. I lay my head on my pillow and closed my eyes and was drifting like a snowflake myself when the shaking began. I thought I'd left seismic activity behind in the Bay Area, but when the inmate in the bunk below got his rocks off it must have registered 6.5 on the Richter scale.

BULL DICK GRAVY

THE FRESH FALLEN SNOW CRUNCHED beneath my boots and the frigid air was pure and sweet as I and half a hundred fellow prisoners were marched to breakfast. The dining hall was cavernous and brightly lit like the bunkhouse. In the center of the room was a floor-to-ceiling tower with a door at floor level and a tinted plate glass window near the ceiling. Inmates sat at rectangular tables, eight to a table, white with white, black with black. Guards patrolled between rows of tables with a somber vigilance. There was little conversation. I picked up a tray and a metal spoon at the beginning of the serving line and was ladled out scrambled eggs and biscuits and gravy by a beefy white inmate with a hair net and filmy blue latex gloves. I saw an empty seat at an all black table. There sat Stan the Man.

This seat taken? I asked.

Stan replied without looking up.

Do it look like it's taken?

I sat. I looked from face to face. No one spoke. No one looked up from their tray. I took a bite of egg and of biscuit and gravy. It was palatable. I gazed around the room. Between rows of tables walked inmates clad in white, with metal bins fastened by straps around their necks. They held ladles and shouted, On these eggs! On this bull-dick gravy! Seated inmates shouted back, Over here! On them eggs! On that bull-dick gravy, brother! And the food-toting inmates came and ladled up eggs and biscuits and gravy. I was reminded of vendors at Giants Stadium in San Francisco shouting, Peanuts! Getcher peanuts! Getcher beer! Getcher peanuts here!

The compact muscular inmate next to me frowned and poked at his gravy with his spoon.

Man, he said to no one in particular, why they call this bull-dick gravy?

Stan the Man wiped his mouth with the back of his hand.

Brother, why you think they call it bull dick gravy? he said.

Brother, I'm askin you, the inmate said.

Think about it, Stan said. What part of the bull is big as your motherfuckin arm?

The inmate narrowed his eyes, then opened them wide.

No, man! I ain't eat no motherfuckin bull's dick!

It's just meat, Stan said offhandedly, taking a bite of his own bull dick gravy.

The inmate stood suddenly and slammed his tray onto the table.

I ain't eat no motherfuckin bull's dick! he shouted.

He glared around the room. Inmates turned their heads. In the tower, the tinted window slid open and the guard inside pumped a shotgun. Stan the Man took him by the arm.

Be cool, nigger, he said.

Sit your ass down, brother, said another inmate at the table. He just messin with you, man. Ain't bull dick. It's just pork sausage.

A hefty guard with long sideburns and a bulbous nose approached.

We got a problem here, Slim? he said.

The inmate sat down slowly.

No, he said. We ain't got no motherfuckin problem.

That's good, the guard said. We don't like problems here in Arcadia.

His icy gaze lingered on me. I could read his thoughts: You're sittin at the wrong table, boy.

The tinted window in the guard tower slid shut. Inmates in the aisles waved their ladles.

On these eggs! On this bull dick gravy!

Eat your breakfast, Brother, Stan the Man said to his irate table-mate. It's getting cold.

Kiss my ass, nigger, came the stony reply.

I was careful to conceal my amusement.

I THRUST MY HANDS DEEP into the pockets of my old blue over-coat and crunched my way down the snow-encrusted sidewalk next to Billy Odum Jr., the inmate who'd slammed the phone down the day I arrived. A thirty-something white guy looking beat up by life— blonde hair thin and greasy; nose broken and bent to the side; lips a twisted snarl—he muttered to himself that it was colder than a witch's tit! He and I and half a dozen other men were led by a sullen guard in a green woolen uniform to a low brick building over the door of which a wooden sign read CLINIC. Inside, another half-dozen men sat on benches in a crowded foyer. We took our places and waited. In the corner was a kerosene stove cranking out heat. In spite of the cold outside, the room was stifling hot. Behind a counter, a hard-looking woman in white, her blonde hair ratted and sprayed, perused papers and puffed on a long, thin cigarette. Smoke hung in the air. On the left side of the counter, a plastic radio played the Statler Brothers' *Flowers on the Wall*. The guard removed his hat and rested his elbows on the counter.

How about a cup of that good fresh Folgers, Marge? he said.

Down a hallway to the back of the building a second guard leaned against the wall, drinking coffee. In the corner opposite the kerosene heater was a dusty water cooler. Crushed paper cups littered the floor. On the wall next to the cooler a sign read: No Smoking!

We were handed a clipboard holding a form that queried our medical history. Beneath the form a flyer warned of the danger of sharing needles and from having sex with one's fellow prisoners. A young, slightly-built black inmate with pleated hair scowled.

They blame that AIDS shit on a motherfuckin monkey from Africa! he said.

A second black inmate, wearing a blue denim baseball cap, nodded in agreement.

It's the fuckin CIA, man!

The first inmate concurred.

It's a motherfuckin honkie conspiracy!

The guard at the counter turned and glared. The inmate in the baseball cap glared back. He took off the cap and put it on backwards.

Turn the cap around, Slim, the guard said.

Ain't this a bitch! the inmate said.

He turned the cap around and folded his arms.

Gimme a square, man, he said to the first inmate, who pulled out a pack of cigarettes.

Hey, can't you read? The guard said. No smoking!

Fuck that, the inmate said, and lit his cigarette.

Can the butt, slim! The guard said.

The inmate looked behind the counter at the woman in white.

The bitch be smokin! he said.

The woman gave him a dirty look, then glanced at the guard. The guard stiffened and called down the hallway.

Johnny!

The guard at the end of the hall came into the waiting room.

Outside, slim, the first guard said. Let's go!

Fuck you, screw! the inmate said, and took a drag off his cigarette.

Both guards advanced. The inmate took a step back. The first guard took him by the elbow. The inmate jerked away.

Get your goddamn honkie hands off me, peanut-butter-neck motherfucker!

Each guard grabbed a wrist of the inmate with one hand, put the other under his arm, and lifted him off the floor. He struggled and yelled to the men on the bench.

Y'all gone let these cracker motherfuckers put me in check?

No one paid attention. He was carried out the door. Soon the guards returned without him and took their respective posts.

I shifted on the bench. Sweat streamed from my armpits, down my ribcage, into my trousers. Periodically, an inmate emerged from the hallway and took a seat, and I would hear a shout in an Asian accent: Nexa! Nexa! Then a plump young woman in white, pleasing to the eye in a wholesome country sort of way, would enter the room and call out a name. All eyes were upon her as she came and went. A young black inmate bragged—under his breath, not to be overheard by the guard at the counter—If I had that fine, white bitch in my crib, I'd be layin me some tall pipe, Jack! The white inmate next to him, long in the jaw and waxen-faced, wet his lips and drawled, If I rammed my piston up that tight young pussy, she'd be squealin like a stuck pig!

My name was called. I followed the young nurse down the hall. I watched how her corn-fed derriere undulated beneath her white cotton uniform like soccer balls in a canvass bag. How, with every step, her calves bunched beneath her white nylon hosiery.

She led me to a small room outside of which the guard, Johnny, stood post.

Sit there, she said, nodding toward an examining table. And roll up your sleeve.

She tied a rubber tube around my bicep and told me to make a fist. She slapped the crook of my arm and deftly slid a syringe into my pulsing blue vein. She kept her eyes on the syringe as it filled with my blood, while I kept my eyes on the buttons of her tunic as they strained to harness the wholesome plenitude of her bosom. I smelled her warm breath, her shower soap; noted the black at the roots of her blondness; the light, white layer of powder, hopefully applied; the thin black line of mascara, carefully drawn; her serious pursed lips. She never once looked at me. I am nothing to her, I thought. A nobody. A bug. I wanted to shout: I'm not like the others! I could show you the world! But in her mind, I knew, I was the same. And no doubt she was seeing all the world she could handle at this point in her simple life. I imagined she was married to the former captain of the high school football team, who might well be a Correctional Officer here in Arcadia, and they afforded a fine little white frame house on their combined salaries, and tooled around on week-ends in his renovated red Malibu, him still showing her off, she attending the local junior college to get further certified, him drinking Busch Bavarian beer with his buddies, ex-high school football teammates, while they watched the games on Sunday—at his place because he has a new fake wood laminated wet bar with a phony stained-glass Tiffany lamp overhead—and they count down to the super-bowl, while he drinks more and more, and likes his life less and less, till one day he hits her and she leaves and raises the kids alone in a trailer, and the youngest son, his pride and joy, grows up angry and confused and burgles and robs to support his methamphetamine habit, and gets busted and sent to the joint still pimply-faced, and gets fucked in the ass by some mean black motherfucker from Chicago, maybe the same one that the guards today had sent to the hole for lighting up in the clinic when after all the bitch behind the counter be smokin, too!

She slid the needle from my vein and swabbed the hole with alcohol and sealed it with a Band-Aid. Put your finger here, she said. Bend your arm, she said. Take off them bib overalls and shorts, she said, and put on this here gown. Tie it in the back. The doctor will be here in a minute.

She closed the door behind her.

I stripped and hopped back onto the waxed-paper covered table in which the butt prints of previously examined inmates remained pressed. The door opened. In came a small doctor in a white frock, a stethoscope around his neck, wearing thick glasses that magnified the orbs of his eyes grotesquely. He cupped my balls in the palm of his small hand and commanded: You cough!

I coughed.

He held a flat stick with one hand and put the fingertips of the other on my lower lip.

You open!

I opened my mouth. He pressed my tongue with the stick and peered down my throat.

Ah! Ah!

He put the plugs of the stethoscope in his ears and put the cold steel medallion of it on my bare chest. He pulled the plugs from his ears.

Good healthy! he declared. Live long time!

He closed the door behind him.

Nexa! Nexa!

Back in my cell, I wondered what had brought the good doctor from the rice fields of Asia to the cornfields of middle America. Had he fled a repressive government? Did he come over on a boat? Did he have a wife and kids? Did they shop at Wal-Mart? Did the local farm boys punch his kids in the face?

There had to be a story there, and I liked a good story.

I put my hands on my stomach. Good healthy, like hell! I pondered my true physical condition: liver long abused by liquor and a litany of controlled substances; brain cells burnt and lost to the void for all time like cinders up a chimney; twenty-five pounds of fat too many; back stiff, poor muscle tone and no aerobic capacity. Well, I was in the right place to change all that. I dropped to the floor and knocked out twenty push-ups. My stomach touched the floor before my chest did, so I turned over and did twenty sit-ups. I felt conspicuous, but no one paid attention.

THAT EVENING I SAT ON MY BUNK with a pen in my hand and a legal pad in my lap. I thought to keep a written account of my incarceration. My mind was a flurry of images and impressions but no coherent point of view. Entreaties to my Muse, Miranda, were met with silence. It was like her to keep me in the dark when I needed the light of inspiration. She was perverse that way. Whimsical. A fairy borne by a wayward wind.

I put down my pen and surveyed the room. In the center isle two bunks away Stan the Man hunkered down in a boxer's crouch in front of a cluster of young inmates. He straightened and brought the big balled fist of his left hand around in a hook and smashed it into the palm of his right hand.

That's right! he declared. I knocked out Buster Mathis! Muhammad Ali couldn't knock out Buster Mathis! Ali need fifteen rounds to beat Buster by decision, but I knocked his sorry ass out cold, Jack!

I doubted the big man's claim. I was a fight fan from way back and knew that Buster Mathis, the heavyweight contender, had been knocked out only once, by Ron Lyle in 1972. His fight with Joe Frazier in 1968 was stopped by the referee, he'd lost by decision to Jerry Quarry in 1969, and again to Ali in 1971, but he'd never been knocked out by anyone remotely named Stan the Man. I felt compelled to call the man out. When he went to the sink in the back of the pen and filled a coffee cup with water, I jumped down off my bunk and got up alongside him and told him what I knew.

He scowled down from his height.

Boy, he said, did you hear me say I knocked him out in a real fight?

No, I stammered, but—

But nothin! I was Buster's sparrin partner. I went two hundred rounds gettin that nigger in shape for Ali. Two weeks before the fight I knocked his sorry ass out. His people sent me home. Didn't want no part of Stan the Man! Who are you, anyway, motherfucker? You a fighter? You don't look like no fighter to me!

I was embarrassed. I'd been out of line. I told Stan that I'd sort of been a fighter, having fought for a community boxing club in Marin County, California, when I was twelve years old. I'd won a few fights. I'd weighed eighty-eight pounds at the time, less than half what I weighed now.

Eighty-eight pounds! Stan scoffed. Nobody weigh eighty-eight pounds. You must have been in the goddamn Flea Weight division!

I felt no malice coming from the man, perhaps even a trace of respect for my audacity. I quipped: I was big for my size.

He laughed.

Flea Weight, ain't nobody big for their size! Ever body the size they is! You can be big for your age, you can be too big for your britches, but you can't be big for your size!

OVER DOMINOS AND TEPID COFFEE, Stan and I talked boxing, me telling him what I knew from Ring Magazine, fights on television, and anecdotes from the few professional fights I'd attended, Stan telling tales from his real-life experience in the game, how he had twice won the Chicago Golden Gloves City Championship, had gotten to the third round of the 1960 Olympics Qualifying tournament, had trained in the Philadelphia gym of Smokin' Joe Frazier, and with Emmanuel Stewart at his Kronk Gym in Detroit, and was being groomed for a title shot himself until late one bonehead night he went to a party with a bottle of gin, a pocketful of pills, and a pistol. A man was shot. Stan did twelve years in a maximum security pen up north. When he got out, his days in the ring were over. He turned to crime and was sent back to the pen.

I knocked out Buster Mathis, he said, but I couldn't beat the street. Street knocked my ass out cold, Jack!

Now here he was in Arcadia waiting to be transferred to a medium security facility nearby where he would coach the boxing team, his predecessor having been sent to a max joint following an altercation that left a guard with a broken jaw. He would finish his sentence, go back to the world, open a gym, and try to hook up with his only boy, Rashan, who hung out with his little hoodlum partners, and carried a pistol in his pocket like his old man had, and sold crack in the neighborhood. He hadn't seen Rashan in five years and might not know him now if he saw him.

I wasn't there when he needed me, Stan said, and now he ain't nothin but a thug like me. He'll be locked up or shot dead one day if I don't help him get his life right. You got babies back in the World, Flea Weight?

I do, I said. A girl named Lola. Six months old.

Best raise that baby up right, Flea Weight. You only get one time around.

THE BEST LAID PLANS

I OPENED MY LOCKER AND REMOVED my bag of books. I looked at each in turn and read its title and remembered when and where I had read it, then tossed it into the center of my bunk: John Steinbeck's *Of Mice and Men*; Graham Green's *A Burnt-Out Case*; Nelsen Algren's *A Walk on the Wild Side*; Albert Camus's *The Stranger*; Ernest Hemingway's *For Whom the Bell Tolls*; Louis-Ferdinand Celine's *Journey to the End of the Night*; J.M. Coetzee's *Waiting for the Barbarians*; Paul Bowles' *Let it Come Down*; Joseph Conrad's *Heart of Darkness*; Nietzsche's *Will to Power*, and Jean Paul Sartre's *Being and Nothingness*. I had grabbed them off the shelf without thinking, when packing to surrender, figuring the chance of finding a good book where I was going was low, but I wondered now if the selections were random after all. They seemed to have in common the theme of alienation from society, the Outsider motif, which was at odds with my newfound urge to engage with life. I couldn't choose; they were yesterday's news. I looked up and saw the black inmate on the top bunk across the aisle staring at me. He waved a book around and yelled something that was lost in the noise of the room. I motioned him over. He climbed down from his bunk, crossed the aisle and came up alongside me. He was short. His hair was slicked back and shiny like that of a '50s Motown artist. He sported a matchstick-thin mustache and one of his two front teeth was gold. The word dapper occurred to me.

Trade you for a book, he said.

He handed me a dog-eared paperback: *Pimp, The Story of my Life*, by Iceberg Slim.

What's it about? I said.

Bout a brother name of Robert Beck who was raised up by his mamma in Chicago. He went to College but he really wanna be a pimp, so he go to pimp school on the streets and gets a degree in whorology. He a chump and a chili ass pimp till he get his coattails pulled by Sweet, the top spade pimp in the country, the Master Mack of all time!

He pronounced of all time the way Mohammad Ali famously described himself as The Greatest. He continued his recap of *Pimp*.

Sweet tell my man he gotta be icy cold like the inside of a dead whore's pussy, so he change his name to Iceberg Slim. Soon he got a fine stable of bitches. Got a tall pile a scratch. Got a new shiny hog. Got vines cost two hundred slats apiece. But like my man say: A pimp's fame is as fleeting as an icicle under a blow torch. One day he find himself in the penitentiary, forty-three years old, ain't got shit to show for all them years of pimpin, so he decide to square up and get his life right. Ol boy get out the joint, move to California and write this book.

I opened the book at random and read:

> *Nigger, you're pretty, but a bleach cream will never be invented that will make you white. So, pimp your ass off and be somebody with what you got. It could be worse, you could be an ugly nigger.*

I had taken Black Literature courses at San Francisco State—Zora Neale Hurston, James Baldwin, Richard Wright, Toni Morrison—but Iceberg Slim wasn't on the curriculum.

All right, I said. Pick a book.

He scrambled up onto my bunk. He looked at the books and frowned.

Pick one for me, he said.

I picked *Of Mice and Men*.

What's it about? he said.

The title is a line from a poem: The best laid plans of mice and men often go awry. It's about planning a better life for yourself.

He climbed down off my bunk. He held out his hand.

Lamar Johnson, he said. I plan to be a pimp.

Dean Davis, I said. I don't have a plan.

Lamar shook his head.

Brother, you don't know where you goin, you gone wind up some-place else!

I looked around the room.

I'll keep that in mind, Lamar, I said. Where do I get coffee?

We make store on Thursday, he said. You got money on the books you can buy what you want. Mud, squares, whams and zooms.

What are those?

Coffee. Cigarettes. Snacks like soda pop and Twinkies.

I've got money on the books, I said, but I need coffee now.

Got to trade for somethin.

Don't have anything.

Lamar went to his locker and returned with a styrofoam cup half full of instant coffee.

When you make store, he said, hook me up with a pack of squares. Double Os.

What are double Os?

Kools.

It's a deal, I said.

He handed me the mud. He needed the cup back. I tore a square of paper from the bag in which I'd brought my books, folded it into an envelope, poured the coffee flakes into the envelope and gave Lamar his cup. He returned to his bunk with his book. I made a little wedge of a spoon from a strip of the paper and spooned a pile of the brown flakes into my cup and filled the cup with hot water from the tap at the back of the pen. I clambered onto my bunk and cracked open *Pimp* by Robert Beck, alias Iceberg Slim. I was soon immersed in another world: the mean streets of the Windy City, Chicago, circa 1930s and '40s, the world of the black pimp, a time of spats and slats and derby hats; of Billie Holiday & Billy Eckstein; of Sarah Vaughn, Nat King Cole, Zoot Sims, Charlie Bird Parker; of Packards & Duesenbergs, and Maggie & Jiggs comic books. When I looked up from the book and rubbed my eyes and looked around the cell-block, I felt I was emerging from one dream and entering another, the gauzy curtain between them no more substantial than the smoky haze that hung in the air. I tried to remember the sights and sounds of the life I'd left behind: the golden hills of the Marin headlands; the fog rolling in beneath the Golden Gate Bridge; the white caps on the water; the twinkling nightscape of San Francisco seen from across the bay; the pretty face of Lucy, the light in her almond eyes; her long legs, her dimpled derriere; the soft sweet breath of Lola—but these, too, seemed like the smoky tendrils of a dissipating dream. I had the disquieting sense of embarking in a flimsy craft on a foggy sea to a distant, foreign shore.

I SKIPPED THE MORNING MEAL. By noon I'd finished *Pimp*. I was impressed that when Beck sat down to write his book, he had something to say. That if he had become a writer first and gotten his degree from Tuskegee and read lots of books filled with the fine writing of others and foregone the pimping game and never known the streets, he'd have become just another brilliant genius wordsmith with nothing real to write about. I felt fortunate to have read the book here in Arcadia, where the characters who peopled its pages milled around me in the flesh.

THAT BITCH! THAT JAZZY JIVE WHORE! My man Iceberg would've put his foot up her funky ass before he turned her out on the street!

Lamar tossed *Of Mice and Men* onto my bunk. He continued his rant.

That sissy bitch, Curly, he better never *ever* go to East St. Louis! They'll turn his pussy ass out in a minute! And that lame-ass, George, why he gotta pop a cap on the ass of his own road doggie? He shoulda shot Crooks! That sorry-ass, busted-back, slop-totin nigger, sleepin in the barn like an animal and kissin the white man's ass! He better never go to East St. Louis, too!

I smiled. Lamar's point of view was not one to be heard in a Modern American Literature class.

How'd you like *Pimp*, Davis? he said.

I liked it a lot, I said. I liked how Beck did it his way, even if he lost it all in the end. I liked how he squared up after, and wrote a good book about it. But I didn't like how he made his money off women who don't feel good about themselves till they've got a foot up their ass. But that's just me. So, Lamar, how come you want to be a pimp if your man Iceberg decided it was a sick life and he squared up?

Can't square up off somethin I ain't did yet! Lamar said.

Makes sense, Lamar, I said.

I could relate. Like Beck, I'd done it my way. I could hardly discourage Lamar from doing the same.

What else you got to read, Davis? he said.

You might like this, I said.

I handed him *For Whom the Bell Tolls.*

What's it about? he said.

It's about a man named Robert Jordan who sacrificed his life for a bunch of wine-swilling gypsies.

Lamar's eyes narrowed.

Sound like a chump thing to do, don't it, Davis?

It wasn't something he planned on doing, Lamar, but shit happens.

Lamar's gold tooth flashed.

Ain't that a natural fact!

JUDY BLUE EYES

THE SMALL GUARD WITH THE BIG VOICE bellowed: Davis! Odum! Psych line walkin in five minutes! Psych line!

I jumped down off my bunk and put on my boots. I'd anticipated this day with a mix of exhilaration and dread. I feared that after a week in a jam-packed holding cell I was losing my identity to a collective consciousness reduced to its lowest common denominator. I wanted to engage with my fellow inmates, sure, but not be lost in the crowd. I anticipated the sweet, narcissistic pleasure of being evaluated and seen for what I was: singular and noteworthy. On the other hand, what if I wasn't? What if I was dismissed summarily as just another case in a caseload?

I would take a book. There might be a long wait on a hard wooden bench and reading would pass the time and sharpen my wit for this much-anticipated encounter with my captors. Should I take Celine's *Journey to the End of Night*? Nietzsche's *Will to Power*?? Sartre's *Being and Nothingness*? I chose the latter. I hadn't read it in fifteen years and vaguely remembered the gist of it, but perhaps my evaluator would appreciate my taste in literature.

I SAT ON A BENCH FILLING OUT A FORM on a clipboard. Down the corridor more inmates filled out forms. Odum sat next to me with his arms crossed and his form left blank.

I ain't tellin these sumbitches a goddam thing! he muttered.

I wondered if what I said could and would be used against me.

Two guards, one white, one black, collected the clipboards and delivered them to an office through the door of which every twenty minutes or so an inmate would exit and another would take his place.

I was the last man called. Let the games begin! I followed the black guard—his name tag read Calvin Green— into a small office. Behind a desk sat a woman in a grey pantsuit staring at a clipboard. Her hair was short and brushed back severely. I guessed her age at thirty-eight, that she was a dozen years out of college, long enough to realize that she was not doing what she wanted with her life, but that it was too late to do anything else.

Please have a seat, Mr. Davis, she said without looking up.

I sat in the chair beside the desk. I put my book down with the title facing the woman. I noticed that her chair was higher than mine, and thought it an absurdly obvious maneuver. Officer Green poured a cup of coffee from the pot on a low filing cabinet against the far wall. He leaned against it with his long legs crossed, seeming at ease. He looked at me without expression, then looked away.

On the wall behind the woman hung framed certificates and a framed print of Edvard Munch's *The Scream*. On her desk were a brass plaque that read Judy Sorenson, MS, LCSW; a stack of manila folders; a framed photo of a boy with his arm around a dog that wore a Chicago Cubs T-shirt; a cactus with little red flowers, and a transparent plastic paper-weight that contained a little white church and phony snow on the ground. The trappings of a banal existence, I surmised. She was pretty despite her pallor and the severity of her expression. She had the straight nose, high forehead and cold blue eyes of her Nordic ancestors. Judy Blue Eyes. I sensed the young girl inside, wanting out. I decided she was sexually repressed, as were all middle-aged women in pantsuits who sat behind their nameplates reading forms on clipboards.

She looked at me with a slow cold blink of her eyes.

Do you know why you're here today, Mr. Davis?

She gazed down her straight white nose at me.

To be evaluated, I said.

If she detected the cynicism in my voice she didn't show it.

Correct, Mr. Davis. To determine to which facility you should be assigned, what would be your most suitable occupation once there, and to determine how our counseling services might facilitate your rehabilitation.

Whatever I can do to help, Ms. Sorenson.

You can answer a few questions, she said.

The limit is twenty, I quipped with a smile that Sorensen did not return, which told me she was determined to remain in charge and feared that my facile intellect might wrest control. But sometimes the best way to be in charge of an encounter was to let the other person think they were. And so I would.

Your address of record is in California. Is that correct?

I smiled. She was repeating the questions I'd just answered on the form.

You'd know better than I do what my address of record is, Miss Sorenson, I said. But I can tell you where I lived before I came here.

Please do, she said.

San Francisco, I replied. Baghdad by the Bay.

I had added Baghdad by the Bay because it had an exotic ring and implied a world where anything goes, and which, no doubt, she knew nothing of.

You're a long way from home, she said.

Just passing through, I said.

Marital status, Mr. Davis?

My marital status, too, was a matter of record, but I'd do it her way.

Married, I said.

And you're still together?

Temporarily separated by circumstance, I said.

But you are together. She'll be there when you get out, is that correct?

Yes, we plan to have a long and interesting life together.

Children?

One. A daughter. Six months old.

You'll miss some very important years, she said.

We'll be in touch, I said, feeling her observation intrusive.

Siblings? she said.

A brother, Brodie.

Any history of mental illness in your family?

No, I lied. Doubtless, Miss Judy couldn't care less about the state of my mother's mind, and I didn't like the term illness attached to it.

Any history of sexual deviation?

I wondered if cross-dressing counted, but my Brother Brodie's proclivities were none of her business.

Before I got married, I said, I deviated from one woman to another as often as I could. Does that qualify?

Sorenson's expression did not change.

I see you have five people on your visiting list—mother, brother, father-in-law, wife and daughter—but have not yet had a visit.

I didn't know I would be allowed a visit before I was permanently assigned, I said.

Now you know.

Do they need an appointment?

Of course not. When a visitor arrives you'll be summoned from wherever you are on the grounds. Nine to five, seven days a week, five visits per month, one hour each.

Really, I said, genuinely surprised.

We encourage visits, she said. They increase an inmate's prospects for rehabilitation, and decrease the risk of recidivism. Is anyone on your list nearby?

Wife and daughter. About thirty miles away.

Give her a call, Mr. Davis.

I resented her commanding tone, but she seemed not to have noticed.

I see you haven't checked the box for racial preference, Mr. Davis, she said. Do you not have a racial preference?

I welcomed the opportunity to restore a bit of flippancy to my replies.

In women, yes. Asian and Hispanic ... but don't tell my wife.

Still no reaction from the implacable Judy Blue Eyes.

I'll just check Caucasian if you don't object, she said.

That's mighty white of you, I said.

I see you've been to college, Mr. Davis.

San Francisco State. Six years.

What was your major?

I deviated from one to another, I said. I tried Psychology until I realized that psychologists analyze the problems of others to avoid facing their own. I tried Philosophy until I realized that philosophers are more interested in creating clever systems of thought, and writing books about them, then they are in knowing the truth. Then I majored in literature.

I see. Six years and no degree.

Am I being charged with Failure to Graduate?

Why did you not graduate?

My last class, a survey of Modern American Literature. The professor would have us believe she was meeting Virginia Woolf for tea after class. I decided she was in a club I didn't want to join.

Judy Sorenson put her clipboard down, and her pen down, and folded one hand over the other. She looked at me with her cold blue eyes.

Have you considered, Mr. Davis, that you may have a fear of success?

I resented the question. I responded indignantly.

Have you considered, Ms. Sorenson, that you may have a tendency to arrive at stupid and presumptuous conclusions?

Her smile was barely perceptible. She noted my file. She looked up.

Mr. Davis, do you feel that you may have a problem with authority, especially female authority?

I don't really care who's on top, I said in a feeble attempt to regain my facade of indifference. But she maintained hers. She turned the page of my file.

I see you have a very high IQ, Mr. Davis.

Not as high as that of my man, Iceberg Slim, I said—one seventy-five!

I glanced at Calvin Green. Surely the man was a fan of the Iceberg. But Green was examining his fingernails.

I'm afraid I'm not familiar with your friend, Mr. Slim, Sorenson said dismissively.

You wouldn't want to be, Judy, I said. He's not your type.

I wondered had she noticed that I'd called her Judy? She hadn't complained.

Do you use drugs, Mr. Davis?

No, I lied again. I knew better than to mention the sea of liquor, the mountain of cocaine and the avalanche of uppers, downers and sideways-rendering substances that had been my staple for two decades. I didn't want to spend the next five years in substance abuse counseling, least of all with Judy Blue Eyes.

Just wine with dinner, I said. I smoked marijuana once but it gave me a headache.

She continued in her maddening measured way.

You were convicted of possessing 500 pounds of Marijuana and sentenced to ten years in the penitentiary, she said. Do you feel that your sentence was harsh?

There was no straight answer to her question. I had never admitted my guilt and now was not the time.

I'm sure the streets will be safer with me not on them, I said.

You understand that you'll receive day-for-day good time and be released in five years if you stay out of trouble?

Yes, I do.

She put her fingertip on the frame of her glasses, slid them halfway down the sharp ridge of her nose, fixed me with a cold blue stare.

You do plan on staying out of trouble, don't you, Mr. Davis?

The invisible man, I assured her. Out of sight, out of mind.

She resettled her glasses and noted my file.

You are aware, she said without looking up, that institutional infractions, including possession of contraband, will result in a loss of good time?

Duly noted.

There was a moment of silence while Sorenson perused my file. I sensed that the interview was coming to a close, and wanted to be the one who brought it there.

Where is this going, Miss Sorenson? I believe that was question number twenty.

One more question, if you please, Mr. Davis.

Sure.

How do you feel about your crime?

My alleged crime, I said. I pled not guilty and went to trial.

And lost.

And appealed.

And lost again.

You want an Act of Contrition?

It would be beneficial for the record, Mr. Davis, if you were, umm … penitent.

I'm in the penitentiary, I said. Doesn't that make me penitent?

I regretted the resentment that had crept into my voice.

You must show a degree of remorse, she said. It's essential to your rehabilitation. Does that make sense to you, Mr. Davis?

You want me to say I'm sorry? I'm sorry I was convicted! Does that make sense to you, Miss Judy Blue Eyes?

I will note your file, Mr. Davis. Thank you.

Am I being dismissed?

You are.

Well, based on our little chat, what sort of assignment should I expect?

I don't assign, Mr. Davis. I evaluate and recommend.

Well, based on your evaluation, what will you recommend?

It's confidential, Mr. Davis. You may go.

One more—

You may go, Mr. Davis.

She looked at Officer Green.

Let's go, Davis, Green said.

I stood.

Don't forget your book, Dean, she said.

Dean! She called me Dean! Now I was getting somewhere! I picked up my book.

Have you read it? I said.

I haven't, she said, but I've read Woody Allen's *Non-Being and Somethingness.*

Touché, Judy, I said. I'd let her get the last word in.

She addressed Calvin Green.

Officer, I'm going to need some assistance when you're finished with Davis. Do you mind?

My pleasure, Miss Sorenson, Green said. And to me, gruffly, Let's go, Davis.

I felt Judy's cold blue scrutiny follow me out the door.

I SAT ON MY BUNK AND BERATED myself. What had I hoped to prove? That I didn't belong here? That I could match wits with an emissary of the outside world? Judy Blue Eyes had seen me coming! She played me for a fool! I closed my eyes and reimagined her as other than the stifled prude she seemed to be. I saw her in her office alone, prior to my entrance. She regarded the stack of manila folders on her desk without enthusiasm. Evaluation Day had long been her favorite, when she'd gotten her kicks watching helpless men struggle to present themselves in a favorable light, or to let her know they didn't give a good goddamn. But today she felt only a creeping weariness. She'd seen every type and didn't expect that in the stack of folders before her she would encounter anything new.

The truth was, she missed being Dame Duesenberg, Dominatrix Extraordinaire, at the Stud Button Leather Club on South Kinky Street in Chicago. That had been a walk on the wild side! She'd assumed the role on a lark to put herself through grad school, but the whips and the chains and the groveling men had pleased her, and revealed a darker side of herself she embraced and was loathe to let go of. Squaring up after getting her credentials had been difficult, and these last ten years being a Licensed Clinical Social Worker in a penitentiary a poor substitute for the life she'd left behind. But perhaps there was someone in the stack today who would amuse her. And after I was toyed with, and summarily dismissed, she leaned back in her chair and turned the transparent paperweight over and watched the snowflakes fall. These trapped little men, she mused, she could see inside their souls! Though her encounter with me had fallen short of curing her creeping weariness, it was mildly entertaining. How pathetic were my attempts to display my worldliness, she thought, as though I were the only prisoner ever to have read a good book or eaten in a restaurant or gotten on an airplane! How foolish my reference to Robert Beck—what she could tell me about her escapades with the Iceberg would knock my socks off! And my flippant remark that I didn't care who was on top—how juvenile!

And, oh, how she had loved springing the degree of remorse trap on me. The smart ones fell for it every time. No, she would not have me sent to a max joint to show who's really in charge. She would keep me right here, have me assigned to the kitchen to make bull dick gravy, or to the slaughterhouse to butcher hogs. Yes, she would keep me here in Arcadia, and there would be plenty of opportunity for further evaluation.

At a knock on the door, she put the paperweight down.

Come in, she said.

Broad-shouldered, narrow-hipped Officer Green entered the room.

She slipped off the jacket of her pantsuit and hung it on the back of her chair.

Calvin, she purred, I'm going to rearrange my filing cabinets. Do you think you can help remove my drawers?

You freaky white bitch, Calvin said beneath his breath as he closed the door with one hand and reached for his belt buckle with the other.

I FELT BETTER HAVING TURNED a dubious encounter with Judy into an amusing anecdote. She was right, though, whichever Judy she was, that I should make that call. I climbed down from my bunk.

Odum was on the phone. He shouted above the noise in the room.

It's me, Billie Odum Junior! Lemmee talk to Ruby Sue! Well, god-dammit, where is she? Where? What time?

He put a finger in his ear.

What? What? With who … ? I Goddam told her I'd be callin!

He glared at me with a twisted face.

Whatchoo lookin at, Bud?

I returned to my bunk and waited while he continued to curse his listener. He slammed the receiver down.

It's all yours, bud, he said as he passed by my bunk.

I went to the phone but another inmate got there first. I stood be-hind him.

Aw, baby, he said. You know how I feel about you! When I get out the joint, I'm gonna treat you right! I just need a few dollars on the books till I get where these cracker motherfuckers gonna send me.

His tone changed.

Bitch, I'll put my foot in your ass when I hit the bricks, you don't come up off that scratch!

He hung up and I took his place. I read the instructions on the wall:

Collect calls only from this phone. Direct dial, credit card and out-of-country calls cannot be placed. Information service is not avail-able. You must know the number you wish to reach. Dial O for the operator. State your name and the area code and number you are calling. The operator will place your call promptly. The operator is instructed to not tolerate profanity or verbal abuse, and will termi-nate your call in that event. AT&T, your long-distance carrier, will discontinue phone service to this institution in the event of repeated infractions. Have a nice day.

I placed my call. Lucy came on the line. The operator said, Will you accept a collect call from Dean Davis?

Pardon me?

Will you accept a collect call from Dean Davis?

A pause, then a hesitant, Yes …

I shouted above the noise.

Lucy, It's me. Dean!

Dean! Where are you?

In some weird place waiting to be assigned.

What? I didn't hear you. There's static on the line.

I put a finger in my ear. I shouted.

Arcadia Correctional Center! About thirty miles away. What? Arcadia Correctional Center! Did you get that? Ok, good, write it down. Listen, you can visit ... I said you can visit! Come tomorrow. Bring Lola! What? I don't know the address. Call the prison. Get directions. I don't know. Call 411 and get the number, then call and get directions. Yes, call them. Come in the morning. Yes, I love you, too. Goodbye!

I hung up and made a cup of mud and settled back on my bunk. It had been nice to hear her voice. It would be nice to see her face. But I wondered if my heart and mind were big enough to accommodate two worlds at once.

SLAUGHTERHOUSE JIVE

 I BRUSHED MY TEETH and combed my hair and wondered what else I could do to get ready for Lucy's visit. I had the fleeting and absurd notion that I might look physically different to her now than I did only a few days ago, that she might not recognize me, and that she might appear different, too, each of us transformed by our abrupt exclusion from the other's universe.

I made a cup of mud and sat back on my bunk. The four TVs played an All In The Family rerun. A few inmates watched and shouted racial epithets at Archie Bunker, others went back to bed and pulled the covers over their heads, some played cards, some hunkered on their bunks rolling cigarettes with state-issued tobacco, Bugler or Little Egypt. One shouted out, Man, fuck this redneck bullshit, I ain't no motherfuckin cowboy! Somebody give me a real square!

Someone shouted back, It's just like rollin reefer, Brother!

A guard entered the cellblock.

Davis! Odum! Johnson! Thomas! he yelled. Work detail! Get dressed and come to the front!

Odum grumbled.

What the fuck does he want?

Lamar frowned.

Ain't this a bitch!

Stan the Man dressed slowly and said nothing.

I climbed down from my bunk and put on my work boots and approached the guard. His name tag read Smith, Oren.

Officer, where are we going?

A slight man with kindly eyes, wispy white hair and a white handlebar mustache, Smith replied, To the slaughterhouse.

Have I been assigned to the slaughterhouse?

This is a work detail, son, to keep you boys busy till you get where you're going.

But I'm expecting a visitor.

When your visitor arrives, there'll be a call over to the slaughterhouse and I'll bring you back.

We were shackled together by the ankles and marched through the driving snow and blasting wind to a waiting Department of Corrections van. We drove out the front gate and a mile down a blacktop road over the frozen countryside, through another gate, and up to an oblong concrete block building painted a sickly mustard yellow. On the right side of the building a civilian in a brown and orange plaid coat, with the help of an inmate in overalls, kicked and slid a dozen or more fat floppy-eared pigs down a ramp hooked to the back of an old green flat-bed truck with wood-slatted sides, into a pen of rusted iron piping, where they sniffed and snorted and bumped into each other in a frantic effort to be somewhere else. When they were all transferred from the truck to the pen, the inmate joined them and continued to kick at them for no apparent reason. He let off kicking and sat himself on a rusted pen rail and lit a cigarette.

Mornin, Smitty, he said to Officer Smith.

Mornin, Carter, Smith said.

He undid our shackles and opened the door of the building and we stepped inside. The air was hot and the stench was foul. I didn't know the smell of death but suspected I smelled it now.

Four steps led down to the cement floor of the building. From the front to the back of it, seven inmates in white aprons stood at their respective stations with legs spread and arms folded, and regarded us with expectant grins. Despite my apprehension, I was amused. I thought they lacked only a spotlight overhead to complete the effect.

Set in the floor at each of the stations was a drain. Overhead, attached to the ceiling, was a pulley track. Immediately to the right of the door a guard with greasy grey hair set in a pompadour looked us up and down. His name tag read Tull, Grover.

Mornin, Smitty, he said. Whatta we got here?

Mornin, Grover, Smith said. I gotcher backup boys.

They another buncha city slickers?

Dunno. Ain't ast.

Any country boys in the bunch, Tull asked us.

I'm a country boy, born and bred, Odum said.

What's your name, country boy?

Odum.

What'd you do back in the world, Odum?

Was raised up on my daddy's hog farm!

Well then, bet you know all about butcherin.

I reckon I could learn you a trick or two.

Doubt that, Odum. Where you from?

Porktown, smack dab on the Kaintucky border, an I'll bet you ain't never heard of it!

I know Porktown, Tull said. Got a gal cousin name of Irma Sue Bean married a Becker boy from Porktown. You know the Becker boys, Odum?

Know Bobby and Joe. Know Irma Sue, too.

Well, there you have it, Odum. You'n me're practically kin. What about you, slick? You from up north?

Lamar Johnson was looking around the facility with grave

apprehension. Tull snapped his fingers.

Yo, slick! Pay attention! I said you from up north?

Nuh uh, East St. Louis, Johnson said.

East St. Louis! All-American City in 1959, did you know that, slick? You boys run it into the ground real good. Got a liquor store on every corner but the stop lights don't work cause you don't pay the lectric.

Tull looked at me.

What about you, boy? Where you from?

California.

California! Where the cars wear bras and the women don't! Are you one of them beach boys?

No.

You're a long way from home, beach boy.

Just passing through.

Tull addressed the group.

Today you boys are gonna find out where the meat on your table comes from. Y'all are gonna turn a truckload a livin breathin warm-blooded animals into enough hams and ribs and chops and loins and sausages to feed a thousand sorry ass convicts like you for a week! Smitty, outfit these boys with some slaughterin clothes.

Smitty led us into a side room and handed out rubber boots, white canvass aprons stiff with dried blood, and elasticized plastic hats like scrub nurses wear. There was a desk and on the desk was a phone—the phone, I supposed, that would ring when Lucy and Lola arrived. Which wouldn't be a minute too soon.

We reassembled in front of Officer Tull.

Boys, Tull said, meet my regular crew who y'all'll be backin up till your sorry asses are shipped outta here. Up front there, that's Leroy.

He pointed a finger at a broad-shouldered black inmate who smiled and held a sledgehammer across his chest like John Henry. To the side of Leroy a ramp led up to a small wooden door hinged at the top.

When the pig come slidin down that ramp, Tull said, Leroy's job is to back it into a corner and swing that ol hammer and crack the pig's skull and knock'm senseless. Outside the penitentiary that job's done with a .22 rifle or a slug gun, but in here ain't no guns allowed, not even in the hands of yours truly. Then Leroy pulls that cable down and wraps the back legs of the pig and I pull this here lever and hoist the pig up. Then Leroy takes his cuttin knife and he cuts the pig's throat and the blood drains into that there drain in the floor. It's tricky business. You got to hit the artery just right or you risk lettin blood back into the meat.

Leroy pulled a knife from the pocket of his apron and pretended to slide it across his own throat.

Then I hit this here switch, Tull said, and the pulley wheels the pig on down the line to Brandon there.

Brandon, a short fat black inmate, took a bow.

Then Brandon takes his cuttin knife, Tull said, and he slices that pig from his butt bone to his neck bone and he puts his hands inside the carcass and scoops the guts out into a wheelbarrow.

Brandon pantomimed a great two-armed scooping gesture from top to bottom. He finished by rubbing his face in his hands and licking his lips and patting his large belly.

Then Brandon rolls the wheelbarrow full of organ meat to the back table where the butchers are, and I pull this here lever and send the pig carcass on down the line to Cletus.

Cletus, a white inmate with a broad head and cold glaring eyes, stood in front of a large steel tub full of steaming water. He held a staff with a barbed head, like a deckhand on a whaleboat.

When the pig is over that there tub, Tull said, I hit the lever and lower the pig into the water and Cletus pokes the pig and gits it turnin over'n over till it's soaked clear through. This softens up the hairs on the pig hide. Then I send the pig on down the line to Bucky there. Bucky saws the head off, and the two front legs off, then he takes a scraper and scrapes off the hair that Cletus done softened up. Two of you backup boys'll hustle up to Bucky and help with scrapin.

Bucky, a fat white inmate with long black hair jutting unevenly from his plastic hat, seemed to have missed his cue. He stared and pulled at one of his earlobes. Tull shouted, Hey, Bucky! Pay attention!

Bucky released his ear and looked up with an open mouth.

Tull said slowly and distinctly, Then Bucky takes a scraper and scrapes off the hair that Cletus done softened up!

Bucky fumbled in his apron pouch and retrieved a small saw and a scraper and displayed them with a doltish grin.

Then, continued Tull, I send the carcass on down to Jonesy there. Jonesy'll split the carcass in two from north to south with a chainsaw.

Jonesy, a very tall, thin black inmate with a full beard, held a small chainsaw in one hand and pulled its starting rope with the other. The chainsaw sputtered to life. He held it high over his head and pressed its trigger till the whine of the motor and the chain reverberated from the roof of the building.

Then, Tull said, I send the split halves to that choppin block at the back of the building, where my two butchers, Ricky and Clarence, turn'm into ribs and chops and loins and such. They got the sharpest knives and cleavers in the Midwest. I call those boys my surgeons.

Tull's surgeons, one white, one black, spun their cleavers and knives expertly, stuck them into the wooden butcher block, and folded their arms across their chests.

And that, gentlemen, Tull announced, is where your meat comes from. Twenty minutes per hog from start to finish, a dozen hogs changed into chitlins and things before the dinner bell rings!

I appreciated the crude theatricality of the presentation. It was surreal and comic at once. I remembered that when I was a kid, the carnival would come to town and I would watch the workers, the carnies, unload and assemble the rides and the games, the sucker booths, the spook houses and freak shows. That night and the next, they would stand by their attractions and invite you in, and on Sunday night they would tear it all down and load it on trucks and hit the road, and I wanted to go with them. I wanted to join the carnival.

Now we'll show you how it's done, Tull said. Smitty, would you tell Carter to send us a big'n down the chute?

Smitty stuck his head out the door.

Carter, he yelled. Send us down a big'n!

There was a chorus of frantic squealing. The flap at the top of the chute burst open and a fat screaming pig slid down the ramp to Leroy's feet.

That there sow weighs better'n 300 pounds! Tull said.

The animal looked around the room with wild, pleading little pig eyes. Leroy backed it into a corner and raised the sledgehammer over his head. As the hammer came down, the pig darted to the side and the steel head of the hammer caught its eye socket with a hollow pocking sound, leaving a crimson crater like an inverted tomato where the eye had been. The pig squealed and dropped to its knees, then flopped on its side and kicked convulsively. Leroy reached up and pulled the cable down from the overhead pulley track, but when he went to fastening the cable around the hindquarters of the pig it suddenly bucked itself up and ran about the room squealing in one-eyed terror. Leroy pulled out his knife and leaped on its back, knocking it off its feet, and plunged the knife into its neck. Blood black as motor oil leaped from the wound and turned to crimson as it thinned itself across the concrete floor and entered the drain. The crazed animal righted itself once more and raced about the room with Leroy clamped to its back like a bull rider, hacking at its neck. Inmates up and down the line shouted encouragement.

On that pig, Leroy!

Kill that motherfucker!

Tull yelled, Leroy! What'd I say about stabbing any ol place and ruinin the meat?

Soon the exhausted and dying animal dropped onto its belly and rolled to its side. A bloodied Leroy slid off and raised his dripping knife overhead, to the whistles and applause of his crew members. Was it my imagination that the pitiful creature had at the very end fixed its one good eye upon me with a gaze at once a plea and an accusation? I decided this was one carnival I didn't want to join.

Officer, I won't do this, I said to Tull.

Are you refusing to work, beach boy?

I'll do something else.

Won't be nothin else. You refuse an assignment, you go straight to the hole for a week.

And there won't be no visit today, Davis, Officer Smith said with a sympathetic tone. Your folks'll be turned away. You won't see'm till you get where you're goin, to a medium security prison or worse.

Damn! I said to myself. Going to the hole was not part of the plan. Flying under the radar was. Being the Invisible Man was. Stay out of trouble, please, Lucy had said. Don't let prison change you. If I went to the hole for refusing to work, I'd be starting my sojourn in the joint a marked man, a malcontent. On the other hand, hadn't I wanted to immerse myself in my new world? How much deeper could I go than into the hole? I could count it a reward for having foregone participation in an obscene gleeful slaughtering melee. I could meditate on the meaning of life. I might talk with the spirits. Perhaps Miranda would make an appearance.

But Lucy was on her way, nervous, excited, Lola beside her, babbling. She would arrive and be turned away, afraid and confused. Or they were here already, sitting on a bench, waiting for the call to be made. Or the call was being made at this very moment and the phone on the desk in the next room was about to ring and make this decision for me.

The slaughterhouse crew had fallen into silence. All eyes in the house were on me. I fancied I could hear the drip, drip, drip of the slaughtered animal's blood sliding into the drain.

It's just meat, Flea Weight, Stan the Man said.

You gone make me do this here bullshit alone, Brother Davis? Lamar said.

What'll it be, son, Smith said.

I imagined a scene five years into the future. I was sitting at a cloth-covered table at La Petite Maison in Tiburon. The fireplace crackled and popped. I ordered the catch of the day with mango salsa, asparagus spears and a crisp Chardonnay. Lucy ordered crab salad, a Pinot Noir, and for Lola, three-cheese macaroni and chocolate milk. Michael the waiter brought crayons and a paper placemat, and Lola scribbled away.

Look, Daddy, she said. I drew a pig!

That's good, Lola, I said. It has a curly tail. But it only has one eye. Why does it only have one eye?

I don't know, Lola said.

Give it another eye, honey, I said.

Okay, Daddy, Lola said, and drew another eye.

Lucy, I said, do you remember your first visit to prison and they turned you away because I was in the hole for refusing to work?

Yes, she said.

I've never told you the story behind the story. Would you like me to?

If you'd like, she said.

I would, I said.

And so I did.

They got a phone in the hole, Smitty?

Not hardly, Davis. No phone, no shower, no mattress. Just a cold steel bunk and one meal a day.

I smiled.

Wouldn't miss it for the world, I said.

Suit yourself, son, Smitty said.

He put me in leg-irons.

I know how you feel, Davis, he said quietly. I'm a country boy myself, but I wouldn't do it either. Not this way.

He led me up the steps and opened the door. The glare of the sun raked my eyes. A blast of bitter cold wind raced past me and across the slaughterhouse floor.

On the desk in the side room, the phone rang.

BOOK II

WHAT YOU SEEK

Go to heaven for the climate, hell for the company.
~ Mark Twain

THE SOUTH HOUSE

EL MUCHACHO LOCO

I RUBBED AT THE reddened flesh of my ankles after my shackles were removed inside the gates of Lime Ridge State Penitentiary, a medium security prison perched high on a cliff above the banks of the Muddy Mississippi. I'd been driven through the rolling snow-covered countryside in the back of a Department of Corrections van in the company of fellow inmate Ruben Choo Choo Rodriguez, El Muchacho Loco, the self-proclaimed soon-to-be Oldest Puerto Rican on the Planet. I had gotten to know Choo Choo in the hole at Arcadia Correctional Center, where I'd spent the last week. As an oasis of peace and tranquility, a refuge from the chaos of the general population, a place to park the soul and meditate on the meaning of life, solitary confinement had been a major disappointment. I was led in leg-irons down a narrow concrete corridor below ground level with my cuffed hands in front of me holding two thin, raggedy blue blankets. Low-watt bulbs in wire cages fixed to the ceiling lit the corridor with a dirty light. To my left was a windowless wall of concrete, to my right a row of cells with barred doors behind which inmates shouted conversations with unseen neighbors or yelled obscenities at me as I passed.

Whatchoo lookin at, cracker-ass motherfucker?

Hey, white boy, suck my dick!

I was shown to a cell so narrow I could touch both sides at the same time. On the left was a steel bunk without a mattress, hung from the wall by chains, and at the rear a low lidless toilet bowl and a stainless steel sink. I sat on the bunk and mulled the finite possibilities of a single pair of blankets: one doubled over and laid down on the bunk as a cushion for my hip, the other to cover with, and no pillow for my head; one to cover with, one to roll into a pillow, and no cushion between hip and cold hard steel; or one to lie on, one to roll into a pillow, and none to cover with. There was no appealing option.

Sometime late in the afternoon—I had no watch, and there was no natural light by which to judge—a guard opened my cell door and let in a young Latino inmate with a wispy mustache, close-set eyes and a silly grin.

Officer, I said, there's only one bunk in here. Why are we doubling up?

Because there's more a you shit-birds than there's holes to put you in, the guard said. So one a you sleeps on the floor.

He clanged the door shut. The new arrival dropped his blanket on the floor and grinned.

Aieee! A roommate! A Cellie in the hole! he exclaimed. This the first time I have a Cellie in the hole, man. Haha. Ain't this a bitch, man? A Cellie in the hole!

During the next seven days and nights, I made the acquaintance of Ruben Choo Choo Rodriguez. There was time for conversation. Time in the hole was like a sea without wind or wave. The only marker of its passing was the single meal a day—invariably a hot dog, a piece of white bread, and a carton of milk—brought at ten in the morning, though it might have been at three in the afternoon: by my third meal, I didn't know if it was morning, noon or night. The bulbs in the ceiling burned twenty-four hours a day; the shouting in the corridor was around the clock; the moments melted into a single unit of time.

Born in the arrabales, the slums, of Mayaguez, Puerto Rico, raised in the barrio of Humboldt Park on Chicago's West Side, and now serving twenty-five years for manslaughter—which he would do half of, and had done two years of already in a Maximum Security Penitentiary up North—Choo Choo had little reason to be happy, but happy he was. His smile rarely left his face, and his laughter erupted frequently and for no apparent reason. I didn't know if it was because of something he said, or something he was thinking, or only because there was laughter inside him that needed coming out. Whichever, it was contagious, and I sometimes found myself laughing, too, and wondering why.

My partners call me El Muchacho Loco, he said. The Crazy Boy. Haha!

I told him he didn't strike me as a murderer and did he mind if I asked what happened.

No, amigo, is all right, Choo Choo said. I had a white compañera, see, a girlfriend. I meet her in the Junior College.

He laughed, as though having a white girlfriend, or else meeting her in Junior College, was the funniest thing in the world.

She lived across town, he said, in a very white neighborhood with her mother and her big brother. I would drive to her house to visit. Her mother was nice to me, like my own mama, but her brother didn't want his sister dating a dirty spic from the barrio. Sometimes he would be with friends, and they would insult me and push me around, and my girlfriend and her brother would argue. I was afraid, so I kept a pistol in my car in case there was trouble. One day I park on the street and get out of the car and here come her brother and his friends. One has a baseball bat. Aiee! I reach for the gun and start shooting. I shoot two of them and one dies. Because they attack me first, I'm only charged with manslaughter, not murder in the first degree. Is why I only get twenty-five years, amigo. No es nada! Es fantastico! Only ten years more, then is back to The Real World and a new life for Choo Choo Rodriguez! Only no more white girls for me, haha. Anyway, man, is plenty of life left. I'm going to live to be a hundred! A hundred and twenty! I'm going to be the oldest Puerto Rican on the planet!

It occurred to me that Choo Choo Rodriguez, El Muchacho Loco, was the first Puerto Rican I had ever met. If there was a Puerto Rican in Sausalito, California, we hadn't lived in the same neighborhood.

DOUBLE BUNKED WITH BILLY

IN MY BRIGHT YELLOW JUMPSUIT in the queue in the chow hall with Choo Choo and other new arrivals—the fish line—I felt like merchandise on display. I looked out over the sea of inmates, four to a table, twenty rows of fifteen tables each, who gawked and jeered at the new arrivals.

Be my bitch!

Put that sweet young thang in my house!

There were those among them with their hair bleached blonde, or fiery orange, worn long and loose at the shoulders or done up in pigtails tied with ribbons, with rosy red cheeks and blue eye shadow.

I took a tray and was ladled up some sort of stew and an iceberg lettuce and sliced tomato salad buried under Thousand Island dressing. I hadn't eaten since yesterday's hot dog, and the fumes wafting up from the stew made my nostrils flare and my stomach rumble. I figured that in the last week I'd lost at least five of the twenty-five pounds I needed to lose to be slim and trim. That and meeting Choo Choo had made my week in the hole worthwhile.

After chow, Choo Choo and I and other fresh fish of the day were issued bedding and clothing and basic toiletries and escorted to the South House, where we would spend the next ninety plus days in doubled-up cells waiting for single cells to become available.

The South House was a hive of controlled chaos, dozens of new arrivals pushing white canvas carts filled with bedding and clothing and personal items in one direction, dozens more departing, pushing carts in the opposite direction. Old partners from the street exchanged boisterous greetings, while guards read off rosters and shouted orders to the arriving and the departing.

Choo Choo was paired with a fellow Hispanic. I was directed to a cell on the other side of the house wherein, on the top bunk, in bib overalls, picking his teeth and swinging his bare feet, sat Billy Odum, Jr.

Well, I'll be Goddamned, Odum drawled. If it ain't Dean Davis, the California Kid! How'd you like the hole, Davis?

Liked it just fine, Odum, I said.

I looked around at my new house. Only slightly larger than the one in solitary confinement, it was made oppressively smaller by Odum's presence in it.

You can pick a bunk, Davis, Odum said. I don't give a damn, but I feel safer on top. The farther I am from them black sumbitches out there, the better!

Bottom works for me, I said.

I made up my bunk while ruing the fate that had thrown Odum and me together. I reminded myself that everything happens for a reason, but I was not consoled. I knew we'd be smelling each other's shit before the day was over.

THE WELCOME COMMITTEE WASTED no time. I met them at the door. The tall one, with short blond hair and a patch over one eye, introduced himself as Captain Jack, and his brawny bearded tattooed partner as Bobo.

I'm Davis, I said. That's Odum on the bunk.

Odum sat up and blinked. I held out my hand. Captain Jack took it thumb-grip style and pumped it like a piston.

All right! he said. That makes thirty of us and only seventy of them!

I wasn't sure if that was the score of a game that began before I arrived or an informal census.

What does? I said.

Captain Jack's smile faded.

What does what? he said.

I felt at a disadvantage, there being but a single eye to betray what the man was thinking.

What makes thirty of us and only seventy of them? I said warily.

You and Odum do, Davis, Captain Jack said as though I were stupid. Two more white boys makes thirty white boys and seventy niggers—well, sixty niggers and ten spics, same fucking thing.

Bobo nodded.

Yeah, same fucking thing, he said.

I wondered how to respond without betraying my lack of sentiment for the demographics.

Right, right, I said. I can see how that might be important.

I immediately regretted my tone. It was not convincing. Captain Jack's eye narrowed.

It's not important to you, Davis?

I haven't given it a lot of thought, I said.

He released his grip. The corner of his lip pulsed in a poor imitation of Clint Eastwood's iconic quiver of contempt.

You need to think about it real fast, Davis. The joint could jump any minute. Your ass is grass if no one's got your back ... or do you think you can ride alone?

I didn't know if I could ride alone but I knew I didn't like Captain Jack and I didn't like being pushed.

I don't know, Captain Jack. What do you think?

I think when the shit hits the fan, Davis, you better know what color you are!

Yeah, Davis, Bobo said, you better know what color you are.

I'll keep that in mind, I said, and returned to my bunk.

Captain Jack looked at Odum.

What about you, Odum? You know what color you are?

White as a bed sheet, Odum said. And a country boy to boot. I'd as soon kill them black sumbitches as look at'em!

You're our man, Odum, Captain Jack said. We'll see you around the camp. And you, Davis, you can bet I'll have my eye on you!

ODUM AND I AND A ROSTER-FULL of new arrivals were escorted to a windowless room with a concrete floor, bare walls, glaring overhead fluorescent lighting, a desk up front, and four rows of four chairs each. There were more inmates than chairs and some sat on the floor or leaned against the wall in the back of the room. On the desk were two stacks of blue-bound booklets.

Standing behind the desk, a tall, slim, clean-shaven youthful white man in a dark suit and tie and white cotton shirt smiled pleasantly. Against the wall, with his arms folded and a stern, disdainful expression on his face, leaned a powerfully built black man in a green

uniform with brass buttons on his shirt, a gold oak leaf on each ep-
aulet and, ludicrously, I thought, a tan Safari Helmet, the kind worn
by British Colonial Officers.

The suited man asked for a volunteer to distribute the booklets. A
skinny white inmate with long blonde hair seated in the front of the
room stood quickly.

I'll do it! he said.

A young black inmate leaning against the wall scowled.

Sit your pussy ass down! he said.

The kid distributed the booklets without looking anyone in the eye.

Thank you, the man in the dark suit said. He addressed the group.

Gentlemen, welcome to Lime Ridge State Penitentiary!

There was scattered cynical laughter and a few nasty remarks muttered low. He introduced himself as Wesley Wainwright, Assistant
Warden of Programs. He praised the rehabilitation philosophy of
the Illinois Department of Corrections and touted the many programs at Lime Ridge State Penitentiary—academic, vocational and
recreational—and its many services designed to redirect the lives of
inmates—Anger Management, Alcoholics Anonymous, Narcotics
Anonymous, Life Skills, Job Preparedness Training and more. It was
a long list. He appealed to the new arrivals to take advantage of
these programs.

Take some knowledge, skills, abilities and professional certification
back to the streets! he said. Escape the cycle of poverty and crime, the
revolving door of recidivism!

Why, a person could become a welder, he said, or a baker, a television technician, an auto body repairman! He could get his GED, an
AA degree! Return to the world ready to make an honest living, be a
decent law-abiding citizen!

He was nothing if not earnest, and I appreciated his apparently
genuine concern. He concluded by referring us to the booklets, which
contained a history of the prison, a naming of its staff and their roles,
a description of its programs, policies and procedures—in short, he
said, everything they needed to know to make their stay in Lime
Ridge a positive experience.

There was more laughter and muttering of obscenities. The officer in the Bwana hat stepped forward. He thanked the Warden for his presentation in a tone that was unmistakably derisive. He introduced himself as Major Drumm, Chief of Security. He put his hands on his hips.

Gentlemen, he said, let me make one thing clear: the Warden's programs notwithstanding, this is not a Trade School. It is not a Community College. It is not a nursery. It is a penitentiary and you are here because you done fucked up and you're paying a debt to society. If you fuck up in here you will only go deeper in debt. You will not go to court. You will not have a lawyer. We are the prosecutor, judge and jury of all infractions!

In spite of the ominous tone of the Major's pronouncements, I smiled to myself and heard the words of Tennessee Ernie Ford: You load sixteen tons, whattaya get? Another day older and deeper in debt!

The Major recited a litany of infractions that would not be tolerated: gang activity, fighting, colored clothing, new tattoos, assaulting a guard or a civilian employee, disrespect of females, being in the cell of another inmate except in the honor dorm, possession of contraband, possession of shanks—sharpened lengths of steel, an offense punishable by a long stretch in solitary confinement, loss of up to a year of good time, and transfer to a maximum security penitentiary—and, finally, refusal to work. This is not a flophouse, he said. You will earn your grits and your bull dick gravy!

Was it my imagination or had the Major's stern gaze lingered on me when he named this final intolerable infraction? He continued.

You were issued a key upon arrival, he said. Keep it with you at all times. When you close your door, it will lock automatically whether you are inside or out. When you are in your cell it cannot be opened from the outside except by a guard. This protects you from thieves and thugs who might want to rip you off. If you are outside your cell and close the door and do not have your key you cannot get in. You must be let in by a guard. If there is only one guard present in the house, he cannot leave the control room to open your door. You must wait for another guard to arrive to let you in. You might be waiting a long time. There will be little sympathy for anyone too dumb to remember their key. Gentlemen, thank you for your attention. Obey the rules. Don't stir up shit. It will be in your best interest to not be in my presence ever again.

He left the room. Throughout his presentation, the Warden cast apologetic smiles at the assembled inmates.

There followed brief presentations by assorted department heads.

The Chaplain informed that all faiths were accommodated in the prison's modern chapel, the envy of congregations in cities and towns across America. The Director of the Health Clinic warned of the dangers of unprotected sex and the sharing of needles. The Mail Room Officer warned that all incoming items were thoroughly inspected for contraband. He instructed in the proper use of Kites—correspondence between inmates and various departments. He held up a four-by-four-inch packet of pink paper.

You'll find these at the front of every control room next to a box with a slot, he said. Write your request and slip the paper into the slot. Kites are for official business, like requesting a library pass or to see a counselor or to get a haircut. They are not for writing love letters to your pals in other houses. They will not be delivered.

The Commissary manager explained the process of making store.

Once a week, he said, you will be escorted to the commissary. There you will mark what you want on a form. If what you want is not available, you will be given a similar item, at the discretion of the inmate clerk. Our return policy is no items are returnable. If you do not have enough money on the books for all items, your requests will be filled until your money is gone. No credit will be extended. A complete list of usually available items can be found in the blue booklet.

Under the weight of so thorough an induction, I felt myself sink one layer deeper into the inescapable fact of my confinement.

THE QUEUE TO THE TELEPHONE extended from the wall to the center of the dayroom. Those inmates fortunate enough to reach their party were soon berated by those awaiting their turn: Give it up, sucker! That bitch don't wanna to talk to you! The guard in the control room periodically reminded inmates of the fifteen-minute limit when other inmates waited in line. I saw Odum cross the day-room and bump into the skinny white kid who had passed out blue booklets at orientation. The kid stepped back with a frightened look and balled his fists at his side. Odum smirked.

Whattaya gonna do? he said.

The kid turned and walked quickly away, his face a mask of shame and rage.

When my turn at the phone came I reached Lucy's answering ma-chine. I was not allowed to leave a message.

Later in our cell Odum paced and his jaw worked.

That white trash hippie sumbitch don't know who he's messin with, he said. You got an extra razor, Bud?

I gave him a state-issued disposable plastic razor, the only kind in-mates were allowed. He twisted it and broke out the narrow blade from the plastic. He got his toothbrush and a plastic lighter and held the flame of the lighter under the handle of the toothbrush till greasy black smoke coiled into the air and the tip of the handle melted. He pushed the thin blade into the melted plastic, then blew on the plastic till it was hard. He wrapped the nasty little weapon in a washcloth, exited the cell and returned momentarily, rubbing his hands together and laughing gleefully.

I skipped the evening meal. The phone line was short. I got through to Lucy. I was not prepared for the flood of her emotions and demand for an explanation for my no-show at her first visit. I reassured her that all was well but I couldn't talk now, others were waiting in line, I would explain everything when she visited. I told her where I was. I hung up just as the skinny white kid was led handcuffed across the dayroom.

It isn't mine! he screamed. I never saw it before!

That night I leaned against the wall behind my bunk and entered into my journal an account of the day. I noted the difference be-tween a *Cellie*, a *Rappee*, a *Road Doggie*, and a *Ride*. A *Cellie* was the inmate with whom one shared one's cell, for better or worse. Regrettably, Odum was my *Cellie* of the moment. A *Rappee* was the inmate with whom one committed one's crime and who was charged with the same *rap* as you. A *Road Doggie* was a more or less syco- phantic inmate who tagged along with another inmate for status and protection. Lennie was *Road Doggie* to George in Steinbeck's *Of Mice and Men*. A *Ride* was a companion of more or less equal status and with a compatible point of view. To address a fellow inmate as one's *Ride* was to bestow respect. One had many *Rides* if he was hooked up with a gang. I had no *Rides*. I road alone.

I noted the meaning of *Good looking out*. If a fellow inmate did you a good turn—warned you of danger, was at your side in an alterca- tion, gave you something you could use—you might have said *Good looking out, Ride*. You might said that he *had your back*.

I put my notes aside and glanced through the blue orientation book- let. I perused the list of usually available commissary items. It was extensive: nonessential toiletries; paper and pens; typing paper; sta- tionery and envelopes; an array of whams and zooms: Top Ramen, Folgers Coffee, soft drinks, peanut butter, Hi Ho crackers, Twinkies, Hostess Cupcakes, Nutty Bars, and more. Also available to order— expect a six week waiting period—were such luxuries as a cassette player, a small black and white television, a fan, and a Hot Pot for boiling water.

White burgundy was not on the list, but I would survive.

I tossed aside the blue booklet and attempted to read a novel, but its account of the outside world and its concerns failed to resonate. Beyond my door, half a dozen boom boxes were cranked to the max. Inmates prowled the corridor shouting obscenities and pounding on doors. Beyond my bunk, to the left of the door, Odum sat on the low, lidless toilet bowl, humming to himself and making dumping noises. A raspy voice over the P.A. system announced: Ten o'clock lock-down! Clear the corridor! Return to your cells! Lock-down!

The announcement was met with a chorus of jeers.

Fuck you, screw! We ain't clearin shit!

Lock your own self down, motherfucker!

The officer in the control room responded with practiced disregard. Gentlemen, if you're not in your cells in five minutes, you'll be sleeping on the floor in the hole for a week. It's up to you.

Odum finished his business and wiped himself and climbed up onto his bunk. I went to piss. I peered into the bowl.

You didn't flush, Odum, I said.

Sorry bout that, Bud, he said. I'll get it next time.

He reached under his pillow and pulled out a length of cloth, pulled it down over the top of his head, tied it under his chin and stuffed a sock between the cloth and each ear. I flushed the toilet. The control room announced: Last call, Gentlemen! Last call for alcohol!

Inmates returned to their cells. A guard came down the corridor, closing and locking doors. The clanging of steel on steel reverberated from the concrete walls. I turned off the light and undressed and slipped under the scratchy blue blanket. Inmates continued their conversation with partners, shouting through the walls. Music from boom boxes coursed through the ventilation system and deposited itself disharmoniously into my cell. Odum's snoring sounded like an argument between an ogre and a troll.

It was going to be a long ninety days till I had my own cell.

ANOTHER TIME AND PLACE

LUCY SAT ACROSS FROM ME at one of a dozen Formica-topped tables, nursing Lola under a blanket. She peered down through an opening in the blanket and smiled serenely. I took a mental picture: Madonna With Child in Penitentiary. To the right of the door a guard with a ruddy face sat behind a desk observing the room. Behind him on the wall a sign listed the visiting rules:

> *No Touching Above the Elbows*
> *No Touching Below the Table*
> *Kissing Only Upon Entering and Leaving the Room*
> *No Visiting Other Tables*
> *Inmates May Speak Only to Their Own Visitors*
> *No Conversation Between Inmates*

To the guard's right, on the bathroom door, a sign with male and female symbols instructed that only one person was allowed inside at a time. To his left was a row of vending machines. On the walls around the room hung inmate art available for purchase by visitors. There were no windows.

She's asleep, Lucy said.

She fastened her blouse beneath the blanket. The blanket slid to her lap. Lola's lips continued to suckle. Her lids were heavy and pink.

Let me hold her, I said.

I cradled her in one arm and touched her cheek. She seemed a cherub with one foot yet in heaven. I kissed her on the forehead and handed her back. Lucy wrapped her snugly in the blanket and laid her in the basket on the table. She seemed suddenly to remember where she was and looked around the room. At a table nearby, a very dark middle-aged African American woman wearing a small round black hat with a small red feather, sat across from a light-skinned African American inmate with blue eye shadow, rosy cheeks and long hair bleached golden like the sun and done up in two braids. Lucy leaned forward and whispered.

Are there female prisoners here?

I glanced at the table and smiled.

That's a guy, I said.

You could have fooled me, Lucy said. You're allowed to look like a girl?

Guys have girlfriends here, I said. They're called Kids. Or Gumps.

You wouldn't ever … you know … would you?

I slid the fingers of my free hand softly up her forearm and circled them slowly in the hollow of her elbow.

I can wait, I said.

She glanced quickly at a beady-eyed white inmate with crude blue tattoos that began at his knuckles, slid under the sleeve of his blue denim shirt, emerged from its collar and continued up the side of his shaved head.

There are some scary characters in here, she said. Are you going to be all right?

I'll be fine, I said. I've made a few friends.

Friends!

I told her about Oh Henry, how all the pretty women got stuck on The Candy Man's stick; about Stan the Man, who had knocked out Buster Mathis; about Lamar from East St. Louis, who aspired to the pinnacle of Pimpdom; about Ruben Choo Choo Rodriguez, El Muchacho Loco, who aspired to be the Oldest Puerto Rican on the Planet. I saw the misgiving in her face. There was much she could not be expected to understand. Upon her arrival, I told her I had been sent to the hole for refusing to slaughter pigs, but faltered telling her why.

It's complicated, I had said. Some day I'll be able to explain.

What do you do all day, she said now.

I watch and I wait. I try not to make anybody mad. When I'm assigned to a permanent housing unit, I'll go to school. They have a Junior College program.

That's wonderful, Dean!

Umm ... I'll be repeating classes I've already had, but it will keep me out of the kitchen.

Lucy glanced at the wall behind me.

Some of the art is good, she said, especially the Mother Goose pictures. So carefully crafted.

I looked.

I guess there's time in here to be meticulous, I said.

I like the one with her wings spread, Lucy said. And the little boy asleep under one wing and the little girl under the other. They look protected and peaceful, while the goose looks sad and motherly and fierce all at the same time.

I like that one, too, I said. Buy it. Hang it in Lola's room. She can grow up under the loving gaze of Mother Goose.

I don't know, Dean. Do I want prison paraphernalia in my house?

The artist gets the money, I said.

All right, she said. But what can you do with money in here?

The state provides essential items like basic toiletries, but there's a commissary for expendable items. They call it *making store.*

What can you buy?

A long list of goodies to make your stay a pleasant one. But you have to have money on the books.

Will you need money?

When I go to school I'll be paid fifteen dollars a month.

Fifty cents a day! That's not enough. How do I put money on the books?

You mail a money order with my inmate number on it. No personal checks.

Where do I mail it to?

I don't know. Ask on your way out.

How much should I send?

I hesitated. I felt bad taking money away that she might need for herself and Lola.

I don't know, I said.

A hundred dollars a month?

I don't want to be a burden.

You supported me in style for a few years, Dean. It's my turn.

All right, I said. I can live well here on a hundred dollars a month. Thank you very much.

The guard came to our table.

Five minutes, Davis, he said, politely but firmly. Wrap it up. Your visitor leaves first. Then you wait for an escort.

I took Lucy's hand. We held each other's gaze.

Give my love to Brodie, I said. And to your dad. Tell them to write. And to visit.

All right, she said.

A tear ran down her cheek.

Can I send you anything else?

An Iceberg Slim novel, I said. And some Elmore Leonard. And some Cormac McCarthy. And a pad of drawing paper and some colored pens and pencils.

I'll never remember, she said.

Write it down, I said.

I don't have pen and paper, she said. They wouldn't let me bring anything in.

Maybe the guard will lend you some.

She went to the guard's desk and returned with paper and pen. She made a list.

Anything else? she said.

A blue jean jacket.

That's not your style, Dean.

It's the only kind allowed in here.

You'll look like one of them.

I am one of them.

You're not, she said.

Well ...

All right, she said. Anything else?

Yes, I said. A case of Oh Henry candy bars. Take them to the County Jail. Tell them they're for the inmate from Alabama.

The County Jail, she said. The inmate from Alabama.

You'll make an old guy very happy.

The guard shouted across the room: Time's up, Davis.

We stood. I took Lola from her basket and rubbed her nose with mine. She awoke and whimpered.

Hi, Lola, I said. Daddy loves you.

I returned her to the basket. Lucy and I embraced.

I'll see you in six months, I said.

It's so long, she said. I'll come sooner.

Save your money, I said. I'll be fine.

But I won't be, she said.

She walked away. She spoke to the guard and pointed at the Mother Goose picture. He took it down and opened the door and handed it to someone on the other side. Lucy turned and waved goodbye with a brave smile on her face. As the door closed behind her, I had the disturbing impression that she and Lola were being phased out of my existence and transported to another time and place. I hoped it was not forever.

THE BOYS ON THE BLOCK

HERMIT CRAB

A HOUSING UNIT AT LIME RIDGE was laid out like a Greek Cross, four corridors of equal length extending off a central, glassed-in security room where a guard on one side sat at a control panel and monitored two of the corridors, A and B, and a second guard sat opposite him and monitored C and D. Each pair of adjacent corridors had a dayroom in common, and each corridor pair was comprised of fifty cells, thirteen down one side of each corridor, twelve down the other side, the missing cell-space occupied by a shower which served twenty-five men. Inmates referred to their cells as their house or their crib.

The polished concrete floor of each corridor reflected the glare of the overhead fluorescent fixtures in great floating shimmering disks of light laid on by years of daily waxing and buffing. Gray steel doors lined the pale green concrete walls on either side, and over the doors were stenciled number-and-letter combinations: 1A, 2A, 3A, 4A, etc. When I entered corridor A in housing unit North One pushing a canvass cart that contained my clothing and bedding and books, I was reminded of the carnival game I'd loved in my childhood: a spinning wheel with holes around its perimeter, each hole marked by a number and color. Customers placed their bets and a mouse was let loose on the spinning wheel till it disappeared down a hole, and the customer who had bet the winning hole won double his money. I was the mouse in hole number 11.

North One 11A. My new home.

I pushed my cart to the end of the corridor where, in front of the open door of North One 11A, stood a short, middle-aged African American inmate alongside a cart of his own, contemplating the now empty cell. Our carts were side by side. He turned his attention from the cell to me.

You must be Davis, he said.

His head was shaved and shiny, his ears small and curved tight like miniature tubas, his blue cotton work shirt pressed and buttoned to the top, his blue cotton trousers creased neatly, his black leather shoes polished and buffed. Fastidious, I thought. Self-contained.

That's my name, I said. How did you know?

It's my business to know who's moving into my house, Davis. Who he is and what he is about.

He spoke slowly and precisely, seeming in no hurry to get to the end of his sentences. He looked again into the seventy-five square feet of empty space he was leaving behind. He sniffed the air. There was something at once mournful and resolute in the man's voice and I was careful to respect the solemnity of the moment.

What's your name? I said.

Mayo. Marvin Mayo.

So … you've lived in this house a long time, Marvin?

I was on the first bus that passed through the gates of this whore camp ten years ago, Davis. This been my only house. Old boy pass away. Moms pass away. My little girl have a baby three times her own self since I come to this house.

I looked into the empty cell.

That's a long time, Marvin. Are you going home?

Marvin Mayo grinned like I'd said something funny and stupid.

Lime Ridge *is* my home, brother. I'm just moving cross camp to the honor dorm.

Lucky you, I said. I hear it's nice over there.

Won't be the same, Davis. This house full of memories and dreams.

I was touched by the man's nostalgia. I felt impelled to ease his passage from one habitat to another.

Marvin, I said, those memories and dreams, they're not stored up in these concrete walls, you know. They're stored up in your heart and your soul. Let me tell you about the hermit crab. The hermit crab is born with a shell on his back. That shell is the only home he knows.

He eats and sleeps and dreams in that shell. One day he outgrows it and leaves it behind and finds a new empty shell that's been left behind by another hermit crab. If it fits, he moves in. He takes his memories and his dreams with him, and when he outgrows that shell he finds another and so forth until he's outgrown his need for any more shells. Till he moves to that shiny white shell in the sky. You're like that hermit crab, Marvin: moving out of one shell into another and taking your memories and dreams with you.

Marvin Mayo was silent a long time.

That's deep, Davis, he said. You tell a good story. I feel a whole lot better now. Lookee here—I want to do you right. You got a blue jean jacket?

I do, I said. It's brand new. Why do you ask?

I'm the tailor in the camp. I was a tailor on the street. Don't nobody do a stitch like Marvelous Marvin Mayo! You give me that jacket, Davis. I'll hook it up real tough. It'll pop your eyes out!

I hesitated. I'd gotten the jacket from Lucy. I didn't know Marvin Mayo. Would I get the jacket back? But where could the man go? And what would he gain by keeping it? And what did he mean, he'd hook it up real tough?

There was only one way to find out.

Okay, Marvin, I said.

I dug down into my cart and found the jacket and handed it to Mayo. He folded it neatly and placed it on top of his cart.

I'll call you over to my shop in a week, Davis, he said. You'll like what you see.

He wheeled his cart around mine. He stopped and took one long last look into the cell he was leaving behind.

It's been a good house, he said. A mighty good house.

BE LIKE BOTHA

IN THE EVENING OF MY FIRST DAY in North One, I sat at a table in the smoky dayroom pretending to read the prison newspaper,

Prose & Cons. I cast cautious glances at the fraternity of men who would be my friends and neighbors for the next few years.

At the table to my left, two black inmates, one portly and bald, the other slight, his hair flattened back and shiny, were absorbed in a game of Chess. The portly one addressed his partner.

Quincy, you gonna move a piece fore the middle of next week?

Move when I be ready to move, Lloyd, Quincy said without looking up from the board.

Goddam, Quincy, a nigger could do his time, come back for another crime, fore you be ready!

Lloyd, how a man sposa think with you steady runnin your mouth?

Jus move *somethin,* turtle ass motherfucker!

In the center of the room sat a shirtless, muscular African American as dark and sculpted as my teakwood bar at home. A threadbare white towel covered his shoulders like a cape. He leaned forward, his elbows on his knees, and stared at the floor between his feet. I felt his smoldering intensity, like heat waves off a two-lane blacktop road in the summertime. Hovering about him, a cinnamon-skinned inmate with blue eye shadow and rosy cheeks braided his hair in tight rows.

Oh, you gonna love this, honey, he cooed like a dove. You gonna be so handsome!

I recognized him as the one I had first seen from the fish line in the chow hall, a Whitney Houston look-alike who would have fooled me in a bar on the street, especially after a few drinks.

At a table to my right, four men played cards. The white one among them, his shaved head milky white and misshapen as a potato, his back a crude blue mural of demons, dragons and snakes, jumped up suddenly and slammed a card into the center pile.

Trump *that,* Cooba, you cocksucker! You little spic!

A plump little Latino inmate with a fine line of facial hair encircling his lips and chin, wearing long-john bottoms and high-top tennis shoes, glared at the pile.

Ain dees a beetch, mon! he said.

On the far side of the room, bolted high up the cinder block wall, a television blared. A long haired white inmate stood on a folding chair flipping channels. Inmates seated below shouted their preferences.

Play The Jeffersons, motherfucker!

No, Charlie's Angels!

Man, fuck them holes! The Bulls playin Boston in the Garden at eight.

An inmate with a towel wrapped around his head like a turban yelled in the direction of the card table.

Yo, Simon, what time it is, man?

Receiving no response, he yelled louder.

Simon! What time it is!

Simon responded while keeping his eyes on his hand.

Why you wanna know what time it is, Andrew? There some place you gotta be?

Just what time it is, man, c'mon!

Time a bitch! Time a funky ho!

Simon, goddam! On your watch, nigger! What time it is!

Time a river! Time a sea! Time drown a nigger like you or me!

Oh, now you a motherfuckin poet!

I can bust a rhyme.

You can bust a rhyme, but you can't tell time, sucker, so go fuck yourself!

Andrew turned back round and nudged the inmate next to him.

Gimme a square, Darnell.

Darnell slid a cigarette pack from his blue denim shirt pocket without taking his eyes from the television.

Shit, Andrew said, Y'all ain't got no Double Os?

What you see is what you get, sucker, said Darnell.

Andrew took a cigarette from the pack, put it between his lips, took two more and slipped them into his shirt pocket.

Gimme some fire, Darnell, he said.

Darnell slid a plastic lighter from his pocket and handed it to Andrew.

You want me to smoke it for you, too? he said.

Andrew lit his cigarette. He looked around the floor at his feet.

Yo! Rhymin Simon, he yelled toward the card table. Slide me that butt can over here!

On the floor by Simon's feet was a coffee can painted red.

What's the magic words, Andrew?

Magic words is, You wanna die, motherfucker?

Uh huh, fool, now you gotta come get this can!

Simon, Andrew moaned, why you make me get up when you right there by the motherfucker? Slide me that can over here, brother, goddamn!

Simon stuck a leg out and shoved the butt can toward Andrew. It slid across the polished concrete floor, clipped the leg of Andrew's chair and flipped over, spilling inky black water and soggy butts onto his bare feet.

Goddam, nigger! he shouted. Lookee what you done did, man!

He yelled across the room to where an elderly, light-skinned black man with a patch of hair like dirty snow sat holding a mop.

Hey, Sylvester, bring that mop over here!

The old man looked up. His head bobbed like a cork in a stream.

Get your sorry ass over here, pops!

The old man shuffled over, dragging his mop behind him.

Mop up this mess, pops!

The old man swished the mop in the mess, lapping sodden ashes onto Andrew's bare feet.

Shit, pops, you moppin my feet, fart ass motherfucker!

He shoved the old man, who stumbled and nearly fell.

I wanted to bop the back of Andrew's head with the mop handle. He was smaller than me. But I knew it was not my place. The culture of the camp was crude, it was in your face, but changing it was not an option. I could only change myself. But wasn't change what I had promised Lucy I would not do?

At that moment, through the D Wing door, strode a tall, slim black inmate clutching a thick black book at his side. His blue cotton pants and work shirt were freshly cleaned and pressed, his black leather shoes buffed to a sheen, his hair cropped short, appearing almost to have been painted on. His round rimless glasses gave him a learned look. He might have come out of the Marvelous Marvin Mayo

School of Impeccable Grooming. He walked to the cluster of inmates beneath the television.

Brother Andrew, he said with a chastising tone, why you shove that old man like he a dog? Don't he have enough burden in this mortal world without your help?

Andrew shrugged.

He alright. Ol boy ain't dead, is he?

Brother, you'll be old and infirm your own self someday. Let's pray folks don't be pushing *you* into an early grave!

Andrew looked back at the television. The old man dragged his mop to the corner, where he sat and pawed at his face as though to remove some fine invisible stuff that clung to it. The tall inmate walked to the center of the room and addressed the muscular inmate having his hair coiffed.

Evening, Brother Botha, he said.

I ain't your brother, Pinklon, Botha said without looking up.

Look like you getting all dressed up for the bright lights on the boulevard, Pinklon said. Guess in a minute you be pimping whores and slamming Cadillac doors!

Botha regarded Pinklon with a baleful look, then resumed his scrutiny of the floor between his feet. Pinklon looked at the inmate braiding Botha's hair.

Brother Botha, why you let this freak put his hands on you? What did the Prophet Mohammed say about men lying down with men?

The Prophet Mohammed can kiss my black ass! Botha said.

Pinklon shook his head in mock dismay.

Such bitter and blasphemous words, my brother!

I done told you I ain't your motherfucking brother!

We are all brothers in the bosom of Allah, my brother.

Botha jumped up. The towel slipped from his shoulders. He poked a finger into Pinklon's chest.

Allah don't mean shit to me, nigger! And you are not my Imam! You are Pinklon! Pinklon the Punk! I rode with you when you were the man. Now you can't wipe your own black ass without Allah saying when and where. So don't talk to me, nigger. I ain't your boy. I'm a straight up gangster, and I'll be a gangster till the day I die! I smoke dope. I fuck freaks. I eat swine. And I kill motherfuckers who get in my bidness. And you ... are in ... my bidness.

The guard in the control room put down his paperback book.

Gentlemen, he drawled, let's don't be getting physical or the whole house will be locked down and you two hombres will spend the night in the hole.

Botha whirled.

Fuck you, too, Hopalong Cassidy motherfucker!

He turned back around to face Pinklon, who pressed the Koran to his own chest and bowed slightly, keeping a wary eye on his adversary's glowering face.

I meant no disrespect, he said. I leave you in peace. A salaam a laikam.

He exited the dayroom. Botha watched him go. He glared around the room. Everyone who had witnessed the exchange now looked away—except me. I was riveted, struck by the force of his malice, transfixed by his face, a warrior's face, adorned by a scar from his temple to his chin, like a string of knots beneath the skin. What vagaries of fate had fashioned a man so bitter, yet so unambiguous? A man who knew what he was about, as I did not. Killing motherfuckers who got in his business notwithstanding, I would do well to be like Botha. He caught me staring.

What the fuck are *you* lookin at?

I blinked. The spell was broken.

Nothing, I said. I'm not looking at anything.

You better find you some bidness!

I can do that.

Find it and mind it!

I turned around. I felt his glare through the back of my head, like the rays of the sun through a magnifying glass. I attempted to read from *Prose & Cons* but the words were meaningless, while six words shone like a beacon of light: You better find you some bidness!

IS IT SOUP YET?

THE DUCTWORK THAT CARRIED fresh air from cell to cell also served as a conduit for sound, especially after lockup when the block was relatively quiet. Then you could hear the strains of music wafting up from radios and boom boxes still playing, and sometimes the clacking of typewriter keys into the wee hours. Such was the case the night before I first met Wilbur.

I thought the faint clacking that echoed each riff of my own on the key board was some kind of aberration, a warping of the atmosphere that caused the sound to be absorbed by, then released back into the night air. Or a warping of the atmosphere between my ears caused by the long succession of nights locked up and alone. Either way, when my passage on the keys was brief, it was followed by a brief rejoinder. When my passage was sustained, likewise its echo. This continued for a half hour, then ceased as though the warp in one atmosphere or another had corrected itself.

The next evening, soon after I settled myself in and commenced typing, there was a knock at the door. I opened it on an inmate I had seen around but never talked to, a wiry, leprechaun-looking guy with a knobby chin, long nose and ears, and eyes set deep in the shadow of craggy brows. I fancied the man might have been born and raised in a tangle of gnarly tree roots. He smiled a crooked smile and said, Is it soup yet?

Is what soup yet? I said.

What you're cooking up.

I'm not cooking up anything.

You know what I mean.

Afraid I don't.

I write, too.

About what?

Necrophilia. Doppelgangers. Time and space. The living dead. Did you hear me talking to you last night?

No.

Through the ventilation system. Clickety-clack. Clickety-clack.

Oh, that was you.

I was letting you know you're not alone.

I like alone, especially when I am.

We're fellow writers. We need each other.

I don't know about that.

Let's read each other's stuff. What do you write?

I keep a journal to pass the time. Character sketches. Bits of dialogue. Incidents and anecdotes. A Boys on the Block kind of thing. There's nothing for you to read.

You should write stories. Reality is boring. Too many rules. When you're doing hard time, you want to create worlds where anything goes. Right now, I'm writing the biography of Mother Goose. She wants it told but she doesn't write, so I'm interviewing her in my cell. Sometimes in her cell, which is next to mine.

I see. Mother Goose is here in Lime Ridge, is she?

Yes. We're lucky to have her. She's a rare specimen. I'm doing her childhood first. I call it Bird Interrupted. When she asked me to write her story I said, Can I borrow a quill? But she didn't get the joke. I'm Wilbur, by the way.

I'm Dean.

I know. Dean Davis. AKA Double D. Busted for dope. Doing a dime, a nickel with good time. Address of record San Francisco.

You know more about me than I know about you.

I work in the Captain's office. I pull records. I know who's who and what's what.

Wilbur looked around me into my cell.

Nice typewriter, he said.

IBM Selectric, I said. Courtesy of my wife.

It's beauty. I use a vintage Remington. It has the soul of an old machine. Would you like to read her bio when I'm done?

Whose bio?

Of Mother Goose! Are you listening?

Sure, I'd like to read it.

It's not up to me, Wilbur said. It's up to her. She might not like you.

I suppressed a laugh.

Well, be sure and let me know, I said.

You bet I will, Double D. We'll talk again.

He glanced up and down the corridor and walked quickly away.

FROM TIME TO TIME, WILBUR would bring me a story to read. He'd knock softly and when the door opened, his eyes would dart left and right like roaches when the lights come on. He'd pull the manuscript out from the front of his shirt and hand it to me and say, You'll like this, then walk away with his hands in his pockets and his head hanging low.

His stories were eclectic and bizarre: tales of animals that gave birth to humans, and of humans who gave birth to animals; of mannequins that mated after the department store closed and gave birth to little mannequins; of plants and trees that uprooted themselves in the night and rearranged the forest floor; of a man and a dog who lived alone together and stared into each other's eyes until they traded places, and the man became the dog, and sat at the feet of the dog who became the man, and sat in the man's chair by the fireplace and smoked his pipe and thought the world was a marvelous place; of planets that communicated with one another telepathically and told jokes about the planets in other galaxies; of the oldest boulder in the world, which served as a repository of every thought, word and deed of every sentient being on earth from the beginning to the end of time, and of the idiot savant who set out to find it; of children who went missing for a day and returned with a hundred years of knowledge and wisdom, which they had to conceal from grown-ups.

His stories were a record of dream states and delirium. His sentences meandered for a quarter of a page, with baffling metaphors and labyrinthine syntax, but always you came to the end of them with a head full of images and ideas and to the end of the story with the feeling of having been somewhere outside yourself, which served one well who was strictly confined.

I had been reluctant to read Wilbur's work at first but soon found myself dropping by his cell, sticking my head in the door and saying: Is it soup yet?

CHICKEN SHACK

I THOUGHT IF EVER I TOLD the story of Old Man Mosley, I should not mention hearing late at night, through the common wall of our adjacent cells, the old man singing in a sweet sad baritone: Swing low, Sweet Chariot, coming for to carry me home. It was too improbable a cliché.

Old Man Mosley had a tumor in his bowels the size of a golf ball. It festered and fumed, and when he walked up the corridor, mumbling and cursing, his flatulence was audible and seemed to quicken his pace like a booster rocket firing, prompting such complaints as, Pops, you a foul dude, you a fart-ass motherfucker!

It was understood by his fellow prisoners that the old man would die behind these walls, no doubt sooner than later. He was twenty years into an eighty year sentence for the shooting death of two teen-age boys who one fine day robbed his chicken shack on Chicago's South Side. They walked into his joint, pulled their pistols, took his money and ran ... and he ran after them firing his own pistol till they lay dead in the street.

Old Man Mosley didn't understand why he had to be locked up.

Those punks pulled their pop guns first, he lamented. Little gangsters think they gone rob my chicken shack!

He believed he would be back on the street someday and would have his self another chicken shack. He told me he was too old to start from nothin. He best get himself a ready-made chicken shack like that one with the old white man with the glasses and the silly grin.

That would be Colonel Sanders, I said. His place is called Kentucky Fried Chicken.

How much a man has to pay for a Kentucky Fried Chicken shack, Davis?

I don't know. It's a franchise. You never really own it. You pay a fee for the license, then you pay a fee every month. And there'd be start-up costs and operating costs.

How much a man need to get started?

A chunk of change for sure.

How much, Davis?

I'd guess a quarter million dollars.

The old man winced and seemed to visibly shrink beneath the weight of all those dollars. But he straightened and shouted defiantly: A quarter million dollars my black ass! I ain't payin no quarter million dollars for no goddam chicken shack! Get my own motherfuckin chicken shack!

He turned and walked quickly up the corridor muttering and cursing and venting noxious fumes.

GRATITUDE

HARRY THE STICK WAS NOT a pretty man. He was square-headed, with deep indents at the temples as might be left by forceps on the malleable skull of an infant. His grey hair was cut flat on top, his teeth were big and square, his lips fleshy, with always tiny white bubbles nestling in their corners like fish eggs. He spat when he said his Ps and Bs and when he spat he wiped his lips and said with shame and anger, Fuck this fucking mouth of mine!

Harry the Stick, so-called because his crime of choice was armed robbery—sticking people up—was passionate about his trade. He wasn't in it for the money, though he made a living at it between gigs as an iron-worker and bits in the joint. No, he did it for the gratitude. He used a forty-five caliber pistol because it was big and square and ugly and intimidating like he was, and put the fear of death in the hearts and minds of his victims, who he called his customers. When he doesn't kill them they are so grateful. He can feel the love. And after getting stuck up by a blockhead like me, he says, and thinking they're going to die and they don't, they got a story to tell their friends for the rest of their stupid lives.

WAXING THE WALLS

TREVOR THE HITMAN HARRIS and I got to the phone at the same time. I reached for it first, but Trevor reached faster and wrapped his big hand around the receiver. We were almost nose to nose and locked in a stare.

I know you ain't crazy, he said.

A tall, young, muscular black inmate who moved with the sinewy grace of a panther, Harris was the Illinois Department of Corrections Light Heavyweight Champion. He was being trained by one-time professional Stan the Man to defend his title. Despite his reputation as a skilled and ferocious opponent in the ring, he had a ready smile and lots of friends.

No, I ain't crazy, I said, withdrawing my hand. I wasn't afraid but I wasn't crazy either and knew there was a time to hold your ground and a time to take a step back. So I took a step back. Harris flashed a big smile and took his hand off the receiver.

I'm jus messin with you, man! he said. Make your call! Who you callin? Your wife and kids? Your mama? Go ahead on, man. Make your call!

Thanks, I said. Yeah, I'm calling my wife.

I didn't feel it necessary to explain but I appreciated the Hit Man's politeness.

I won't be long, I said.

I called Lucy. I got her machine and couldn't leave a message. I motioned for Harris to come get the phone. He sat at a table with two other inmates playing cards and gestured for me to join them.

You play Tonk? he said.

I'm learning.

I need a partner.

I sat. The other two men at the table, one a lean, middle-aged African American with eyes like dark marbles and a ragged scar on his cheek, the other a stone-faced shirtless Hispanic, did not introduce themselves. We played without conversation. Whenever the

Hispanic got trumped, he would exclaim: Ain't dees a beetch, mon! The Hit Man and I won two games in a row. The Hispanic and his partner left the table.

Come to my crib, Brother Davis, Harris said. I got somethin for you.

I followed him to his cell. The guard was looking the other way. I slipped inside. The first thing I noticed was the sparseness. The man owned nothing but the bare necessities and these were meticulously arranged: bed, made uptight and smooth like a military bunk; black leather work boots polished brightly, high top tennis shoes and rubber shower shoes, all lined up like soldiers on parade; state-issued green metal cabinet with a single shelf, on which were his underwear folded in little squares, socks snugly bundled, and his boxing paraphernalia—mouth piece, hand wraps and Jockstrap. From the bar across the top of the cabinet hung two sets of blue denim work clothes, creased sharply, and a pair of long-john tops and bottoms folded precisely in half. On the stainless steel shelf over his sink, in a neat row, evenly spaced, were his toiletries.

The second thing I noticed was the sheen: the floors, the walls, the ceiling, all sparkled with a fine shining patina.

Bright, I said.

I waxed it, he said, surveying his handiwork with a satisfied smile. Got me some floor wax from the porter, put it in a pan, got me a mop, waxed it all up real nice!

Shiny, I said.

Take this, he said. Do yourself right.

He handed me a skinny joint and a red plastic lighter.

I went to the window in the back of the cell, took a few tokes and blew the smoke out the window. I handed the joint and the lighter back.

Thanks for the high, I said. I appreciated the gesture. It was generous and unexpected. I liked The Hit Man. He seemed to want little and was nearly content. Whatever brilliance he demanded of life he seemed to get from waxing the walls of his cell … and maybe from waxing his opponents in the ring.

He stuck his head out the door. It's all clear, Brother Davis, he said.

Thanks for the buzz, I said, though I didn't feel it much. No doubt there was more dynamite in The Hit Man's fists than there was in his reefer.

BUCK ROGERS OUTDATE

I TOLD REGGIE BROWN ABOUT the view from the top of Mt. Tamalpais in Marin County, California, when the sun goes down: how it glows like a red hot nickel when it slides beneath the sea; how cargo ships long as city blocks and tall as ten story buildings pass beneath the Golden Gate Bridge en route to the Port of Oakland, carrying who knows what from the far-flung corners of the world; how when the fog rolls in, the screech of the seagulls and the cottony moan of the fog horns reminds me of the Zen flute playing of Tony Scott.

Reggie Brown told me about the view from the window of the 10th floor apartment in the housing project, Cabrini Green, on the Near North Side of Chicago, where he was born and raised: the mobs of black youth, bored, restless, and angry, fighting in the street; of little girls in pigtails, his little sister Maddie among them, skipping rope on sidewalks littered with glass chips that sparkled in the sun; of his big brother Deontay cooking up pork steaks for sale out of an old barrel cut sideways and hooked up for grilling; about the cops, like nazis in their checkered flat hats and black leather coats, breaking the bones and the heads of his partners with their big old nightsticks; how, when the wail of the sirens mixed with the sounds of the shooting and the shouting, it reminded him of Stevie Wonder's *Living for the City*.

I showed Reggie Brown a photograph I'd taken of my older brother, Brodie, a Poetry Professor at San Francisco State, standing with the poet Lawrence Ferlinghetti on the sidewalk outside City Lights Books in North Beach, San Francisco. The guy on the left is Ferlinghetti,

I told him. He owns the bookstore. The guy on the right is Alan Ginsberg. He wrote a famous book, *Howl and Other Poems*, published by Ferlinghetti. The guy in the middle is my brother, Brodie. He wishes he was famous, too.

Reggie Brown showed me a photograph of himself and two of his partners posing on a balcony of Cabrini Green, taken by his brother, Deontay, on the day they named themselves The Cabrini Green Gangsters.

That's me on the left, Reggie said. The shortest of the shorties. I was twelve.

Twelve-year-old Reggie, in blue jeans, striped tennis shoes, a pullover shirt with a stripe across the chest, and a baseball cap on backward, stood with his feet apart and his arms folded, staring at the camera, trying to look not so short and not so young.

Next to me is Randall, Reggie said. He was fourteen then. I was in love with his sister.

Fourteen-year-old Randall was a head taller than Reggie, with long legs in black denim trousers, high top tennis shoes, and a hooded sweatshirt. His arms, too, were folded, and on his face was a mix of defiance and uncertainty.

That's Terrence on the right, Reggie said. He was fifteen. He was our Chief.

Terrence was tall and slim, in faded blue jeans and tennis shoes, and a zippered nylon windbreaker with a Chicago Bulls logo on the front. His expression was one of supreme indifference.

Reggie Brown told me how he picked their gang name: he liked to watch Super Hero television shows and read Super Hero comic books. He liked Flash Gordon and Buck Rogers, how they lived in a future impossibly faraway. He liked The X-Men and The Fantastic Four. He liked Captain America and The Teen Titans and Wonder Woman. He liked The Green Hornet. He told his partners, Lissen up, Yo! We're from Cabrini Green. Let's be The Cabrini Green Hornets! Randall hooted and rolled his eyes, and Terrence said, Nigger, you better come up off that comic book bullshit, Reggie. We straight up gangsters, not some jive ass white folk superheroes!

And Reggie said, All right. All right. How about just the Cabrini Green Gangsters? And Terrence said, Now you makin sense, Youngblood!

Reggie Brown told me how, two years later, the Cabrini Green Gangsters delivered a kilo of cocaine to a white man they didn't know, an undercover narcotics agent, and when two of the agents' partners came busting through the door with their pistols drawn, Reggie and his partners pulled theirs, too. When Reggie opened his eyes in the hospital under guard four days later, he was the only one from the shootout left alive. At the age of sixteen, he was sentenced to three consecutive one hundred year terms for the murder of three of Chicago's Finest.

He told me his outdate was the year 2274. I could only shake my head.

Damn, Reggie, I said. That's a long fucking time!

He smiled ruefully.

It's a Buck Rogers outdate, for damn sure, Double D!

NASTY PUSSY LIPS

THE GYM LINE RETURNED and the corridor erupted with the raucous repartee of testosterone-fueled men fired up from playing hoops and pumping iron. I closed my eyes and listened:

Leroy, get your monkey ass up! How come y'all tell me you goin to the gym, then you don't go? Good for nothin lazy ass nigger!

That South House, they straight up bums, man! Cain't play no hoop cuz they alla time be fightin with they own motherfuckin selves!

I tol that chump, You jump in my shit one more time, Ah bus yo motherfuckin head, Jack!

Yeah, what he say?

Aw, he jus be tremblin an shit, his pussy ass!

Whooee! Buster, you done pumped up them pecs for real! Look like the incredible Hulk!

Like the Hulk's momma, you mean!

Like the Hulk's ugly brother!

I got your momma in my crib, sucker. Got your daddy, too. And you, chump, I got your ugly brother in my jockey shorts! Come over here and give him a kiss, he turn into a big prince!

Buster, get that shit back in your pants! Goddamm, boy, you crazy!

A big fist pounded my door and a booming voice bellowed, Double D! Open the fuck up, man! I got to talk to you!

I had come to be called Double D by a few of the boys on the block. The atmosphere of the South House, where I'd spent ninety days double-bunked with Billy Odum Jr. while I waited for a single cell to open up, had been one of chaos and impermanence. Every day a dozen men leaving, a dozen others taking their places. Belligerence and aggression ruled, with little regard for the peace of mind of others. But in North One, where the average length of stay was three years—so I'd been told—and some of the inmates had been in the Unit since Lime Ridge State Penitentiary was built on the banks of the Mississippi more than a decade ago—there was a tendency to accommodate a new arrival, who might be your neighbor twenty-four seven for a very long time. There were plenty of surly, antisocial inmates to keep the place from being an absolute Peaceable Kingdom, but there were limits to the amount of disruptive behavior that was put up with before its perpetrator was put in check by his neighbors, or lost his coveted single cell and found himself back in the South House doubled up, or else shipped off to another joint.

I made it a point to be personable, yet discreet, and soon had my share of pals among the boys on the block. Double D. It spoke of fellowship, which pleased me.

I opened the door. Buster's hulking torso blocked the light from the corridor. He joined his fists at the naval and flexed his pecs alternately till they bounced on his bare chest like talking drums.

Double D, he said, I want you to be my girlfriend. I want you to clean my house.

You can't afford me, Buster, I said.

Buster was a handsome young man the color of coffee with cream.

His hair was cropped close, his forehead broad and smooth. His eyes, though expressive and playful, scarcely concealed a deranged enthusiasm for violence. But I had nothing to fear. Buster was a Baby Huey, a nice guy if you were nice to him, and I was. I showed him respect. I supplied him with whams and zooms—though not every time he wanted them—and I listened to his conversation, wherever it wandered. I knew that he was the oldest of nine siblings, that he loved his Granny, and his Golden Retriever, Rosco, who was four years old when Buster came to Lime Ridge three years ago, and he loved fried frog legs and corn fritters washed down with Old Milwaukee beer. Born and raised in the rolling green hills at the Southern tip of the state, far from the mean streets of the Windy City, he was what you'd call a country-ass nigger, though not to his face.

He stroked his cheek and turned his head from side to side.

Look at me, Double D, he said. Mohammed Ali wish he had a face like mine!

I'm busy, Buster, I said. What's up?

Gimme some whams and zooms, Double D. I'm hungry.

I'm all out, I said.

Don't be holding out on me, Double D!

Let me see, Buster, I said. I might be overlooking something.

I reached behind the towel draped over my grey steel cabinet and pulled out a Hostess Twinkie.

You're in luck, Buster. This is my very last one. I wouldn't give it to anyone but you.

Buster unwrapped the Twinkie and pushed it into his mouth. I watched him chew. I said, You wanted to talk to me about something...

He wiped his lips.

About Belinda, he said. That bitch! And about Daryl, my motherfuckin cousin.

What about them?

We both done the crime, see, but I'm doin the time, while he's out there stickin it to Belinda in the back seat of my motherfuckin Eldorado. An that bitch Belinda sposa be home takin care a my kids...

Buster—

… stead a flappin her nasty pussy lips for my goddam cousin …

Buster—

… in the back seat of my motherfuckin Eldorado!

Buster! What can I do for you?

I need your help, Double D. My daddy, his tight ass, momma say he ain't gonna come up off one more red cent to pay my lawyer. He say he got eight more babies to pay for. Say if I ain't done what the D.A. say I done, I must be locked up for somethin I done they don't know about. Say the chickens come home to roost, don't they, boy? Fool act like I ain't his own flesh and blood, which maybe I ain't, but twelve goddamn years, Double D! How the hell I'm gonna do twelve motherfuckin calendars in this whore camp? My dog will be dead! My Granny will be gone! I'll go out my motherfuckin mind! I'll do something crazy!

He waved a clenched fist in the air and looked around for something crazy to do. He shouted, I swear I will!

I was stricken with pity. Buster could bench press 500 pounds but against the nebulous forces of the Universe he was powerless.

Buster, I said, how can I help?

I need a PPCR, Buster said.

What is that?

A Petition for Post-Conviction Relief.

Isn't there a Legal Clerk in the library for that kind of thing?

That homosexual-ass honkie don't know shit, Double D! He sucked dick for that job! He did me a PPCR one time and it didn't make a lick a sense. There's this part about Daryl, his simple ass, it was his idea, but the way the clerk say it, sound like it was my motherfuckin idea!

And just what are the legal grounds for a PPCR in your case, Buster?

The legal grounds I can't do this no more!

I doubted if the grounds that Buster couldn't do this no more were sufficient to file a Petition for Post-Conviction Relief. Buster and a few million other inmates coast to coast couldn't do this no more. But it wasn't about getting Buster out of the joint, only about giving him hope for a minute, a respite from despair, like wetting the parched lips of Jesus on the cross, knowing he was going to die anyway.

All right, I said. I'll do it.

You will? Straight up?

Straight up, Buster. Bring your file by in the morning. I'll go to the library after lunch. I'll write up something that makes sense and might get some attention. Maybe how you have eight brothers and sisters and your momma needs all the help she can get. You never know.

I eased the door shut a few inches.

I've got to go, Buster, I said. I'm working on something of my own. Bring your shit by tomorrow.

Buster held out a fist.

I'll tighten you up when I make store, he said. You know how we play it.

I bumped his fist with one of my own.

Don't worry about it, Buster, I said. What goes around comes around.

That it do, Double D. It's a two-way street. Daryl, his country-ass, he gone find that out.

I'm sure he will.

Belinda, too, that whore, that funky bitch.

Yes …

Flappin her nasty pussy lips for my goddam cousin in my mother-fuckin Eldorado!

Yes, yes, good night, Buster, GOOD NIGHT!

I put my hand on Buster's chest and pushed gently. I closed the door. I put a fresh piece of paper in the humming IBM Selectric and typed across the top: Nasty Pussy Lips.

PAPERBOY

IN THE BACK WALL OF EVERY CELL in Lime Ridge was a narrow vertical slit of window that opened onto a courtyard or a field beyond. A handle below the window allowed it to be rolled open several inches. I sat on my bunk and leaned against the back wall and inhaled deeply the sweet, frosty air that streamed through the window. It was three hours earlier on the West Coast and I imagined the sun sinking into the ocean like a molten slug, turning pink the fog that slithered under the Golden Gate Bridge like a mindless amorphous creature from beyond the horizon.

From the corridor outside my cell sang a strong defiant voice:

Extra, Extra, read all about it!
I want some pussy and I'm gonna shout it!

A moment later there came a knock.

Pauly, what's up?

Damn, Double D, it's cold in your crib!

I had the window open, I said. I like fresh air.

Pauly was tall and lean as a lamp-post. His long hair, parted in the middle, framed a face youthful yet hard, his cold blue eyes a closed door to a cold heart. Boy Interrupted. His sleeveless denim shirt hung open on a bare chest adorned by a screaming eagle etched in blue, its wings spread nipple to scarlet nipple. Clutched in its talons, an unfurling banner read: Harley Davidson Motorcycles. His long arms rested in the door frame like the eagle's wings.

Double D, you got a pack of squares till I make store?

All out, Pauly, I said. Got to make store myself.

Well, shit piss fuck, he said.

We'd had a few friendly but guarded exchanges in the months since I had arrived in North One. Pauly knew I was here for dealing dope, that I had acquaintances in the camp of all colors and persuasions, attached myself to no group and no group claimed me. Pauly had advised me that maybe I could ride alone … until the shit hit the fan, and then, echoing the one-eyed Captain Jack, I'd better know what color I was. Meanwhile, nobody was complaining.

I knew that Pauly was doing his second bit, both times for breaking and entering, and that he was in the auto body program learning skills that would allow him to customize motorcycles—chop hogs— for his partners for dope money and beer. He came by occasionally to borrow a pack of squares or a shot of mud, and would sometimes let his guard down and linger for conversation. He took great interest in all things California: surfing and skiing; sling-shot dragsters; Satan worshipers; the Hell's Angels; beaches, bikinis and Hollywood. I detected a certain wistfulness, a mourning for missed opportunities, and it pleased me to paint a pretty picture of the Golden State. Pauly regularly borrowed parts of the Sunday *San Francisco Chronicle*, to which I was subscribed courtesy of my father-in-law, Wally. He especially liked the Far Side cartoon, which spoke to his opinion that the world was twisted and incomprehensible.

Pauly looked down the corridor. From the last cell on the left, its door wide open, came the lyrics of the Michael Jackson tune *Beat It*, cranked to the max.

That spook on the end don't cool it with his ghetto blaster, Pauly said, we'll put his ass in check! Tape earphones to his nappy head, make him listen to Sammy Hagar all night long. Or Led fucking Zeppelin. Drive his monkey ass nuts!

That would do it, I said.

Goddamn boogaloo bullshit all fucking day and night!

I said nothing. Pauly sighed.

This is some crazy ass shit, Double D. It just doesn't make sense.

It was a small, unexpected moment of commiseration and I wondered over what—our common plight in the penitentiary or the generally crazy conundrum that was life itself? Whichever, I could only agree.

That it is, Pauly, I said.

We lapsed into silence. Pauly slipped off his shirt and spun around.

Check this out, Double D!

Adorning the upper left quarter of his back, etched in exquisite detail, in brilliant blues, greens and reds, was a fantastic, flying, fire-breathing creature, all scales and claws and crazy eyes, raised up on the welt of swelling caused by the thousands of needle-pokes it must have taken to create it.

I admired the artistry. It wasn't your typical, crude blue prison tattoo.

Who's the artist? I said. Where does he get the colored ink? And the gun?

I hoped I wasn't asking too many questions but Pauly seemed not to mind.

Berserker, he said. On B-Wing. He had a shop on the street. He makes his own tattoo gun out of stuff he finds in the joint: a motor from a tape player, a ballpoint pen, a guitar string. He's a fucking genius. A screw brings him the ink. They were pals on the street.

Berserker … is he the dude with the braided beard and the broom straws through his nipples?

Yeah, that crazy mother.

I heard he ate a lizard on the yard.

Yeah, because Bobo bit the head off a snake.

I said nothing. I could only imagine.

It was a small lizard, Pauly said.

You've got some heavy duty partners there, Pauly.

One hundred percent Honkie! Take no shit from nobody! That spook on the end is gonna find that out!

The conversation stalled. I had no doubt the inmate on the end would get his. Years ago in a max joint up north Pauly and his pals, led by the feared and revered Otto Mann, had wrapped their torsos in magazines held tight with duct tape and launched a frenzied attack, a fierce and bloody melee of score-settling and retribution that lived on as a page in the book of prison lore.

I felt the gulf between our worlds. Pauly must have felt it, too, but he lingered.

He wants to hook up with you, Double D.

Who does?

Berserker.

Me? Why?

He wants to kick it about the business. He did a little dealing out the back of his shop. I told him you were big time.

Those days are over, Pauly. I'm all squared up.

You say …

It's a fact.

So … you'll do what when you hit the bricks, Double D—get a job? He said job like it was a disease you didn't want to come down with.

That's the plan, I said.

You crack me up, Double D. After all the dough you made!

I thought about all the dough I made and didn't have now.

I had my fun, I said.

Pauly looked down the corridor, then back at me. His smile was wry.

I almost had a job once, he said.

Yeah?

Yeah. I saw this old black and white gangster movie with James Cagney and Edward G. Robinson. There was this kid, see, a paperboy. It was winter and he wore a wool scarf and a little flat hat that buttoned down in front. He had freckles and a gap between his teeth. When the gangsters knocked off a brewery or shot up an after-hours joint, the next day the kid would hold up a paper and yell: Extra, Extra, read all about it! And the paper would spin out of his hand and stop in front of the camera so you could read the headlines about the heist the night before.

So you got a job as a paperboy?

No, but I liked that kid: Extra, extra, read all about it! Cracked me up.

Pauly, I said. You know Buster on B-Wing?

Seen him around. Hard to miss.

He's got Double Os. He'll hook you up.

That spook doesn't like me. I stay out of his way.

He's cool if you're cool. Tell him I sent you. Give him this.

I turned to my desk and wrote a note and folded it and gave it to Pauly.

Right on, Double D, Pauly said. I'll get 'em back to you when I make store.

No hurry, I said.

Pauly turned to go. He looked back.

You should hook up with Berserker, Double D. Can't hurt to kick it.

I suppose not, I said.

If you wanna get high, Pauly said, he's the go-to guy in the North House.

In that case, Pauly—set it up!

CRY OF THE VALKYRIE

INMATE ERIC BERSERKER BORG claimed to trace his lineage to the days of Harold Fairhair, first King of Norway, circa 900 AD. His ancestors, he informed me, were of an especially vicious breed of Viking Warrior called Berserkers who worshipped the Norse God Odin and fought in a trance-like state induced by ingestion of the psychotropic Russian mushroom amanita muscaria and copious amounts of mead. While thus intoxicated, a state called berserker-gang, they fought with the strength and ferocity of wild animals. They would cleave an enemy in two with a single blow of a broad-ax or sword. Impervious to pain, they ate their own shields; they swallowed burning coals; their limbs continued to fight after being severed.

Harold Fairhair owed much of his dominion to the employment of Berserkers as shock troops when sending his army into battle.

Borg told me about how his motorcycle club, The Berserkergangers, would gather in the woods at night around a roaring fire, ingest the drug Phencyclidine, PCP, commonly known as Angel Dust, drink co-pious amounts of vodka, strip to the waist, and in a frenzied state fight each other till the sun rose over the tree line. On more than one occasion, they roared away on their choppers leaving the ravaged body of one of their own behind.

Their savagery was legendary and they were feared by other clubs as far east as New Jersey.

Borg was tall and brawny, blue-eyed with a wide nose, wavy orange hair to his shoulders, and a full beard braided to his navel. Pieces of broom straw pierced his nipples. I imagined him in a horned helmet, his big-knuckled hands and his thick, tattoo-covered forearms swing-ing a broad-ax at my torso, cleaving me in two.

I had seen him on the yard huddled with others of his sort. They seemed of another race, from another time and place. They seemed to be waiting ...

He told me his ambition was to die on the battlefield and be selected by the Valkyrie—fierce female virginal Viking warriors who descend from the sky on fiery steeds and decide who will live and who will die and who will be spirited away to Valhalla to again drink copious amounts of mead with his fellows and to revel in the glory of Odin. At the moment of his being chosen, Eric told me, the Northern Lights will blaze across the sky and announce his ascension into Valhalla.

Berserker's blue eyes bore into mine, inviting me to share in his vision. I wondered if the Northern Lights descended as far south as Illinois. Berserker reached out suddenly and grabbed my forearm.

What a fucking waste, Davis! he said. I could fill that arm with creatures seen only on the far side of Nifleheim. I have been there and back!

I assumed Nifleheim was some bleak nether region in Norse Mythology. Berserker's intense stare told me he hadn't been back from there for very long. I attempted to withdraw my arm slowly but it was held in a powerful grip. I was wary of making any sudden moves or saying something offensive.

I've almost gotten tattooed a few times, Berserker, I said cautiously, but I've always declined, worried I'd change my mind and wouldn't like it anymore. Then what? You can't wash them off. But I do love the art. In fact, I once painted faces at festivals and fairs, of flowers and fairies, lions, tigers and bears. On the faces of children. Nothing like what you do, though. I've seen Pauly's creature—wowza, you're a fucking arteest!

Berserker released my arm.

Davis, he said, you must be kidding me, Bro—that's how I got my start! Painting kids' faces! I set up a booth at County Fairs up and down the state. Kids and their mommies and daddies would line up half a fucking block.

Is that a fact, I said, imagining Berserker's bulk towering over a tiny child, the protective parent looking on apprehensively.

I did the cute little animal stuff, too, he said. Then I started doing dope and having visions and my pictures got weird: demons and creatures and clowns with crazy eyes. The kids liked it but the parents didn't. I went out of business. I couldn't do cute anymore. I became an apprentice at a tattoo parlor. Bikers liked my shit. I opened my own shop. Between my art and dealing out the back door, I made lots of dough. I bought a chopper and started the Berserkergangers. Well, fuck a duck, Davis! Let me do you, man! No charge.

Let me think about it, Berserker.

Okay, you think about it, Berserker said a little peevishly. You come around when you're ready.

He unraveled one of his beard-braids and from the midst of its twining pulled out a thin joint. He turned on the small electric fan atop his grey metal cabinet and directed the streaming air to the window in the back of his cell. He handed me the joint and a plastic lighter.

Blow it out the window, he said.

Together we finished the joint, alternately toking and blowing the smoke into the wintry darkness beyond. The weed was deceptively smooth and sweet and I felt immediately altered.

Let's talk business, Berserker said.

I didn't want to talk business, but I would listen.

What do you have in mind? I said.

I sat on the toilet and listened while Berserker sat on his bunk and stroked his beard and proposed that his people in Illinois ship top grade Columbian weed to my people on the West Coast. He said Mexican weed was trash, we both knew it. Those beaners had gotten lazy. They'd had a monopoly too long. But Columbians were smart. They put out a product that was pretty, and potent and the price was right, and with his source on the Gulf of Mexico and my market on the West Coast, we could both make serious money right here in the penitentiary!

For a moment I allowed myself the fantasy of doing business from behind bars. It seemed a natural extension of my outlaw days. But if ever I were to do business again, would it be with a man who ate lizards on the yard and aspired to be borne into Valhalla by Virgins on fiery steeds? Well, maybe. It had a certain appeal. But I would never know. Wary of offending my host a second time, having declined his offer of a free tattoo, I told him I was flattered by his proposal, that a few years ago I would have died to have a good Columbian connection, but unfortunately my operation was now-defunct; I no longer had a market on the West Coast. After I was busted I spent all my time and money appealing my conviction. My people had since gone their way. But if I were looking for a partner, Berserker would be my first choice.

He looked at me sideways.

All right, Davis, he said, I'll buy that, but if anything changes you let me know. I won't be hard to find. Meanwhile, you want to get loaded, I'm your man. Pauly will tell you when I'm holding.

I appreciate that, I said, and I did. I'd gotten what I came for: a source for reefer in the joint and having made the acquaintance of a character unlike any I was likely to meet on the streets of Sausalito. I felt like a fortunate man.

I also felt very stoned. In the cell with Berserker my high had grown slowly, imperceptibly, like a stalk of bamboo. Now my heart raced and my feet didn't touch the ground. The corridor was hazy with cigarette smoke and steam from the shower, an eerie nether region the inhabitants of which walked in slow motion and spoke an alien tongue, like refugees from Dylan's *Desolation Row*. I was greeted by several as I made my way to the sanctuary of my own cell but their words were nonsensical and I could only smile lamely and say, You bet.

A FEW TIMES REMOVED

ABEL CARTER'S CLAIM TO FAME was that his great-great-grandmother had been a slave on a cotton plantation owned by the great-great-grandfather of President Jimmy Carter. A light-skinned African American with short white hair dusting his head like a layer of soot, a twinkle in his eye, and false teeth that were sometimes present in his mouth and sometimes not, Carter claimed the President to be his cousin a few times removed. While the truth of his claim could not be verified, it was undoubtedly true that he cooked up one hell of a batch of hooch.

Carter said there'd been a liquor still in his family going all the way back to the Civil War, and even though prohibition ended fifty years ago, folks in the hills of Georgia preferred his family's bathtub gin to the store-bought kind, it was that good. When Carter migrated to Chicago a long time ago and got locked up for an unspecified crime for an unspecified number of years, he had brought his moonshine-making skills in with him. At irregular intervals he cooked up a gallon or two of exotic brew for distribution among those inmates fortunate enough to be on his shortlist of clientele.

His concoctions were always delightful: some combination of apples, oranges, raisins, prunes, canned pineapple and fruit cocktail—whatever had been on the chow hall menu the previous month, and was made available to him by his contact in the kitchen, Stan the Man, introduced to him by me, hence my inclusion on Carter's list.

I felt the Universe smiling whenever the availability of Carter's hooch and that of Berserker's cannabis coincided.

GHETTO CHILD RUNNING WILD

A BLACK HEAD BOBBED IN THE WINDOW like a balloon on a string. Willis! What might he want now? Whams and zooms? A shot of mud? A pack of squares?

Willis grinned and waved a cup in little circles. I opened the door. From the last cell on the left, its door wide open, came music cranked to the max, careening off the concrete walls like a banshee released from a bottle. I winced.

What's up, Willis? I said.

What's up with you? Willis said.

I asked you first.

I ast you second.

C'mon, Willis.

Gimmee shot a mud, old man.

I'm not old, Willis.

Old as my momma.

Willis was a lanky, angular, forlorn-looking kid whose crude braid-ings of bristly hair flopped from his head like corn stalks left to rot in the rain. His eyes were small and close together like a ferret's, his teeth too big for his mouth. He wore a frayed and food-stained long-john top and long-john bottoms cut off above his knobby knees. I had been doling out coffee and snacks to Willis since I'd arrived on the cellblock months ago, and no doubt Willis thought me an easy mark to get over on, but that isn't the case. I knew that if Willis didn't get the occasional treat from me, from whom would he get it? He had no partners in the pen, nothing to barter, no game to run, and the dollar a day he was paid to scour pots and pans in the chow hall didn't go very far. I complied with his frequent requests but first engaged him in some light-hearted banter to practice the local dialect, and to allow him to feel he'd paid in some small way for the hand-out.

You owe me a hundred shots already, Willis, I said. A man could do his time, come back for another crime before you make store.

Man, why you put me through these changes?

Why you come around with your hand out every day?

'cause you got it like a Big Dog! Got it like the Shan of Iran!

God bless the child that's got his own, Willis.

Just give me a shot of mud, old man!

What's the magic word, Willis?

Magic word is, Give it up, sucker, fore I pop a cap on your ass!

You must have worried your poor mamma to death.

Ol girl too busy turnin tricks! Johns steady coming through the front door day and night!

While you be sneaking out the back door to hang with your hood-lum pals.

Ghetto Child runnin wild! Now you gonna come up off that mud, old man?

Satisfied that Willis has paid his dues and would not feel that he had gotten over on a chump, I took his cup and turned to the gray steel cabinet flanking my gray steel desk. I knew how Willis liked his coffee: two spoons of flakes, one of powdered creamer, and four cubes of sugar.

Two more cubes! Willis said.

You're pushing your luck, son, I said.

I added two more cubes and poured steaming water from the hot pot on the cabinet, stirred the coffee and handed the cup to Willis.

Willis, I said, what are you going to do when I'm gone?

Do my time. What I'm sposa do?

I mean about mud and squares and whams and zooms.

Find another mark like you to get over on!

Not likely, I said.

I looked down the corridor to the source of the booming music and remembered Pauly's threat to strap earphones to the nappy head of the perpetrator and torture him with the music of Sammy Hagar or Led Fucking Zeppelin. I would not want Willis to suffer that fate.

Willis, I said, is that your music playing so loud down there?

I ain't got no box, Willis said. Gone get me one, though, soon as old girl put some money on the books. Get me a baaad box!

Whose is it?

Corn Dog Watson. He a straight up crank. That nigger don't listen to *nobody*!

I decided to have a talk with Mr. Watson.

Thanks for stopping by, Willis, I said.

I'll tighten you up soon as old girl put some money on the books, Willis said.

I know you will, I said.

I watched Willis lurch up the corridor. There was a glitch in his hip. One leg swung wide as he walked, and he spilled coffee with every step.

A DOZEN ROSES FOR CORN DOG

I WALKED TO THE LAST CELL on the left. I was determined to be civil. I believed that every person had a core that craved recognition and respect. Give it and you make a friend. I stuck my head in the door. Rumpled clothing littered thè floor and the desk and the bunk, where the occupant lounged in his underwear reading a magazine. I hailed him over the music.

Yo, Mr. Watson!

Corn Dog Watson lowered his magazine. His face was set in a permanent frown. A clear plastic shower cap hugged his head.

What the fuck you want? he barked at me.

I parried the man's tone of ill will with a smile.

I'm Davis, I said. Down the way in 11A.

Corn Dog's scowl deepened.

Did I ask your name or where you live, motherfucker? I said what the fuck you want?

How do you like your new digs? I inquired brightly, looking around to indicate the cell and the house and the camp beyond.

What the fuck are you—the Welcome Wagon? I done asked you three times what the fuck you want.

I abandoned my good neighbor approach and got to the point.

I'm wondering if you might turn your music down a bit.

What ... you don't like music?

I like music well enough, but—

But you don't like rap music. Is that what you're saying, white boy?

I didn't take the bait.

It's not the style of music I object to, Mr. Watson. It's the volume. I can't hear myself think.

Corn Dog tossed his magazine onto the floor.

You in the penitentiary now, fool, he said. You want it quiet, you should have stayed at home!

I couldn't argue the point, though staying home was not an option. I forced a smile.

Just thought I'd ask, Mr. Watson, I said. You're going to do what you're going to do, but remember: What goes around comes around.

He rose from his bunk and stepped quickly toward me. We were the same height but he was younger and leaner and meaner. He put his face close to mine.

Man, don't give me that jive ass bullshit about what come around go around! You think I give a goddamn you can't hear yourself think? Y'all can think about this: I don't kiss the ass of no damn cracker. I'm a real live nigger! Ain't no house nigger. Now get your ass out my crib before I put something up in it!

I was startled. I stepped away.

I can do that, Mr. Watson, I said. You enjoy the rest of your day.

Back at my cell I analyzed the encounter. Why was I put off my game by the man's belligerence? Had I withdrawn out of fear for my safety or simply demonstrated that discretion is the better part of valor? I chose to believe the latter. I wondered, too, if there might not have been something a tad disingenuous in my approach. I decided no, that extending recognition and respect to my fellow man would always be the best policy, straight up cranks like Corn Dog Watson notwithstanding.

I WAS PLEASED WITH HOW THE PALE GREEN OF the pencil lead and the darker green of the felt tip pen conspired to make the stem of the drawn rose curve across the white of the envelope as though it were real. And how those thorns, like the horns of a rhino, with a yellow highlight on one side, and a shadow on the other—how you could almost feel their prickly point! And how the pink of the pencil lead delicately applied, and the darker red of the pen to carve deep shadows in the folds of the petals—how you could almost feel the loving velvety texture of the rose in bloom!

YO! BROTHER DAVIS!

I sometimes left my door open while I worked so that anyone

passing by could stick their head in my cell and kick it about what-ever, but the last thing I expected this morning was a visit by Corn Dog Watson, and especially to be addressed as Brother Davis. I put the pen down and pushed the envelope away.

Mr. Watson, I said. What's up?

Call me Corn Dog, Brother Davis, Watson said. Cornelius Corn Dog Watson! Listen here ... about last night ... you were straight with me and I get all up in your face like a rabid dog—shame on me! But like I said, I'm a real live nigger! Ain't no house nigger. Niggers down here think they done passed through the Pearly Gates! Got they pretty green lawns and the yard to walk around like holes on the stroll. Got colored TV in the dayroom. Got ice machines. Even got pizza delivered to their house! But I don't go for the okeedoke, see. I get me some real live partners down here from the North, we gonna make the joint jump and all a y'all white devils be saying, Watch out for Corn Dog and his crew! But you and me, Brother Davis, we straight. Ain't we straight?

I wanted to believe that Corn Dog's apology was genuine. I wanted to believe that my practice of extending respect and recognition up front had paid dividends after all. But I detected a wily undercurrent in Corn Dog's tone. Did he think that because my approach was civil I was a chump to be gotten over on? And how could I be Brother Davis and one of the race of White Devils in the same breath? I told myself to be careful. I extended a closed fist.

We're straight, Corn Dog, I said.

Corn Dog bumped my fist with a fist of his own.

All right then, he said.

He looked past me into my cell at my desk where my envelopes and colored pens and pencils were splayed.

What you hooking up there, Brother Davis?

I was pleased to share my work. It had been a labor of love.

Let me show you, I said. Come on in.

Corn Dog admired the rose I showed him.

Look at them thorns! he said.

Let me tell you about thorns, Corn Dog, I said. Thorns on the stem of a rose are like life itself. The rose is soft and bright and beautiful. The rose is love. Thorns are the price you pay for love. They tell the world: If you want a piece of the rose, you go through me!

That's deep, Davis, Corn Dog said. I got me some bitches back in the world would dig a rose like that. I think you and me can do business.

I was put on my guard. I said, What kind of business, Corn Dog?

You wait here, he said. I'll be back.

He returned from his cell with a picture frame, heart-shaped, fashioned of red and white squares of paper tightly woven, with an oval base and handles on each side like those on a victory cup.

I hook these up with the paper from packs of squares, he said. I do red and white from Marlboros and green and white from Double Os.

I marveled at his handiwork. I thought it an example of craftsmanship only possible in the penitentiary, or in a Third World country, where there was more time than money.

Let's make a deal, Corn Dog said. Flowers for picture frames. You like red and white or green and white?

Umm … red and white, I said. I have a picture of my wife and baby that will look really sharp in a red and white frame like this one.

Take it then, Corn Dog said, and I'll take that rose on your desk.

That one's for my wife, I said. But I can draw you a new one. I can do a yellow rose with orange trim, or a red rose with purple trim, or a pale pink rose with red trim, or any color rose with no trim at all. Whatever you want.

You decide, Brother. You're the artist. I know you'll hook me up real tough.

You bet I will, Corn Dog. I'll make it special.

Square business, Davis.

We shook to seal the deal.

I WAS HAPPY WITH MY WORK. I'd stayed up well past midnight drawing Corn Dog's rose. Roses *plural* because in a gesture of magnanimity, I'd put one in each of three corners of the envelope and connected them with a single serpentine thorny stem. And I'd improvised a faint shadow behind rose and stem so they seemed to float above the white of the envelope. I was sure Corn Dog would be impressed.

And he was.

It's hooked up real tough, Brother Davis, he said, but where's the others?

What others?

The other eleven. The deal was a dozen roses for a picture frame.

A dozen? I didn't hear a dozen.

I can't help what you didn't hear, Brother.

I hesitated. I tried to recollect the exact verbiage of the conversation. Had Corn Dog said flowers for picture frames? A rather ambiguous phrase I would have done well to clarify. But hadn't he also said, You take that one—meaning the frame in my hand—and I'll take the rose on your desk? That sounded to me like a transaction of a single frame for a single rose. Was Corn Dog trying to get over on me? Or might there have been something in his vernacular or diction that caused me to misunderstand? I wasn't sure but I was sure I would not have traded a dozen roses for a single frame.

If that was the deal, Corn Dog, it was a bad one. You take the frame back. I'll keep the envelope.

Don't want the frame back, sucker. Want the rest of my roses!

You got three of the best roses I have ever done, I said.

Corn Dog tried a different approach.

Man, how long it take you to hook up them roses?

All day and half the night, I said.

Took me four days to make that frame. Now how is that a good deal for me?

I thought Corn Dog had a good point—if what he said was true. He didn't strike me as the patient craftsman type and he might not have made the frame at all, but only traded for a pack of squares. Or ripped it off another inmate. But I decided to give him the benefit of the doubt.

Tell you what I'll do, I said. I'll make you another three-rose envelope just like that one and you'll have gotten half a dozen of the finest roses on the planet for a single picture frame.

You must think I'm a chump, Davis.

I don't think you're a chump at all, Corn Dog. I think you're one hell of a businessman who doesn't want to be gotten over on. Can't blame you for that. I think if we do this deal, neither of us is a chump, and we are two of the smartest motherfuckers in the camp. What do you say?

I say you a smooth talking devil, Brother Davis.

Is it a deal?

It's a deal!

We shook a second time.

That night as I drew Corn Dog's next round of roses, my closed door did not entirely shield me from the music cranked to the max that came from the open door of the last cell on the left.

The next day when I went to deliver the roses, I found Corn Dog's cell vacant. I got the low-down from Buster. Last night Corn Dog was discovered by Woody the Screw bound to his toilet with duct tape, his hands behind his back, earphones taped to his head. He had refused to identify his assailants. This morning he went to the dayroom and attempted to punch Pauly in the face. Pauly didn't retaliate but merely retreated. Berserker grabbed Corn Dog from behind and held him till the screws came and cuffed him. He was in the hole and would likely be shipped back to the max joint from whence he came. As he was led away he screamed: I'll be back! I'm a real live nigger! All a y'all gone find that out! Me and my partners gone make this joint jump!

Shit, Double D, Buster concluded, that crazy mother couldn't make a bullfrog jump!

I would keep the triple-rose envelope and the red and white picture frame fashioned of cigarette package paper by Cornelius Corn Dog Watson. They were prize pieces of prison memorabilia.

DIVINATION BY DUNG:
THE FLYING FECAL FINGER
OF FATE

A BALL, A BELL, A BUTTERFLY, A SHIP,
A TREE, A STAR

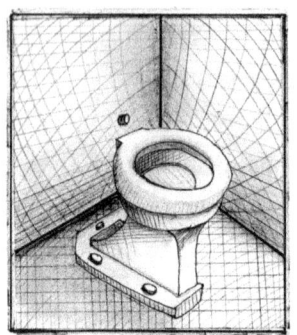

RANDY BONE'S CASE had been sensational when it occurred twenty years ago and it was still being talked about when I arrived at Lime Ridge State Penitentiary in the Autumn of 1984. Bone was seventeen when he raped and murdered his fifteen-year-old girlfriend ... that is, the fifteen-year-old he wanted for a girlfriend but who declined to be, or at least declined his advances on that fateful day. Not getting what he wanted, he took it anyway—tore it off, in the vernacular of the joint—then cut the girl up, put the pieces of her body in the trunk of his Volkswagen Beetle—his lovebug—and drove around the Windy City all night, till he ran out of gas in a busy intersection during morning rush hour. There he sat staring blankly till Chicago's Finest took note of the ensuing traffic jam, and the blood still dripping onto the pavement, and hauled his sorry ass away. He was tried as an adult and sentenced to die in the electric chair. He spent ten years on death row at Statesville Maximum Security Penitentiary before his sentence was commuted to life without the possibility of parole.

Bone had been a lanky and goofy kid when he committed his foul deed, five feet ten inches tall and a few ounces shy of 140 pounds with his clothes on, weak and easy prey, and because dissectors of young girls get no respect even in the max joint, Randy Bone was soon on the receiving end of what he had dished out, taking it up the ass on a regular basis, being passed around as a kid from gang Chief to gang Chief. But he tired of the role, went to the gym and hit the weights, and by the time he was sent down to Lime Ridge, he'd transformed himself into a strapping six feet two-inch 220-pound man, and no one's kid anymore. I gave him credit: he didn't like being a punk and he did something about it.

But he remained a goofy kid. He had an adolescent grin and wispy blond hair with bangs like a prep school student. When he thought something was funny, especially a sick joke, he'd stick the pink tip of his tongue between his teeth and slither it like a serpent's. When talk turned to the attractive nurse newly assigned to the medical unit, he'd said, I wonder if she's ever been raped? I wonder if she'd like to be? I wonder if she'd like a barbed-wire enema?

The word was that Bone was a shit-eater from way back and had been caught licking an inmate's asshole in the mop closet of the gym. Not that his fondness for feces rendered him entirely unsavory. The population of Lime Ridge manifested the gamut of personality traits that might be considered disordered in the real world but which inside the walls just put the color in the colorful character.

I had first-hand knowledge of Bone's unseemly fetish. I went round to his house one evening to pay back a shot of mud. I looked through the slit of window in his grey steel door and saw him on his knees in front of his toilet bowl. I knocked. He opened the door.

Here's your mud, Randy, I said.

Thanks, he said.

He had a weird gleam in his eyes. He put his face close to mine.

They're just like tea leaves, he whispered.

What are? I said.

You'll see. Come in. Close the door.

I looked up and down the corridor. No screw in sight. I closed the door behind me. Bone stepped to the toilet bowl.

Look, he said.

I looked over the rim of the bowl and saw a rag-tag assortment of turds, all shapes and sizes, like a flotilla of cargo ships.

Well, what do you see? Bone said.

Shit? I said. Could it be shit?

Yes, but what does it tell you? What does it say?

That you're regular? That your colon's firing on all six cylinders, but your brain isn't?

No, smart ass! About the future! Your fate! Your fortune! About what might be going down in your life! I've found a way to see!

Ah! I suddenly realized that Bone was talking about prognostication. A month earlier I had loaned him *The Prophecies of Nostradamus*. He'd read it cover to cover and said he couldn't find what he wanted. Shortly thereafter, according to the inmate librarian, Bone ordered a bunch of books on fortune telling, including one on tea leaf reading. Apparently he'd found what he wanted and was now sharing with me his innovative new system of fortune-telling: Divination by Dung.

That's terrific, Randy, I said. How does it work?

He explained in so many words that Divination by Dung, like tea leaf reading, is a very personal and subjective process, that what a configuration of crap conjures for one petitioner will differ from what it conjures for another. One concentrates on the arrangement and a pattern or shape emerges, one that speaks to one's subconscious mind, to one's hidden hopes and fears, one's predispositions. Interpretation of the symbol or shape is then made intuitively.

I see, I said. Something like a Rorschach inkblot test.

Yes, he said. Or one could refer to a lexicon of standard symbols with predetermined meanings, which didn't exist yet but he was working on compiling one.

Can't wait to read it, Randy, I said. Say ... why are all the turds floating? Not all mine float.

They're not all from the same dump, he said.

He explained the difference between his system and that of traditional tea leaf reading, how with tea leaf reading a cup of tea is prepared without using a strainer, the leaves float on top, you drink off most of the tea, swirl the cup so that the leaves stick to the side of the cup, then you pour off the remainder of the tea. The formation of clinging leaves is ready for reading. Simple, any fool could do it. But in the more elaborate process of prepping for Divination By Dung, one had to collect a sufficient number of turds that float. And yes they are rare, he agreed. There were tricks, of course, for increasing their occurrence—for example, eating fast and swallowing air with your food—but in spite of such tricks one should expect to put in a few hard days of dumping. One defecates, then looks for a floater, sets it aside and flushes the rest. When enough have been collected they're returned to the bowl, the bowl is stirred, and when the waters have stilled—let the reading begin! Or, he explained, an advanced Oracle of Ordure, such as he had become, might choose to read while there is still current in the bowl and the floaters drift slowly along, changing their relationship to one another, hence changing the shapes and symbols to be observed, a more challenging method, he said, but so much more true to life because life is not static but always moving and changing.

That's some deep doo doo, Randy, I said. So, what does the current configuration of crap say to you?

Let's stir the waters and see, Bone said.

I sensed his eagerness to share. He knelt down in front of the toilet bowl and stirred the water with his index finger, then licked the finger dry. The floaters followed one another lazily around the bowl like promenaders on the boardwalk, like holes on the stroll. He closed his eyes and took several deep breaths, in through his nose, out through his pursed lips, with a little whistle. He opened his eyes and stared at the procession intently.

Ah, he said, I see a butterfly!

Which means ... ?

That overdue happiness is coming my way. And there! A bell!

Meaning ... ?

Meaning a favorable turn in love or business. I could use that. And there's a ball, which means a desire to travel. And there's a ship, meaning a long and leisurely journey. And there's a palm tree, signifying wealth and a vacation on a beach. And above the palm tree a star, meaning success, adulation and praise. Hot damn, Davis! A ball, a bell, a butterfly! A ship, a tree, a star! What a great reading. I'm glad you stopped by! You've brought me luck, my friend!

I wanted to say, Randy, from shit you get shit, so don't hold your breath till you're on that beach, basking in adulation. The only thing you can count on is the final curtain coming down. But I knew that Bone knew that already; he'd had plenty of time to think about the jam he was in, and who was I to remind him of reality if he preferred to escape it through one fantasy or another? If he found solace imagining that floating fecal matter arranged favorably might alter his fate? From my point of view we were all victims, even the lowest of the low, the most foul, forlorn and forsaken fuckers on the planet: victimized by the lack of a key, by a missing piece, by the absence of a blueprint, an instruction manual, a map of the soul; by too much of one chemical, too little of another. Undoubtedly one or more of these conditions applied to Randy Bone and now he was paying a heavy price. To borrow a hackneyed phrase, We all have our cross to bear, and I was not inclined to render another man's cross heavier by so much as a splinter of wood.

Randy, I said, I'm glad I came by, too.

Just then his face contorted.

Argh, he said, a crocodile is forming!

Is that bad?

It means beware of false friendship, he said. Beware of betrayal. Damn! And there's a vase. That means a secret is being kept from me.

He got up off his knees. He mumbled something to himself. He glanced quickly at me, then looked away. He turned left, then right, in small half-circles of agitation on the few square feet of floor that were available to him. The mood of the cell had darkened. I had had enough. I had some reading to do and a journal entry to make and I'd shared Randy Bone's world long enough for one evening, so I took my leave.

CROCODILE

A FEW DAYS LATER RUSTY THE DRUMMER paid me a visit.

Double D, can you spare a shot of peanut butter?

Sure, I said. Would you like some crackers with it?

No, he said, I won't be eating it.

Alright, I said.

Aren't you going to ask why I want peanut butter if I'm not going to eat it?

Sure, I said. Say, Rusty, why do you want peanut butter if you're not going to eat it?

To make a turd, he said.

Of course, I said.

Rusty the Drummer was so-called because he had been one, a drummer, in a famous rock band in the sixties. To the select few he deemed worthy he would show off the photograph collection that documented his friendship with a litany of luminaries from the rock world: Rusty with Mick Jagger, with Tina Turner, with Suzi Quatro, Joan Jett, Jeff Beck, David Bowie, Pat Benatar ...

I first saw Rusty in 1968 at the Avalon Ballroom in San Francisco. Or was it the Fillmore West? I'd done the decade right, and the details were hazy. I was propped on an elbow on a pillow on the floor of one of those venues, enjoying one of the many joints circulating through the crowd, and listening to a soon-to-be-famous rock band play a twenty-minute number that would climb the charts and set an all-time record for sales. Rusty played the drums that night. He was busted years later, his career on the skids, for receiving a couple of kilos of cocaine he'd shipped up to himself from his cliff-side Hideaway in St. Croix, U.S. Virgin Islands. He had a picture of that, too, his Hideaway, and invited me to come down and visit when hey were back in the real world, though I suspected Rusty had lost possession of his Shangri-La just as he'd lost possession of his status in the Wonderland of Rock Stardom. Here in the joint he was just another dude, no one special. The un-esteemed. And not likely ever to be esteemed again. These were the eighties, and in his own words, who needed a burnt-out drummer from the stone age? The ship of fame and fortune had dropped him at a seedy port called Lime Ridge State Penitentiary and sailed away without him. He seemed to me to resent being banished to the bottom of the dung heap and to be always looking for someone lower than himself to dump on.

Aren't you going to ask why I'm making a turd out of peanut butter? he asked.

Sure, I said. Say, Rusty, why are you making a turd out of peanut butter?

A present for a friend, he said. Can I come in and make it here?

Sure, I said.

I looked down the corridor for screws. All clear. I stepped aside. Rusty slipped into my cell and closed the door behind him. I took a plastic jar of peanut butter from a cardboard box under my bunk.

Ah, chunky! Rusty said. Got a plate? Got a spoon?

I moved my typewriter and a stack of books to the floor and got a plastic plate and spoon from the box. I angled my desk lamp low, encircling the plate in a pool of light. Rusty took a seat. I stood behind him. His hair, long and dark and full in his photos, was now thin and streaked with grey, tied back in a straggly ponytail. He took a deep breath. If his tank top had had sleeves, I thought, he would have rolled them up.

This will be my first turd, he said.

You'll do fine, I said.

He spooned great dollops of peanut butter onto the plate. He took the mound between the palms of his hands and rolled it into a ball, then into a tube. He laid the latent turd-shape onto the plate, leaned back and looked at his product. It was crude.

I think you need to taper the ends, I said.

He grunted agreement and tried to roll one end at a time into a point like the tail of a snake, but the turd broke off in the middle.

It's too soft, I said. It needs a binder.

I took a carton of Wheaties from the box. Rusty flattened the mound of peanut butter onto the plate, poured a pile of Wheaties onto the flattened mound, and kneaded the mess like dough. It squished between his long white fingers, the once-famous fingers of Rusty the Drummer, now those of Rusty the Neophyte Sculptor of Scat.

It feels more solid now, he said.

He rolled the mash into a ball, then into a tube, then tapered the ends without breaking the tube. He laid the semi-fashioned form down carefully.

It's still not right, he said.

It needs texture, I said. It's too smooth.

I need a pencil, he said.

In the drawer of the desk, I said.

He carved crevices into the surface of the turd. He worked meticulously. Beads of sweat broke out on his forehead. The hand holding the pencil shook. I put my hand on his shoulder.

Relax, I said. You can do this.

He put the pencil down. It was quiet in the room, an eternal stillness. He sat back and regarded his work. He shook his head.

It's straight like a spear, I said. It needs to curve.

He leaned forward and bent the turd into a semi-circle.

Too much, I said. It looks like a Smiley Face.

He decreased the curve into that of a crescent moon.

Better, I said.

It's still not right, he said.

It's bland, I said. Uniform in color, like baby shit. Adult shit is not so pure. You need to darken it. Funk it up a bit.

I retrieved a container of cocoa from the box.

Try this, I said.

Rusty poured the dark powder onto the plate, then rolled the turd across it with his fingertips. The cocoa adhered in splotches.

It needs to be spread out, I said. Try rubbing a little water on it to dissolve the cocoa and spread it out.

He wet his hands at the sink and worked his fingers across the turd, dissolving the cocoa, distributing it evenly. The transformation was miraculous. The Maestro of Manure had worked his magic. We had before us a flawless replica of a natural human turd!

It's time to deliver, Rusty said. I need something to cover it up with.

I tore off the page of the *San Francisco Chronicle* that contained The Far Side cartoon. Rusty wrapped the plate in the page like a platter of cookies.

Care to witness the presentation, Double D?

After you, I said.

He exited the cell. I followed him out.

It was the hour of the evening when supper was over and inmates had returned from the chow hall, the yard, the gym and the library, and the housing unit teemed with inmates who lingered in the corridor, kicking it, drinking coffee and smoking, leaning against the walls in white cotton boxer shorts, or towels wrapped around their waists. Cigarette smoke hung in the air like low lying cirrus clouds. Cell doors were left open to circulate the stale air. Rock, rap and country music played simultaneously from boom boxes set on the corridor floor. Rusty walked by Randy Bone's cell. The door was open. He looked inside.

He walked to the end of the corridor and looked into the dayroom.

He returned to Bone's cell, entered and placed the perfectly crafted piece of shit onto the rim of the toilet bowl. He went back up the corridor, opened the door to the dayroom and yelled with a tone of outrage and revulsion.

Bone, what the fuck, man! If you're going to leave your shit laying around, close your fucking door!

Bone yelled back.

What are you talking about?

You know what I'm talking about, Bone. Jesus fucking Christ!

Randy came down the corridor and looked into his cell. He stared a long time. His face turned red. His eyes narrowed.

This is not fucking funny, he said. Not fucking funny at all!

Curious inmates gathered at the door of his cell.

Bone, you a foul dude! said one.

You a sorry ass motherfucker! said another.

I stuck my head in the door as though I had no idea what was happening. When I saw that dark mound hunkered on the rim of the toilet bowl like a giant slug, I was suddenly compelled to enact a long-forgotten adolescent joke. I shouldered my way into the cell.

What is this? I asked. Umm … looks like shit!

I leaned over and put my nose to the turd.

And it smells like shit!

I pinched a piece off and rubbed it between my thumb and forefinger.

And it feels like shit!

I dabbed my feces-laden finger onto my tongue.

It tastes like shit, too! You know, I think it is shit! Sure glad I didn't step in it!

There were titters from those who recognized the joke, exclamations of disgust from those who didn't.

Rusty stepped into the cell.

That looks good, Double D. Let me try some!

He poked a finger in the turd and licked it. He closed his eyes.

Man, he said, that is some good tasting shit! Randy, what have you been eating?

A new arrival stuck his head in the door.

What's going on here?

Double D and Rusty be eatin Randy Bone's shit!

I saw the joke was getting out of hand. I didn't want it said that Rusty and I had been reduced to the rank of shit-eaters. When word gets around, the Big House isn't so big.

It's not real, I said. It's a joke. It's peanut butter.

Looks real to me.

But it's not. Here, try some.

I scooped a fingertip of the phony feces and offered it to the doubting inmate. He backed away with a pained look.

I ain't eatin nobody shit!

It's not shit, I said. Just smell it.

He smelled my fingertip warily.

Smells like peanut butter, he said.

It is peanut butter, I said.

I still ain't eatin it, he said.

I extended my finger toward Bone.

Try some, Randy, I said.

I hoped feebly that the man would appreciate the humor of a joke he'd just been made the butt of. He slapped my finger away.

Everybody get the fuck out of my house! he shouted. Rusty, take that shit with you. You're not fucking funny!

Rusty scooped the turd onto the paper plate and exited the cell chuckling. Bone gave me a cold hard stare.

Crocodile, he said.

Crocodile.

A few days later, Bone dropped by my house.

Got a shot of mud, Double D?

Sure, I said.

I handed him a half-full plastic container of Folgers instant coffee.

I only need a shot, he said.

I have more, I said.

Alright, he said. I'll pay you back when I make store.

Don't worry about it. Say, listen … Randy … the other day … about the joke … it wasn't my idea … it just happened.

Bullshit ain't nothing, he said with a wave of his hand, as if to say if he couldn't handle a little sick humor how could he handle knowing he'd be taking his last breath behind an iron door, and that a ball, a bell, a butterfly, a ship, a tree, a star, and all the phony happiness they foretold, were no more than pieces of shit going round and round in his toilet bowl?

Anyway, he said, it was a beautiful turd.

It was, I agreed. It was Rusty's work.

Fuck Rusty, Bone said.

Yeah, fuck Rusty, I said.

Thanks for the mud, Bone said. See you around.

Yeah, see you around, Randy. Thanks for stopping by.

THE GOLD MEDAL

SEEK AND YE SHALL FIND

ABDUL AND I SAT SIDE BY SIDE on plastic chairs outside his cell conversing above the discord of competing boom boxes blaring *I Still Haven't Found What I'm Looking for* by U2 and *You've Got Another Thing Coming* by The Clash. Abdul's long legs were crossed at the ankles, the fingers of his slim and delicate hands laced in his lap. His hair was short and receding, forehead broad and smooth, eyes bright and inquisitive yet suggesting a remote space within, forever inaccessible to others.

The first time I saw Abdul I was still in South One, double-bunked with Billy Odum Jr. The camp was caught in the icy grip of winter. I walked the cinder track around the yard with my black knit cap pulled low over my ears, the collar of my fleece-lined blue denim jacket up, and my hands thrust deep into my pockets. The sky overhead was a grey steel slab, the earth beneath my feet frozen hard as the concrete floor of my cell. Shadowy guards watched from the windows of their towers, riot guns resting in the crooks of their arms, as a few hardy inmates braved the bitter wind—The Almighty Hawk—to walk the quarter-mile loop of frosted cinders, in the center of which a lean black inmate, shoeless and clad in blue cotton trousers and a tank top, practiced yoga asanas on a blanket. During the hour I walked the track he held six positions, transitioning from one to the other with practiced, athletic grace. When End of yard! Return to your cells! crackled through a loudspeaker, I watched as the yogi walked by carrying his rolled-up blanket, still barefoot on the brittle earth, deep inside himself, oblivious to my attention.

Or so it had seemed to me at the time.

I next saw Abdul one evening shortly after being assigned to North One. I sat in the dayroom playing Chess with a new inmate, Quincy, who took an incredible amount of time during his moves, allowing me to reflect on the state of my affairs. I had reached an impasse. I vowed to Lucy to remain unchanged, to be the same Dean Davis when I returned as I was when I arrived, but I found that prospect disagreeable. I was in search of a new me. Like Quincy, I was waiting to make my move.

Through the far door of the dayroom, the yogi had entered, lean and graceful, shirtless above blue denim trousers and rubber shower shoes, with an expression I had since come to know: pensive and purposeful, yet supremely indifferent. He carried a big book and surveyed the room until he saw a middle-aged white inmate sitting alone. He sauntered over and took a seat and slid the book across the table. I watched the inmate open the book and go to the parts to which Abdul directed him.

I perceived the man to be the proverbial intellect forged in the fires of doing hard time. The font and dispenser of knowledge and wisdom. Soon he stood, leaving his book behind with the other inmate. As he passed through the door of the dayroom, his gaze met mine and the shadow of a smile played upon his lips. I was certain we would meet.

Now here we were, having a serious conversation about my search for meaning. He studied my face.

So, Dean, he said, what is it you are looking for? Redemption?

His tone was at once solicitous and detached. If he wasn't doing forty years to life for first-degree murder, he might have been a celebrated psychoanalyst in a book-lined office on the 20th floor of a high rise overlooking Lake Michigan. Since the time he introduced himself to me in the dayroom, we had become friends and exchanged brief biographies. Born James Harvey Dixon and raised in the predominantly middle-class black neighborhood of Groveland, on Chicago's

South Side, Abdul had been a standout high school student, president of the Drama Club, and a star pitcher on the baseball team. He attended Northwestern University on an athletic scholarship where his academic interests ranged from Theatre to Religious Studies. Among his many heroes was the great baseball pitcher, the willowy Satchel Paige, who, it was said, could throw a baseball through the eye of a needle and who, like Muhammad Ali, was famous for doing what he said he was going to do. Abdul's realization that through the ages black athletes were relegated to the back pages of the history books— and that his people were being brutalized on the streets of Chicago— awakened his political consciousness and he became a zealous champion of social causes, an articulate apostle of the oppressed and the dispossessed. Enlisted into the ranks of Elijah Muhammad's Nation of Islam, he disavowed his slave name, Dixon, took the name Abdullah, Servant of Allah, and repudiated his beloved game of baseball, which he had come to perceive as the pastime of slave masters.

His devotion to Islam ran deep. There he found his voice, and there he thought to find the absolute truth of existence. Simultaneously he was experimenting with hallucinogens, mescaline and peyote, a practice not endorsed by the Nation. Between his religious fervor and his frequently altered state, he slipped through the cracks of reality and entered what he calls his Demon Days, during which time he took a human life. He did not disclose the circumstances and I didn't ask. Afterward, in solitary confinement, where he spent the first five years of his sentence in rapt meditation, he had an awakening causing him to forsake the Nation of Islam and to affirm there was no religion higher than the truth. Now he was neither Muslim nor Christian nor Buddhist, but only a pilgrim seeking the truth ... or, rather, waiting for the truth to reveal itself. It will find you when you are ready, he said. Meanwhile, he did his yoga, studied esoteric principles and practices, contributed to the sporadically published inmate paper *Prose & Cons*, wrote poetry and plays, worked as inmate assistant to the progressive Warden of Programs, Wesley Wainwright ... and was happily once again a Cubs fan.

Redemption? I replied. No. I have no regrets, Abdul. I knew what I was doing. I put my freedom on the line and lost, and when I knew I was coming here, I prepared myself for a new kind of adversity that would forge a new me, only to find that if I mind my own business and don't cross anybody, I'll probably be safe for the duration and go home the same person I was when I arrived. That is just not acceptable. I need to make something happen. I need to assert my will. I need a symbolic victory!

Well, Brother Dean, Abdul said with a knowing smile: Seek and ye shall find.

Seek and ye shall find. Words that would have been a worn and sappy platitude coming from anyone else seemed to have the ring of truth coming from Abdul.

How will I know when I find what I'm looking for? I said.

It will make itself known, Dean. Because what you seek is seeking you.

I WENT TO THE GYM THE NEXT DAY in a Seek and Find frame of mind. It was a fine gym, comparable to that of a well-funded high school in Marin County, with all the amenities: full-court basketball with six hoops; pull-down bleachers running the length on both sides; showers and lockers; a boxing ring; and at the far end, free weights and benches. But the comparisons stopped there. Surly guards watched with wary eyes while inmates raced up and down the courts pushing and shoving and shouting racial epithets. Lifters awaiting their turn on the chest-press bench harangued the grimacing inmate struggling beneath a bar loaded with forty-five-pound plates: Get your money, motherfucker! Get that bitch off your chest!

Next to the boxing ring was Stan the Man, lacing up the gloves of Trevor the Hit Man Harris, Department Of Corrections Light Heavyweight Champion. He and I were housemates in North One. Stan and I met at Arcadia Correctional Center, where I'd awaited a permanent assignment and he'd awaited shipment to Lime Ridge to coach the team. An amateur fighter myself at a young age, and a steadfast aficionado of the Sweet Science, I proposed to Stan that if we happened to be assigned to the same prison, I would like to join the team. Stan had laughed.

Already got a team where I'm going, Flea Weight, he'd said. Them young bloods mean and hungry and you old and fat.

Thirty-five is the new twenty-five, Stan, I said. And I can lose the weight.

When you get where you going, Flea Weight, you best join the Ping Pong team.

You don't know what I can do, Stan, I said.

Know what them young bloods can do, Flea Weight—tear you a new asshole.

Now here was Stan, lacing up The Hit Man.

Flea Weight! he said. What House they put you in?

North One, I said. Same as The Hit Man.

You sign up for Ping Pong yet?

He climbed into the ring with Trevor. He held a pair of padded focus mitts, giving Trevor moving targets, forcing him to dig deep into his arsenal of jabs, hooks, crosses and uppercuts. He put down the mitts. They each donned headgear and mouthpieces. Stan put on a pair of gloves and they sparred a few rounds. Trevor looked sharp against the larger man, but Stan took everything Trevor could deliver.

You hit like a sissy! he said. You hit like a bitch!

A small crowd of inmates put down their basketballs and barbells and gathered around. Stan and Trevor traded leather. They were sweating when they finished. Stan pulled off his headgear and spit out his mouthpiece and addressed the spectators.

Who wanna go a round with The Hit Man? Any y'all young bloods out there? Someone get they pussy ass up here! No? I didn't think so!

An impulse came over me.

I'll go a round with The Hit Man, I said.

There was a moment of silence in the crowd.

You a fool, white boy! someone said.

Stan looked at me and shook his head.

Flea Weight! he said. Get your dumb ass up here. We'll show you what it's all about.

I climbed into the ring with a strange exhilaration. Stan laced up my gloves and headgear and rinsed an old mouthpiece in a bucket of water and put it in my mouth. The Hit Man grinned. Stan directed us to opposite corners. He got in the center of the ring, held his hands out between us, then brought them together.

Time! he yelled.

From across the ring, Harris came toward me like a machine in slow motion. I moved in slow motion, too. The sounds from the crowd seemed to come from underwater. Harris, a southpaw, left-handed, jabbed with his right. I was right-handed, and knew enough to fight a southpaw circling to his left, out of range of his left hand. We closed the distance and Harris pushed out a probing jab. I dropped my left shoulder and let it sail by, pivoted my hips and dug a hard right hand into his rib cage. I heard a muffled grunt through the weird acoustics in my head. I pivoted the other way and hooked a left into his liver. I straightened up to admire my handiwork, and Harris leaped forward quick as a cat and brought his left across the diagonal and cracked it on my forehead. My knees buckled and I took a wobbly step back. He followed with a vicious right hook that grazed my temple and turned my head half around, then another left cross that landed like an anvil on my cheekbone. I knew better than to escape a fusillade of punches by back-pedaling in a straight line, but I did it anyway, and Harris's next overhand left caught me smack in the mouth. My back met the ropes and I had nowhere to go but down and out when Stan the Man leaped in between us and waved Harris away.

See what I'm talkin bout, Flea Weight? Stan said, pulling off my headgear.

I'm alright, I said, more embarrassed than hurt.

I'll fight that white boy! someone yelled. Lemme in the ring!

Oh, now you bad, you little pussy ass! Stan yelled back.

I licked blood from my lip. Stan unlaced my gloves.

Ass whuppin ain't shit, Flea Weight, he said. You done just fine. Just need practice is all. I took a few shots back in the day my own self. They make me a better man. Now listen up. I'm giving you some inside information. Warden Wainwright puttin on a show—the Olympics! That's right. In July. Same as the real one in Los Angeles. Be track and field, soccer, hoops, baseball, and boxin. Be givin out medals. Gold, silver, and bronze. You start trainin now, Flea Weight, lose twenty, twenty-five pounds, you might be ready.

A gold medal! I saw it around my neck, my hand raised in victory. I was sure that with hard training and the right state of mind I could beat the Hit Man or whoever else they put in front of me. I had months to mold myself into a lean, mean fighting machine—and I would!

There's a Mexican brother name of Chico in Orientation, Stan said. Used to box back in the world. He a tall welterweight with fast hands. I'll get him hooked up to your house so y'all can train together. Sign up sheets come out this week. Get signed up, champ. We see what you made of in July!

THE NEXT DAY ABDUL AND I SAT in the dayroom drinking instant coffee out of liter-sized plastic mugs. The dayroom was clamorous as usual, but I'd grown accustomed to it. The din was no more disturbing than the drone of a housefly on a hot day, or the barking of dogs down the street. Abdul's unbuttoned blue cotton work shirt hung open, revealing his lean and molded torso. I put my hands on the swell of my gut and thought: This will have to go. It will be gone!

I told Abdul about the pending surrogate Summer Olympics and the opportunity to win a gold medal. I marveled that what I'd sought had wasted no time finding me.

Is that so? he said.

What … you don't think it's what I'm looking for? Seems to me to be the perfect symbol of victory.

He tapped the fingertips of one hand against the fingertips of the other.

It might seem to be, he said, but might it not be compatible with the evolution of your soul?

I thought it a weird question. I waved a hand.

I don't know that evolving my soul is what I'm trying to do here, Abdul. My ambition is a bit more secular. Winning the gold will make me feel good about myself, and that's good enough for me.

Abdul nodded.

Very well, he said. Let's make it happen. Let's put the power of the Universe on your side. Wait here. I have something for you.

Abdul left the dayroom. It occurred to me that I sat at the very table at which he had delivered a book and advice to an inmate on the eve of my first day in this cellblock a few short weeks ago. I had sat and observed from the table on the far side of the room. I imagined myself sitting there now, observing myself sitting here. I had the eerie feeling that time had folded back on itself like a serpent eating its own tail.

Abdul returned. He slid a book across the table. *The Science of Mind*, by Ernest Holmes.

From this book, Abdul said, you'll learn of the Law of Mental Equivalents, which states that one manifests in the material world results equivalent to the power of thought with which one addresses the impersonal universal mind.

I was impressed as always that Abdul could deliver an esoteric concept so precisely in casual conversation.

Sounds deep, I said, feeling the heft of the book, a weighty tome.

It is deep, Dean, Abdul said, but once understood, its truth will seem obvious. For now, what you need to grasp is that your word is law. Spoken rightly, your word commands the Universe to manifest the outcome you desire. Your mind and the universal mind are inseparable. You want to manifest a gold medal. Your desire does not contradict any other law of the universe. Therefore if you command the law rightly, for better or worse you'll have your medal.

For better or worse? Sounds ominous, Abdul.

The Law is impartial, Dean. It works as well for Genghis Khan as for Gandhi. For Mother Teresa as for Ivan the Terrible. Whatever you want, command the Law and you will have it. But there's no guarantee you'll be satisfied. There is often a great disparity between what one wants and what one needs. But we won't talk about the evolution of your soul now, Dean. We'll just help you get what you want.

Read the chapter on Principles, and the ones on The Law of Mental Equivalents and The Laws of Attraction. Then read Meditations. Study the author's sample affirmations. Write one of your own. And from now until that medal is hung around your neck, repeat the words of your affirmation every night in your cell. Let them be the last words you speak before you fall asleep. And bear in mind always the mantra: Conceive, believe, achieve!

I stayed up late reading *The Science of Mind*. I composed my affirmation. As instructed by Ernest Holmes, I fine-tuned it to be first person, present tense, and a statement of unambiguous power and purpose.

> *My opponent is crushed!*
> *He cowers and crumples beneath*
> *the barrage of my blows.*
> *He cannot endure the power with which I pummel him.*
> *He is caught by an overhand right, which buckles his legs*
> *and robs him of the will to rise.*
> *The gold medal is placed around my neck.*
> *My arm is raised in VICTORY!*

I read it over and over till I knew it by heart. I played the scene in my head till I could feel it in my bones: the bobbing and the weaving; the rolling of my shoulders; the forward motion on the balls of my feet; the recoil of energy up my arm when my overhand right found its mark. I felt the weight of the medal as it was placed around my neck. I felt my arm being raised in victory.

In this mental diorama, my opponent was a form without a face, an unknown quantity. A few days later the sign-up sheets came around, a thick pile stapled to the bulletin board, a sheet for every event, and for boxing, a sheet for every weight division. I was the first to sign up for light heavyweight. The following day there was a name under mine. The form had a face: Trevor the Hit Man Harris! That evening we passed in the corridor. He waved a fist in the air and said with a playful grin, Be the same way next time that it was the first time, sucker!

At the end of the week I met Chico Hernandez. Chico was a welterweight, 147 pounds. He had the high chiseled cheekbones, hooked nose and raven black hair of his Mayan ancestors. A fine line of scar tissue ran from his left eyelid upwards, neatly bisecting his brow. His gaze was penetrating. We sat in the dayroom.

Stan says you're very fast, I said.

Si, muy rapidamente, Chico said with a self-assured smile.

Chico had come out of Ciudad Juarez, across the border from El Paso. He'd fought a bit in the rough little clubs in Juarez, where boys as young as thirteen mauled each other for money, like roosters or dogs. He'd gotten sidetracked from boxing by the allure of easier money in El Norte. He'd been apprehended in the Windy City receiving a shit load of reefer his uncle had sent up. On the day of his release he would be met by immigration authorities and accompanied back to the border.

I told him a little about my business on the West Coast. About the time I'd spent seventeen days on the seventeenth floor of the Holiday Inn in downtown Chula Vista waiting for a load of dope that never arrived because my supplier in Tijuana, Pepé, had crossed the wrong hombre and been persuaded to jump out of a plane without a parachute. Chico found this amusing and suggested we hook up when we were back in the world.

Thanks, but no thanks, amigo, I said. I'm out of the business. My only business now is winning this gold medal.

The next day we went to the gym together. Stan was training his team.

Stan, I said, I've hooked up with Chico here. When can we get in the ring and spar?

Stan shook his head.

Can't get in the ring, he said. Can't nobody use the ring but the team. Can't get in the ring. Can't put on the gloves.

What? But why?

Crowd control, Flea Weight. Warden can't be havin fifty y'all motherfuckers slappin each other upside the head. Y'all can hit the heavy bag, the speed bag, the focus mitts. Y'all can jump some rope, and shadow box. But y'all can't be lacin up no leather, no sir.

But the team gets to spar! How fair is that?

Fair don't mean shit, Flea Weight. Anyway, the prison team ain't allowed to fight in the Olympics.

But Trevor's already signed up!

Trevor a joker, Flea Weight. He jus messin with your head. He on the team, so he ain't eligible.

I felt duped by the Universe. By some cosmic sleight of hand, the biggest barrier between myself and the gold medal had been removed, and I hadn't even broken a sweat. But maybe The Hit Man wasn't the baddest man in the camp after all. Who else might be out there standing between me and my goal? The sign-up sheets would be collected in June. I'd find out then.

Chico and I commenced training the very next day. We pounded the heavy bag till it bounced and swung like a condemned man dropped from the gallows. We hit the focus mitts till our shoulders burned and sweat stung our eyes and the whapping of our blows echoed off the concrete walls of the gym. Chico was fast, and it was all I could do to move the mitts around and keep ahead of his swift combinations. His speed and accuracy improved my own. We skipped rope for ten rounds of three minutes each, twice a day, forwards and backward, left and right, till our footwork would have been the envy of Fred Astaire. We ran the cinder track side by side, stride for stride, completing twenty laps in the allotted hour, our breath billowing in the frigid air. In the weight room we did high repetitions of light weights to build muscular endurance and to not bulk up and diminish our speed. In the cellblock we did push-ups and sit-ups on the floors of our cells, and some clandestine sparring, open-handed when the guard wasn't looking. Trevor contributed his expertise, teaching us techniques I did not learn as a twelve-year-old amateur in Marin County, nor Chico in the alleys and clubs of Juarez.

Each night alone in my cell I recited my affirmation. When I did not feel like training, when the days were long and fatigue settled over me like a heavy blanket, I recited another brief but powerful admonition to myself, gleaned from the pages of *The Science of Mind*: Be firm and ye shall be made firm!

By the end of May I was made firm. The pounds had melted away like spring snow. I was down to one hundred seventy pounds. The veins on my shoulders and biceps stood out like the blue line highways on a road map. My abdomen rippled like the undulations of a corrugated tin roof. I was ready!

ON THE FIRST MONDAY OF JUNE the sign-up sheets were collected. Other than myself, only two inmates were listed for light-heavyweight, one from the East House named Rinaldi, and one from the South house named Antwon Evans.

I asked around and learned that Rinaldi was a tall white boy who had boxed as an amateur and won the Chicago Golden Gloves in 1979. He had a reputation for rumbling in the streets and never backing down. He played hoops for his house and could run up and down the court all day. He was a bad man who got respect from all races.

No one knew about Antwon Evans, except that he minded his own business. A quiet man. Because there were three of us in the light-heavyweight division, one would get a pass into the next round, two of us would fight each other, and the winner would fight the man who got the pass. I wondered who stood between me and the gold medal—the bad man, the quiet man, or both? Time would tell.

THE BAD MAN

ON FRIDAY OF THAT WEEK I JOGGED the loop of track alone. Spring had arrived. It was the kind of day to make a man forget he was an involuntary guest of the Department of Corrections. Between the shimmering pubescent blue-green blades of grass on the lawn inside the loop, clumps of purple and yellow flowers pushed up to an azure sky. Bees buzzed between the clumps. And across the fields between the camp and banks of the mighty Mississippi, a mound of clouds billowed above a dark line of trees.

In the center of the yard, pedophiles, who had lately gotten Jesus, sat in a circle reading from the Bible. A gaggle of Gumps—gender-challenged inmates with bleached hair, cheeks made rosy with strawberry Kool-Aid, and eye shadow fashioned of the ashes of burnt match heads—sunned themselves in tailored denim short shorts, and watched the shirtless, tattooed weightlifters on a slab of concrete across the way flex themselves and do squats and presses and curls with rusted barbells. On the handball court, Latino inmates sped to and fro on fancy footwork, slammed a hard rubber ball against a concrete wall, and cursed en Español.

I ran smoothly, speeding up, slowing down, imitating the flow of energy required in the ring, when a shirtless inmate broke away from a group on the grass and pulled up alongside me. He was fair-haired and blue-eyed, tall, trim and muscular. On his chiseled bicep was a tattoo of a snarling pit bull with a spiked collar and a caption that read No Place to Hide.

You Dean Davis? he said.

Maybe, I said. Who wants to know?

Rinaldi, the man said.

He stuck out a hand. I took it. His grip was powerful, his fist big and bony. No doubt he could palm a basketball.

Heard you been asking around about me, he said. Whattaya wanna know?

What I'll be up against.

No, you don't wanna know that.

But I do.

I'll be your worst nightmare, Davis. I'll be all over you like flies on shit.

Is that right?

That's right. Just you and me, brother, no place to hide.

You won't have to look for me.

Oh, are you a mean motherfucker, Davis? You don't look mean to me. You look like a nice guy, and I want to apologize in advance for kicking your ass.

Bring it on, I said.

We did half a lap in silence. Rinaldi picked up the pace. I matched him stride for stride, till he picked it up again and on his long legs, and with his basketball court-conditioned heart and lungs, he was quickly ten yards ahead of me. He slowed and we fell back into a rhythm. I was glad the fight would be three rounds, not ten or twelve.

Dean, Dean, the lean mean fightin machine, Rinaldi crooned. I feel so bad! We might be pals someday, you and me. Old motherfuckers on the block kickin it about back in the day, and I'll say to you, Yo, Davis! You remember that night in the penitentiary I knocked your sorry ass out? No hard feelings, alright?

Rinaldi stuck his hand out again. I shook it.

I'll see you in the ring, I said. I won't be hard to find.

He laughed and ran off the track, back to his circle of pals.

I imagined his story. His mother Sonja was Swiss, hence his blue eyes and blond hair. She was a chambermaid at a tourist hotel on the shores of Lake Maggiore in Northern Italy where she'd met his father, Cosimo, a commercial fisherman. They emigrated to Chicago, USA, where Cosimo's cousin Antonio got him a job on a boat on Lake Michigan. They hoped to get a piece of the American Pie. They dreamed their son would go to college, but he got his education on the mean streets instead, and was now in the penitentiary where he intended to kick the ass of Dean Davis.

That night in my cell I recited my affirmation with heightened fervor.

THE QUIET MAN

RINALDI HAD GOTTEN THE PASS into the second round. I would fight Antwon Evans. The quiet man. Chico and I hung out at the house waiting to be called to the gym. We wrapped each other's hands. We shadow-boxed. Gym line was called. All inmates not working or restricted were allowed to attend. The bleachers filled rapidly with rowdy spectators psyched for a night of violence. Near the front of the gym a section was roped off for guests of inmates. Guards provided security to these citizens in street clothes who sat nervously within their dubious haven of safety, some in the company of the inmate they came to visit, others alone waiting to watch their loved one fight.

The dressing room was crowded with fighters. Each was given a new mouthpiece, but gloves were in short supply and had to be rotated between bouts. I sat on a folding chair. I looked around the room. There he was, no doubt of it: Brother Antwon Evans. A light-skinned African American my size, with close-cropped hair and handsome features, a good physique, broad shoulders and erect posture. But a little soft around the middle, I thought. He had no tattoos, no facial hair, no hint of aggression in his attitude, no aura of bad intentions.

I imagined his story. He was not a tough guy off the streets of an urban ghetto, but grew up in a small town down-state, a tolerant community a hundred miles south of the Windy City. He attended the local public high school, the only Negro in the student body, had the status of mascot and was given the nickname Snowball. He'd gotten his varsity letter in track and field, led his team to the County Championship, and finished Junior College with an Associate's Degree in accounting. He'd carved out a little niche for himself as an independent bookkeeper for several businesses in town, when he overestimated the town's estimation of him and took on as a girl-friend the daughter of a white city councilman. Under dubious cir-cumstances, he was charged with and convicted of rape, and now here he was, surrounded by skinheads and bikers and gang-bangers, and his hostile in-your-face big city brethren who looked down upon him as a country ass nigger. With this tournament he hoped to prove to the world, and to himself, that he was a real live nigger just like them. Yes, he hoped to make a statement. But I had faith that it would not be made at my expense. Evans looked my way. Our eyes met. I could see the hope there, but not the faith, and faith trumps hope every time.

Chico and his opponent, a pudgy African American affecting a comic appearance in blue denim dungarees with pant legs cut off at the knees and a baseball cap on backwards, were called to the ring. I was Chico's cornerman. I preceded him up the steps to the ring apron, stepped on the bottom rope, lifted the middle one, and Chico slipped through. He sat on his stool and I rubbed his shoulders.

Buena suerte, amigo, I said. Good luck!

Stan the Man stood in the center of the ring with a microphone in one hand and a notepad in the other, which he read from in a booming announcer's voice.

Ladies and gentleman, in the welterweight division, in the red corner, fighting out of the Windy City, weighing in at one hundred and forty-five and one-half pounds—Gerald the Assassin Jaaackson! And in the blue corner, also fighting out of the Windy City, by way of Cuidad Juarez, Mexico, weighing in at an even one hundred and forty-seven pounds—Chico the Gangster Gonzaaalez!

He called the fighters to the center of the ring, plucked off Gerald Jackson's baseball cap, tossed it to his corner like a Frisbee and gave his final instructions. I exited the ring, pulling the stool behind me. Chico and Gerald returned to their corners. The bell rang and they came out fighting. Jackson fought with the tenacity of a bulldog, and had a good chin but little else, and Chico danced around him deftly, peppered his face with pinpoint jabs and powerful right hands, piled up points and won a unanimous decision.

Back in the dressing room, Chico laced me up. He'd be my cornerman. A pair of middleweights was called to the ring. I couldn't see the fight but could tell from the roar of the crowd it was a good one and that it went the distance. They returned soon after, one boisterous and boastful, the other dejected. Evans and I were summoned.

I entered the ring and went to my corner. I looked out over the crowd. The middleweight fight had been a thriller and the crowd was riled and rowdy. I saw Rinaldi, who'd come to see who'd be on his dance card the following week. I saw Abdul, who'd come to witness my defining moment, if there was to be one. There were Buster and a few others of my neighbors in North One. There was Botha with some mean looking partners. There were a few white faces scattered here and there. Chico splashed water on my neck and back.

Kick ass, amigo! he said.

Stan the Man held his microphone and read from his roster.

Ladies and gentlemen, we bring you light heavyweight action! In the blue corner, fighting out of Coal Town, Illinois, weighing in at one hundred and seventy-two pounds—Antwon the Executioner Evaaans! And in the red corner, fighting all the way out of San Francisco, California, and weighing in at an even one hundred seventy pounds—Dean the Destroyer Daaavis!

Stan called Evans and me to the center of the ring and gave his instructions.

I'm the referee, he said. I'm the man! Y'unnerstan? I say break, y'all break. Punch after the break, I take a point away. Someone get knock down, other man go to a neutral corner until I finish my count. Any questions?

Evans and I shook our heads.

Who the man, Davis? Stan said.

You're the man, Stan.

That's right! Who the man, Evans?

You're the man, Evans said.

That's right! Now touch gloves, go back to your corner and when the bell ring—come out fightin!

Evans and I touched gloves and went to our corners. The bell rang. I sped across the ring. Evans back-pedaled with a look of alarm. I closed the distance, bobbing and weaving. I flicked out a jab. It fell short. Evans threw one of his own. It landed but it had no pop. I jabbed again, hard on the nose of Evans, snapping his head back, distracting him from what came next, a right hook brought up from the floor that finished as a right cross flush to the point of his chin. He sagged into the ropes and sat down on the bottom rung. He looked like a bum on a park bench feeding the pigeons. I waved my glove in the air and exhorted him to rise, like Ali when he stood over a stiffened Sonny Liston in Lewiston, Maine, in May of '65.

Get up, sucker, I said, so I can hit you again!

That brought a chuckle from the crowd.

Stan waved me into a neutral corner and began his count.

One ... two ... three ... four ...

Evans paid no attention. He seemed to be trying to remember his address.

Five ... six ... seven ...

When Stan got to seven, Evans looked at me. His spirit was crushed. His hopes were dashed. He lacked the will to rise. He looked away.

Eight ... nine ... ten.

Stan waved the fight over. He went to the ring apron and leaned over the ropes and spoke to the judges and the timekeeper. He motioned me to the center of the ring and raised my hand.

Ladies and gentlemen, he announced, we have a winner by knockout in twenty-one seconds of the first round—Dean the Destroyer Daaavis!

I climbed through the ropes. I saw Rinaldi in the crowd. He pointed a finger at himself, then at me. I followed Evans to the dressing room. He looked at his face in the stainless steel mirror over the sink. I stood behind him. His gaze met mine.

You could have gotten up, I said. You could have gotten up.

He looked away.

THE NEXT DAY ABDUL AND I SAT at one of the many small round concrete tables lining the perimeter of the yard inside the cinder track. The sun shone brightly onto Abdul's face and glinted off the pigment of his skin. I saw flecks of copper there, and of gold, bronze and burnt umber, of lavender and magenta and cobalt blue.

An African American inmate I had never seen before approached our table.

Dean the Destroyer! he said. My man! Give me some skin, bro!

He held a hand out palm up. I slapped it and turned my hand over. He slapped it and went his way.

Abdul's tone was droll.

I see you have a new alias, Dean, he said. And a new reputation.

So much for being the invisible man, I said.

Did you not feel intimidated by the crowd? A white man knocking out a black man in front of three hundred boisterous black inmates?

I didn't think about it, Abdul. I just took care of business.

Very good, Dean. Your attitude will serve you well in future endeavors.

What endeavors might you have in mind, Abdul?

Whatever the Universe delivers, Brother Dean.

I was not put off by Abdul's equivocation. There was never a time when he did not have something in mind. He would be forthcoming when it suited his purpose … and he always had a purpose.

So tell me, Dean, he said, how did it feel at the moment your fist found the face of Mr. Antwon the Executioner Evans, and you put him onto his beehind?

Terrific, Abdul, I said. My overhand right hurtled through the air like a heat-seeking missile. I can still feel the force of the impact. And when Evans sat on the bottom rope like he was waiting for a bus, I knew my word had become law. But something was missing. Before the referee reached the count of ten, Evans looked me in the eyes, and I saw that he could have gotten up. I was pissed and disappointed that he didn't.

But didn't your affirmation say he'd be robbed of the will to rise?

Yes, but it was too easy. I felt like I was the one being robbed.

Abdul stroked his chin with his fingertips.

Umm … so, despite the fact that you gave a perfect demonstration of the law, knocking out The Executioner was not the defining mo-ment you sought?

No, it wasn't, I admitted.

Abdul put a hand on my shoulder.

Patience, Grasshopper, he said. We shall see what we shall see. Perhaps what you seek is yet seeking you.

That must be it, I thought. The Universe has a plan. The path to the gold medal is being cleared for the ultimate test that will make my quest a worthy one.

Just you and me, brother, no place to hide.

A FUNNY THING HAPPENED

THE NEXT DAY THE SCHEDULE WAS POSTED for the second round of matches. Something was amiss: Rinaldi would be fighting Evans.

I found Stan in the gym.

Stan, what's up? I'm supposed to fight Rinaldi. Evans is out of it.

Stan shook his head.

Evans ain't out of it till he fight Rinaldi, he said. If Rinaldi win, Evans get the bronze cause he a two-time loser, you and Rinaldi throw down in the finals, and the winner get the gold and the loser get the silver. Now, if Evans beat Rinaldi—which I don't suspect— then Rinaldi get the bronze cause he didn't beat nobody, Evans get the silver cause he beat Rinaldi, and you get the gold because you beat the man who beat the man.

But Rinaldi got the pass, I said. That's the same as a victory in the first round. Then he fights the winner of the second round, which was me, and the winner gets the gold, the loser gets the silver and Evans gets the bronze. That's how round-robin tournaments work.

How it work is, I'm the boss, Flea Weight. But don't be trippin on the details. After Rinaldi take care of business, you and him gonna mix it up for the gold.

Fine, I thought. The Universe has its ways.

ALL DAY LONG THE SUN HAD BEAT DOWN through a sultry haze. The second round of matches would be held in a tropical hot-box. My fate was out of my hands. When I wasn't in Chico's corner, I'd be in the bleachers watching. No doubt Rinaldi would dispose of The Executioner, and the following week he and I would be staring at each other across the ring.

The flyweight and bantamweight bouts were lively. Little guys full of fury and bad intentions. I went to the dressing room and laced up Chico. I walked him to the ring. He won a spirited match against a scrappy but over-matched fellow Mexicano named Lupe. I walked him back to the dressing room, toweled off his sweating head and shoulders, and unlaced his gloves. I saw Evans sitting alone. I sat beside him.

Here, I said, you'll need these.

I laced him up. I saw in his eyes the hope that had failed him before. I felt he could use an infusion of faith.

You can do this, I said. Just don't quit! He's going to come at you with everything he has. Cover up. Let him wear himself out, then pick your shots. Remember Ali versus Foreman, Kinshasa, Zaire, 1974. Rumble in the jungle! Do the rope-a-dope, man!

I didn't know if he heard me. I patted him on the back.

Just don't quit, I said.

I looked around. I didn't see Rinaldi. I left the dressing room. There he was, fully dressed, sitting in the roped-off spectator section between a stout middle-aged woman in a lime green pantsuit, who dabbed at her neck with a handkerchief, and an attractive young girl in a yellow dress whose hand rested on his hand, which in turn rested on her knee as on the armrest of a throne. I got his attention. He spoke to his guests and came over. His blue denim shirt hung limply, with softball-sized circles of sweat staining the armpits.

Rinaldi, I said, you're fighting in a minute. What's up?

Fuck a whole lot of fighting, Davis, he said. My ma's here. And my girl. Anyway, I'm mellow, man. Know what I mean?

But if you don't fight, Evans wins by default, and he gets the silver and you get the bronze.

Guess I don't give a shit, bro.

Come on, Rinaldi, you can take this guy out in the first round. Then come back and enjoy the show with your Ma and your girl. They'll be impressed.

You don't get it, Davis. I am mell*oow*! Can you dig what I'm saying?

What I dig is, if you don't fight Evans and win, you don't fight me next week … but maybe that's how you want it.

Rinaldi gave me a Fuck You look. He went back to his ma and his girl, said a few words, and went to the dressing room. I took a seat in the bleachers. I watched the middleweight bout, a brawling affair that deteriorated into a wrestling match and brought jeers from the crowd. Then Rinaldi and Evans were up.

Stan announced grandly: Ladies and gentlemen, we bring you action in the light heavyweight division ...

Rinaldi and Evans faced each other across the ring. Rinaldi paced
like a bull in a pen. Evans eyed him warily. The bell rang. Evans put
up his guard and took two timorous steps forward. Rinaldi charged
across the ring and commenced to wail away. Evans retreated with
his gloves held high.

Don't quit, Evans, I yelled. Just don't quit!

Rinaldi pinned him on the ropes and launched looping lefts and
rights to his head and body. Evans leaned back and took the shots on
his gloves, and on his elbows held close to his ribcage.

Now get off the ropes! I yelled. Throw some punches!

Evans slid out sideways and danced to the middle of the ring with
Rinaldi in pugnacious pursuit. Evans poked out a powerless jab,
and a flimsy right cross, and Rinaldi again backed him into the
ropes, going up to the head and down to the body with a barrage of
blistering blows. Evans was being broken down. It was just a matter
of time.

Then a funny thing happened. Rinaldi stopped throwing punches.
He wobbled to the center of the ring, put his hands on his knees and
vomited. His mouthpiece fell into the mess. The spectators groaned.
Evans stayed on the ropes with his gloves up. Stan the Man came
over.

Are you all right? he asked Rinaldi.

Rinaldi nodded and put his hands in front of his face. Stan called
for a rag. He picked up the mouthpiece with the rag and brought it
to Rinaldi's corner and the cornerman cleaned it with water from a
plastic bottle. Stan returned the mouthpiece to Rinaldi, wiped up
the mess, threw the rag out of the ring and motioned the fighters
together.

Fight! he commanded.

Rinaldi remained in the middle of the ring with his hands up, unsteady on his feet. Evans stayed on the ropes with his hands up, looking at Rinaldi.

Go get him, Evans, I yelled. Hit him now!

Evans advanced cautiously.

Hit him! I yelled.

Evans threw a straight right that went between Rinaldi's gloves and bounced off his forehead. Rinaldi fired back feebly. His mouth was open and he gasped for air.

Go downstairs, Evans! I yelled.

Evans dug a left hook into Rinaldi's ribs. Rinaldi's hands came down and a new surge of vomit spilled over his lips onto his chest. Evans hit him with a right cross that turned his head around and sent his mouthpiece across the ring like a fluttering moth. He hit him with a stiff jab that split his lip, and a rivulet of blood mixed with vomit and saliva flowed from his mouth onto his pants and the canvas mat. Rinaldi turned away and wobbled to the ring apron, draped his arms over the ropes, and looked out at the crowd. Blood and vomit flowed freely. The audience heckled and hooted.

You a bum, Rinaldi!

You a bitch!

You a sorry ass motherfucker!

He responded to the ridicule with a pathetic, apologetic, blood-and-vomit-drooling smile. The crowd erupted with laughter. Evans stood in the middle of the ring with his hands down. Stan stepped between Evans and Rinaldi and waved the fight over. He went to the ring apron and leaned over the ropes and spoke to the judges and the timekeeper. He returned to the center of the ring and held up Evans' gloved hand.

Ladies and gentlemen, he announced. We have a winner in the light heavyweight division! At two minutes twenty-four seconds of round number one, the opponent is unable to continue and the referee stops the fight. The winner by technical decision—Antwon the Executioner Evaaans!

I followed Evans to the dressing room.

You didn't quit, I said.

Thanks, he said.

The light of redemption shone in his eyes.

Rinaldi was nowhere in sight.

THAT NIGHT I WENT BY ABDUL'S HOUSE. I peered into the narrow slit of window in the grey steel door. It was dark inside, but a figure moved about. I knocked and the door was opened by a short balding black man.

The fuck you want? he snarled.

Where's Abdul? I said.

Do I look like the goddam missing person's bureau to you, lame-ass motherfucker?

He slammed the door shut. I shouted out to no one in particular.

Hey, where's Abdul?

Transferred to the Honor Dorm, Double D, someone shouted back.

Until I could hook up with Abdul at another time and place, I would be left to contemplate the turn of events myself.

THE NEXT DAY I RAN THE YARD ALONE. I remained thoughtless. I listened to my heartbeat, and to the crunch of my footfalls on the cinder track. I passed a cluster of inmates from which Rinaldi broke away and ran up beside me.

Hey, I said.

Hey nothin, Rinaldi said. You fucked me up, dude!

How did I fuck you up?

You made me look like a fool in front of my partners, and my Ma and my girl.

That wasn't me up there in the ring, I said.

But it was you that ran your fuckin mouth! I told you I was mellow but you didn't get it. Look—

He held out his arm and showed me the needle marks on the inside of his elbow.

My girl brought me some smack, he said. I was cruising, dude! I was in no fuckin shape to get in the ring in that heat, but you thought you'd be clever with that bullshit about me not wanting to fight you next week.

Well, what can I say, Rinaldi? One day we'll be old motherfuckers on the block, kickin it about back in the day, and I'll say, Hey,

Rinaldi, remember that time you got your butt kicked in the penitentiary because you didn't want to fight me?

Funny, Davis. I would've knocked your sorry ass out.

Maybe there'll be an '88 Olympics, I said.

Not for me, he said. I'm paroled in '86.

Then we'll never know.

Fuck that, Davis. You want a taste of the smack? I saved you some. China white. And a clean point just for you.

No thanks, Rinaldi, I said, but I do appreciate the offer.

And I truly did. It was a gesture of respect that I would not soon forget.

THE FOLLOWING SATURDAY I WATCHED the final matches with a certain detachment. My fighting days were over. Chico's opponent was a slick and powerful and popular Puerto Rican gang banger named Tito. The intensity of their match was the embodiment of the long-standing rivalry between Mexican and Puerto Rican boxers. Both were knocked down twice and got back up and gave as good as they got. Chico's speed gave him a slight advantage, and his split decision victory by a narrow margin was not well received by the Puerto Rican contingent, who outnumbered all other Latino inmates in Lime Ridge by a four-to-one margin. Chico was proud of his victory and graciously praised the prowess of his vanquished opponent.

After the last match, three wooden boxes of differing heights were placed in the center of the ring. Stan summoned the winners by weight division, and the color of their medals, and they mounted their respective boxes. Warden Wainwright hung a medal around the neck of each and shook his hand. Stan shook his hand, too. Chico's award was met with jeers from the Puerto Rican fans and vigorous applause from the Mexican. Rinaldi was called to receive his bronze medal, but his pedestal remained empty. Antwon Evans bent low to receive the silver. The Warden shook his hand. Stan the Man shook his hand. I shook his hand, too, and saw in his eyes that faith had supplanted hope.

When the gold medal was hung around my neck, I felt the weight of it, familiar, as though it had been hung around my neck many times before, which it had, in the diorama of my affirmation night after night in my cell. I shook the warden's hand and that of Stan the Man.

Feel better now, Flea Weight? Stan said.

You bet I do, Stan, I lied.

Because I didn't.

I felt nothing at all.

TIME PASSED AND THE DRAMA SURROUNDING the surrogate Summer Olympics of 1984 slipped silently into the annals of my personal history. I ran into Rinaldi occasionally, in the gym or on the yard, till he was cut loose in '86 and the subject of the tournament never came up. I guess he really didn't give a shit.

Chico's performance earned him a spot on Stan's team and he won the Department of Corrections welterweight title in '85. He was paroled in '87 and sent back to Cuidad Juarez. I got one letter from him in pidgin English. He'd found a promoter, was undefeated in his first four professional bouts, and was invited to train at Emmanuel Steward's Kronk Gym in Detroit, but his criminal record and visa issues would forever keep him south of the border.

The Hit Man continued to box for the team, and defended his title twice before he was busted for reefer, lost a year of good time, and was shipped to a max joint in the North, where no doubt his cell is the shiniest on the block.

I never saw Evans again. Quiet he came. Quiet he went.

WHEN I NEXT SAW ABDUL the grass on the yard was frosted over and the shadow of the almighty hawk lay once more upon the land. We hadn't had a conversation since his move to the Honor Dorm. He sat now at a small table in the prison's modest library, his hands folded in his lap, a look of abiding contentment on his face. I took the chair opposite him and slid *The Science of Mind* across the table.

Thanks for the loan, Abdul, I said. I now have a copy of my own.

There's a lifetime of learning between those covers, he said.

There is, I agreed. I'll be absorbing its lessons for a long time.

How are the boys on the block? Is Old Man Mosley still with us?

He's hanging on.

Has Buster's PPCR come through?

No. I don't imagine it ever will, but there's always hope.

And Botha—is he still giving you the evil eye?

I stay out of his way. He's an angry man. He might have plenty of things to be angry about, but one of them should not be me. I must represent something disagreeable to him.

Could be you're having too much fun, Dean. Some people are offended by those who enjoy life.

I wish there was something I could do for the man.

We became silent. I waited for Abdul to decide the direction of the conversation. He was never not going somewhere with his train of thought and I had always been gratified to go there with him.

How about that U.S. Boxing Team, Dean? he said. Nine Olympic gold medals. Imagine!

That's quite a haul, I agreed. But I'll bet the boycott by the Russians, East Germans and Cubans, the teams to beat, took some glitter off the gold.

Yes, the Universe has a way of spinning an event. So tell me, Champ, was winning that gold medal the victory you had sought?

I had expected the question. I had a weird feeling that no time had passed since our discussion at the table on the yard about my speedy dispatch of Antwon the Executioner Evans.

No, I said. It was an empty one. I got what I thought I wanted, but when the medal was put around my neck it felt like a cosmic joke. I could almost hear the Universe laughing.

Abdul laughed now as though he shared in the joke.

Dean, he said, one of my favorite deities is the Laughing Buddha. His needs are simple. He wants for nothing. He throws his meager bag of possessions over his shoulder and laughs his way down the road of life.

What does he think is so funny?

He's not attached to the outcome of events, and he's amused by those who are.

How does that jive with the precept to conceive, believe and achieve, Abdul? What's the point of wanting something, then not caring if you get it?

The point is to harmonize your endeavors with the intent of the Universe that all sentient beings spiral upwards toward perfection and the annihilation of self. When your efforts further your fellow man on his journey toward the divine, the farther along you'll be on your own. In my estimation, Dean, you've progressed beyond the need to gratify your ego with vainglorious pursuits, and are ready to put the needs of others above your own.

I dug my heels in like a blindfolded burro being led down a steep mountain pass. I had a saddlebag of needs of my own still to satisfy. The divine could wait.

Thanks for the rave review, I said, but I'm not as far along as you think. I give respect and recognition to my fellow man, but if I get what I want without depriving them of what they want, that's good enough for me.

Abdul's smile was indulgent.

Fair enough, Dean, he said. You'll know when you're ready. Meanwhile, there are a couple of developments here in the camp that might be of interest.

I'm listening.

Option number one: I'm starting a theatre group, The Players of Conviction. There's a lot of untapped talent behind bars. I intend to provide an outlet of expression for the oppressed, the luckless and the lame of spirit.

Plenty of those here, I said. I suppose the Administration appreciates your keeping the natives from getting restless.

You would think so, but the masters get nervous when the people speak. If you want to keep the downtrodden down, don't give them a voice. Major Drumm was especially opposed. He doesn't want to see anyone improve their station in life, least of all one of his own people. He's twisted that way. But Warden Wainwright pushed it through. He's the last of a breed. The tenor of criminal justice is changing, with less emphasis on rehabilitation and more on incarceration. An ill wind blows through the House of Corrections, Dean. Enjoy the relative calm in this camp while you can. You're in the eye of the storm.

I felt a quiet thrill at the prospect of a stronger wind blowing.

Are you writing your own plays? I asked.

I am. But first we'll do some classics—*Hope Is the Thing with Feathers*; *The Telltale Heart; The Zoo Story*—to hone the skill of the players, and to lull the Administration to sleep. After which I'll introduce my own stuff, material with a message.

Abdul's sly smile surprised me. I saw a side of him I hadn't seen before: the anarchist, the agitator, the firebrand he must have been before he succumbed to his Demon Days. I wondered if he, too, wearied of the doldrums at the eye of the storm, and yearned for a more vigorous wind to blow. I returned his smile.

Well, no doubt you've aligned your personal mind with the Universal, I said, and will manifest the results you desire, so I won't say break a leg, Abdul. I'll only say: Conceive, believe, achieve!

Perhaps you'd care to join us, Dean. If you're looking for a new you, there will be plenty of roles to play.

I was intrigued. My Danté Allegro alias had been amusing and had given me a look at another side of myself.

What's option number two? I said.

Lime Ridge has been designated an extension of South East Illinois University. It's been a pet project of the Warden for years. Qualified inmates will take two courses per semester, leading to a B.A. in Liberal Arts. You need sixty undergraduate credits to enroll.

Are you going for it?

I'll be busy with the Players of Conviction. A degree can wait.

Two terrific options, Abdul, I said. I'll have to give this some serious thought.

I'm sure you'll make the right decision, Dean, but whatever you choose, remember—beware the Laughing Buddha!

I laughed.

Abdul laughed, too.

We three had a good laugh together.

PAULY STOOD OUTSIDE the cell of Berserker keeping guard. I sat on the edge of Berserker's bunk and opened the book *Demons and Deities*, by Charles Lesserman, Ph.D., to the page containing the picture of the Laughing Buddha. I showed Berserker my sketch of the Buddha encircled by the words Conceive, Believe, Achieve.

I'd like the Buddha to be golden, Berserker, I said. He has the light of the sun shining through him. The light of joy.

I can do bronze, Berserker said.

Okay, bronze, Berserker. You're the artist.

That I am, he said.

He sat on his folding chair in front of me and swabbed my right bicep with alcohol.

What made you change your mind, Davis?

I want something I know will always be true, Berserker. And I want a tangible record of my time in the joint, so I don't wake up one day wondering if it was all a dream.

The electric motor of the tattoo gun whined like the hum of a hornet's nest. The needle burned like fire.

It is all a dream, Davis, Berserker said. A dream within a dream.

I wondered at the sudden perspicuity of a man I thought I'd gotten to know.

I wondered if anyone knows anyone, truly.

LOLA SQUIRMED IN LUCY'S ARMS. She would get down and practice her newly acquired walking skills, but the rules did not allow children to wander the visiting room. There was a lull in our conversation. Lucy was disturbed by my tattoo, not because she opposed the art, but because my explanation of its meaning, and my account of the quest for the gold medal and why its attainment failed to satisfy, were rambling and unintelligible.

She was further disturbed when she noticed, two tables away, an inmate with his penis in his lap.

Oh, my God, she exclaimed. That guy over there has his dick out!

I looked. I laughed.

That's Hit Man Harris, I said. He's in my house. He's the State Champion I was telling you about. The one who almost knocked me out. He's a joker, all right. He wants you to know his dick is bigger than mine.

Well, it is!

You don't have to look, Lucy.

This place gives me the creeps, she said.

It does have its cast of characters, I agreed.

I told her about Randy Bone and his innovative new system of prognostication, Divination By Dung. I told her about Abdul, who had the power to fold time back upon itself and make a year gone by seem like a moment ago. I told her about Wilbur, who wrote bizarre stories he claimed were channeled through him by denizens of another dimension. I told her about Martin Mueller, the billionaire who claimed Lime Ridge was in the basement of his country estate and took an elevator down to his cell each day to produce a manuscript that would change the course of the evolution of mankind and earn him a high place among his brethren-to-be, the Illuminati. I told her we were invited to be guests at his mansion. He and his wife, Millie, would wine us and dine us, and we'd take in a play. I told her about Crazy Carl, who tormented Mueller with gibberish, and that there was some sort of sinister psychic bond between them that made the walls of the corridors crawl with malevolent energy.

Lucy frowned.

I'm worried about you, Dean, she said. You're having too much fun in here.

A line from a Crosby, Stills & Nash tune ran through my head: If you can't be with the one you love, honey, love the one you're with.

I avoided further mention of life in Lime Ridge. I asked about Wally. He'd only visited once. The place made him uncomfortable. He hated to see me here. He wrote occasionally, beginning his letters, Yo! Danté! And he had subscribed me to The *San Francisco Chronicle*, knowing I loved the verbal pyrotechnics of Herb Caen.

He continues to drink, Lucy said. He's killing himself.

I asked after Brodie. He, too, had only visited once, but he took my calls, during which he complained about life and marveled at my enthusiasm for it. Lucy said his moods were up and down like a roller coaster. He had a new guy friend every week. He took her around to his favorite clubs on Castro Street, where she felt more comfortable and less harassed with a gay male crowd than a straight one. We discussed the antics of Lola, and the trials and tribulations of raising a child alone. And when we had exhausted what few subjects were common to our disparate lives, the conversation stalled and my thoughts wandered to North One. I wondered what they'd be serving in the chow hall for supper. I hoped not what was laughably called Swiss Steak—you could run a pencil through the arteries that were found inside a slab of it. I wondered if I'd go to the yard afterward. I'd come to love these sultry Midwest summer evenings, the chirp of the crickets, the blink of the fireflies, the heat lightning sliding silent as prayer across a darkening sky. I wondered how I would render this visit in my journal tonight when alone in the sanctuary of my cell, and which would seem more real to me in the future, the visit or my written account of it.

BOOK III

THE GUMP REPORT

*Homosexuality in Russia is a crime and the punishment is seven years
in prison, locked up with the other men.
There is a three year waiting list.*

~ Yakov Smirnoff

THE PROPOSAL

YOU HAD TO GIVE THE MAN CREDIT: to leave the haven of academia and walk through those big iron gates alone, and cross the camp unescorted to the red brick building where he taught a course in Cultural Anthropology twice a week, and to deliver his lessons to a group of cynical convicts, would have discouraged a lesser man.

I felt for the Professor when my classmates scoffed at his proposal— that in lieu of the final exam next week they could do a paper on such topics as gang activity, drug use, and sexual activity, based on inter- views with fellow inmates. He would instruct them in the protocol of ethnographic data collection, their findings to be included in a paper presented at the Annual Conference of Cultural Anthropologists in London in September of that year, and they named as contributors. It would be such authentic material!

He was pointedly informed by his students that, authentic or not, inmates interviewing inmates on such topics would not be appreci- ated—by the inmates or the Administration.

The Professor had blushed. Of course! he said. What was I think- ing? I forgot where I was! Well, we'll just put an optional bonus ques- tion on the exam asking your opinion on any of these topics—and there are no wrong answers, of course. Now, where were we … ?

He then shuffled through his papers as though the faux pas had never occurred.

I would miss the Professor, his spunk and his open-mindedness. And I would miss these classes. I had embraced them with more en- thusiasm than any of those I took during my years at San Francisco State. Unfettered by the concerns of the outside world, I had become totally immersed. Lucy, too, approved. For once I was engaged in an activity that made sense to her. But next week's class would be my last. I and Randy Bone, my sole fellow graduate, would be award- ed our degrees from Southeastern Illinois University at a ceremony presided over by Warden Wainwright, and attended by a coterie of Prison and University officials. We'd have our picture taken, there'd be a little write-up in the prison paper, *Prose & Cons*, and I would still have eighteen months of my sentence to fill with meaningful activity. I needed to remain engaged.

AT THE END OF THE EXAM the following week I waited while my fellows students left the room.

Officer, I said to the guard, I need five minutes to get some clarification of an assignment. Okay?

Five minutes, Davis, the guard grunted as he stepped into the hallway.

The Professor stuffed exams into his briefcase. He seemed subdued, perhaps yet disheartened by the demise of his proposal. I looked forward to lifting his spirits with one of my own.

Professor, I said, I really enjoyed your class.

Thanks, Dean, he said. I enjoyed your participation ... and your moral support.

You did all right, I said. The guys can be direct, but I know they respected you.

Do you really think so?

Yes, you brought the far-flung corners of the world into this little room. They'll miss it. I know I will.

The Professor looked around at the bare walls.

So will I, he said. Don't laugh, but I feel like I'll be on the outside looking in.

Inside or out, I said, we're all doing time somewhere.

He smiled.

Given a choice, he said, I'll do my time on the outside, thank you.

He snapped his briefcase shut.

Yes, it's been a great experience, he said, but I do regret that my research paper won't happen. It would have been my pièce de résistance!

He pointed a finger into the air and attempted a French accent. I felt a welling up of goodwill.

It can still happen, Larry, I said.

He narrowed one eye.

How do you mean? he said.

I mean I propose to do the interviews for you.

But your classmates seemed to think it was a bad idea.

They're here for the long haul, I said. They've got to cover their butts. Me, I'm just passing through. The worst that could happen is the Administration shuts me down. I can handle that.

What's in it for you, Dean?

Amusement, I said. And memories. Someday my life will be ordinary. My neighbors will be retired professional people who pay their taxes and have opinions about the current state of affairs. I will look back on this experience and think: Damn! Did I really do that?

Are you sure … ?

I am.

Then I'm grateful. Thank you!

You're welcome. I suggest we limit the interviews to a single topic. There's only one of me. Do you have a preference?

The Professor put his fingers to his chin.

Umm … I think the study of sexual activity behind bars would be of significant interest to the, uh, Academic Community.

The Professor had often alluded to the subject in class, wondering how the role of the Gump—inmates who provided sexual gratification to fellow inmates, whether by choice or coercion—compared to the role of the Berdache, males of Plains Indian tribes who assumed multiple gender roles and were appreciated for their contribution to the community. Were Gumps treated with similar regard, or with contempt? He could research the Berdach, but did not have entré to the world of the Gump. He'd been quick to point out that he himself had no gender identity issues, and even displayed his wedding band to prove it! That had gotten a few snickers from the class.

Excellent choice, I said. The Administration tolerates sex in the joint. I'll find plenty of inmates willing to have a conversation around the subject, and we'll get some of the gang stuff and the drug stuff as collateral material. How much time do I have?

I need to submit a draft of my presentation to the Committee in

August, he said. I'll need to assimilate your observations with my own. Will eight weeks be enough time to gather the raw material?

Yes, and it will be raw, Larry. If an inmate says, Suck my dick, motherfucker, it goes into my report. You can edit the vernacular if you want, but what I hear is what you get.

I wouldn't have it any other way!

I'll send the notes of each interview as they're done. I have a friend on staff who'll carry them out and mail them. In eight weeks you'll have *The Gump Report*.

The Professor opened his briefcase. He took out a business card and a pen. He wrote on the back of the card. His hand trembled slightly.

Here's my University address, he said. And my home phone number. Call collect if you have questions or concerns ... or if you just want to talk.

I put the card in my shirt pocket. The guard stuck his head in the door.

Let's go, Davis!

I held out my hand. The Professor took it.

Thanks again, he said.

The pleasure's all mine, I said. You'll have the notes from the first interview soon.

I can't wait!

Davis! the guard barked.

All right! All right! I'm coming!

TOMMY'S NUTS & BOLTS

TOMMY FIT THE PROFILE of a middle-aged, middle-American, god-fearing, semi-articulate white man doing hard time. We weren't pals but I had sat at the same table with him for a few hands of Tonk, and had gotten an impression. Approaching him directly would have been imprudent, so I approached a mutual acquaintance, Wilbur Walsh.

Oh, yeah, he's your man, Wilbur said. He's a card-carrying bigot and homophobe who won't mind giving you his opinion—if he trusts you. See, Dean, Tommy's a little paranoid.

That Tommy was paranoid was an ironic assessment because Wilbur was forever looking over his shoulder to see if he was being spied upon. The wry smile that curled his lips when his eyes flitted left and right seemed to be saying they would never catch him because he was way too goddamned smart for the bastards!

And he was smart in a wily sort of way. Cunning and discreet, he could count as an ally every type of inmate, from puffy white child molester to the Imam of the resident Mosque—or a card-carrying racist homophobe like Tommy, who'd been locked up a long time, for just what Wilbur didn't say. He only told you what he wanted you to know. He was a joker that way.

But he'll trust you, Dean, Wilbur said, because I'll tell him you're all right. Bring him some hooch. He likes his liquor. It'll loosen his tongue. He can't get it from Carter. Carter doesn't like his attitude. He can rub you the wrong way.

TOMMY LEANED AGAINST THE WALL behind his bunk in boxer shorts and a tank top displaying his hairy pits. He was clean-shaven, with a nose like an eagle's beak and thinning hair combed straight back. A silver cross hung from a chain around his neck.

I sat on a piece of plywood placed over the toilet bowl, with pen and paper in one hand, a quart plastic jug in the other.

What'd you bring me, Davis? Tommy said.

I recognized the challenge in his tone. A demand for toll from the troll beneath the bridge.

Some hooch, I said. Abel Carter's new batch. Lots of pineapple.

I don't like that black son of a bitch, Tommy said. I don't like his attitude.

He makes good hooch, I said. This batch, it's so good if you stuck a little umbrella in it you'd think you were in the Bahamas.

Never been to the Bahamas, Tommy said. Never been east of Illinois.

I handed Tommy the jug. He unscrewed the cap and put his nose to the spout. He grunted approval.

There's some cups behind the towel, he said. And grab a couple cigars while you're at it.

I pushed aside the white towel draped over the grey metal cabinet next to the toilet and took out two plastic glasses and two cigars. I held out the glasses. Tommy filled them, took one for himself and put the jug on the floor.

There's a lighter on the desk, he said.

I lit our cigars. I puffed appreciatively.

Very nice, I said.

Can't get Panatela's like these in the commissary, Tommy said. They were brought in by a screw pal of mine. His old man knew my old man. He's a customer of my hardware store, Tommy's Nuts & Bolts. You ever been to Tommy's Nuts & Bolts, Davis?

I'm not from around here.

Where you from?

California.

California! Where the cars wear bras and the women don't!

Where had I heard that catchy phrase before? I wondered. Oh, yeah—Grover Tull, ringmaster of the Arcadia Correctional Center Slaughter House Family Circus.

You ever been to California, Tommy? I said.

Never been West of Illinois, Davis. Never saw the point.

Never Been East. Never been West. Ever been North to Chicago?

What's up there? Just spooks and spics! I got everything I need down the road a few miles—a wife, two kids and the best damn hardware store in the Midwest!

The black and white television on top of the cabinet was turned on with the volume off. Blue smoke drifted in the flickering light.

Wilbur tells me you're all right, Davis, Tommy said. That you're not a snitch or a snoop.

That's right, Tommy.

Because if you are, you're wasting my time. I'm a businessman. Time is money. I got to know when to invest and when to cut my losses.

I understand. I appreciate your time.

Wilbur says you're writing a book.

I'm doing an assignment. The professor might write a book.

Is he going to use my name?

That's up to you, Tommy.

All right by me. I don't care what the world thinks. I know what I did was right.

It's not about what you did, Tommy, but what you think about sex in prison. A Boys Behind Bars kind of thing.

Why you want to know about Gumps for anyway, Davis?

Not me. The professor. He's an anthropologist. They study the weird shit people do. He thinks what goes on in the joint is interesting.

I'm all in favor of education, Davis. I've got two kids in college. They're smarter than me. Ain't that how it oughta be? If the next generation isn't smarter than the last, the human race gets dumber and dumber. I don't think that's God's plan. You believe in God, Davis? I want to know who I'm talking to if I'm going to bare my soul.

No need to bare your soul, Tommy. I'm just looking for your take on men fucking men in the joint. What you think about it.

I think it violates the law of God! Tommy said. You believe in God, Davis? You didn't say.

I leaned against the wall behind the toilet. The flush button poked my spine. I leaned forward and thought about my answer. I didn't want the interview to go far afield too soon.

I know something is going on, Tommy, I said, but I don't know what. Guess I'll just wait and see.

Wait and see! What did Jesus say about people who are luke-warm? He'd as soon spit'm out of his mouth!

Well, I hope he'll find it in his heart to keep me in his mouth till I know what it's all about, I said.

It's all about family! Tommy said, his tone that of one scolding a naughty child. It's about your wife and kids!

I said nothing, not wanting to fan the flames. I sipped my drink.

You got a wife and kids, Davis?

A beautiful wife and a baby girl, Tommy.

They waiting for you out there in California?

You bet they are, I said.

Then count yourself a lucky son of a bitch, Davis!

I do, Tommy. Every day.

I got a wife and two kids, Tommy said. If it wasn't for knowing they're out there waiting, I don't know if I could handle this time.

He finished his drink.

Ready for another, Davis?

No, I'm good.

He poured himself another. I took a deep breath. I picked up my pad and pen.

Let's start with your first encounter with homosexuality in prison, Tommy, I said. Do you remember your first encounter?

Tommy stiffened.

What encounter? he said. I didn't have no fucking encounter!

Not you personally, I said. I mean the first time it came to your attention. Do you have a story?

He regarded me through narrowed eyes. He took a deep drag from his cigar. He exhaled and watched the stream of smoke break up and roil crazily in the flickering light.

Yeah, he said. I got a story. About the County Coroner. You've got to be elected Coroner, you know. This guy was a war hero and he got himself elected. Then he gets caught fucking a corpse!

That's fucked up, I said, scribbling notes. I felt a good story coming.

Tell me, Davis! And the guy had a kid my age. Messed his mind up real good. Think about it. Your old man, who you thought was a hero, a man's man, and the sick fuck gets caught with his dick up a dead man's butt!

It was a male corpse?

That's the point, Davis! All that dead pussy laying around and he picks a man to screw!

So what happened?

The sick fuck had friends in City Hall. The charges were reduced to destruction of property. He lost his job but got a new one as Deputy Sheriff. A couple years later I shot some creep who had it coming and I'm in the County Jail waiting to be sent to the max joint. There's two of us in the bullpen, me and a kid about eighteen, Joey. He's a burglar, a three-time loser. He's going to the max joint, too. I'm laying on my bunk in the dark, thinking about my wife and kids. I hear keys jangling and the door opening. I hear a voice cooing. Joey, Joey, I want to make love to you! It's the ex-coroner turned Deputy Sheriff. The kid whines, Leave me alone! The deputy says, Please! The kid says, I'll tell the Sheriff! The deputy leaves. The next day, the kid tells the Sheriff but the Sheriff doesn't do shit. A couple years later, the deputy's charged with soliciting sex from an underage kid at a fancy hotel in Chicago. The charges are dropped. I happened to read about it. I connect the corpse case and the under-age kid case and the Joey case and I write a letter to the local paper. They print an article. The deputy's fired. I did my fucking duty!

I wondered how much credence to give Tommy's account. Was it normal for a man to be gay and a pedophile and a necrophiliac all at once? I didn't know what was normal in the world of skewed sex, but did it matter that Tommy was an unreliable narrator if his stories were good?

Tommy continued.

Later, I see Joey in the max joint. He's been turned out, turned into a Gump. That was fifteen years ago. He's here now, in Lime Ridge. He delivers pizza in the Jaycees program. He was King B's kid for a while. Their cell was next to mine. I could hear them talk their lovey-dovey fuck shit. Made me sick! One day Joey decides he isn't a Gump anymore, he'll kill anyone who says he is, including King B

Ali. King B finds this funny, but he cuts Joey loose; there were plenty of other young punks around. So Joey starts pumping iron, puts on fifty pounds of muscle, but so what if a faggot pumps a little iron and looks like Arnold Schwarzenegger, Davis? Whatta you got? A big muscle-bound cocksucker is all!

Tommy made a face like he had a foul taste in his mouth. He slumped against the wall. He took a drag off his cigar and mumbled a few unintelligible words to himself while the smoke curled from his mouth. He sat up suddenly.

Yeah, he said, then there was Big Bo Johnson. This was back in the day. Big Bo was a regular Gump playboy. Had a different kid every month. He was getting out soon and wanted one more go round before he went. Had his eye on this little white-boy in the serving line, who's maybe a faggot, maybe not. The kid hadn't made up his mind. Bo hears the kid likes reefer. He offers him reefer to meet him in the toilet at the gym. There's a peephole with a flap over it between the screw's office and the toilet. The screw sees the kid on the toilet with his legs up, and Bo on his knees licking the kid's butt. Screw doesn't bust these perverts. He just closes the flap. I know because the screw is a pal of mine. He used to come into my hardware store, Tommy's Nuts & Bolts. You ever do business at Tommy's Nuts & Bolts? That's right, you're not from around here. When you get out, Davis, go to Tommy's Nuts & Bolts. Best damn hardware store in the Midwest. I opened the doors in '64. Me and Shirley. That's my old lady. I knew the business, she knew the books. What a team! We opened another in '66 and one more in '67. That's almost a quarter century of Tommy's Nuts & Bolts, Davis, and still going strong, thanks to Shirley! She's still doing those books. Hell, Davis, if it wasn't for her, I don't know if I could do this time. A man could lose his mind. You got a woman waiting for you, Davis?

There was no point telling Tommy he had already asked that question.

You bet I do, I said.

Then count yourself a lucky son of a bitch!

I do, I said. So, tell me, Tommy, why do you think there's so much homosexual activity in the joint?

Because the Department of Corrections condones it, Davis. They figure the more dicks getting sucked, the fewer shanks getting stuck in someone's rib cage. When they tell the press, We ain't got a homosexual problem here, they really mean there are plenty of homos to go around; you want sex in the joint—no problem! They should be writing letters to the families of homos telling them their boy is taking it up the ass! I see a faggot, he's giving head one day, the next day he's in the visiting room holding his wife's hand! With his daughter on his lap! I want to say, Pardon me, mam, is that a dick under your dress? Because that's what your old man is getting in here! Homos shouldn't be allowed in the population at all, Davis. They should be put into a special unit and fumigated like the Jews!

Tommy finished his drink. A drop ran down his chin. He leaned forward.

And there ain't none of this I'm the man, you're the bitch, bullshit, Davis. If you pitch, you catch! If you deal, you shuffle! If you flip, you flop!

He refilled his glass.

Ready for more, Davis?

I held out my glass.

Sure, Tommy, I said. I appreciate your point of view. It is unambiguous.

Goddamn right, Davis. Some things, there ain't no two ways about it!

You're a natural storyteller, Tommy, I said.

He took a sip of his hooch and licked his lips. He stared into a corner of his cell and murmured:

> *You are my sunshine, my only sunshine,*
> *you make me happy when skies are grey.*

I used to sing that to my kids, Davis, he said.

So did I, Tommy, I said, remembering the happy face of Lola when I sang it to her during Lucy's last visit six months ago. Had it been that long? I allowed myself this moment of commiseration with Tommy; for all our differences, we had separation from our kids in common.

Kids! Tommy shouted suddenly. Why they gotta call these scummy Gump faggots kids, Davis. I've got two kids in college, a boy and a girl. The boy's a real scholar, spends all day in the library reading. He's an athlete, too, at the University of Illinois on a football scholarship. A regular Renaissance man! And my little girl—I still call her my little girl, she's a big girl now—she's good with numbers like her mom. She's gonna be a CPA. She'll work for some big-ass outfit, make more money in a year than I'll make in a lifetime off Tommy's Nuts & Bolts, but that's how it oughta be, ain't it? If the next generation ain't smarter than the last, we'll turn back into monkeys. Me and Shirley, we love kids, Davis, but I'll tell you what: if I found out my kids were homos I'd kill them! I'm a businessman, Davis. Time is money. You got to know when to invest and when to cut your losses.

Tommy returned his gaze to the corner and crooned—

Rock-a-bye baby, in the treetop
When the wind blows, the cradle will rock

—then shouted: Yes, Sir! I'd throw their faggot asses out the window!

I fidgeted with my pen. I looked down at my pad. I took a slow deep breath.

So, Tommy, I said, do you think Gumps are born that way or does some weird experience like being molested as a child, or having their booty torn off in the joint make them what they are?

Tommy poked his index finger in the air.

I'll tell you a medical fact, Davis. Every fetus is a female first. Then, if they're going to be a boy, their little balls drop into their little ball sack, and bam, they're a boy! And sons of bitches who think they can just decide to be a girl, they're mentally fucking ill! They can't change their minds, Davis! It wasn't their mind that decided those little balls would drop in the first place, now was it? No, it was the mind of God! You believe in God, Davis!

I reminded myself that as an ethnographer I was to remain objective, but I couldn't help concluding that Tommy was hopelessly unhinged.

I believe the Universe is a mysterious place, Tommy, I said carefully.

That doesn't make any goddamned sense, Davis! Tommy said.

He waved his hand in the air.

I suppose not, Tommy, I said. I just mean the truth is way bigger than me right now. I'm waiting for some kind of revelation, but it's not up to me when or where or what.

I hoped this would satisfy Tommy's obsession with whether or not I believed in God, but Tommy wasn't finished.

Yeah? Well, who the fuck is it up to, Davis?

I hesitated.

Tommy leaned forward and shouted.

Ha! That's what I'm talking about, Davis! You wouldn't be waiting for God to show his face if you didn't fucking believe in him, now would you? I didn't think so!

He leaned back against the wall, a triumphant smile on his face. I gave him credit for his attempt at logic, faulty as it was, and hoped the subject was put to rest but he continued.

Do you know who's gonna burn in the Hell Fires of Damnation, Davis?

No, who … ?

Doctor fucking Dick is who!

Doctor Dick … ?

You've seen him on the yard, walking the track alone, muttering to himself like some old nutso.

I believe I have, Tommy. So he's a real Doctor?

The sick fuck makes boys out of girls and girls out of boys.

You mean he does sex change operations?

He does the Devil's work. He will burn in hell. Him and all the butt fuck faggots and ass lickers and the killers of little children!

Well put, Tommy, I said. I thought his tirade a marvelous string of phrases delivered with the oratorical flourish of a Revivalist Preacher, and I wrote them down. I also made a note to make the acquaintance of Doctor Dick.

Tommy finished his drink and poured himself another.

You ready for more, Davis?

Not yet, I said.

Where was I? Tommy said. Have I mentioned Minnie?

I don't think so.

Minnie Mouse. In the East House. Know why they call her Minnie Mouse, Davis?

No, why?

Because her ass is so tight, it squeaks! Used to anyway. Or so I'm told. What else do you want know, Davis? You want to know why the library is overrun with filthy fucking faggots?

Sure, I said.

Because the civilian librarian, Freddy, he's a faggot, too. He signs up faggot inmates. The library's one big Gump dump. When they're not putting away books or filing cards, they're giving head between the aisles or in the mop closet. Faggot Freddy gets kick-backs from King B Ali and the screw at the door looks away. I've seen it. You wouldn't believe what I've seen.

Tommy leaned forward and spoke with a worried tone.

I wonder if libraries in colleges are the same way, Davis. I've got a boy spends half his life in the library. Is he safe? You been to libraries in the real world—should I be worried?

I think your boy will be all right, Tommy, I assured him. In the real world, most librarians are straight.

Tommy leaned back against the wall. He regarded me sideways.

What do you know about it, Davis? Let me tell you. First of all, most faggots have defective faces. Look at Freddie's twisted mouth. Look at Minnie's lousy complexion. Little craters. You can bet she's had small pox. You gotta look close to see.

Tommy finished his drink. The jug was nearly empty.

Ready for another? he said.

No, thanks. I've got to get back to my house and type this up.

He refilled his glass.

Anything else, Davis? he said.

Yeah, Tommy. It seems like most of the time in the joint you see a black man with a white kid. Why do you think that is?

Easy, Davis. Back in the world, the black man loves white women, especially fat blond women. He thinks he's getting over. But the truth is, we'd as soon throw those white trash whores out the window! In the joint, those little white Gumps are getting what they deserve—their butt holes reamed by a donkey dick! May they be stricken with AIDS. Let me tell you a medical fact, Davis: AIDS came from monkeys. African monkeys. Niggers haven't been down from the trees too long their own goddamned selves. If you want to know how long a nigger's been down from the trees, look at his knuckles. You ever buy a horse, Davis?

Never have, I said.

You want to know how old a horse is, Davis, you look at its teeth. You want to know how old a tree is, you cut it cross-wise and count the rings. You want to know how long a nigger's been down from the trees, you look at his knuckles!

I was tempted to say: That doesn't make any goddamned sense, Tommy! He would likely not provide another revealing anecdote, only more racist and homophobic diatribe. I closed my notebook.

You want some more of this, Davis? he said.

No, I'm good.

He upended the jug and gurgled the dregs. He licked the last drops off the spout, settled back against the wall and sang to himself:

> *Tommy and Shirley were lovers,*
> *Lordy, how they did love*
> *Swore to be true to each other*
> *True as the stars above*
> *He was her man,*
> *he wouldn't do her no wrong ...*

I stood.

Thanks for the interview, Tommy, I said.

Anytime, Davis, he mumbled. You're all right by me. When you get out of here, you go by Tommy's Nuts & Bolts. Ask for Shirley. Tell her you're a pal of mine. Tell her I said you get ten percent off any item in the store. Light bulbs, screwdrivers, whatever ...

Thanks, I'll do that.

Make that twenty percent, Davis. You're my kinda guy.

Thanks, Tommy.

Let me know when your book comes out.

I will, Tommy.

Turn off the TV on your way out, would you, pal?

You bet, Tommy.

WILBUR WAS A JOKER all right. Told you what he wanted you to know when he was ready. So I shouldn't have been surprised when he told me after the interview that Tommy was doing life without parole for killing his wife and kids. Threw them out the window of the 17th floor of a fancy hotel in Downtown Chicago. One at a time, according to witnesses: the mother, the little girl, the little boy. Then he went uptown to a night club with his old man's .38, shot the owner six times, sat down with a bottle of scotch and drank till the cops arrived.

The motive was never established.

It was all over the Chicago Tribune, Wilbur said, but I guess you weren't reading the Chicago Tribune fifteen years ago.

Guess not, I said.

And did he tell you his old man was the County Coroner?

No. He didn't.

I WAS MOVED BY TOMMY'S TALE. By the depth of his delusions. I regretted that the truth would die with the man. I smoked half a joint, turned on my typewriter and composed a facsimile of his life. It was plausible and engaging, provided motivation for his mortifying deeds, forgave him his sins and granted him a kind of immortality. What else? Maybe nothing. Doubt clouded my brain like a fog. Maybe I was the one being delusional. Tommy was going to die here. Would the man in his fiftieth year buried alive behind these walls give a good goddamn that someone wrote a story about him that didn't get the facts right? I felt dirty, like a grave robber, or a Coroner fucking a corpse. What right did I have to leave these men behind and take the nuts and bolts of their souls back to the blue skies of California and resurrect their anguished lives when it pleased me, turning them into stories for someone else's voyeuristic reading pleasure?

I felt like a rat scouring the cellars of the souls of the damned, nibbling at the crumbs of their despair.

I stood and looked at myself in the warped stainless steel mirror above my sink. I wagged my face back and forth like a bobblehead. I slapped myself and laughed.

You're wasted, I said to myself. And you're getting stupid. There is no answer. Just carry on. You're committed to *The Gump Report*. Give the Professor what he wants, take what you want, treat the men you interview with respect and empathy, and if the Universe is willing, everyone gets something out of it.

Or not. Time would tell.

I pulled back the covers of my bunk and took my clothes off. I turned off the lights and went to bed and wondered who was next.

I set my sights on Doctor Dick.

DOCTOR DICK

THE SKY WAS A HAZY BLUE and the summer sun beat down on the small round concrete table on the yard where the doctor and I sat. Between us lay a worn medical text entitled *The Principles and Practice Of Gender Dysphoria Management: An Illustrated Guide to Hormone Replacement Therapy and Transsexual Surgery* by Richard Ryback, M.D., Ph.D. I had leafed through it, read a few chapter names—Functional and Aesthetic Surgery of Male Genitalia; Epidemiologic Considerations; Methodological Issues—perused the abundant, luridly picturesque anatomical illustrations, and set it aside.

I had often seen the doctor walking the yard alone, talking to himself, his hands behind his back, occasionally unjoining his fingers and flinging a hand out before him in a dismissive gesture, as though casting corn to a flock of chickens. A fifty-something surgeon with a slight frame, wispy blonde hair, milky blue eyes, creamy white skin and a pockmarked face, doing a dozen years for an unspecified Medical Malpractice offense, and known to fellow inmates as Doctor Dick, he had readily agreed to an interview. He seemed flattered and eager to share his expertise and his point of view. Twenty years of practice, he had said, and I have to go to the penitentiary to be asked for an interview!

He sat with his legs crossed at the ankles and his long white fingers laced in his lap.

Let me make this distinction, he said: A transgender person suffers gender dysphoria, which is to say he or she is at odds with what is between his or her legs. Biological sex is a matter of the flesh; gender is a matter of the heart or spirit. One is born with the genitalia of a man, for example, but knows for certain that one is a woman. A transsexual is a transgender who transitions from the wrong to the right genitalia, or at least to the preferred Secondary Sex Characteristics, under the care of a medical professional such as myself. So let's be clear on this point, Dean: I do not make men into women and women into men. I align the spirit and the flesh, allowing men and women to be who and what they truly are.

I scribbled on my notepad. My bare forearms soaked up the sun's heat stored in the stone tabletop.

Correcting the mistakes of nature, I said.

Yes, Dean, but I'm inclined to believe that the spiritual entities responsible for choosing the parts that will make up the whole of a person before jettisoning him or her onto this mortal plane have mismatched those parts on purpose.

I was surprised at the man's Theosophical point of view.

Fascinating theory, I said, but hardly amenable to the scientific method.

Do you find it hard to imagine?

Not at all, Richard, I said. I have a Muse, Miranda, who inspires me on occasion. She came to me one day as though she were assigned. She abides in a zone of her own. She and your entities could be neighbors. Do you think they might take some perverse pleasure watching the mismatched person suffer an identity crisis for their own amusement?

No, Dean, I believe that the forces behind gender dysphoria are benevolent. Transgender folks, because they struggle with their identity, are farther up the ladder of spiritual evolution than their heterosexual counterparts who are, on the whole, complacent.

So you view gender dysphoria as a gift from the Gods?

A Golden Apple, Dean.

Interesting, I said, turning the page of my notebook.

So, Richard, I said, a person born with the parts of a man, who is at heart a woman, if he—or rather *she*—likes men, then he—or rather *she*—is not homosexual at all, but heterosexual?

Excellent observation, Dean.

And if that man—or woman at heart—likes women, he—or *she*—is not heterosexual at all but a lesbian with a penis?

A valid conclusion.

And a person born with a vagina, who is at heart a man, and who likes men, is homosexual?

Semantically speaking.

Fascinating! I said. So many possibilities!

Quite …

So, Richard, how is the realignment of the misaligned effected? I asked.

Doctor Dick then delivered a lengthy exposition of the technicalities of Hormone Replacement Therapy and of Sex Reconstruction Surgery. I struggled to get it down. I was not so concerned with the medical particulars as with the character of the man who explained them. His story. He concluded that those who choose to undergo Sex Reconstruction Surgery—vaginaplasty for transwomen and phalloplasty for transmen—must undergo a diagnostic phase administered by a Mental Health Professional, which he happened to be, in addition to his other qualifications. Prospective patients, he said, must be deemed psychologically fit because this change sometimes, though rarely, leads to regret, anxiety, depression and suicide.

I require that my patients live as one of their targeted gender for at least a year prior to surgery, he said, to determine if they're comfortable in the role. Don't buy the shoes before you've tried them on. In most cases, my patients have been living the life for more than a year when they come to me, and following surgery they almost always report decreased gender dysphoria. They are aligned and happy, and I am happy to have intervened on their behalf.

He smiled and fiddled with his fingers, the pale, slender fingers of a pianist or a priest.

Richard, I said, I've observed that a few of the men in here are referred to as she, even by inmates who disparage them, whereas others are considered punks, just boys who suck dicks. Why is this?

Because those few who are perceived to be female truly are, Dean, and this is recognized intuitively at the deepest level, even by your typical macho Neanderthal inmate.

I have to concur, I said. With certain inmates I feel a definite female presence. So tell me, Richard, you're known to your fellow inmates as Doctor Dick. Are some of your former clients now here in Lime Ridge?

Yes. Eight. Only three of whom outwardly assume the role of female: Sunshine, Candy and Maria.

I've seen Sunshine around, I said, putting down my pen. She's always flirting on the yard. She has a bevy of suitors. I haven't met Candy but I know her keeper, Otto Mann. We had classes together. I've seen them together on the yard—an odd couple, the white supremacist gang leader and his girlfriend, strolling arm in arm. Maria is in my housing unit but we've never talked. What a face! I would mistake her for Whitney Houston if I didn't know better.

She's stunning indeed, the doctor said. If she didn't have the protection of King B Ali and Botha and Mother Goose she would be fought over, used and abused. Because she was my patient on the street I almost feel she has been stolen from me, appropriated, but Mother Goose and I are kindred spirits in that protection of kids is paramount, although I do find her tactics duplicitous. One wonders if the end justifies the means.

What work did you do for Maria on the streets?

Hormone Replacement Therapy in preparation for surgery, but I got locked up and she came in soon after.

Unfinished business ...

Yes. We'll be released a year apart. We'll resume treatment then.

So she's still physically a male. She has all the parts ... ?

Of course. Would she be in a men's institution if she didn't?

Right. What am I thinking? And the other five of your former patients who aren't visibly transgender ... ?

They don't want to be known as homosexual, Gump, faggot, punk, queer, or whatever other derogatory label might be put upon them by their fellow inmates who are, in the main, as you know, crude Neanderthals. They choose not to be forced into the role of sex provider against their will. They avoid association with me to preserve their anonymity, just as I do not associate with them or known transgender folks of any persuasion to avoid being labeled homosexual myself. I am not the most masculine of men; I do not wish to be preyed upon, not that I'm a prize. My status as Doctor Dick grants me a certain immunity.

Why have so many of your patients become convicts? I asked.

Most had little money on the streets, he said. Given the lack of support from family and community, and the high cost of treatment, and substance abuse engendered by depression, and just to survive day to day, they engaged in various petty criminal activities. They sold sexual favors. They stole. Often when I drove home from the clinic I would see them on the street corner soliciting.

And by such means your patients could afford your services?

Most could hustle up the cost of Hormone Replacement Therapy. Those who could not, I treated pro bono. I turned no one away. Few could pay for Sex Reconstruction Surgery. On occasion, I financed an operation.

That seems very generous.

There were those who were crying out for alignment. I could not deny them.

It must have set you back a few dollars.

That and legal fees, but I'll survive.

Of the one thousand men in this camp, Richard, how many do you believe have participated in sex with another inmate?

Six hundred.

Really! Are you sure?

I watch. I know.

Why so many?

Supply and demand. The vacuum created by the absence of biological females is filled by individuals willing to assume the role. On the outside, homosexual activity is stigmatized and marginalized. It is found in discrete enclaves, apart from the mainstream. But in here it is pervasive. It is woven into the social fabric. Individuals so inclined are given the green light to be gay. And once they come out they are in demand, they have power. Take Sunshine. I call her case one of Situational Transvestitism. On the street she was a husband, married with children, a closet bisexual who favored her feminine side. We discussed her options. She declined to come out.

She couldn't handle the disapproval. But once locked up, she was free to be herself. She became highly visible, sought after and fought over. She was in it for the whams and the zooms and the status. She took great pleasure in not putting out. A penitentiary prick tease. A dangerous game but it drives up the price. After a spate of gang warfare, she became the property of King B Ali. When King B was shipped downstate to Lime Ridge to keep the peace, she came, too, she and Maria, as part of the deal. She's in my unit. Her cell is on my side. She keeps the door open and herself on display. She practices the Psychology of Conspicuous Consumption. On her shelf and sink and desk are signs of her status: books and magazines she has no interest in, nor ability to read, and boxes of cosmetics and commissary items, and of whams and zooms, many of which are empty. She enjoys frustrating her suitors. She's not required by her keepers to be promiscuous. Her value, like that of Maria, is enhanced by her relative unavailability.

Is Sunshine friends with Candy and Maria?

She and Maria are rivals and mutually catty. You'll rarely see them together, but because they are both kept by King B and under the wing of Mother Goose, they are discouraged from trashing one another in public. Both dislike Candy immensely. She was something of a celebrity on the street, a successful female impersonator. They see her as a privileged white bitch and a racist who, if she wasn't kept by Otto Mann, who is respected by all—well, most—white inmates, and by the guards, most of whom are white, she would be a prize for any black leader to claim, probably King B Ali.

I don't imagine that would go over well with Sunshine and Maria.

The King would have his hands full keeping the peace in that harem.

Richard, I imagine the life of a Gump as an unending quest for identity. You'd have to have a strong sense of self to stay sane.

Yes, Dean, in here homosexuality is a subculture within a subculture. On the street there is a better chance to be gay while maintaining a normal existence. You can have a relationship with your partner, have your career, your society, much like a straight couple. But in here transgender inmates identify primarily with their sexual orientation. They have no choice. It's hard enough that one has to adjust to being a prisoner; compound that with the adjustment to being a transgender prisoner, or wondering if you are, then add to that the issue of race. Take Maria. She's half Puerto Rican and half African American. Puerto Ricans disown and disdain her because she's a punk faggot who freaks off with blacks, who in turn disdain her because she's a bitch and a hole, and white inmates disdain her because they are, in the main, as you know, racist, homophobic Neanderthal brutes.

Maria seems pretty well adjusted, I said.

She's an anomaly. She's dealt with identification issues on all fronts and stays sassy and tough. Some of her spunk she brought into the world with her, some she owes to the nurturing and tutelage of Mother Goose.

What about kids who were not gay on the outside, but were pretty and weak and forcibly turned into punks?

There is less rape in prison than is commonly believed, Dean. What is more common is coercion. Some of these kids were tough and fought for their right to be male. Others accepted the role and wonder if they haven't been homosexual all along. A few others are turned out early, accept the role, then rebel against it, hit the weights, get mean and fight back. They're left alone because they're no longer worth the trouble. Joey the pizza delivery boy comes to mind. And Randy Bone.

I know Bone. He's in my house. We graduated together. A graduating class of two. Forever bound.

I saw your picture in *Prose & Cons*. Congratulations.

Thank you, Richard. So, tell me, why the proliferation of transgender inmates in the library and as teaching assistants in the educational programs? One can't help but notice.

As a group they are more qualified than most, more likely to have acquired office skills or to have taken certain courses in school, while their macho counterparts were playing basketball and selling drugs and sticking up people on the street. Also, office work is more suited to the constitution of a gentle transgender person.

This seems a bit sexist, in a skewed way, I said. I wondered how much of the doctor's account was accurate. He was, after all, in spite of his professional status, prone to his own biases and misconceptions. But again I was less interested in the facts than in the characters of my interviewees and the stories they told.

There's a kind of transgender nepotism, the doctor said. They pull each other in. The library is a safe haven. They have society there.

Homosexuality in here is so open, I said. How does the Administration view it?

They have a hard time telling who is who and what is what. The logistics of housing transgender inmates is confusing. They label transsexuals as homosexuals which according to the medical profession they are not. Until a few months ago the policy was that no more than two would be housed in the same unit and not on the same side. The policy is now that they shall be celled together in the mistaken belief that since both are homosexual they won't freak off with each other. But that is hardly true, especially if one is passive and one is aggressive. There is no end to the variations of who might be freaking off with whom. Many transgender persons when they enter prison declare themselves gay to get a single cell, thereby avoiding being celled with exploitative, bigoted, or otherwise undesirable individuals. Cook County jail used to house them in a separate wing. This was abolished as discriminatory. They were then housed in the mental wing, though the American Psychiatric Association declared fifteen years ago that homosexuality was not mental illness. They have since been put into population, as they are throughout the system. The Placement Office here has a list of known homosexuals, which was once tacked up on the wall, visible to anyone who might be visiting the office. This list has since been taken down, consequent to a grievance filed. But in the main, Dean, deviant sexual conduct is tolerated because it's the only kind there is in here, and to blatantly take it away from the population would cause violent dissent.

I scribbled some notes. I turned a page.

What of the high incidence of black dominance of white kids? I said. Some suggest this is backlash for the oppression of slavery. Would you agree?

It's not that simple, Dean. Some of our black brethren are angry, and revenge is sweet, but often white kids prefer black keepers. They see themselves as deviant and alienated from the white mainstream. Having a black daddy enhances their deviance and increases the shock value of the statement they seek to make. Also, they seek protection. A white kid with a white daddy might feel less safe and secure, and for good reason. White inmates, because they're in the minority, have a harder time protecting their property, and especially their claim to a kid. And you'll rarely see a white man with a black kid, especially if the white man is a racist. Neither blacks nor whites appreciate it. It takes a special kind of white man to keep a black kid.

But surely in some instances, I said, a white kid would choose a black daddy, or they would choose each other, out of mutual affection.

Of course, the doctor said. We're not discounting true love. We are merely saying that the dynamics of romantic relationships in prison are atypical due to the preponderance of sexual predators and other sociopaths. It's a rough place to be a kid, white or black.

I see. So are black inmates or white more likely to continue homosexual activity after release?

Urban blacks are, it has been my observation, because homosexual activity in prison is more an extension of their society on the street than that of Caucasians.

What happens when the transgender inmate, white or black, is released and returns to the streets?

The doctor uncrossed and recrossed his legs under the table.

If he was engaged in homosexual activity before he came in, he said, he'll continue to be. If he was turned out in here, he might to all appearances resume a straight life—get married, have kids—but he will have developed another side of himself that needs to be satisfied. He may participate in the Tea Room Trade, having clandestine rendezvous in public places, or visiting sordid districts in the city, unbeknownst to his wife and friends. Yet he will be most vociferous in the condemnation of homosexuality, while harboring a deep resentment of those who turned him out in prison. Or—and this is more common—he will discard his homosexual lifestyle like a suit of clothes and leave it in prison where he found it.

I see. And what of your macho types who regard themselves as straight because they do the poking and don't get penetrated themselves? Who tear off the booty, then go back to the world with their heads held high and their chests puffed out like nothing happened?

The doctor scowled.

I would dearly like to give those Neanderthals a taste of their own medicine! he said.

I wondered if the good doctor hadn't already administered a taste of one's own medicine by way of an involuntary vaginoplasty on some Neanderthal strapped to a table in a clandestine operating room, sedated for days on end. I imagined the satisfaction he might have felt, hovering under the bright lights, slicing and dicing. I wondered, too, at the man's own sexual proclivities.

Richard, I said, if it's not being too personal, what can you tell us about your sexual identity

Asexual, Dean. Indifferent. Always have been. When my peers came into puberty their actions astonished me. I entered this world with the equipment of a male, which developed on schedule, and to all appearances I was a young man. But I lacked libido. I was not attracted to either sex. Consequently, I found the behavior induced by the onset of raging hormones shocking and mysterious. My curiosity evolved into my profession. If I did not spend most of my waking days observing the peculiar sexual antics of my fellow man I would probably be a bird watcher.

I laughed. I imagined the doctor deep in a forest alone, in search of a rare bird.

Richard, I said, has there never been a significant other in your life?

No, Dean, I've been fortunate to remain undisturbed by the carnal desires that afflict my fellow man. Left in peace to practice my craft. There's a reason placid rhymes with flaccid, my friend.

I looked at my watch. The end of yard approached.

Richard, I said, what of your legal status? Will you be allowed to practice your craft after your release?

I had touched a nerve. The doctor glowered.

My license is suspended, he said. Not revoked. I will practice again!

He unjoined his hands and thrust them upward. His pale white fingers fluttered against the blue sky like a pair of doves released. As if in concert, the loudspeaker in the guard tower crackled.

Yard is over! Return to your units! Yard is over!

I closed my notepad, pleased with the wealth of insights and anecdotes and information I had captured.

Richard, I said, thank you for sharing.

Thank you for caring, he said.

His tone was ironic. He seemed suddenly to be enveloped in a fog of melancholy. He uncrossed his legs and rose slowly from the table. I detected his shift of mood. I wanted to lift his spirits.

Richard, I said, your comments will be included in a presentation in London to a gathering of preeminent Cultural Anthropologists. Because of your credentials, I imagine your contribution might be seen as an interdisciplinary effort.

He smiled.

That would be nice, he said. Will my name be used?

If you'd like.

I would, he said. Richard Ryback M.D., Ph.D. Don't leave off the Ph.D.

Certainly not, I said, rising from the table. By the way, Richard, what do you do when you are not aligning misaligned gender? Do you have a pastime?

I do, he said brightly. I write poetry. Well, limericks, really. Would you like me to recite something?

Sure, I said.

He held a hand out before him as though addressing an invisible audience. His expression became grave. His voice lowered an octave and he paused dramatically between phrases as he recited:

> *There once was a lass from Salinas*
> *Who had a magnificent penis.*

She said to her beau:
It's so nice to know
That we have two dicks between us.

He raised his face to the sky and laughed. It was the first time I had heard him laugh.

I like it, Richard, I said. It's to the point, and a prime example of deviant ribald humor.

Well then, here's another, he said eagerly. May I?

Please do!

He gathered himself and recited:

My nipples are north of my navel.
My Johnson is north of my knee.
The nose on my face
Is in the right place,
But there's a hole
where my soul
Ought to be.

He waved a hand.

Yes, I know, Davis, he said. As poetry it is wretched, but it pleases me.

He laced his fingers together behind his back and walked in the direction of the housing units. I fell in beside him.

Actually, Richard, I said, I found it poignant.

Yes? Well, it's better when sung, Davis. It can be sung to the tune of *My Bonnie Lies Over the Ocean.* Would you like me to sing it for you now?

No, thank you, Richard, I said, suspecting the offer was facetious.

But that evening while I typed my notes, I sang the poem to myself, and it rambled through my brain for several days after.

MOTHER GOOSE

MOTHER GOOSE HAS AGREED to see you, Wilbur told me at the door of my cell one simmering summer night. She liked the book so much, he said, that she almost creamed in her pants. She'll want to party with you now more than ever!

That Mother Goose would cream in her pants and want to party with me now more than ever were not what I had in mind when I gifted her the book, but only that she agree to an interview. Previously, Wilbur had told me I would not be allowed to read the short biographical piece, *Bird Interrupted*, that he claimed to have written for and about Mother Goose.

She's shy, Wilbur had said. She likes you and wants you to like her, and doesn't know if you will after you read it. She doesn't know where your head is about certain things.

Not being allowed to read *Bird Interrupted* had been just fine with me then because, for all I knew, Wilbur was crazy, and a biographical piece about Mother Goose was a product of his strange imagination. But I had since learned that Mother Goose was inmate Frankie Waters, a large and powerful yet matronly black inmate who sometimes scowled with the dark heart of Idi Amin, at other times seemed as amused as the Laughing Buddha. She painted pictures of the nursery rhyme character, Mother Goose, and sold them in the visiting room. Lucy bought one on her first visit. A prize piece of prison memorabilia, it now hung in the bedroom of our little girl, Lola.

When I had agreed to do *The Gump Report* for the Professor, I immediately thought of Waters who, Wilbur informed me, had spent the last eighteen years procuring kids for gang Chiefs in numerous facilities within the Illinois Department of Corrections. He—or, rather, she, because like certain others of her persuasion, she radiated a powerful female persona in spite of what was in her pants—she would be a wealth of inside information. But she declined to be interviewed, citing the sensitivity of the subject.

But it's not really about the sensitivity of the subject, Wilbur told me. That's a ploy. Nothing she does or has done is a secret in the joint. It's about her sensitivity. She wants you to like her. Give her something nice to soften her up. She might change her mind.

So I called Lucy and asked her to send by Express Mail the biggest, fattest, most picture-laden hardback book of *Mother Goose Nursery Rhymes* she could find. I had Wilbur deliver the book and a note assuring Mother Goose that her experiences were remarkable and of interest to the world and ought to be documented, and anyway I liked a good story and was sure she could tell a few.

While awaiting a response, I interviewed Tommy and Doctor Dick, and crossed my fingers that Mother Goose would concede, suspecting she would provide material as unique and engaging as theirs had been.

She asks two things, Wilbur said now: That you read *Bird Interrupted* first and that your meeting be less like an interview and more like a friendly chat.

Sure, I said, thrilled to have gotten the nod.

Wilbur looked up and down the corridor. He undid the top button of his shirt, reached inside, pulled out a manuscript and handed it to me.

The words are mine, he said, but the story is hers. Tomorrow at seven. Go by her cell and knock. Happy tales.

Wilbur turned and walked quickly up the corridor with his hands in his pockets and his shoulders up around his ears. I lay back on my bunk and read.

BIRD INTERRUPTED

WILBUR, HONEY, I WILL ONLY TELL YOU now about a single day in my life, the one that changed me forever. It was Good Friday, the week before Easter, 1959. I was seventeen. Barbara called and said, Come over, Frankie. I have something for you. I had known Barbara for ten years. She had been my baby sitter. She read nursery rhymes to me and showed me the pretty pictures. I liked *Mother Goose* best. I liked *Little Bo Peep* and *Little Boy Blue* and *Jack Be Nimble, Jack Be Quick.* I especially liked *Robin and Richard.* I memorized it:

> *Robin and Richard were two pretty men,*
> *They lay in bed till the clock struck ten;*
> *Then up starts Robin and looks at the sky,*
> *"Oh, brother Richard, the sun's very high!*
> *You go before, with the bottle and bag,*
> *And I will come after on little Jack Nag."*

We played house. Sometimes I would be the mommy and sometimes I would be the daddy. And we cut out paper dolls and dressed them in skirts and blouses and panties and bras.

I was too old now to be baby-sat, but we were still friends. She was five years older than me and had her own apartment. She met me at the door and took my hand and led me to the couch. We sat side by side and she smiled at me in the strangest way.

Frankie, she said. Put your arm around me.

She unbuttoned her blouse and exposed her breasts. They were very beautiful.

Do you want to touch them? she said.

Oh, yes, I said.

They were warm and smooth and firm. I squeezed them and felt their weight. She closed her eyes and a moan escaped her lips. My blood was boiling and my prick was an iron rod. I pulled her face to mine and our lips met in a long and passionate kiss. I put my other hand on her knee and slid it up to her crotch. Her panties were soaked in the boiling lava of love. I slid my fingers under them and stroked her swelling cunt lips. I slid my fingers inside and she began a slow and rhythmic rolling of her hips. My seventeen years of virginity were about to be over.

Or so I thought. Suddenly, Barbara pushed me away and stood up and left the room. She returned with a magazine. She sat beside me with the magazine on her lap and her hand on the cover. She slid her hand down slowly, revealing the beautiful face of a woman, then her long neck, then her beautiful full breasts and the shadow of her navel and her narrow waist and—and her big, hairy prick!

I was too shocked for words.

Frankie, she said, it's always been my wildest fantasy to see a man dressed as a woman. Would you do that for me now?

Wouldn't you be happy to have me just the way I am? I said.

But even as I said it, I began to feel the excitement of pleasing her in this freaky way.

Baby, I said. I'll do anything you want.

She led me to her bedroom and told me to take off my clothes. She took dresses from her closet and asked me to pick the one I thought was most sexy. I thought happily of our days cutting out paper dolls and dressing them on the floor of my childhood bedroom. I chose a blue chiffon backless dress with a plunging neckline and a slit up the front. Barbara opened a dresser and got out sky-blue silk stockings and blue garter belts and blue panties with ruffles around them and a lacy bra. I put them on. She stuffed tissue into the bra cups. She approached me with a pair of scissors and a wild gleam in her eyes.

Barbara, I said, what are you going to do?

Relax, Frankie, she said, I won't hurt you.

She cut a hole in the panties and released my bulging love tool.

Sit here, she said, pointing to the stool in front of her vanity. She made up my face with lipstick, eye shadow, powdered rouge and blue eyeliner, and snapped dangling earrings onto my lobes. My face was framed in the glittering lights of the vanity mirror, and I could have kissed myself! She slipped the dress over my head and led me to a full-length mirror. I was in another world as I stared at the luscious creature I had become. She must have been pleased with her handiwork, too, because she pulled my face to hers and kissed me like I had never been kissed before. She slipped her hand through the slit in my dress and grabbed my aching, throbbing penis. I pulled her toward me but she pushed me away and said, No, not yet. She went into the bathroom and closed the door. When she returned, she was naked. My eyes roamed over her naked beauty, but when my gaze fell upon her womanhood, I saw not a warm inviting vagina, but an eight-inch dildo!

This is for you, she said, and led me to her bed and pushed me onto my back. I was too dumbfounded and too intrigued and too excited to resist. I felt like something new and wonderful was happening in my life. That my true nature was emerging from a secret place.

She kissed me from head to toe and sucked hard on the knob of my throbbing tool. Waves of bliss shot through my body. Before I knew it, my legs were up around her shoulders and she was easing her monstrous dildo into my pristine virgin booty hole. She pushed hard and violent pain caused me to beg her to stop, but we both knew I didn't mean it. She told me to relax and I would experience unbelievable agonizing pleasure. Soon the pain gave way to a feeling of ecstasy that filled my mind, body and soul. I responded to her animal thrusts with an equal vigor. I cried out her name and begged her to fuck me harder. She pounded the dildo into me relentlessly, pulling it back and slamming it to the hilt. She arched her back and screamed that she was coming. As she convulsed and shook, I felt my own self explode, and my love juices flowed for what seemed like eternity.

When Barbara rolled onto her back, the dildo slipped from my ass. I looked at her womanly body, her beautiful face and round, firm, full breasts still heaving from the effort of fucking me, but my eyes rested on the dildo and I found myself wishing it was not a rubber imitation, but real flesh.

I kissed Barbara good night at the door. I knew I could not be satisfied by more of the same. As I walked home I began to gyrate my hips in a most feminine yet natural way. The transformation was complete. I was now a woman with the needs of a woman and my need at the moment was to find a real man.

I PUT THE MANUSCRIPT DOWN. I laughed. Wow, I thought, that was positively pornographic! But I wondered at its veracity. Could the transformation of Mother Goose really have been caused by a single erotic encounter? Without an iota of preceding transgender inclination? Had Wilbur's fertile imagination spun the event for dramatic impact? But it didn't matter. It was a great story and introduced the character of Mother Goose in wham bam fashion, and told me who I was about to kick it with, and I couldn't wait … though I waited with a certain trepidation.

YOU ARE SUCH A NICE MAN! gushed Mother Goose as I stepped inside her cell on the appointed night. A kind and generous man!

Her cell was cast in the bordello-red glow produced by a cloth draped over a lamp. The night was sultry, and the scent of body odor and jasmine hung in the air. Inmate Frankie Waters, aka Mother Goose, sat on her bunk leaning against the wall, fanning herself with a paper fan in one hand and clutching a large hardback book to her chest with the other.

Come in, Mister Davis, she cooed. Close the door and sit by Mother Goose and we'll read nursery rhymes together!

She patted the bunk beside her.

I'll just sit here on the toilet with the door open if you don't mind, I said. You know the rules.

Rules! Mother Goose said.

The rule prohibiting an inmate from being in the cell of another inmate with the door closed was only selectively enforced. I had broken it routinely myself, but I invoked it now because I felt uneasy being closed in with Mother Goose. At six feet four inches tall and 250 pounds, she was a formidable figure even on the yard or in the dayroom but here in her tiny cell she loomed. Her head was large and shaved and shiny, her eyes round and brown, her nose broad, her lips large and purplish, her skin tinted grey, like a cup of cocoa left to sit overnight. She wore a blue denim shirt with the sleeves cut off, unbuttoned and tied together at the bottom, the knot resting in the crater of her naval, scanty pink shorts, and a blue ribbon around her neck.

There's a reason rules rhyme with fools, my friend, she said. Now you just shut that door and come sit by Mother Goose!

Her tone was gentle yet imperious. I closed the door and sat on the bunk facing her, my yellow legal pad and pen in my lap.

Should I call you Frankie or Mother Goose? I said.

My friends call me Frankie.

All right, Frankie. Call me Dean.

Dean, she said.

I remembered Wilbur's dictate to keep it casual.

I like your paintings, I said.

Thank you, honey, she said.

My wife bought one, I said. It hangs in our little girl Lola's bedroom. She'll grow up beneath the warm, maternal gaze of Mother Goose.

Dean, that makes me so happy.

I used to paint, too, I said.

Did you!

Yes, faces.

They are so hard to get right, Dean. All of my Mother Gooses look the same. But my children, my darlings, I try to get inside their little hearts and bring their feelings out. Did you paint with oil, Dean?

No, I said. With watercolors. On the faces of little children: lions, tigers and bears, flowers, fairies and clowns. I would set up a booth at fairs and festivals. I charged a couple dollars each. I was pretty good. Like you, I looked for what was special in every child. Some were ferocious and I made them into animals. Some were charming and I made them into fairies. Others were little jokers and I made them into clowns.

Did you look into their eyes?

I did.

Honey, we have so much in common.

I wondered whether to share the photograph I'd brought. Would it be an act of bad faith? Would Brodie feel betrayed? No, I decided.

There could not be a more kindred spirit than Mother Goose.

Frankie, I said, I read Wilbur's biographical sketch of you. It was entertaining. Thanks for sharing. Here, I want to share something with you.

I removed the photograph that was tucked into the back of my notepad and handed it to Mother Goose.

The building in the background, I said, is City Lights Bookstore in San Francisco. It's famous in the poetry world. The guy on the left is the owner, Lawrence Ferlinghetti. He published a book by Alan Ginsberg called *Howl and Other Poems*. That's Ginsberg on the right. He's gay. The guy in the middle is Brodie, my brother. He's gay, too. He was in love with Ginsberg, but Ginsberg didn't love him back.

That's a terrible thing, Mother Goose said.

It is. He was crushed.

Is your brother a poet, too?

Yes. He published one book of poetry. It was not well received. He was crushed by that, too. He's brilliant but doesn't believe in himself. He quit writing. He teaches at San Francisco State. He hopes to discover the next Alan Ginsberg among his students. Anyway, when I read your story, it reminded me of a certain moment in my life.

Tell me about it, Dean, Mother Goose said. Her tone was tender and warm.

I had come home early from school, I said, and I heard a rustling in my parents' bedroom. They were out of town. I snuck up the stairs to investigate. There was Brodie, all gussied up in my mother's clothes, dancing in front of the mirror. He was so embarrassed. He begged me not to tell mom and dad. I didn't, of course, but they discovered his pastime somehow anyway. The old man blew his top. There'll be no faggots in my house, he said. Brodie left home under a cloud of shame and guilt. They didn't speak again, and a year later the old man died. Brodie was inconsolable.

Mother Goose looked at the photograph.

He's had a hard life, she said. Thank you for sharing. I like to think that whatever doesn't kill us makes us stronger. He should write again. He has much to say.

She handed the photo back.

Look at this, Dean, she said.

She opened the book of nursery rhymes to a place saved by one of many scraps of paper inserted between pages.

One of my favorite pictures, she said. I've copied and sold it several times.

I leaned forward but was looking at the picture upside down. Mother Goose patted the bunk beside her.

Sit next to me, she said. I don't bite—though I have been known to nibble a bit.

Her smile was mischievous.

I swung around and leaned against the wall beside Mother Goose. I felt her large naked thigh against my own. I noticed below the book the prominent bulge of her genitalia in her faded pink shorts. I leaned forward to see the picture: An illustrated Mother Goose in a frilly, pointy bonnet, a blue ribbon around her neck, her wings spread, under the left wing a sleeping boy, under the right a sleeping girl.

They are so sweet, said Mother Goose. So safe and warm and happy.

Frankie, this is amazing! I said. That's the very picture that hangs in my little girl's bedroom!

I'm not surprised, Dean, honey. Some things are meant to be. May I read you a few of my favorite rhymes?

Sure, Frankie, that would be nice.

She opened the book to a saved page.

This one is called *Myself.* Your brother would like it.

She read slowly, running her large, well-manicured finger beneath each word:

> As I walked by myself,
> And talked to myself,
> Myself said unto me:
> "Look to thyself,
> Take care of thyself,
> For nobody cares for thee."
> I answered myself,
> And said to myself

In the self-same repartee:
"Look to thyself,
Or not look to thyself,
The self-same thing will be."

Her voice was soft and assured, her pronunciation precise.

Such good advice, she said. Don't you think?

I do, I said.

I'm sure you've heard this one before, she said. It's called *Birds of a Feather*:

Birds of a feather flock together,
And so will pigs and swine;
Rats and mice will have their choice,
And so will I have mine!

She repeated the last line: And so will I have mine!

She turned to the next saved page.

You'll like this, Dean, she said. It's called *Dance to Your Daddy*:

Dance to your daddie,
My bonnie laddie;
Dance to your daddie, my bonnie lamb;
You shall get a fishy,
On a little dishy;
You shall get a fishy when the boat comes home.

Do you like fish, Dean? You look like a man who likes fish to me.

I hesitated. It was a loaded question.

I like halibut and salmon and sea bass, I said. And scampi and scallops and crab. I'm a seafood kind of guy. Whatever comes off the boat.

Whatever comes off the boat, she said. Very good, Dean.

She turned the page. She waggled her large head.

This one is so funny, she said. It's called *Four Stiff Standers*:

Four stiff standers,
Four dilly-danders,

Two lookers,
Two crookers,
And a wig-wag

Isn't that funny, Dean?

It is clever, I agreed.

This next one, though, is not so funny. I can hardly read it without crying. It's called *Why May Not I Love Johnny*:

Johnny shall have a new bonnet,
And Johnny shall go to the fair,
And Johnny shall have a blue ribbon
To tie up his bonny brown hair.
And why may I not love Johnny?
And why may not Johnny love me?
And why may I not love Johnny
As well as another body?

Mother Goose put the book aside and dabbed at her eyes.

You see, Dean, I had a young lover named Johnny once, a sweet pretty boy of sixteen. After our first time together, I gave him a blue ribbon, and he would tie his hair back with it. He was shy and afraid and confused. His parents didn't approve that their little boy should have a friend so big and so black and so queer! They were brutal to him, so mean that he took his own life. My heart was broken. I tied a blue ribbon in my own hair and didn't take it out for a year. Of course that was back in the day when I had hair—

Mother Goose rubbed her hand across her bald head and laughed ruefully.

But old Mother Goose still has her pleasures, she said, and recited without referring to the book:

Old Mother Goose,
when she wanted to wander,
Would ride through the air
on a very fine gander.

She picked up the book and read from the last saved page:

If you are to be a gentleman,
As I suppose you'll be,
You'll neither laugh nor smile,
For a tickling of the knee.

She put the book down and put a big hand on my knee. Her smile was lewd.

Are you to be a gentleman? she said.

I had anticipated this moment of reckoning. I put my hand on hers and removed it from my knee.

I don't think so, I said.

She sighed.

You can't blame a girl for trying, she said. I've had my eye on you since you came through the fish line almost four years ago. I thought, *There is a mighty fine gander*! But I could see you knew who you were. You wouldn't be giving it up for anyone without making a fuss.

That is correct, I said.

But I could have it anyway, Dean, honey. I could have you held down and could tear off your booty till the cows come home. Or the boat does. But that's not what I be about. Like your brother, Brodie, I prefer my lovers to love me back.

I appreciate that, Frankie. I'm flattered. If I were so inclined, you'd be the first gay man I'd freak off with.

Mother Goose frowned.

Is it because I'm old and fat and black and ugly?

None of the above.

If I was young and pretty and fair skinned like Maria … ?

Wouldn't matter, Frankie. It's just not my thing.

You can tell Mother Goose.

I am telling you.

She picked up her fan. She looked at me sideways.

Why you want to know about Gumps for anyway, Mister Davis?

It's not for me. It's for a Professor of Anthropology.

Anthropology! Such a big word. My, my!

It's the study of humanity, Frankie. The weird things we do. Like freaking off in the joint.

And you're not a little interested your own self?

I'm interested in everything in the world, Frankie.

Well, I don't know about everything in the world, Dean, honey, but I do know about freaking off in the joint, and since you have paid for an interview—she patted the book with her big hand—what would you like to know?

I took up my pen and notepad, relieved to get down to business. Frankie, I said, is it safe to say you were a happy, practicing homosexual before you were locked up?

Oh, yes, Dean. I was a happy queen in the '60s. You could always find me in the bars and clubs of Boystown in Chicago and I never missed an annual Halloween Drag Ball! I was voted runner-up for Best Dressed in 1968. I remember my outfit: a slinky blue dress with shiny sequins and a plunging neckline, and a big floppy hat piled high with feathers, the kind like Mae West wore. Do you know what she said?

What who said?

Mae West, Dean, honey. Are you listening?

No. I mean yes, I'm listening. What did she say?

She said: When I'm good I'm very good … but when I'm bad I'm better.

Nice line, I said, and wrote it down.

But I wasn't only a party girl, honey; I was an activist! I joined the Third World Gay Revolution for black gay men. We picketed the Normandy on Rush Street because they wouldn't let us dance together. Can you imagine a law that says you have to have a license for boys to dance with boys! We picketed till they went to City Hall and got a license. My feeling was, Dean, who needs a sexual revolution if you can't dance! And I marched in Chicago's first annual Gay Pride Parade in 1970. I twirled a baton. Oh, I was so young and happy!

Her smile faded. Her tone became melancholic.

But it was my first and last parade, Dean, she said. That year, for the second time, my life changed forever.

What happened?

A murderous mood came over me. I went upside the head of a white City Councilman who had abused a sweet young boy I was watching over. Up one side and down the other. I was charged with assault with intent to do great bodily harm and they were right about my intentions, Dean. That honkie motherfucker, excuse my language, he used to be a handsome man, but he ain't handsome anymore!

So you went from happy and gay on the streets of Chicago to locked up gay in the penitentiary. What was your first impression?

That there was a whole lot of freaky sex going on! And a whole lot of meanness, too! All those big nasty queens telling boys what to do, and the gangs fighting for control like dogs over meat. Those poor babies! It made me mad and sad at the same time!

But you didn't have your booty tore off?

No.

Because you were big and mean yourself?

I wasn't so big back then. I was tall and skinny. But I did have a dark side. My first day in population, the meanest, blackest, handsomest negro on the yard came up and said to me, You real pretty, girl. You gone be mine! I said, Oh, you think so! He said, Girl, we can do this the easy way or we can do it the hard way! And I said, Nigger, we can do this no way at all because you touch me I will fuck you up for life! You won't sleep another day without me standing over you with a razor in my hand! We stared each other down till he smiled and said, Baby, I think you and me can be friends. After that he treats me real nice. Has hot food sent to my cell. And reefer, and whams and zooms. Pulls my coattails about life in the penitentiary for a black gay man. He lets everyone know: This girl is mine! That man was Botha, Dean, who is right here in this house.

I know Botha, I said. I don't think he likes me.

He doesn't like a lot of people, but if he does he's your friend for life.

Frankie, what do you think is the percentage of homosexual activity in the joint?

Half and half.

That seems high. Why is it so high?

Because the Department of Corrections don't pay it no mind. They want their prisoners happy and not cutting each other up.

But why do so many men freak off with each other in the joint?

Who else you going to freak off with? If you can't smoke Camels or Kools, you smoke Bugler or Little Egypt. When you're locked up a hundred years and someone wants to freak off, you freak off. If you leave the moral principles on the street, there's no reason not to. Anyway, men are freakish by nature. They freak off whenever they can.

But some get it tore off against their will …

Yes, you have a thousand men running around with hard dicks all day, along comes a pretty boy, he's going to give it up.

But not everyone gets it tore off …

No, some are turned out already and they're happy they can be themselves. Others are just little whores who give it up for reefer or heroin. But some are afraid. They pretend to be straight, but they get found out. Someone knew them on the street, or they can't hide who they are, least of all from Mother Goose. I tell them, Listen, honey, you're going to be turned out anyway, so why not give it up and make a place for yourself here. This is your new home.

And you help them give it up the right way?

Yes, so they don't get hurt.

Frankie, Let's talk about nature versus nurture. Do you feel that people are born homosexual, not shaped by society on the street or in the joint?

Honey, a girl is a girl. You come into this world looking like a boy but there is a little girl inside you crying to get out. You're confused; you don't know what you're about. But when you go to prison, you are free to be yourself. Prison is a good place to be who you are. Whether you're a gay man, a gang banger or a white racist, there's a place for you here.

What of those who come in closet gay and get turned out, then go back to the street?

They're going back to the world of rules for fools, and folks saying they are sick. Society makes you out a sick person. You see yourself a sick person. You see other gays as sick persons. You hate them for re-minding you that you are sick. Pretty soon you tear each other apart. Call each other bitches. You got to be strong not to be a sick bitch. I am not a sick bitch. I am a queen! I am a strong proud black gay man who is a queen by nature and by choice! You call me a sick bitch, I will go up one side of your head and down the other!

I was startled by the vehemence of Mother Goose. Her rapid trans-formation from warm and tender to Holy Terror. I made notes while I collected my thoughts.

So, Frankie, I said, a Gump might go back to the world and pretend to be straight?

Yes, but he will sneak out his crib at night, go do it on the down low.

The down low?

Yes, he's ashamed of who he was in prison, but he's hooked on freaky sex. He does his freaking off in toilets and parks and bath-houses, then goes back home to the wife. Some who sneak around are so confused, Dean, they can't wait to get back to the penitentiary where they can let the freak out! They might even do a crime on pur-pose so they get locked up again.

Are gay men treated differently in the joint than on the street?

In the joint you are normal. But how you are treated depends on how you carry yourself. On the street or in the joint, if you act like a tramp, you'll be treated like a tramp. But if you're true to your man, if you know what you're about, and you take care of business, you'll be treated like a lady.

But not all men who freak off want to be seen as or treated like a lady, I said. A lot of men in the joint have sex with other men but don't consider themselves homosexual. Isn't that right?

It's all about are you a top or a bottom, honey. Some men think if they're on the top doing the screwing, they're the man, and the one on the bottom is the bitch. Funniest thing is when two men want to be on top. They fight about who's on the bottom! But if you flip, you flop, honey. If you pitch, you catch. You freak off long enough, you'll be swapping spit in a minute. You'll be wanting some dick up your ass and you'll be having some dick up your ass real soon! Now some gay men, Dean, they only want to be on the bottom. I say, Girl, you got ten, twelve inches of swinging dick down there, why you don't want to be tearing some booty up?

Mother Goose put her hands on her belly and laughed heartily. The Laughing Buddha carved in ebony. I was relieved that she had transited back to lovable and gay.

Frankie, I said, do you think more black men are freaking off in prison than white men?

Yes, but only because there are more black men in prison than white. Freaking off is not about color. It's about where you come from. In the city we have whole freak neighborhoods. We have freaks on street corners. We have clubs and parades. You don't have honky tonks for gay cowboys and farmers. A farm boy wants to freak off, he has to sneak off behind the barn. But now he's in prison, he can freak off anywhere, anytime. But he's afraid. He sees black gangsters and big ugly queens like me. A young country boy isn't tough the same way as a young blood off the bricks is. Maybe he wrestled in the dirt and had fist fights with other farm boys and scraped his knuckles, but in the joint it's all about sticking and stabbing and murdering motherfuckers. A black boy off the street can run his game on a country white boy any time. Talk him onto his knees.

Frankie, in your experience, what kind of man makes the best lover?

I like a seafood sort of fellow, Dean, honey. One who likes whatever comes off the boat.

Her smile was at once charming and disarming. She added, But I do prefer white lovers, Dean. They are more romantic. A black lover wants to be King Kong. He wants to get a nut, then walk away and beat his chest. He doesn't like it sunny side up, his partner's swipe rubbing all up and down his belly. I'll swap tongues with a white boy any day.

How about you and Botha, Frankie? Are you still lovers?

No, that fire is out, but we are friends for life. He's got Maria and whoever else he wants from the fish line. I make sure of that.

That's right, Wilbur tells me that in Statesville you were the proud procurer of kids for gangs. How did that come about?

Came about because you can't put just anybody in a cell with just anybody else. You've got to know who's who and what they're about. Are they hooked up with a gang? Which one? Are they straight? Do they freak off? Do they want to? You can't put rival gang members together, or a freak with a homophobe. The Administration knew that I knew what was what, and they made me cell house clerk. I advised who got put where. I would watch the fish line, pick a kid, send him to a gangster's house where there's color TV and a cassette player and whams and zooms and reefer. The fish feels like he died and went to heaven. Then we send another gangster around who says, Hey, punk motherfucker, you ate our food, you smoked our dope, you got to pay up. But since you ain't got nothing, you can pay up in booty! The fish is scared now. He talks to his cellie, who he thinks is his new best friend. Cellie says, Don't worry, I know someone who can help. He sends for me. I tell the fish, You're going to be turned out anyway, your booty tore off, you should give it up the easy way. You'll be treated real nice. Then I take him to a Chief, tell him to show the Chief a good time. If the Chief likes the kid, he keeps him for himself or assigns him to a lieutenant to freak off with or be put on the stroll. If he doesn't please the Chief he's put into a cell where there might not even be a radio. Of course, while I'm working the fish, I get all the booty I want.

Did you perform this service for all the gangs?

Yes, I had a system. On some days one gang would get first choice from the fish line, on other days a different gang would. It was all about being fair. Also, a Chief could say what kind of kid he wants— black, brown, white, skinny or fat.

And you would fill the order?

If I could.

Did you ever feel the fish was being tricked or taken advantage of?

Tricked for his own good, honey. Young boys still come to me and ask my advice how to come out. I pull their coattails, teach them how to behave and be dignified. And inmates who want to freak off but don't know where to go will ask my help. I hook them up.

Matchmaker Extraordinaire, I said to myself as I wrote.

Were there other services you provided, Frankie? Anything in particular you're proud of or remember fondly?

Party nights, Mother Goose said. Party nights reminded me of the Normandy on Rush Street when life was good.

What were party nights?

In Statesville there were two twelve man cells side by side. We called them the Ballroom. I organized parties for gangsters and their kids. There was dope and liquor and soft lights and music and dancing. If a gang had a beef with another gang, they would leave it at the door. There was peace and love.

Frankie, what were your rewards for providing these valuable services?

Lots of dope. Whams and zooms, bricks of squares, toiletries and cosmetics, and respect from gangs and the Administration. But most of all just knowing my boys and girls were not being used and abused and having their booties tore off. I would take them under my wing and keep them safe. And because I painted my pictures, I became known as Mother Goose.

Frankie, I find you to be a romantic person with a big heart. All those kids to watch over and have your way with. Did you ever fall for one in particular?

I did. One time a fish so fine came down the line, I just had to have her for myself. She was sugar and spice and everything nice, and she knew what she was about. It was her first time locked up and she was afraid but she brought her own brand of sassy. I kept her for three months until I was sent to Lime Ridge. Then King B Ali kept her till he tired of her sass, and he gave her to Botha. Then when King B was sent down to Lime Ridge to keep the peace, he took Botha and Botha's kid down, too, as part of the deal. So here we all are, together again, King B and Botha and Mother Goose ... and Maria.

Maria! I knew she was the one, Frankie. Sass drips off her like honey.

You've been noticing Maria, have you, Dean?

I notice everyone. She's hard not to notice. She's a Whitney Houston look-alike. Anyway, Frankie, Wilbur tells me you're going home soon.

I hope you find true love and never come back. What are your plans?

I'll be forty-six years old, Dean, old and gay and don't know nothing but the streets and the penitentiary. I will help young boys who want to come out. I will protect them and guide them and I will make a living off of giving them a life. It's all I can do.

Frankie, don't sell yourself short. You have talents and experience that apply in the real world. You've been a skilled negotiator under adverse conditions. You've been a matchmaker. You've put together block parties. There's a field called Event Planning. There are dating services. Or—

Mother Goose frowned.

I will watch over my kids! she nearly shouted. And if anyone tries to hurt them, I will kill the motherfuckers! I will kill them dead! And if the pigs want to shut me down, I will kill them, too. Because I am not coming back to this place. Not … fucking … ever!

I was startled by her sudden transformation. I closed my note pad.

Frankie, I said, I can't thank you enough. What you've given me tonight is priceless. And the Professor will be thrilled. But most of all, I feel I've made a friend.

Mother Goose smiled shyly.

I'm so glad, she said. Do me a favor and sign my book.

I signed it and handed it back. She read aloud:

> *To my new friend, Frankie, alias Mother Goose, guardian of the weak and afraid. Keep doing what you're doing—and may you never come back to this place!*
> *Dean Davis*

She clutched the book to her chest.

This makes me so happy, she said.

The control room speaker crackled:

Eight o-clock count, return to your cells! Eight o'clock count!

I stood.

Okay, Frankie, I said. I'm out of here. Thanks again for the conversation.

We'll talk again, Dean.

I hope so, I said.

I opened the door.

Oh, Dean, honey, Mother Goose said—one more favor?

Sure, Frankie ... what?

She smiled her lewd and lascivious smile.

Don't let your wig wag sag!

MARIA MIRANDA

I WENT BY BERSERKER'S CRIB FOR A JOINT, to Abel Carter's for a pint, and back to my cell to get stoned and to put the notes of last night's interview of Mother Goose in order. I decided that when the writing was done and the house was quiet, I just might jerk off. I wasn't fond of the practice because in the aftermath I felt desolate, my imagined lover dispersed like mist in a breeze, but I was especially horny tonight and periodic relief was a practical matter.

I never lacked for inspiration. I might dwell on memories of my most erotic nights with Lucy, of which there were plenty. Or on memories of nights with paramours who preceded her, and there were plenty of those, too. Or I might revisit the night I'd spent on a houseboat moored off Sausalito in Marin County, California, with my Muse, Miranda. Earlier that day I'd bought a hit of acid off a street dealer on Telegraph Avenue in Berkeley outside a Tibetan Curio Shop where I'd purchased a pendant, seven charms on a chain, thought to stimulate mystical insight. I dropped the acid in the evening when alone on the boat I was tending for a friend out of town, and thought I would sit on the deck in a rocking chair and watch the sun go down, and the seagulls dip and soar over the white-capped waves on the bay, and across the bay the lights of the San Francisco Skyline as they blinked on silently and twinkled like fairy dust. But as the acid took effect, and I rocked and pondered the unfolding panorama of the bay, I became obsessed by the number seven. I saw a group of seagulls cavorting in the salty air off the bow of the boat and there were seven of them. I saw a cluster of sailboats make their way in the rough waters from Alcatraz to the Embarcadero, and there were seven of them, too. Even the forlorn cottony moan of a foghorn emanating from the roiling sea-smoke beyond the Golden Gate Bridge sounded in groups of seven. There was something mysterious going on, and I was seized by the notion that I should capture its meaning in a poem of, yes, seven lines. But as I sat at the typewriter on the desk in the main room of the boat that served as study, parlor and boudoir, my fingers poised on the keyboard in rapt anticipation of cosmic revelation, nothing happened. The doors of perception had slammed shut rudely in my face. I went out to the deck and searched the sky, where the stars had arranged themselves neatly into clusters of seven.

Miranda! I called out. Miranda! I need you!

My supplication was met by silence.

I called again and again until I had called out seven times, then heard a soft voice behind me:

I'm here.

I turned, and there in the dark interior of the boat, glowing softly like a Luna Moth in moonlight, stood Miranda.

Come closer, she said.

Her voice was soft and sweet. I thought of honey, dripping. I seemed to float across the distance between us. She put a hand on my arm. I put a hand on hers. She was real, all right, ephemeral as a fairy, yet her fleshly presence no less corporeal than that of any of the women I had been with, and the comeliness of her carriage no less alluring than that of any nymph conjured by the brain of Botticelli. Miranda! Her eyes were like nothing I had seen before, portals onto an imponderable swirling cosmos. I would have left my wife and children for her if I had had them to leave.

Your need is very great, she said. A poem of seven lines that unlocks the secrets of the universe!

I put my hands on her hips. I stroked her willowy torso.

My need is great indeed, I said, but not for lines of poetry.

When I came the final time, tossed on a sea of bliss, dawn had broken and I was alone on the boat. I untangled myself from the twisted blankets and the sweaty sheets and went to the deck. Off the bow five seagulls dipped and soared in the salty air. A trio of sailboats leaned their sheets into the wind. A foghorn sounded twice. If Miranda had bestowed the secrets of the Universe upon me that night they were lost to me now, but I would not soon forget the pleasure of carnal knowledge raised to the level of mystic rapture. It was a memory that served me well when, on nights like this, I just might jerk off after a good bout of writing.

BERSERKER'S DOPE WAS ALWAYS GOOD, as prison-grade reefer went, but tonight it seemed especially potent. I smoked half the joint and stowed the other half in the shaft of a pen. I didn't want to be so high I couldn't make sense of my notes. And I hoped no one came calling because I was not in the mood for conversation.

I popped a Johnny Mathis cassette into my player and sat cross-legged on my bunk sipping hooch and reading my notes and hoping there wouldn't be a knock on my door anytime soon.

Bam! Bam! Bam!

I looked through the vertical slit of window in the grey steel door: Buster gestured for me to open up. I gestured for Buster to go away.

Open up, Double D, he yelled. I got to talk to you!

I groaned and opened the door.

Buster, what's up? I said.

He looked into my eyes.

Goddamn, Double D, he said. You lit up like a Christmas tree! Gimmee some a what you got!

I ain't got none of what I got.

You got some. Gimmee some!

It's all gone.

Ain't gone.

I done smoked it all up, Buster. Maybe next time.

I need me some dope, man. Where can I get me some?

I couldn't say.

You a foul dude, Double D, holding out on me like that.

I'm not holding out, Buster. I'm just plain out is all.

I felt bad not sharing, but I might want to smoke later and didn't feel like going back to Berserker's crib. Anyway, if I didn't say no to Buster half the time, the man would be at my door every day.

Buster looked up and down the corridor. He shook his head.

A foul dude, he said, and walked away.

I WAS PLEASED BY THE NARRATIVE in my notes, but something was missing: it wanted a famous final scene. I wondered from where one might materialize when there came another knock at my door. Scowling through the window was the hard dark face of Botha.

Damn! What could the man want? In three years he had never come around to my house. My heart skipped a beat. I put my notes and my hooch aside. I opened the door. I might have been looking into the cold yellow eyes of a Panther.

What's up, Botha? I said.

You got thirty minutes, Davis.

For what?

To do your business.

Behind Botha stood Maria, smiling coyly.

When I knock twice, Botha said, your time is up. Thirty minutes!

He stepped aside. Maria stepped around me, trailing a scent of perfume. She purred: Ain't you gonna close the door?

Her hair was bleached a fiery orange, parted in the middle and done up in pigtails behind each ear. She wore a tight white sleeveless tee shirt which accented the slight swell of her breasts—Doctor Dick's unfinished business—and the nub of her nipples. Her slim legs protruded from faded blue jeans cut off close to a pubic mound as smooth as that of a young girl. I knew from Doctor Dick that Maria retained the full complement of male genitalia and wondered how she achieved this effect. Was her prick pulled back tight and tucked somehow between the cheeks of her derriere? But I'd rather not know. What I did want to know was what she was doing in my cell tonight.

Why are you here? I said.

Mother Goose sent me.

Why?

Said you was gonna paint my face.

Maria raised her hand and held out a tin box of watercolors and an assortment of brushes.

I was amused. Mother Goose, ever the matchmaker. Rats and mice will have their choice, and so will I have mine! What the hell, I thought. I hadn't done a face in years. I took the paint and brushes.

Have a seat, I said, pointing to the bunk.

Maria sat primly, erect, her legs pressed together, her hands on her knees. I removed the bar of soap from the plastic dish on the sink and rinsed the dish and filled it with water and put it on the bunk next to Maria. I poured half my hooch into a plastic glass and extended it to her.

Care for a taste?

Her smile was coquettish.

Are we having a party?

Just being a good host, I said. Cheers.

I raised my glass. She touched hers to mine. She sipped. I drank mine down. I pulled the chair out from under my desk and turned it around and sat facing her, the tin of paints in my left hand, a brush in my right. Johnny Mathis promised that someday there'd be a time for us. When chains were torn by courage, born of a love that's free.

You knew I was coming, didn't you? Maria said.

No.

Then how come you playing Johnny Mathis?

I like Johnny Mathis.

He's my favorite.

He's good.

He's gay, you know.

I didn't, I said.

I like how he sing Maria, she said. Like it so much is why I pick Maria for my name. Now you gonna paint my face, or just look at me like a fool?

I have to look so I know what I'm painting, I said.

What do you see?

That you have a terrific complexion, coppery.

Canelo, Maria said.

What's that?

What my daddy used to call me when I was still a boy. It means cinnamon in Spanish.

You're Hispanic?

My daddy Puerto Rican. My momma black.

It's a beautiful blend on you, I said. Do you speak Spanish?

I can say puta.

What is that?

Bitch. Whore. Slut. It's what the Latin Kings call me. They don't like Puerto Rican gay boys. If it wasn't for Botha and King B Ali and Mother Goose they would cut my face.

I looked at her face, the straight white teeth, the pink tongue, the skin like cinnamon.

That would be a shame, I said. It's such a pretty face.

Are you flirting with me, white boy?

No, I'm just saying ...

You are.

I'm not.

You want me to suck your dick?

No.

You do.

I don't.

I could start yelling and Botha would come in and beat your ass!

I don't think so, I said. The door is locked. The only one coming in would be the screw. Then we'd both spend a few days in the hole, and maybe we'd lose our single cells and you would end up back in the South House doubled up with a Puerto Rican gang banger and faraway from Botha and Mother Goose. Would you like that? I didn't think so. Now hush up, girl. I'm working.

But I wasn't so sure I wanted her to hush up. Her voice was soft and sweet, like honey dripping. I thought I'd heard it once before.

Maria, I said, I do believe your face is the first nonwhite face I ever painted.

Boy, where you from!

A little town called Sausalito. Not many colored folks there.

Ain't never heard of no Sausalito.

It's far, far away, I said.

I rinsed yellow paint from my brush and dabbed it into the blue. Johnny Mathis sang, Small world, isn't it?

So, Botha looks out for you, does he? I said.

Nobody mess with Botha, Maria said. He too mean. Treat me bad sometime. He say, Bitch, when I call, you come! I don't like that.

I cleaned the blue from my brush and dabbed it in the pink.

What you painting me as? Maria said.

You're not any one thing, Maria, I said. You're a tiger, but a pussy cat, too. And there's a little Peter Pan in you, and a bit of Tinker Bell. And something mysterious that I can't quite get. The real you.

Mother Goose say you can look in my eyes and see my very soul.

Not quite, I said.

Come closer, she said.

I need distance, I said. I need perspective.

Look into my eyes.

I need space to see your face.

Look into my eyes, she commanded.

She brought her face close to mine. I smelled cinnamon and honey and musk. I looked into her eyes. Was it the potency of Berserker's reefer or the recollection of a night on a houseboat in Sausalito that caused me to see, as through a mystic portal, an imponderable swirling cosmos. I pulled my face back suddenly.

Miranda! I said.

Miranda? My name Maria! Why you call me Miranda?

Did I?

Outside my door, Buster yelled, Double D, who you got in there?

I heard Botha say, Buster, come back later.

And Buster say, Don't be puttin your hands on me, motherfucker!

And Botha say, Come back later!

And Buster say, Nigger, you ain't shit!

I recognized the mix of defiance and caution in Buster's tone. He was a big man who liked to mix it up. Maybe he could thrash Botha in a fair fight, but Botha was a straight up stone-cold killer, and Buster knew that if he put the hurt on Botha, his own life wouldn't be worth a brick of squares.

I'll be back, he said.

I looked at my watch.

Maria, I said, if you want me to finish your face you better behave.

I want to see it.

See it when I'm done.

I applied the finishing touches. I liked what I saw. I held my paint-brush aloft with one hand and twirled an imaginary Dali moustache with the other.

C'est magnifique! I said.

Maria got off the bunk and stood in front of the mirror over the sink. She looked a long time.

I'll never wash it off, she said.

You'll have to wash it off in the morning, Maria. You can't leave the house looking like that.

Then I'll never leave the house again. I'll have Botha bring me food.

Silly girl.

Botha's big fist pounded twice.

Maria, I said, your car is waiting.

I put down the paints and the brush and opened the door. Maria sashayed through it.

What he do to you, girl? Botha said.

He make me mysterious.

He sure did!

I closed the door. Buster knocked.

Daddy Dean! I didn't know you throw down on the Gump side, Ride!

It's not what you think, I said.

I know what I saw.

I know what you didn't see.

I appreciated the timing of Buster's previous interruption and his near altercation with Botha. I figured I owed him one.

Wait here, I said.

I retrieved the remaining half joint.

Is that why you held out on me, Double D … so you could freak off with that little faggot?

We were having a conversation is all.

Have it your way, Daddy Dean. Thanks for the reefer. What goes around comes around.

That it do.

We'll tighten you up on the flip side, Ride.

I know you will, Buster. Enjoy the dope. It's fire.

I returned to my notes. Where was I? Oh, yes, a famous final scene. I rolled a fresh sheet of paper into my typewriter. I turned up the volume on my cassette player. Johnny Mathis avowed that he'd never stop saying Maria, the most beautiful sound he'd ever heard.

CANDY & THE MANN

OTTO MANN AND I WERE HOUSED in different units on opposite sides of the camp. I hadn't seen Mann since the last session
of our Anthropology class together. I sent a note through a mutual
acquaintance:

> *Herr Mann,*
> *You might remember the Professor's proposal that we do an*
> *ethnography in lieu of a final exam for the Anthropology*
> *course, and we shot that idea down. I've decided to do one*
> *anyway. I'm interviewing a few folks, and if you would be*
> *willing to sit down and kick it for a minute or two, your*
> *point of view would be appreciated.*
> *Herr Davis*

Mann wrote back:

> *Evening yard, tomorrow.*
> *Herr Mann*

I was feeling feisty, fired up for the interview. I wondered if I
shouldn't be more apprehensive. After all, Mann was a notorious
Gang Chief and avowed white supremacist with a reputation for settling disputes with a sharp end of a shank, wielded by himself or by
one of the dozens of soldiers he commanded. But I felt safe enough.
I'd known Mann for a year as a fellow student in the camp's College
Program. We were friendly rivals for the best grades in class. I usually prevailed, which brought a tight-lipped smile to his face, and a
begrudged and sardonic comment like, Congratulations, Herr Davis.
You must have stayed up all night studying to beat me.

Mann had taken to addressing me as Herr Davis, and I reciprocated
with Herr Mann, because it kept our relationship at once friendly and
at a respectful distance. I had often felt the urge to kick it with him

on the subject of racial supremacy, but thought it prudent not to go there. After all, I'd been cautioned on more than one occasion that when the joint jumped I'd better know what color I was.

Mann was an anomaly as gang bangers went. Raised on the predominantly white North Side of the city, he'd been a student at Loyola University, a capable member of the University's tennis team and a regular on the NCAA circuit. He was a budding proponent of white supremacy and when he and a couple of similarly bigoted fraternity brothers went on a frenzied killing spree on the predominantly black South Side, only the color of his victims' skin, his old man's seat on the City Council, and his Uncle's seat on the Circuit Court kept his sentence down to eighty years, of which he would do forty, and had done twelve already.

Entering the Maximum Security Penitentiary up North and confronting the harsh reality of being one of an oppressed minority—Caucasian—he formed a coalition of the scattered white population and founded the largest white prison gang in the state. Having shanked a few rival gang members since, and recalcitrant fellow Caucasians, and taken his share of hits to his torso and limbs, he was referred to as The Mann, revered by a few, respected by all, and now semi-retired to the relatively sedate confines of Lime Ridge State Penitentiary, where he contented himself with study and the company of his paramour, Candy.

I WALKED THE TRACK UNDER THE WATCHFUL eyes of the guards in their towers. The sky was overcast and grey, the air muggy and motionless. Shirtless inmates lounged in the grass or circled the track, some strolling leisurely, others jogging singly or in pairs. I passed the slab that served as the weight-lifting area where two groups of inmates, one white, one black, pumped iron on their respective benches. The clang of steel on cement rang in the air. I passed the handball court, where inmates slapped the small hard ball against the cinder block wall, and grunted and cursed en Español, among them Choo Choo Rodriguez, El Muchacho Loco, who shouted, Yo, Señor Davis! My cellie in the hole! Que paso, amigo? I smiled and waved and walked on. I rounded the curve at the top of the track and there, approaching, sauntering, was Mann, tall, lean and muscular, flanked on one side by his kid, Candy, long-legged and lithe, who clung to his arm like a schoolgirl, and a middle-aged white guy I had seen around and knew to be Italian but had never met. Mann smiled thinly.

Herr Davis, he said. Walk with us.

His tone was at once courteous and commanding. I fell in beside him. Candy and the other inmate followed behind. We approached a round concrete table on the grassy side of the track.

Let's sit here, Mann said.

We sat in a small tight circle, Candy on the left of Mann, the Italian on the right, and me directly across. Mann's blond hair was cut short, faintly oiled and combed straight back. His eyes were a smoky blue, his face intelligent and smooth, but for faint wrinkles around his thin lips. Bruises the size of a puckered mouth showed above his collar.

Do you know Candy, Herr Davis? he said.

Candy's long, shiny, pecan-colored hair was parted in the middle, pulled back from a high smooth forehead, slung over the front of her shoulder and tied with a yellow ribbon. Her brows were thinly penciled in a high arch over drooping blue lids. The faint shadow under the ridge of her cheekbones echoed the shadow of a mustache above her lips. And the nibbles on her neck matched those of Mann.

We've never met, I said.

Charmed, I'm sure, Candy said in what I guessed was an imitation of Bette Davis, remembering Doctor Dick's disclosure that Candy had been an accomplished female impersonator back in the world. She held out a limp-wristed hand, palm down. I wondered if I was supposed to kiss it. I took it and shook it gently.

This is Jimmy, Mann said, nodding to the Italian.

Jimmy, with his slight frame, dark, straight, combed-back hair commencing high on his forehead, his pointy nose and chin and narrow mustache over thin lips, reminded me of the character Fredo in the movie The Godfather. He nodded.

Jimmy, I said.

Jimmy's from Cicero, Mann said.

Where is that? I asked.

Chicago, Jimmy said. Al Capone lived there. A long time ago. Capone and my old man were pals. Now it's niggers and spics in Cicero. A fuckin crime!

Jimmy's Italian, Mann said. He thinks he's white. I keep telling him, Jimmy, a whop ain't white.

Sicilians ain't white, Jimmy corrected. My people are from Bergamo, up North. In Bergamo, Italians are white.

We'll let you be white, Jimmy, Mann said. But Davis isn't here to talk about race, is he? Davis and I were in school together here in the camp. He kept me up all night trying to beat him at grades. Now he's gone off and graduated and left me all alone. Some pal, huh? He's doing a report and this is an interview. Davis, I'm not surprised you're doing the report. You march to a different drummer. Davis rides alone, Jimmy. He's done all right so far. What's your report about, Herr Davis?

Sex in prison, I said. A Boys Behind Bars kind of thing.

Who chose the topic, Davis? You or the Professor?

It was mutually agreed upon, I said.

Candy, you okay with this? Mann said. You want to talk about freaking off with Herr Davis?

Candy smiled.

I've never freaked off with Herr Davis.

Don't be smart. You want to talk about it with him?

I'll do anything you want, Candy said, and in the voice of Bette Davis, added: I'm the nicest Goddamn Dame that ever lived!

Jimmy, Mann said, you can put your two sense in any time. That okay with you, Davis?

Sure, I said. I'm after the big picture. Every opinion counts.

I'm a straight white male, Davis, Jimmy said, but I don't give a shit where someone puts their cock and balls. Otto and Candy here, I love these guys. I knew Candy back in the world. I managed a joint on Clark Street. We did female impersonators. Candy does Bette Midler, Bette Davis, Marlene Dietrich, Marilyn. Wasn't nobody she couldn't do. She packed the house. She had her own dressing room.

This is my lucky day, Candy, I said. I'm glad you're here. Your point of view will really put a spin on things. So let's start with, Is being a female impersonator the same as pretending to be a female?

Not at all, Candy said. It's about pretending to be the person you're pretending to be. How she crosses her legs, smokes her cigarettes, drinks her drinks, licks her lips. Take Dietrich. You want to impersonate Dietrich, you don't try to be female. Men loved her because she was a sexy broad, but women loved her because she looked good in pants. She had no gender. She had an empty face. You filled it with your dreams. Do you know how hard it is to impersonate an empty face?

I can only imagine.

Candy can do anyone, Jimmy said. Candy, do Marilyn. Do *Diamonds Are a Girl's Best Friend*.

Candy feigned shyness.

I haven't sung in years, she said.

Come on! Jimmy said.

My hair isn't right, she said. My lips aren't right. You have to put on a face to do Marilyn.

Don't be shy, Jimmy said.

She's being coy, Mann said.

Oh, all right, boys, if you insist, Candy said.

She sang *Diamonds Are a Girl's Best Friend*. I was impressed. She perfectly channeled Monroe's breathy coquettishness.

What'd I tell you, Davis! Jimmy said.

Candy, Mann said, how come you sing for Davis but you don't sing for me?

I sing for you!

When do you ever?

I sing for you every night, Candy said ... don't I?

She turned and said to me: I married a German. Every night I dress up as Poland and he invades me.

Bette Davis?

Bette Midler. She's a laugh riot.

Candy put her hand on Mann's forearm. She said in the voice of

Bette Midler: Men's brains are smaller than those of women so they can fit in their penises.

Mann pulled his arm away.

Funny girl, he said, but the wrinkles at the sides of his mouth belied his feigned irritation. Candy looked at me and said in Midler's voice: But enough about me. What do you think about me?

You're good, I said. But Herr Mann, what about you? You don't seem to be the type to have a gay lover. How were you on the street?

Straight white male, Mann said. Red-blooded American Boy.

What changed your mind?

You're looking at it, Mann said, nodding to Candy. I wasn't into having a kid. I thought they were faggot trash. Then I saw Candy in the fish line and I flipped. She was my fantasy of a hot broad, and a prize specimen of the white race, and I knew those fucking boogaloo gang bangers would pounce on her the minute she was put into population. I had juice with the Captain. He owed me a favor. I said, You put her in population with those spooks, Captain, there will be a war, guaranteed. You put her in my cell there won't be a problem. He put her in my cell and the rest is history.

Candy touched Mann's shoulder and said in Midler's voice: I have my standards. They're low but I have them.

You're on a roll, baby, Mann said with a faint trace of pique.

Candy, I said, you lived an open and, I assume, satisfying gay life on the street. Suddenly you were locked up. What was that like?

Candy opened her eyes wide.

Like going to hell! she said. I was scared. But the Administration knew what I was about. They put me into Protective Custody.

When you look as good as Candy does, Mann said, and you're white, and you carry yourself with class, and you play upon your helplessness, you get help, just as an attractive helpless female on the outside.

Gays who are not pretty, Candy said, who are ugly and trampy and have no class, they get no special consideration. They're thrown into population to be fought over like scraps of meat. Especially if they're black.

There's nothing worse than a black faggot, Mann said.

Nothing worse, Jimmy agreed.

When you came out of Protective Custody, I said, and were put into the general population, what was that like?

I was escorted to my cell. There were jeers and catcalls up and down the block. It was like, Hang on to your seatbelts, it's going to be a bumpy night.

Bette Davis?

Very Good, Herr Davis. My cell door was opened and standing inside was a tall handsome white boy who said I was now under the protection of him and his mob. And to be nice. And he would be nice. And we've been nice together ever since.

Candy looked at Mann with gratitude and affection.

When I was transferred down here to Lime Ridge, Mann said, I arranged for Candy to come with me. And here we are.

Now you want a piece of Candy, you go through The Mann, Jimmy said.

But no one gets a piece of Candy except me, Davis, Mann said. She's not my property. I don't peddle her ass up and down the block like some nigger pimp ... not yet anyway.

He looked at Candy. She punched him on the arm.

Candy, I said, how would you compare the status of homosexuals in here to that of women in general on the outside?

Conditions are much worse in here than for females in the real world, Candy said. In here you are treated with less respect. You're kept in your place. You have no rights. Your opinions and viewpoints are dismissed.

She added in the voice of Bette Davis: When a man gives his opinion, he's a man. When a woman gives her opinion, she's a bitch.

Oh, is that how it is for you? Mann said coldly.

Candy faced Mann.

Well ... sort of, she said.

I could cut you loose, Candy. Then you'd see how important your opinion is.

I wondered if they were going to fight. I didn't want to break up a happy home.

Candy turned to me.

Conditions are much worse in the max joint, she said, where a punk is just a punk. Lime Ridge is a haven for gay boys compared to there. And Otto does cut me a lot of slack.

She turned to Mann. She put her hand on his.

Is that better, baby? she said.

That's better, Mann said. Not many kids are treated as well as I treat Candy, Davis. And she's treated with respect by everyone else because she's mine.

Not only because I'm yours, Otto, Candy said somewhat peevishly. I'm not just any punk.

She turned to me.

Otto has status, Dean, but I have my own because I carry myself with class. I have a dignified demeanor. I'm not a slut. I don't associate with punks who were turned out in prison. They are punks. The lowest of the low. They can never be my equal. I knew what I was about before I came here.

Candy's right about that, Mann said. If she didn't have class, she wouldn't be my kid. I knew when I saw her in the fish line that day, this kid has class.

I'm from the old school, Davis, Jimmy said. I think turned-out punks are scum. But I love these guys. Candy here, you bet she's got class.

So, Candy, I said, what must it be like to come out in here? It must be a whole other experience than coming in gay as you did and knowing who you are.

New kids have no real women to model after. They're taught tricks of the trade by their peers, others who were turned out inside, or by the few who came in gay. They might be taught how to do make-up using black felt tip pen for mascara and eyeliner, Kool-Aid for blush, and baby powder to take the highlights off the cheeks, like the stage make-up called Stein's Powder.

Candy's a make-up magician, said Jimmy. When she does her face, she can be any fucking body she wants!

So, Candy, you get called upon to help the newly-turned-out make the transition?

Candy frowned.

Dean Darling, she said, you're not listening. I have nothing to do with those who are turned out in here. They are punks. They have no class. They are on their own. They can help each other or they can go to hell!

Yeah, you're not listening, Davis, Jimmy said. They're faggot trash. They can go to hell.

They're confused, Candy said. They don't know who they are. They don't know how to act. Let me tell you about Willy. He was here six months. Apparently straight. Even fooled me. One day Willy went to the gym to meet Sunshine. Sunshine does make-up, too, not as good as me but not too bad for a black trash faggot. Willy goes back to his unit all dolled up and announces in the dayroom: I'm a woman! My name is Wilma! The screw says, Willie, are you out of your fucking mind? Willy—now Wilma—catches so much flak she can't handle it. She tries to hang herself and gets shipped to the Bug House. Such a fool!

Yeah, she was out of her fucking mind, Jimmy said.

A bug from day one, Mann said.

I scribbled my notes and asked of no one in particular, What is the position of the Administration on transgender inmates?

They don't want trouble, Mann said. They like a smooth sailing ship. If they came down on the sex game, they'd have a mutiny on their hands.

When I came in, Candy said, I was called to Internal Affairs. They said if I didn't make my sexual preference a problem for them, I wouldn't be harassed. They suggested I find a single man to be with, or an organization. Otto made that happen and here we are. Now we're given every consideration.

But until you're hooked up you'll be fought over, Mann said. You'll give the Administration a PR problem. They appreciate Candy and me. We set a good example.

Not like that stupid bitch, Sunshine, Candy said. She thought she could be a free agent. She caused a war. King B Ali won. Now you want a piece of Sunshine, you go through King B.

Why do you see mostly white kids with black men? I asked.

A white punk hooks up with a black man for protection, Mann said. If you hook up with a white man, unless that white man is me, or another Caucasian with cojones, you don't get protection. Some black gang banger and his nigger buddies will tear off your booty and there's nothing you can do about it.

You got to understand the mentality of a nigger, Jimmy said. He was born in the state hospital. He was raised on welfare. The State's his mommy and daddy. When he gets to the slammer, it's all about gimme, gimme. He thinks he's got something coming. He's a natural-born taker.

I can tell you this, Candy said, a white kid that fucks a nigger is white trash. No self-respecting white man would have anything to do with her.

I wonder, I said, if centuries of oppression, of his women being ripped off by white slave masters, might motivate the black inmate to dominate the white kid.

It's not about revenge, Davis, Mann said. It's about status. A nigger knows the white race is superior, and freaking off with a white kid or marrying a fat white bitch back in the world is as close as he'll ever get to being white himself.

I felt a line of questioning open up that would not be prudent to pursue, but I opened it in spite of myself.

Do you think, Herr Mann, that the racial superiority you espouse is based on scientific evidence? That there's something inherent in the genes? Studies suggest otherwise.

Mann narrowed his eyes.

I don't need no fucking evidence. Davis. I know what I know.

I just mean to say that your belief isn't rational, and I know you to be a rational man. I wonder if your point of view isn't a bias derived from childhood—the influence of family, friends, the media, the hood—that you've retained despite your intelligence. Take me, for instance. I came up believing that the Republican Party was the One True Party; that Episcopalian was the One True Religion; that the National League was the One True Baseball Organization and the

American League was a pale imitation. I was born a Giants fan and could never be a Cubs fan kind of thing. But I got out into the world and discovered that when I thought for myself, the world was a big place, full of possibilities.

And now you're a Cubs fan, Herr Davis?

No, I'm just saying—

You're saying I can't think for myself?

No, I'm suggesting you're not a True Believer. That something else accounts for your point of view.

And you have a theory about what that something else might be, Herr Professor?

I do. It's been said that the strength of a man can be measured by the strength of his enemies. If one chooses an enemy to measure his own strength by, he would choose a strong enemy, would he not? One he respects for being at least his equal. He would not choose an adversary who is inherently inferior. What would be the point?

So you're saying I hate niggers because I think they're as good as me? Maybe better?

Something in Mann's tone said I was about to cross a line. How rational was it to debate racial supremacy with a white supremacist in the penitentiary, the man's home and castle, especially to win the debate in the presence of his paramour and his partner? I altered my approach.

I'm suggesting, Herr Mann, that you're motivated by something far nobler than a belief in racial supremacy. That you have the mentality of a true warrior, the quintessential conquering hero. That you're a courageous man and a capable leader who is willing to put his life on the line for his people, and I applaud you for that. I am privileged to know you. I am humbled in your presence.

I knew my remarks were ingratiating but I hoped they were made sufficiently tongue-in-cheek for the astute Otto Mann, if not Candy and Jimmy, to appreciate them for what they were: a graceful exit from a subject entered into inadvisably. Mann's thin-lipped smile told me I may have dodged a bullet. He reached across the table and put his hand on my shoulder.

Herr Davis, you must have stayed up all night composing those lines.

And half the morning, I said.

He dropped his hand.

Do you have any more questions about boys behind bars, Davis?

Only a few, I said. Candy, how is it for Gumps who are turned out in here, then go back to the world?

Some will lead a double life, she said. Lovey-dovey at home with the wife and kids, then they'll sneak off downtown for a little hanky panky with the first punk they can find. You've seen them in here, all slutty, then they get straight for a visit.

How about you, Candy? Will you have any adjustments to make?

I'll be the same Candy I was when I came in—dignified and classy.

And the best damn female impersonator on Clark Street! Jimmy added.

You'll be back on stage, Candy?

Packing the house, she said.

She slipped into the voice of Bette Davis: I will not retire while I've got my legs and my makeup.

Herr Mann, how about you?

I've got twenty-eight years left, Davis. When I hit those bricks I won't give a shit about freaking off with anyone.

But suppose you got out tomorrow, I said, and Candy got out, too. Would you still be a loving couple? Or would the allure of a natural-born woman be too much to resist?

Mann looked at Candy, then back at me. His voice was cold.

We'll never know, will we?

He rose from the table.

Candy, Jimmy, you guys keep Herr Davis company. I'll be back.

He walked to the center of the yard, where he joined a huddle of other inmates, among them Captain Jack, Berserker, Bobo and Odum.

Jimmy leaned across the table.

You've got more balls than brains, kid.

Candy had been staring at me while I debated race with Mann.

Dean, darling, she said, I think you made him mad.

She looked toward the huddle of Mann and his mob.

Neanderthals, she said, echoing Doctor Dick's assessment. A bunch of ill-mannered brutes. They're jealous. They don't like Otto spending time with me. They should let him be. Hasn't he done enough? But they're getting restless. They want something to happen. And something will. They'll get what they want. And soon. You'll see.

Jimmy looked at Candy. He shook his head slowly.

Candy, he said, don't say too much.

Candy turned to me and smiled.

I never know how much of what I say is true, she said in the voice of Bette Midler.

Candy, I said, you're quick with the one-liners. I love it, but I wonder if always being someone else is a way of not being who you really are?

Darling, she replied, if you're going to be my psychoanalyst, I get to lay on your couch.

Dietrich? Midler? Davis?

No—Candy, she said.

Botha and Maria strolled by. I hoped Maria would not acknowledge me but she did, with a teasing smile and a delicate fluttering of her fingers. Botha scowled. Candy gave Maria the evil eye. I read Maria's lips: Bitch!

Mann returned just as loudspeakers in the guard towers blared: End of yard. Return to your units! End of yard!

Jimmy, walk Candy back to the house, he said.

Jimmy and Candy got up to go.

Candy, Jimmy, I said, thanks for your contribution to *The Gump Report*. You'll be famous one day.

Famous I don't need, Davis, Jimmy said. Keep my name out of it. We'll see you around.

I'll take fame, Dean, darling, Candy said. Whatever I can get. I want it all and I want it delivered.

Dietrich?

Midler. She's a laugh a minute. Nice to meet you, Herr Davis.

She held her hand out as she had at the beginning of the interview. I shook it gently. She and Jimmy strolled away slowly like all the other inmates returning to their houses who had plenty of time to get there and nowhere else to go. Mann looked down at me.

Herr Davis, did you get what you came for?

All that and more, I said.

I gathered up my pen and my note pad like someone who had dropped his dollar bills and wanted to retrieve them before the wind blew them away. I rose from the small round table.

That's right, you did, Mann said. And now you owe me. We'll be in touch.

He sauntered away. Tall. Erect. Imperial. There were some people in this world in whose debt you did not want to be, and Herr Mann was probably one of them.

CLOSING THE BOOK

IT WAS TIME TO CLOSE THE BOOK on *The Gump Report*. It had gotten too close and personal. I had only to gather an array of diverse opinions briefly articulated to complete the report, then I'd wrap it up and find some other way to do my time.

HELL YES, I GET HEAD SOMETIMES, Double D. Ain't no shame in my game! I just close my eyes and pretend it's Belinda. Did I tell you about that bitch Belinda flappin her nasty pussy lips for my goddamn cousin?

Yes, you did, Buster.

In the back seat of my Eldorado!

Yes ...

By the way, how's *your* girlfriend ... Daddy Dean? Haha!

BAABAR MALIK MUHTADI, servant of the Sovereign Lord, Imam of all Muslims in Lime Ridge State Penitentiary, formerly Pinklon Thomas, infamous Chief of the People's Gangster Nation, waved his copy of the Koran in my face and proclaimed: The Sharia of Islam is quite clear on the subject, My Brother. When a man mounts another man, the throne of God shakes! Kill the one who is doing it and also kill the one to whom it is being done!

That seems rather severe, I said, but it might solve the problem of overcrowding in our nation's prisons.

PAULY PUMPED HIS FIST in a phallus-stroking motion. I don't give a damn how a dude does his time, Double D, but five fingers and a little Vaseline does the trick for me. I wouldn't touch a Gump with a ten-foot pole if I was doing life without parole!

What about Otto Mann and Candy, I said. What do you think of them?

Pauly shook his head.

It's weird to me, Double D, but if Otto wants to play Mister and Missus Mann with a faggot, that's his business. He's paid his dues. Long as I know he's got my back when the joint jumps, you know what I mean?

BERSERKER GRIMACED AND PRETENDED to barf. Have you seen those fucking hickeys on his neck? he said. You just know they're swapping spit! Makes me sick! And he's going to lead us into battle when the shit hits the fan?

RODNEY JOHN CLOVER, SO THE STORY WENT, could pull a tractor with his teeth. A hulking dim-witted farm boy from the bottom of the state, Rodney John didn't like queers, colored folks, big city white boys telling him what to do, or anyone who thought they were smarter than he was, which was a whole lot of people. Rodney John, sitting at a table in the dayroom watching *Charlie's Angels* on the television set mounted high on the wall, turned to me and frowned.

Why you wanna know about that dumb stuff, anyway, Davis? he said.

The academic world wants to hear your opinion, Rodney, I said.

My opinion is anyone who wants to talk about that stuff is sick! Anyway, I'm going home in a few days. I don't have time.

We could do it now.

I'm watching Charlie's Angels.

We could meet in the library tomorrow.

I don't go to the library. I don't like books or the butt fuck faggots who touch them with their filthy hands.

Or on the yard—

Rodney John stood and looked down at me.

Just get away from me, Davis, before I get really mad.

Sure, Rodney, sure. Thanks, anyway … and good luck out there in the world, huh?

Yeah, yeah, yeah, he said, and returned his attention to *Charlie's Angels*.

I WAS SUMMONED TO WARDEN WAINWRIGHT'S office. I had not seen the man since the graduation ceremony, where he gave a small speech to the assembled and had been effusive in his praise of Bone and me. He hoped many more inmates would follow in our footsteps. Our pictures were taken in caps and gowns, holding our diplomas before us like trophies.

Have a seat, Mr. Davis, the Warden said.

He leaned back in his leather desk chair with wooden armrests. He wore a white short-sleeved shirt and a dark green necktie. He was slim, his shoulders squared, his flaxen hair parted on the side, his eyes clear and bright, his face lightly tanned. I guessed him to be a runner. I could see him running along the shoulder of a two-lane county road on a summer morning, or on a dirt path between corn fields, a brown and white collie loping at his side.

He leaned forward and put his elbows on his desk and laced his fingers together. His tone was earnest.

Davis, it has come to my attention, and to the attention of the Major, that you have been conducting clandestine interviews with fellow inmates on the subjects of gang business and homosexual activity. What can you tell me about this?

I had been waiting for the hammer to fall and was only surprised it had taken so long. I did not wonder who or what had brought the matter to the attention of the Warden and the Major. The walls had eyes and ears. Nevertheless, I did not feel in jeopardy. No one had roused me from my sleep in the middle of the night and the Warden's tone was not threatening.

Academic research, Warden, I said. For an Anthropology Professor in the College Program.

I thought as much, the Warden said, leaning back in his chair.

And the interviews weren't clandestine, I said. They were quite in the open.

But unauthorized.

I didn't know they had to be authorized.

Ill-advised then, Davis. The Major wanted to shake you down. I told him that wouldn't be necessary, that I would address the issue.

He will, however, note your file.

I shrugged.

The interviews are over, I said. No harm done.

The Warden smiled.

Very good, he said. Then the issue has been addressed.

I appreciated that the Warden had my back but refrained from saying, Good looking out, Ride.

He leaned forward.

The truth is, Davis, I approve. I'm in favor of academic research and I'm sure your findings are unique. I see the lives of these men from a limited point of view. I'd like to see them from yours. Will there be a published report?

I'm told there will.

Can I get a copy?

Don't know why not, I said. I'll tell the Professor. He'll appreciate your interest.

Wonderful. Thank you. Here, I have something for you.

He opened his desk drawer and handed me a photograph: Randy Bone and me in caps and gowns, grinning, holding our diplomas. A graduating class of two. Forever bound.

I SAT AT A TABLE ON THE YARD composing bawdry limericks. I leaned back and gazed at a cloudless blue sky. A tiny speck of a bird winged its solitary way toward the horizon. Higher still, a larger speck plummeted toward the smaller and they met in a silent explosion of feathers. A single speck winged its way to the horizon and disappeared. A small feather fluttered to my feet. I reached down and picked it up—it would make a fine bookmark to separate what has been read from what was yet to be read—just as a pair of big boots trundled into view. I looked up. Rodney John looked down. The sun was directly behind his head.

Davis, he said, does the academic world really want to know my opinion?

I put the feather in the pocket of my blue denim work shirt.

Yes, Rodney, I said. Every opinion counts. Even yours.

Well, I've changed my mind, Davis. I'd like to tell the Professor what I think.

The project is over, Rodney, I said. I've sent the Professor all my notes.

I'd like to tell the Professor to his face, Rodney said. I'm out of here tomorrow. I'll be staying on the family farm close to the College. We could meet somewhere.

I'll tell you what, Rodney, give me your telephone number. I'll call him. If he wants to meet he'll call you.

Rodney John gave me his number. I called the Professor collect. The Professor's wife answered. She hesitated, then accepted the call.

One moment, please, she said with a quavering voice. I'll get my husband.

I had an eerie feeling, as though I'd just made contact with a creature from another planet. I hadn't talked on the phone to a person other than Lucy or Brodie or Wally in three years.

The Professor came on. I told him about Rodney's offer. I described him as a handsome strapping lad, an Adonis with a low IQ and a pronounced opinion about sex in the joint. I added that he was something of a loose cannon, and cautioned the Professor to meet him in a public place. The Professor was delighted.

TWO WEEKS LATER, WILBUR brought me a copy of the local paper, the Lime Ridge Record. Some news about your Professor friend, he said.

I read the article Wilber had circled in red:

> Lawrence K. Whitehall III, Professor of Anthropology at Southeastern Illinois University, was found beaten and unconscious in his room at the Marriott Hotel on Sunday morning. "I knocked and no one responded," said the housekeeper, Eloise. "I went in and there he was, draped over his bed. It was awful." Professor Whitehall was taken to Lime Ridge State Hospital, where he was treated for lacerations to the head and face, and possible concussion, and was held overnight for observation. A resident of Lime Ridge, he claims to have no memory of the

events of the night before and no clue why he had checked into the hotel.

His empty wallet was found in the parking lot, and his car recovered a few miles out of town. Local authorities are investigating but have not identified the assailant.

I wondered at my culpability. Had the Professor, against my advice to be cautious, rendezvoused with Rodney at the Marriot for a bout of extracurricular activity? Or, having concluded his interview, arranged to meet with a prostitute who brought along a burly male companion who beat and robbed him and left him unconscious? In which case, he had to say he remembered nothing. Or had he quarreled with his wife and fled to the Marriott and was waylaid by an accomplice of the maid, Eloise? And being concussed, he truly didn't remember? I would never know.

IN SEPTEMBER OF THAT YEAR the findings of *The Gump Report* were included in a presentation in London to an International Symposium of Cultural Anthropologists and subsequently published to plaudits in an anthology of cutting-edge ethnographies. I was cited in the report for the boldness and scope of my fieldwork.

Soon after publication I received a copy of the Anthology signed by Professor Whitehall, and a note thanking me again for my contribution. The Professor added that he had sent a copy to the Warden. No mention was made of the beating he took at the hands of an unknown assailant.

BOOK IV

ASCENSION

Man is free at the moment he wishes to be.
~ Voltaire

DOWNTOWN BROWN

WHY I SING THE BLUES

IN THE PHOTO TAKEN BY BOOKER T WILLIAMS, civilian foreman of Lime Ridge State Penitentiary's welding shop, I stand next to a five-foot tall, multi-tiered plant stand constructed of steel tubing and plate. I am trim with a narrow waist in blue denim pants and a blue denim shirt with the sleeves rolled-up to my elbows. My right arm is draped over the top plate of the plant stand as though across the shoulders of an old friend. My hair hangs past my ears, my mouth is circled by a well-groomed mustache and beard, and there is a complacent smile upon my face. I felt pretty good about myself. I had labored over the blueprint in the solitude of my cell, and fabricated the plant stand in the shop with my own two hands. Except for painting faces, there was not a time in my life when I had so coordinated my mind and body to conjure up much of anything.

The plant stand is one of a half dozen I had constructed in the previous four months. It is now in the office of the Director of Vocational Programs, G. Scott Fuller. Another is in the office of the Assistant Warden, Wesley Wainwright, three are on the patios of the homes of the Major, the Captain, and the Lieutenant—gifts for their wives—and the sixth is in the home of the Chaplain, who has no wife.

In addition to the plant stands, I designed and built four coffee tables, three garden trellises, two latticework benches and a half dozen trailer hitches. When demand for my designs became too great for my own two hands, Booker T assigned two inmate assistants to lighten the load. I drew up the blueprints at night in my cell and by day supervised my helpers, who did the cutting, the bending, the grinding and the welding. I stopped counting the pieces my crew and I put out

… all for the staff of the penitentiary, all with materials paid for by the State, which is to say with taxpayers' dollars.

Booker T was amused by the production and pleased that his protégé had mastered his craft so well and so quickly. He didn't give a damn about taxpayer dollars but he did give a damn about his shop and his students, so when there wasn't enough scrap metal for them to practice on and learn their trade because it was going out the back door, and the Director of Programs wasn't able or willing to increase the shop's budget to buy more, Booker T closed the show.

They'll just have to buy their damned plant stands at the garden store in town, he told me.

I thanked him for the photo and the opportunity.

I LIKED HOW THE HEFT OF THE HAND-HELD grinder made taut the tendons in my wrists, and the veins of my forearms stand out like cables; how when the spinning wheel bit into the steel held fast by the vise bolted to the workbench, the high whine of the biting formed a concerto with the slow yawning roar of the carbon arc gouging gun, and the angry buzz of the stick welders coming from behind the heavy canvass curtains of the welding booths; how the spray of metal shavings and sparks from the grinding arched across the shop like the tail of a giant electric rooster.

I flipped my protective goggles to the top of my head, pulled off my heavy leather gloves and admired my handy-work, just as Booker T emerged from his office.

Yo! Davis! he yelled. When you've got a minute!

The first time I had been summoned to his office, a few months into the program and before the Plant Stand Factory enterprise, I wondered if I'd done something wrong.

Close the door and have a seat, he said then, indicating a worn leather armchair in the corner.

A sixty-something black man with a compact frame, hair the color of cigarette ash beating a slow retreat to the back of his head, and a soft light in his eyes that said he forgave the world its many transgressions, he sat with one booted foot resting on his desk. The scent of cigar smoke, sweet and musty, hung in the air of the small, window-less room. And of old coffee. And singed leather. And of the gases produced from the welding and cutting processes: aldehydes, diiso-cyanates, phosgene and phosphine. A revolving fan on a low-slung grey metal cabinet stirred this stew of aromas and ruffled the edges of the stack of papers on the desk. From a cassette player next to the fan, BB King declared that as long he was paying the bills, he was paying the cost to be the boss.

Booker T said nothing. I sat in the armchair. I glanced around the room. On the back wall was a framed certificate reading Hobart School Of Welding Technology, Troy, Ohio, 1947, and a framed poster in orange and black of six sharply-dressed African American musicians on stage playing horns and drums and piano. On the desk was a silver-framed photo of Booker T in a charcoal grey pinstriped suit, with an edge of red handkerchief poking from its pocket, over a shiny plum-colored shirt and a yellow silk tie, beside a woman in a plum-colored dress, a string of pearls nestled in her ample bosom, and a grey bouffant gracing her plump and smiling face. I was sure I had seen that suit somewhere before.

Would you care for a cup of coffee? Booker T said.

No thanks, I said. It's a little hot for coffee.

He swung his leg down, withdrew a thermos from a drawer, and filled the cups on his desk.

It's never too hot for my kind of coffee, he said.

He slid a cup toward me. It was cold to the touch. An ice cube bobbed on the surface. I took a sip.

Ahh … fortified, I said.

My own formula, he said. Two parts espresso, one part gin and a splash of coconut milk. Just between you and me, of course.

Of course, I said. My lips are sealed.

Confident I wasn't being called onto the carpet, I settled deeper into the armchair. I sipped my coffee. Booker T remained silent. I looked at the photo on the desk.

Booker T, I said. That suit you're wearing in the photo? My father-in-law wore the same outfit one night. And before that I saw it on a writer on the boardwalk in Atlantic City.

Booker T's smile was sly.

I'd say those two gentlemen have mighty good taste in clothes, he said.

My father-in-law said the same thing about the writer, I said.

I'd say your father-in-law has a mighty fine sense of humor.

Booker T sipped his coffee. I looked at the certificate on the wall.

Troy, Ohio, 1947, I said. That was a long time ago.

He regarded the certificate.

Seems like a lifetime to me, he said.

His tone was bittersweet.

Is that your hometown? I said.

Born and raised, he said.

You still have people there?

Not a one, son. Moms and the old boy drove off a bridge into a flooded creek one night. Big sister, Nadine, when she was seventeen, she run off to Harlem and was never seen nor heard from again. Big brother, Maurice, he moved to Cleveland, had his self a rib joint and lots of pretty women, till he got his self shot being carjacked at a red light early one morning in a neighborhood where he didn't belong.

I wondered how to respond. It was a longer litany of misfortune than I was prepared to commiserate about.

So ... how'd you end up here in the boonies, Booker T?

He swung a leg up onto his desktop.

Don't live in the boonies, he said. Live in St. Louis proper and commute an hour each way.

I see. What brought you to St. Louis proper?

Charlie Wilson. I met him at Hobart. He knew I was all alone in the world. He said to me, Booker T, come out to St. Louis when you finish the program. I said, Charlie, what's in St. Louis? The blues is, Booker T, Charlie said. And lots of pretty women! Charlie hooked me up with the Pipe Fitters Union. Took me around to the clubs. I met and married the prettiest woman in town, Lucille. We raised two fine boys. Thirty years later I retired with a pension and signed on to this Lime Ridge gig. A sweet deal.

Lucille … is that your wife?

It is. She used to tease me BB King named his guitar after her. I said to her, Lucille, is there something I ought to know about you and BB?

My wife is named Lucille, too. Well … Lucy. Do you call your wife Lucy?

The first time I called Lucille Lucy she got all high and mighty. Told me, Don't be calling me no Lucy. My name is Lucille. After she'd been living in my house a while and me paying the bills she said, You can call me Lucy at home, but I'm still Lucille when we go uptown. But if she was mad at me at home and I said, Aw, now, Lucy, baby, she would say, Don't be calling me no Lucy, Mr. Booker T Williams! My name is Lucille!

Is that the little lady in the photo?

He looked at the picture.

She was little when I met her, he said. Then she got big from living the good life with Booker T, bless her soul. Then she got little again there at the end. Just seemed to melt away, like a candle burning down.

His smile was rueful.

She passed a year ago, he said.

I'm sorry to hear that, I said.

We had a good life, Davis. Raised two fine boys. Here, let me fill your cup, son.

I extended my cup. Booker T filled it.

Instinct told me not to ask about Booker T's two fine boys, but he had mentioned them twice and perhaps was angling for an opportunity to say more.

Did your two boys stay around St. Louis to keep their old man company?

They're keeping their Momma company about now, Booker T said. The oldest, Leon, he went to Vietnam and never came back. I told him before he went, Leon, you don't have to go to no Viet Nam. But he said, Daddy, I'm a Sergeant in the United States Army. I'm sworn to protect my men. I go where they go. And he went and never came back. His baby brother Freddy got a little wild after that. Got hisself shot by a policeman for resisting arrest. Young man never could say, Yes sir, No sir.

I detected the strain of bitterness in Booker T's forgiveness of the world's transgressions.

You've lost a lot of people, I said.

I have a few friends left, he said. They want to hook me up with this gal or that, but my heart isn't in it. Wherever I go reminds me of Lucille.

The conversation stalled. BB King declared, I've been around a long, long time. You know I've paid my dues!

I looked at the poster on the wall.

Booker T, the poster says Leo's Five but I count six.

Booker T replied without turning around.

The man up front, that's Leo Gooden. The five cats behind him are Leo's Five, the house band at The Blue Note, Leo's club in East St. Louis. I met Lucille there. When St. Louis clubs closed for the night, folks crossed the river to the Blue Note. You'd find big stars on the stage: Miles Davis. Lou Rawls. Red Fox. Bill Cosby. Ike and Tina Turner. I knew Tina when she was a young girl named Anna Mae Bullock. Knew Ike when his band, The Kings Of Rhythm, played the Club Manhattan in East St. Louis. Ike and Tina played for dances at my boys' High School.

You have a place in history, I said.

Might see Chuck Berry there, too, Booker T said. Chuck has a big farm in Wentzville, just outside of St. Louis. Me and Lucille got married on the porch of his old farmhouse. There was rhythm and blues and lots of booze till the sun peeked over the trees. Chuck was mighty fond of Lucille. He said to me, Booker T, you better keep your eye on that gal, you don't want to lose her to a better man. I kept my eye on her all right but it seems I lost her to a better man after all.

He gazed upward and laughed a low ironic laugh.

Do you still go to the Blue Note? I said.

It closed in 1964, he said. Leo died a year later. Charlie Wilson the year after that. But enough about this old man, Davis. How about you? Do you dig the blues?

I felt embarrassed. As Danté Allegro I pretended to own a Blues Club in Chicago, yet knew too little about the genre to have a proper conversation.

I grew up on Psychedelic Rock, I said. The San Francisco sound. You might find me tripping on psilocybin in the sun at a concert at Golden Gate Park or at The Fillmore Auditorium or The Avalon Ballroom. When Grace Slick sang *Feed Your Head* she was talking about me. I was at the 1967 Monterey Pop Festival where the Jefferson Airplane and The Grateful Dead and Janis Joplin played on stage together. But something happened, Booker T. The music died. It was *Bye Bye Miss American Pie* for me.

I don't know about all those folks, Davis, but I know you got to get next to the blues. The blues never die. You love, you lose, you sing the blues. Just how it is.

I reflected on all that Booker T had loved and lost. I vowed to give Lucy a call that night. I finished my drink.

You want another, Davis?

I slid my cup forward. Booker T filled it.

I'll bet I can tell you something about the blues you don't know, I said.

Booker T gave me a sideways glance.

What can you tell me I don't already know, Mr. Davis?

I can tell you about Johnny Otis. You know Johnny Otis?

Know he wrote *Willie and the Hand Jive*.

Do you know he wrote *With Every Beat of My Heart*?

I do.

Do you know he wrote *Roll with Me Henry* for Etta James?

Know that, too.

Do you know he played with Charlie Parker and Count Basie?

What else can you tell me?

I can tell you he discovered Big Mamma Thornton.

Keep going …

I can tell you he's a white man.

Booker T's eyebrows went up.

That's right, I said. He's Greek. Born in Berkeley, California, raised in Vallejo in a black neighborhood where his father ran a grocery store. His last name was Veliotes. He changed it to Otis when he was a teenager because it sounded black. He said if he had to choose to be white or black, he'd take black. It was all about the culture.

Well, I'll be damned! Davis. For a man who don't know about the blues, you sure know a lot about Johnny Otis!

I interviewed him for a journalism class, Booker T. He was playing at a club in San Francisco. We had a few drinks.

Booker T swung his leg off his desk.

You have a cassette player in your cell, Davis? he said.

I do, I said.

Take these, he said.

He got a shoebox from the cabinet behind him. It was full of cassettes.

There's lots more where these come from, Davis. You take them back to your house—and get next to the blues, boy!

AND SO I GOT NEXT TO THE BLUES. I listened to that first box of cassettes for a month, then swapped it for another. And another. And once or twice a week I was invited into Booker T's office to lounge in the worn green leather armchair and drink iced coffee with gin and a splash of coconut milk, and kick it about the blues. Or whatever else came to mind. On one such occasion, Booker T made a modest proposal.

How much time you got left, Davis, he said.

Eleven months and twenty-one days, I said. Not that I'm keeping track.

I want you to stay on after you finish the program, son. You learned your trade real fast, you ain't got a bigoted bone in your body, and your conversation is good. Maybe you'll consent to be my inmate assistant till they cut you loose.

You bet I will, Booker T!

I was honored and pleased. I needed a place to finish my time in Lime Ridge. The shop had come to feel like a second home, and the old green leather armchair in the corner of the office mine alone to lounge in, because I had never seen anyone else in it.

Until today.

Today it was occupied by Wesley Wainwright, the young and earnest Assistant Warden of Programs. He did not get up when I entered.

Close the door, Booker T said.

I closed the door.

Have a seat, he said.

From the cassette player on the cabinet came Otis Redding's version of *I've Got Dreams to Remember*. I sat on the cold metal folding chair in the corner opposite the Warden. I knew him to be a progressive penologist with the well-being of inmates at heart. You too can escape the revolving door of recidivism was his oft-heard aphorism. He had promoted the surrogate Summer Olympics of 1984 and presented me with my gold medal; established the Bachelor's Degree program with SEIU and presented Randy and me our diplomas; interceded on my behalf when Major Drumm wanted to shake me down for conducting ill-advised interviews of inmates for *The Gump Report*; kept the prison paper *Prose & Cons* alive even after the ludicrous attempt by several misguided inmates to use its antiquated press to print counterfeit money; pushed through Abdul's drama group, The Players of Conviction; was currently making plans to have outside speakers present during Black History Month in February of next year; and by dint of his efforts on behalf of the Lime Ridge Chapter of the Jaycees, the prison's closed-circuit cable television system had been recently installed.

Davis, Booker T said, how would you like to be a movie star?

Crazier things have happened, I said. Maybe I'll do that some day.

Don't have to wait, Davis. You can be a movie star right here in Lime Ridge.

How is that?

The Warden wants to make a commercial.

About what?

Booker T looked at the Warden. The Warden sat up straight and assumed his signature earnest demeanor.

Davis, he said, every night at 8:00 o'clock, hundreds of men are staring at televisions in their cells or in the dayroom, waiting for nonsense like *The Terminator* or *Dirty Harry* to play on closed circuit. While we have their attention, why not give them some valuable information about what our vocational programs have to offer and persuade them to enroll?

The Warden's raised eyebrows said, Don't you think that's a good idea?

I think that's a good idea, I said. But where do I come in?

I would like the pilot commercial to feature the welding program, Davis. I would like you to write it. And be in it.

Why me?

Because you understand the importance of goal setting and achievement, Davis. And the creative possibilities of the welding trade. I would have it done professionally but it ought to be an inside job, as it were. Inmates addressing other inmates. And you were recommended.

By whom?

James Dixon, my Inmate Assistant. Seconded by Booker T, of course.

Ha! James Dixon, alias Abdul! Ever the framer of the fortunes of others. He and I hadn't kicked it since my graduation from SEIU. I felt his presence across the timeless void.

What do you think, Mr. Davis?

It was an easy decision to make.

I'm your man, Warden, I said. But I'll need complete creative control. I won't want to be censored.

I was being facetious but the earnest Warden shook his head.

I can't promise that, he said. The script will have to be signed off by myself and by Major Drumm.

It will not be incendiary, Warden. It will not rouse the rabble, nor promote the fabrication of shanks.

The Warden frowned.

And you'll have to keep it clean, he said.

Of course, I said. We wouldn't want to offend our audience with salty language.

We don't know who else might view it someday.

Who else might?

We don't know.

All right then, I said. Strictly PG—Parental Guidance Suggested.

Thank you, Davis.

You're welcome, Warden. How much time do I have?

How much time do you need?

A week? I've never written a commercial.

A week is good. Give it to Booker T. He'll give it to me. The Major and I will read it, then we'll all get together. And Davis—

Yes?

I appreciate your sense of humor, but the Major may not.

Duly noted.

The Warden extended his hand. I took it.

Thanks for your contribution, he said. I can't wait to read the script. And remember—keep it clean.

It will be nothing if not clean, Warden, I said.

THE SKY WAS A FROSTY BLUE, the air sweet with the scent of dying leaves and wood smoke. A flock of geese in V formation honked and winged their way south. Booker T and I were escorted to the Warden's office by an unimposing guard with long sideburns, who strolled nonchalantly and whistled as he walked.

The Warden's office was nestled in a warren of administrative buildings near the front gate. I had been there once before, a year ago, when called in and reprimanded for *The Gump Report* interviews. I felt a thrill of anticipation: I'd be on the other side in less than a year.

The ambiance of the Warden's office was in stark contrast with that of Booker T's. Absent were the down-home aromas of cigar smoke and old coffee; the sharp odor of ozone released by the burning and cutting of metal; and the guileless tone and temperament of the blues. Rather, there were the artificial scents of Lemon Pledge; of the oil used to shine the wood of the glass-doored bookcase against the wall; of the aerosol air freshener recently sprayed. In the left corner was a tall potted tropical plant with shiny leaves, bearing clusters of small red flowers; on the rear wall a framed diploma evincing the Warden's Master of Arts Degree in Criminal Justice and Criminology from Loyola University, Magna Cum Laude; on his desk a framed photo of a thirty-something blonde in a starched blouse, and two blonde children, a boy and a girl, on either side of her timid oval face. From speakers in the ceiling wafted the pallid strains of Smooth Jazz.

I didn't begrudge the Warden his fastidiousness, maybe even envied it some. He was that unlikely concurrence of perfect nature perfectly nurtured. No doubt his hearth and home, the confederation of his family and friends, were as meticulously maintained as his office. I was reminded of the scene in Herman Hesse's novel *Steppenwolf* in which the protagonist Harry Haller contemplates the shiny parquet-floored vestibule of a widow's flat, with its potted azalea and araucaria—the very essence of bourgeois cleanliness, of neatness and meticulousness, of duty and devotion shown in little things—with a mixture of admiration and dread. I conceded that the world could do with a few more Warden Wainwrights and a few less Major Drumms.

With the arrival of Booker T and me, the room was suddenly crowded. Major Drumm, in his short-sleeved khaki safari suit, his legs crossed, his bulging arms folded, his bwana hat dangling from the tips of his fingers, leaned against the wall in the left corner next to the tall potted tropical plant, looking ludicrously like he'd just emerged from the bush without a scratch or a drop of sweat. He contemplated the new arrivals with the cold implacable expression of a third world military officer planning a coup.

The Warden, smiling eagerly, rose from behind his desk.

Davis, he said, meet Bill Dobratz.

A well-groomed young man in tan slacks, tasseled loafers and a pale green polo shirt sat in a brown leather armchair to the right of the Warden's desk.

When Bill isn't teaching fractions in our GED Department, the Warden said, he's shooting videos of the weddings or birthdays of friends, or of Little League games, or of lawn parties. He'll be our cinematographer. Bill, this is Dean Davis, scriptwriter and star of our first commercial.

Dobratz stood. He held out his hand, withdrew it, and held it out again. I surmised that he'd never shaken the hand of an inmate. Was he afraid something might rub off? I took his hand.

Howdy, Bill, I said.

He smiled thinly.

I've never met Hollywood Royalty, he said. They don't often make it out to the Hinterlands.

I returned the smile.

Just passing through, I said.

I imagined the story of Bill Dobratz: born and raised in the region; graduated from the local high school where his grades and his SAT scores were good enough for a scholarship to the nearest State University, where he got a degree in math that landed him his well-paid gig at Lime Ridge; a wife who teaches English or History or Home Economics in the High School where they'd met, or is the dispatcher for the County Sheriff's Department; a trio of tousle-haired tots attending the same elementary school as had their parents; two cocker spaniels; a riding mower; a station wagon in which to take vacations to the cheesy lodge clear on the far side of the state; softball on weekends, and amateur videos of the insipid social outings of family and friends. And what else? Oh, yes, a print of Norman Rockwell's *Runaway* on the mustard yellow wall above the mantel of the river rock fireplace in the family room.

But I checked myself. I was not being fair. For all I knew, Dobratz had been a Sergeant in Vietnam, saved the lives of a dozen soldiers, was wounded, captured, escaped, returned home with a Medal of Honor and a severe case of Post Traumatic Stress Disorder, which he overcame sufficiently to go to college on the GI Bill and become the compassionate teacher he now was, unlocking the mysteries of mathematics for the challenged and compromised inmates of the State Penitentiary. Or he'd joined the Peace Corp and gone to the Amazon and snatched the infant son of the Chief of the local tribe from the jaws of a twenty-foot boa constrictor and been made an honorary Chief-for-life.

So give the man his props, Davis! I berated myself. Why was I type-casting these guys? Was it because of the proximity of the front gate, and my being on the other side of it soon, and having to be something other than what I once was, and not knowing what that something other might be?

Dobratz resumed sitting. Booker T took a place in the corner opposite Major Drumm. He put his hands in his pockets and assumed the amused and tolerant expression I had come to know so well.

Bravo, Davis, the Warden said. Bravo! I think the script is terrific. It has the right combination of serious and compelling message laced with humor.

Glad you like it, I said.

But the racist and sexist jokes have to go, he said.

Why? You don't think they're funny?

Funny, but not appropriate for our audience. Getting a laugh at the expense of one another is not the kind of humor we want to encourage. Our goal is to elevate, not to denigrate. The Major agrees with me on this.

But I don't, I said. I think they're especially appropriate for our audience, which doesn't have a hell of a lot to laugh about. If they can laugh about themselves and each other it might make the pain go away. Or not. But no problem. I'll keep the humor in and the racist and sexist jokes out.

Thank you, Davis.

You bet, I said.

Who is Choo Choo Rodriguez? he said.

Inmate Ruben Rodriguez, I said. In East One.

Is he in the welding program?

No.

Wouldn't it make sense to choose a fellow student to be your co-star?

Choo Choo's a natural, Warden, I said. He's got the personality we need: a fun-loving guy with an irrepressible spirit. He'll provide levity. The audience won't want to be talked down to or conned in any way. Also, he's Puerto Rican. We need a Caucasian, an Hispanic and an African American, so everyone can identify with someone.

And the African American is me, Booker T said. Only you can write me out, Mr. Davis.

Booker T, we need you! You're proof that if a man sets a goal and works hard, he can have the good things in life.

I wouldn't feel right someone putting words in my mouth.

Fair enough. How about when Downtown Brown puts that microphone in your face, you just say what you want?

Booker T reflected.

All right, he said. I can do that.

Thank you, Booker T, I said.

Major Drumm looked at me.

We can't have an explosion in the welding shop, he said. Not even a fake one.

I can address that, Dobratz said. Special effects. You'll only see it on tape. You'd never know it wasn't real.

Drumm regarded Dobratz without expression.

Bill is a master of special effects, the Warden said.

The Major looked coldly at Wainwright. I felt the tug of the power struggle between them.

The suit is a problem, the Major said. Regulations forbid inmates from wearing civilian clothes before the day of their release.

I wondered what Drumm would do if there were no one in this world to beat down, foil or frustrate. Booker T regarded the man with scarcely concealed contempt.

With all due respect, Major, I said, a suit won't allow me to go through a dozen steel doors and over a forty-foot fence. It isn't Superman's cape.

The Warden cleared his throat.

I can sign off on an exception to that regulation, Major, he said. Provided there is added security, of course.

Where do you propose to get a suit, Davis, the Major said.

I got a suit for Davis, Booker T said. We're the same size. It'll fit him real good!

There you have it! the Warden said. Davis, you revise the script.

I'll have Rodriguez assigned to the welding program. Take a week to rehearse. Then we'll shoot.

He looked around the room.

Anything else, Gentlemen? No? Then this meeting is adjourned!

THE SHOOT WAS SHROUDED IN SECRECY. Students were given the day off under the pretext of repairs to the shop. Two guards flanked the exit door and a third posted outside. I stood in the center of the shop wearing a charcoal grey pinstriped wide-lapel suit, a red handkerchief poking from its breast pocket, a shiny plum-colored shirt, and a yellow silk tie. It was in fact the very outfit Booker T wore in the photo on his desk, and that my father-in-law, Wally, wore the night of our farewell dinner at La Petite Maison four years ago, and that Gay Talese had worn on the boardwalk in Atlantic City. My hair was cropped close and combed back, my facial hair shorn to a pencil-thin moustache. My left hand was in my pocket, my right hand held before my face a microphone fashioned of shop scraps painted black, bearing the logo LRSPTV—Lime Ridge State Penitentiary TV. My smile was frozen as I waited to go live. I looked like a cross between a street-smart news announcer and a gigolo. Standing behind me, Choo Choo Rodriguez wore a rawhide protective apron and protective helmet and held at his side like a pitchfork an acetylene torch, striking a pose not unlike the Iowa farmer in Grant Wood's painting American Gothic, without the wife. Behind Rodriguez was a haphazard pile of metal scrap, and two large green cylinders.

The scene was lit from the left by a photographer's reflective lighting umbrella. In the center, ten feet in front of me, Dobratz peered through the viewfinder of his tripod-mounted video camera. To the right of the scene, sitting on a folding canvas chair, Director imprinted across its back—a surprise gift for the occasion from his wife—Warden Wainwright, in a white polo shirt and a tan baseball cap, looking in his youthful enthusiasm like the Director Ron Howard, leaned forward and shouted: Lights! Camera! Action!

A few takes and a half hour later, a triumphant smile on his face, he shouted: It's a wrap!

FINGER FOOD AND HIGH SOCIETY

THE PRESCREENING AND RECEPTION in the chapel were surreal. I hadn't expected finger food and High Society. Wesley Wainwright, ever the event planner.

The chapel was spacious and contemporary in design: the floor a blond hardwood buffed to a sheen; the ceiling vaulted and crossed with a latticework of beams from which hung two large fans leisurely turning, gently pushing the incense-laden air; two columns of contoured wooden pews twelve rows deep, each pew accommodating four of the faithful; a blood-red carpet running between the columns and up three steps to a stage, stopping before a boomerang-shaped altar hewn of the same polished blond wood as the floor; and, attached to a beam overhead, canisters casting circles of light onto the stage and the altar and onto the wall back of the altar, where hung in a gilded frame a print of Salvador Dali's rendition of Da Vinci's The Last Supper.

High in the walls left and right, circular stained glass windows big as bicycles tires, lit from within, scattered shards of light in primary colors to the far corners of the chapel. Along the left wall a row of framed symbols in black evinced the Administration's resolve to accommodate a diverse array of belief systems: a crucifix; the Star of David; the Islamic star inside a crescent moon; the Chinese Yin Yang; the Greek letters Alpha and Omega; the American Indian Thunderbird; the Egyptian Ankh. And following this parade of symbols, a framed print of the Laughing Buddha, plump and jolly, a sack of scant possessions slung over his shoulder; a print of the Hindu Deity Lord Krishna lounging in the grass by a quiet lake, blue-skinned, sweetly androgynous, swathed in a saffron robe, crowned by a wreath of flowers, poised to serenade with his little flute the Brahma bull supine to his left, and the lamb to his right; and next to the Krishna print, a Frankie Waters original: Mother Goose in a pointy orange hat, a blue ribbon round her neck, sheltering sleeping toddlers beneath her wings.

At the rear of the chapel, two guards, one lanky and loose-limbed, the other short and round and mustachioed, flanked the entrance door, looking at once curious and bored. A second pair of guards sat silently and unobtrusively in the back pew. In the front pew, Choo Choo and I wore prison blue denim, and Booker T his olive green shop clothes, his signature subtle expression of reluctant forbearance on his face. In the adjacent pew sat Warden Wainwright with his wife, Marianne, and the Missus Dobratz, Cathy, who waited to be joined by husband Bill, who fussed at the altar with the VCR and television set. The wives, dressed in evening wear, sat primly, little purses in their laps, brave smiles on their lips. I imagined Marianne Wainwright's response when her husband proposed they make of the evening not only a celebration but a healing affair, a reconciliation of the forthright with the fallen. But what did they do? she would have asked. What were their crimes? Well, murder and drug dealing, he would have replied. But they are really very nice people, Marianne, and they deserve recognition, so let's give them a chance.

At a knock on the door all heads turned. The taller of the two guards let in Stanley Stan the Man Thomas who, when he wasn't training fighters in the gym, ran the night shift in the kitchen. He pushed a stainless steel cart draped in white linen up the red carpet to the stage.

The Warden rose and announced cheerfully, The caterers have arrived! So, Mr. Thomas, what have we got here?

Stan pulled off the white linen and lifted a stainless steel lid.

We got little meatballs, he said. Sweet and sour!

He replaced the lid and pulled off another.

We got chicken wings, he said. Teriyaki!

He replaced the lid and pulled off another.

We got deviled eggs, he said. With little red paprika flakes!

And here, he said, indicating a large stainless steel bowl on the bottom shelf of the cart, we got fruit punch with pineapple juice and orange peels and lemon peels and pears, and what all else I don't remember.

Wonderful! the Warden said. Push it over there out of the way. We're about to start. Have a seat and enjoy the show.

Stan draped the linen over the cart and pushed the cart to the side of the chapel.

Flea Weight, what crazy shit you hooking up now? he whispered to me as he passed.

You'll see, I said, but keep it to yourself.

What I'm gonna see, Flea Weight?

Gonna see a star is born, Stan. Two stars. Three stars. But keep it to yourself. This is top secret stuff!

He shook his head.

You about a trip, Flea Weight, he said. He took a seat next to me.

Bill Dobratz finished fiddling with the VCR and the television set and went to the side of the stage and dimmed the lights. In the near-dark, the prisms of light cast by the stained glass windows shone more brightly about the room and on the faces of the audience.

We're ready! Dobratz announced.

He took a seat next to his wife and pointed the remote. The television flickered on.

There I was, Downtown Brown, smiling my urbane anchorman smile. To my left was Booker T. Behind me was Choo Choo Rodriguez in full welding shop regalia. I spoke into the microphone.

Welcome to another edition of LRSPTV's award-winning news magazine, *Uptown, Downtown, Get Out of Town*. I'm your host, Hugh Downtown Brown. Today our cameras take us to the welding shop of Lime Ridge State Penitentiary's highly regarded Vocational School where we will hear from foreman Booker T Williams, known affectionately as The Boss, who will tell us about the benefits of a career in welding, and from student Ruben Choo Choo Rodriguez, who will give us a demonstration of his newly acquired skills.

Downtown Brown turned and put the microphone to the mouth of Booker T.

So, tell us, Booker T, what has a career in welding done for you?

Booker T peered into the camera.

My message to all you good brothers is simple—skills pay the bills! Pay your way and set yourself free. Ain't no screw telling me what to do. I do what I want cause I'm the boss of my life. I earned every dollar in my bank account and it is a tall stack! I married the foxiest woman in St. Louis and raised up two fine boys on welding money. I got myself a two-story townhouse in the Central West End, got a walk-in closet full of suits good as any worn by Mr. Downtown Brown here. Got me a pool table and a pinball machine and a juke-box and a wet bar. I drink the best gin money can buy, drink it morning noon and night if I damn well please! I drive me a Cadillac Coup De Ville twenty feet long, that is paid for, ever last dime, and The Man can't lock my black ass up for driving it!

Booker T pointed his finger at the camera.

So pay the cost to be the boss, y'all. Sign up for welding school and get you a piece of the pie!

He went off camera. Downtown Brown addressed the audience.

Thank you, Booker T, for that inspiring testimonial. And now let's hear from student Ruben Choo Choo Rodriguez who will give a demonstration of his newly acquired skills.

Brown stepped back and put the microphone to the helmet of Choo Choo.

Mr. Rodriguez, he said, would you please tell the viewers what you have gained from your experience in Lime Ridge State Penitentiary's Welding Program and what a graduate can look forward to?

Choo Choo remained silent and immobile.

Mr. Rodriguez?

Still no response from Choo Choo. Brown knocked on his helmet.

Choo Choo, are you in there?

Choo Choo lifted the visor of his helmet. He wore dark aviator goggles and earplugs. He pulled the plugs out and left the goggles on.

Whatchoo want, Boss?

I'm not your boss, Choo Choo. I'm the host of LRSPTV's award-winning news magazine, *Uptown, Downtown, Get Out of Town.*

Oh, Geraldo Rivera! Pleased to meet you, man!

No, I'm your host, Hugh Downtown Brown.

Downtown Brown! You a famous dude! Not as famous as my man Geraldo, but you know …

Choo Choo turned and looked at the camera.

Hey, we really on national TV, man?

Yes, we are, Choo Choo. Thirty million viewers are watching us right now.

Aiee! That's a lot of peeps!

It certainly is, Brown said smugly.

Hey, Mr. Brown, Choo Choo said. I'm famous, too!

Is that right, Choo Choo? Famous for what?

Jokes, man! I'm a stand-up comic. You want to hear a joke?

Well, if it's a short one.

Okay, gimme that—

Choo Choo grabbed for the microphone. Brown pulled it away.

I'll hold the mike, he said. You tell the joke.

Okay, okay, Choo Choo said. Don't get so uptight!

He faced the camera.

See, this black dude and this white dude and this Latino dude walk into a bar—

Brown put his free hand over Choo Choo's mouth.

Sorry, Choo Choo, he said. I'm afraid *Uptown, Downtown, Get Out of Town* is not the proper forum for ethnic jokes. We have our standards at LRSPTV.

But this joke, see, it makes fun of everybody!

Nevertheless, Brown said, I'm afraid a portion of our viewing audience would be offended.

He turned to the camera and added, Not to mention our sponsors.

Okay, okay, Choo Choo said. How about a lesbian joke, man? I got a great lesbian joke.

No, Choo Choo, I'm afraid that, too, would be considered offensive.

All right, all right, how about a animal joke? Would a animal joke offend any portion of your viewing audience?

Well, I suppose an animal joke would be acceptable. But make it quick. We have a demonstration to do.

Okay, here's a animal joke, Mr. Brown. What's the difference between a dog and a fox?

Brown stroked his chin.

Umm, the difference between a dog and a fox … ?

That's right. A dog and a fox.

I don't know, Choo Choo. What *is* the difference between a dog and a fox?

About five drinks! Ha, ha, ha. Get it, Mr. Brown? A dog and a fox? Five drinks?

That was funny, I must admit, Choo Choo, Brown said. And now, perhaps you'd be good enough to tell our viewers about the skills you've acquired since you've been a student in the welding program here at Lime Ridge.

Choo Choo frowned.

Whatchoo mean, Boss?

I mean what have you learned to do?

Oh, you know, a little of this, a little of that …

But precisely what, Choo Choo?

Choo Choo reached inside his helmet and scratched his nose.

Well, he said, I can make one piece of metal out of two, or two pieces of metal out of one. I can make two pieces of metal out of four, or four pieces of metal out of two. I can make—here, hold this, Mr. Brown.

Choo Choo handed his torch to Brown and counted on his fingers.

I can make eight pieces of metal out of four, or four pieces of metal out of eight. I can make—

But what else, Choo Choo? Brown said. Surely you build and repair things.

Oh, sure, Mr. Brown: battleships, bridges, skyscrapers, space-stations, stuff like that.

Brown looked around the shop.

What!? You do all that in here?

Oh, no, Mr. Brown. When I hit the streets I'm gonna do all that. In here I'm learning technique. Without technique you are nothing, nada, nobody … you know?

Well, perhaps you'd be willing to give our viewers a demonstration of your technique.

You bet, Mr. Brown! I'm gonna show the peeps the right way to use the oxy-acetylene torch. But first I got to connect my torch to my tanks. Gimme this back.

Cho Choo took the torch from Brown. He looked at the camera.

Thirty million people, aiee!

He turned toward the two large green tanks topped with a cluster of dials behind him. He fiddled with the dials. He hit them with his fist. He kicked the tanks. He wacked them with his torch. Brown turned to the camera.

I'm sure Mr. Rodriguez will have his equipment in order soon, he said with an apologetic tone.

He turned back around to face Choo Choo, who was frantically flicking a striker in front of his unlit torch.

Are we about ready, Choo Choo?

Yeah, but this striker, man. We got us a bum striker. You got a light, Mr. Brown?

Brown reached into his pocket. He handed Choo Choo a lighter.

Choo Choo, he said, are you sure this is the proper way to—

Choo Choo flicked the lighter at the tip of the torch. There was an explosion, courtesy of Bill Dobratz special effects. When the smoke cleared Choo Choo was standing alone. His helmet was blown off. The glass of his goggles was shattered. His hair was standing up. His face was smeared with soot. He stared into the camera, blinking rapidly. He looked down at the floor in front of him.

Mr. Brown, he said, are you all right? Mr. Brown? Hey, Downtown, you don't look so good!

He faced the camera.

I think I messed up Mr. Brown pretty bad!

He bent down out of camera view and came up holding the microphone. He grinned.

I guess Downtown won't be needing this anymore.

He blew into the microphone.

Testing! Testing! he said.

He looked at the camera. He pointed his finger at the audience.

Hey, all you peeps out there in TV Land, he said. It's the Choo Choo Rodriguez Show—and have we got some jokes for you!

The television screen flickered off.

Bill Dobratz went to the side of the stage and turned up the lights.

Warden Wainwright stood abruptly.

Terrific! he said. What did I tell you, Marianne? Is it Oscar worthy or what?

Marianne agreed that it was. There followed a litany of fatuous proclamations: that Booker T was a natural, a diamond in the rough; that Choo Choo was a lock for Best Supporting Actor; that I would be seen on the big screen soon, and that, wasn't it funny, here they were standing on the red carpet already!

Booker T excused himself, citing the long drive home. Stan the Man served up the finger food and the fruit punch, and the gathering served up small talk around the boomerang-shaped altar beneath the Dali print. Small because the discomfort level was large. The wives were out of their element. There was no protocol for an affair of this sort. No precedent. And the punch had no punch. Booker T's gin would have jazzed up the proceedings and loosened a few tongues. Or Abel Carter's hooch.

I found myself talking to Marianne. I held a plastic cup of punch in one hand, a sweet and sour meatball skewered on a wooden tooth-pick in the other, and was looking into the attractive and intriguing face of Marianne, and she was talking. I knew she was talking because her mouth was moving, but I didn't hear the words because I was thinking about her bosom. There was no escaping that it was beautiful. She had dropped her napkin and bent to pick it up and her blouse had fallen away and afforded me a full-on view of her breasts, trimmed in lace.

I imagined she had come to my cell, a gift from her husband for having brought glory to Lime Ridge. She was escorted by Botha, who said, Davis, you've got thirty minutes to finish your business.

That would not be enough time for what I would do with Marianne.

A threadbare red towel tossed over the desk lamp softened the light in the cell to a rosy glow. Roberta Flack sang *The First Time Ever I Saw Your Face.* I stood behind Marianne, swaying to the music and to the heady scent of her perfume and the musk of her body odor. I unbuttoned her dress, slipped it over the sensuous swell of her hips. It fell to the floor with a whoosh. Her panties were brief, diaphanous.

I unclasped her brassiere, slid it down the slender silky flesh of her arms, reached under them to cup her breasts in my trembling hands. She reached behind her, caressed my cheeks, ran her long-nailed fingers through my hair, pressed her firm round dimpled derriere into my stiffening member and moved. She *moved*. I put my hands on her shoulders, turned her around, the better to see her face. On it now was not the look of longing I expected, but one of bewilderment. I saw over her shoulder, at the end of the altar, Dobratz and his wife and the Warden being regaled by the manic humor of El Muchacho Loco. I looked back into the face of Marianne. She had stopped talking. Had she asked me a question and was waiting for an answer? I hadn't heard a word, lost in my lusty daydream of romance in my cell. Might she have asked how I was enjoying my halcyon days of detention? My junket in the joint? Or if I planned to return to the daring world of outlaws, drugs and money? Doubtful. More likely she had asked if I had someone waiting. That would have been a safe subject on which to alight.

Lucy, I said.

I'm sorry?

Lucy. I have a wife named Lucy. She's waiting for me.

Well, that's … wonderful.

She replied in a way that told me she had not asked about who I might have waiting, but I stammered on.

And a little girl. Lola. Lucy and Lola. They're waiting.

I'm so glad, she said.

And you? I said.

Me?

Children, I mean. Do you have children?

Well, I … yes … two.

Marianne's hesitation told me she was not comfortable sharing details of her personal life with a felon, one of the fallen, his intelligence and talent notwithstanding. Which was fine because I had little interest in her, truly, nor in the lives of any of my captors, except for Booker T. They were shadow figures who lived in a world as diaphanous as Marianne's fantasized panties. I thought how, a few years ago, I would have tried to impress her that I was not like the others, the conquered, the crushed. Now I was more interested in how the boys on the block would react to my Downtown Brown commercial. I couldn't wait to see their faces when they saw me in Booker T's suit. I decided I would watch it with them in the dayroom when it debuted.

Last call for treats, y'all!

Stan the Man's announcement was a signal for the party to break up. There were different excuses for an early departure. I guessed the couples would convene at the local pseudo-swank watering hole for cocktails and conversation about the evening's affair. I would go to my cell and make a journal entry.

There commenced a round of handshaking and leave-taking and what I detected as an effluence of unspoken relief. I managed to get Dobratz aside.

Great working with you, Bill, I said. We're one hell of a team. This has been our baby. I'd like to get a copy of the video. I'll give you my wife's address. You can send it there. She'll reimburse for the postage, of course.

Dobratz frowned.

That might be a problem, Dean, he said. The tape would be considered contraband. There are rules about images and recordings being exported from the prison.

I was tempted to quote Mother Goose—There's a reason rules rhyme with fools, my friend—but I only said, Of course. I understand. Think about it, Bill.

I will, Dean.

Great job on the special effects, by the way. That explosion—wowza!

Thanks, Dean.

You're welcome, Bill. Good night.

Good night.

Boy Scout, I thought, as I walked back to my housing unit escorted by the loose-limbed guard, who bobbed his head to a tune only he could hear. The sky overhead was black and riddled with stars. My breath billowed in a frosty plume. I had come to appreciate the bracing Midwest winter. It brought blood to my cheeks.

But this would be my last.

Come what may.

AT EIGHT THE NEXT EVENING I sat with half a dozen inmates beneath the television set mounted high on the dayroom wall and awaited the premiere of Downtown Brown. I was near giddy with anticipation. On the screen, Archie Bunker was getting the last laugh. An inmate stood on a folding chair and flipped the channel changer, while seated inmates shouted their preferences.

It's eight o'clock, man, turn on the movie!

Fuck the movie. The Bulls playing Golden State.

The Warriors are sissies! Yo, Double D, you wanna see your sissy ass team get jacked up by the Almighty Bulls?

I want to watch the movie, I said.

You got a TV in your crib, man.

I get lonely sometimes.

We'll send Marie over. You be alright.

I don't think so, Buster.

Randy, what's the movie tonight?

Psycho.

Let's watch *Psycho*.

Done saw *Psycho* a dozen times, man. Play the Bulls.

Fuck the Bulls. Who say we watch *Psycho*?

Psycho!

Psycho!

Psycho!

See what I'm talking about?

The inmate on the chair turned to the movie channel. I watched myself smile into the camera and welcome viewers to another edition of LRSPTVs award-winning news magazine, *Uptown, Downtown, Get Out of Town!*

I'm your host, Hugh Downtown Brown, I announced.

There were perplexed looks on the faces of my fellow viewers.

Double D, is that you?

It's not me.

Is too you.

It's not me. It's Downtown Brown.

Look like you.

Looks like me but it's not.

The fuck it ain't! You even cut your hair and shaved your beard!

I can cut my hair and shave my beard if I want. It doesn't make me a newsman, now does it?

Y'all shut the fuck up! I'm watching the commercial.

We listened to Booker T espouse the benefits of a welding career.

I want some of what he's got!

It ain't free, motherfucker!

We watched Choo Choo do his shtick.

Who the spic? He crack me up!

It's that loco little Rican from East One.

He a funny dude, man.

Double D, it is too you.

Alright, it's me, I said.

Where you cop them threads, man?

They belong to Booker T.

Oh, man, he just blew up Downtown Brown!

What they pay you to be Downtown Brown, Double D?

Pay me nothing. I did it for kicks.

The commercial ended. Violins played behind the opening credits of *Psycho*. Janet Leigh, in white brassiere and satin slip, lounged in bed with her paramour. All eyes were on her milky white flesh—save two, which I felt boring into my back. I turned. Across the room sat Botha, glaring.

You about a fool, Davis, he yelled. A straight up fool!

The inmates looked his way, then back at the television, perhaps feeling safer in a room with a knife-wielding Anthony Perkins than with Botha. My pulse quickened. I crossed the dayroom and sat at the table next to his. I was close enough to see his yellow eyes and the light reflecting off the beads of his scar. He straightened.

Why do you think I'm a fool, Botha? I said.

You think you in Hollywood, Davis!

I know where I am.

You think the penitentiary your personal playground! Think you can do whatever you want!

I do what I can wherever I'm at.

Why you tell a nigger prison school gonna save his life? Some of these men doin life!

And some will go back to the world one day.

Ain't goin back to the same world you going back to, Davis. It's a world you don't know nothin about.

That's a fact, Botha, but it can't hurt to take something with you wherever you go. Like Booker T says: Skills pay the bills. But you're not being straight with me. You said four years ago to find me some business and mind it, and that's what I've done and you don't like it. I don't know why you don't but that's not my problem. It's your problem.

I don't have a problem, Davis.

You have a problem, Botha. I hope you figure it out.

I could jack you up.

It wouldn't make you feel any better, I said. You'd still have your problem.

He stared at me hard.

I'm not finished with you, Davis, he said.

He walked through the door to B-Wing. I watched him go. I felt good that I'd stood my ground, but I wondered if I had furthered the evolution of his soul or further hardened his heart.

I returned to my seat beneath the television. Buster looked at me.

Damn, Double D! That nigger straight up don't like you!

You can't please everyone, I said.

On the screen Janet Leigh in black brassiere and black satin slip packed her suitcase and prepared to flee with forty thousand dollars in stolen money. I would stay for the famous bloody shower scene.

The next day Bill Dobratz dropped by the welding shop.

What's your wife's address, Dean? he said.

You're a good man, Bill, I said.

It was our baby, Dean, he said. And don't worry about the postage.

NATION OF THE DAMNED

OUTSIDE IN THE DARK, WIND AND RAIN buffeted the building that housed the small prison library. Inside, under bright lights, surrounded by books, Abdul and I caught up on our conversation.

Well, Mr. Downtown Brown, Abdul said, are we ready to add one more alter ego to your growing list?

We sat at the very table in the library as we had three years earlier, following my less than gratifying gold medal victory in the Summer Olympics. Then, Abdul proposed I become involved in his new drama group, The Players of Conviction. He intended to provide an outlet of expression for the oppressed, the luckless and the lame of spirit. Being none of these, I had declined, choosing instead to pursue a Bachelors Degree courtesy of the prison's recent affiliation with Southeastern Illinois University, which pursuit represented unfinished business. Since then, Abdul produced three plays and I earned my degree and, as a practical matter, a certificate in the welding program, yet it seemed no time had passed and the present conversation was merely an adjunct of the previous, without a moment's lapse, as though Abdul dwelt in a timeless realm where everything happened at once. There is only the present moment, he once remarked. Chronology is an illusion that binds the mind of man and prevents him from knowing his true nature. When I asked how to reconcile this doctrine of Everything Happens at Once with the mandate to imagine the future and make it happen, he advised that to escape the wheel of life one must first live it.

What do you have in mind? I said now.

I've written a play, Abdul said, and the time is right to produce it. February is Black History Month. Warden Wainwright plans an evening of celebration in the gym. There will be a sermon by a Baptist Minister of some repute who will praise the progress of civil rights and denounce the evils of racism, followed by my play. In front of a packed house.

And my mission, should I choose to accept it?

To play the role of a racist white cop whose greatest pleasure in life is to break the heads of black gang bangers. He will represent everything the audience despises and holds responsible for their miserable lives and their incarceration. He will be the symbol of four hundred years of oppression, and the focal point of their hatred. Do you have any idea where I can find a Caucasian crazy enough to play the part?

I laughed.

I'll ask around, I said.

Come now, Dean.

I thought you liked me.

I wouldn't ask if I didn't.

Is it safe?

Trust me.

I was filled with a sense of perilous anticipation that brought to mind the last line of Camus' *The Stranger*:

> *All that remained to hope was that on the day of my execution there should be a huge crowd of spectators and that they should greet me with howls of execration.*

All right, Abdul, I said. You've found your crazy Caucasian. What's next?

We meet four nights a week in the Vocational Building. We have two months to rehearse. I would like you to request a transfer to the honor dorm. There's a cell opening soon.

Why would I want to do that, Abdul? I like North One.

Reggie Brown is there, Dean. He plays a major role, and you do several key scenes together. He can help you tweak your part.

I remembered Reggie Brown from my early days in North One. Cofounder of the Cabrini Green Gangsters, he was doing 180 years for the murder of three of Chicago's Finest. He had transferred to the honor dorm shortly after Abdul had.

And you'll like the honor dorm, Dean, Abdul said. It's quiet. There's no lockdown and no lights out. Free movement twenty-four seven. Go to the gym or the library without escort. No restriction on cell visitation. After the play, we'll get you back to North One. What do you say?

I say: Move over, Downtown Brown!

THE ONLY OTHER IN THE CAMP

I SENT A KITE TO THE PLACEMENT OFFICE requesting a transfer to the Honor Dorm. I was informed that cells there were limited and allocated according to the ratio of ethnicity in the camp. The cell opening soon would be assigned to the next African American on the list. There would not be a white cell opening in the foreseeable future.

I asked Mother Goose, inmate assistant to the Placement Officer, to run interference.

The Placement Officer is a white boy, she said. He'd like to help a fellow honkie but a rule is a rule. Everyone in the Honor Dorm is doing hard time. Someone practically has to die before a cell opens up. This is an equal opportunity Penitentiary, Dean Honey. If we gave a black cell to a white boy we would have a race riot. Now, if you were Chinese or Eskimo or Apache Indian, you'd be the only one of a kind and would go to the top of the list.

I was frustrated but I reminded myself: Seek and ye shall find. That night before going to sleep I appealed to my subconscious mind, repository of all knowledge, past, present and future, to find a way. I awoke before dawn to the whisper of my muse, Miranda:

A Romanian Gypsy is one of a kind.

A Romanian Gypsy is one of a kind …

I sat bolt upright in bed. Of course! That's it! I'm not white! I'm *other*! I sent a kite to the Records Office:

In honor of my mother, whose heritage is Romanian Gypsy, and who is ill and not long for this world, I request that my racial preference be changed to Other. This in no way is meant to disparage my own Caucasian roots, of which I am duly proud, but only to honor my ailing mother.

My request was approved, with an FYI that I was officially the only

Other in the camp. I reapplied to the Honor Dorm and was moved to the top of the list. Mother Goose informed me that I would be transferred to my new cell in a week. But Dean, honey, she added— somebody ain't gonna like this!

PORTRAIT OF A PRISON CELL

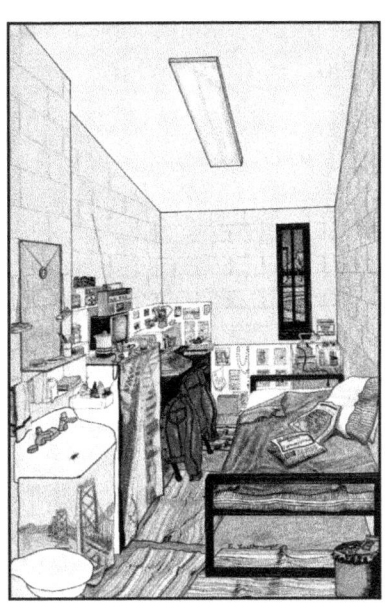

MOTHER GOOSE GAVE ME colored pens and pencils and a twelve by sixteen-inch drawing pad. Booker T gave me a week off from my duties in the welding shop. I sat ten hours a day for seven straight days on the cold concrete floor of the corridor outside my cell and rendered in meticulous detail the cell and its contents, down to the leafless branches of the trees visible through the narrow vertical slit of window in the back wall through which I had watched and felt and smelled the seasons change more than a dozen times; down to the titles on the spines of the many dog-eared books that had been my faithful companions for more than a thousand nights; down to the letters and the images on the front page of the *San Francisco Chronicle* dated November 12th, 1987; down to the knots in the laces of Lola's first pair of tennis shoes, sent to me after her first birthday; down to the wave in Lucy's hair in the photograph in the heart-shaped frame crafted of cigarette package paper by Cornelius Corn Dog Watson, the self-proclaimed *real live nigger* who years ago had vowed to return and make the joint jump; down to the stitching in the blue denim jacket hooked up real tough by Marvelous Marvin Mayo, tailor extraordinaire and previous occupant of the cell who himself had moved on to the honor dorm.

Because the marks made by the pens and the pencils were not erasable, I could make no mistakes. I would meditate long and hard on a feature of the cell, and when it was fixed in my mind I would put my hand to paper and capture it quickly and surely. Fellow inmates stepped over and around me, sometimes stopping to marvel at my work.

On the morning of the eighth day, I transferred my belongings to a white canvas cart. I rolled-up my portrait of North One 11A, secured it with a rubber band and laid it gently on top. I stood a long while regarding the now empty cell, then turned and pushed my cart up the corridor, down which came a new inmate pushing a cart of his own. It's a good house, I said in passing. A very good house.

THE HONOR DORM DAYROOM was deserted, but for an elderly black inmate pushing a mop. I went to the control room window.

Dean Davis, I said. I have reservations.

The officer behind the window didn't smile. He looked at a roster on a clipboard, gave me a key on a string and said, 2B. The porter gave me a silent nod when I rolled my cart across the floor to B-Wing and found cell number two. I transferred my belongings from the cart to the cell and began reconstructing my crib. Hermit Crab Redux. At the door appeared a light-skinned African American inmate, shirtless, with a shock of hair like a small explosion had gone off in his head.

What the fuck are you doing? he said.

I'm moving in, I said.

The fuck you are! My homeboy Lonnie moving in.

I don't know about that.

I'm telling you about that! This cell assigned African American, not Caucasian.

I'm not Caucasian.

Man, what are you talking about?

I'm talking about the box for racial preference, brother. I checked other because they didn't have a box for None of the Above.

That's some jive ass bullshit, white boy. And I ain't your brother!

Suit yourself.

Where I know you from?

Couldn't say.

I know—you're that chump ass newsman, Downtown Brown.

No. I played the part of Downtown Brown. In real life, I'm an inmate same as you.

I know what time it is now. You been freaking off with the Warden. That's how you got this crib, ain't it?

I wanted to say something rude, but a civil tone had served me well thus far and now was no reason to abandon it.

We'll get this straightened out, I said.

Ain't about straighten out, sucker. It's about *gettin* out. Now get your lame ass out Lonnie's house before I go upside your motherfuckin head!

While I considered what to say or do, Stan the Man appeared. He towered over my antagonist.

What's all this noise about? he bellowed.

Ain't none of your business, Stan.

I'm making it my business, Nathan. You messin with my sleep! I'm up all night fryin bacon and scramblin eggs for your sorry ass. I know you don't want me scramblin your nappy head, too!

Nathan scowled at me.

This ain't over yet, newsman, he said.

He walked away. Stan watched him go. He shook his head.

Flea Weight, he said, what kind of shit you stirrin up now?

Not me doing the stirring, Stan, I said. But I wondered if it were true.

We'll kick it later, Flea Weight. I'm going back to bed. Welcome to the honor dorm!

THAT EVENING AFTER CHOW Abdul came by with a copy of his play.

Feel free to mark it up, he said. And listen to this cassette. There's one stanza from each of seven Stevie Wonder songs in the order they appear in the play. Imagine a stanza playing at the beginning of every scene and a final one playing as the curtain comes down. Imagine being Sergeant O'Reilly, Dean. Be one with his bigoted heart. And welcome to The Players of Conviction!

I sat on my bunk and looked out the window in the back wall of my cell. My window on the world. I was twenty yards to the perimeter fence and beyond it the street lamp-illumined parking lot for prison employees, visitors and vendors. To the right I could see the front entrance, a double set of glass doors through which employees passed now and got in their cars and turned on their lights and went their merry way. To their homes. To the nearest Road House. To wherever they fancied. They were free to choose. Freedom was a funny thing. I had steeled myself against the reality of my confinement by asserting that we are all doing time on one side of the fence or another, yet all free on either side, too. That freedom was a state of mind. But the mundane freedom of getting in your car and turning that key and driving on down the road, driving till you ran out of gas and money if that's what you damn well pleased ... well, that was the kind of freedom that would have to wait. At this moment, on this side of the fence, I had a play to read and I was free to mark it up. I turned my back to my window on the world and put my pillow between myself and the wall and read.

THE NATION OF THE DAMNED

THE SETTING

IN THE HOUSING PROJECTS, and on the streets of Chicago, two rival gangs, The Chosen Folk Nation and The Cabrini Green Demons, compete for control of the drug trade. They run amuck, shooting up the projects at night with Uzis. Citizens sleep in their bathtubs to avoid being hit by stray bullets. Elevators are disabled and cops must run up dozens of narrow stairwells to get to the upper floors where the gangsters have cut holes in the walls to escape from one room, and from one building, to the next. They use sniper fire to pick each other off and to keep the cops at bay. When two cops from the Gang Intelligence Unit are killed, the Unit's response is ineffectual. Soon, it is business as usual for the gangs.

SCENE I

The headquarters of The Chosen Folk Nation.

Stevie Wonder's *Village Ghetto Land* plays. We meet Chief Devon the Duke Alexander and his Warlords, Shaka Zulu and Mad Dog. They are all about Money, Murder and Nation Building. They are making new contacts with the Italians for heroin, and with the Columbians for cocaine. They're winning the turf war with their rivals, The Demons. They're making inroads into the suburbs and the boardrooms of the city. Within The Chosen Folk Nation, there is tension between Devon and the ambitious Shaka Zulu.

SCENE II

The headquarters of Chicago's Gang Intelligence Unit.

Stevie Wonder's *Black Man* plays. We meet Captain Percy the Bull Drummond, a beefy black cop who lords it over his own men, and has a special disregard for black gang bangers. We meet Officer Keene O'Reilly, a white cop of Irish descent, and the only white member of the gang-busting unit whose contempt of black gang-bangers rivals that of Bull Drummond. We meet O'Reilly's partner, Robert Hurley, a liberal African American who understands how the culture of the street can turn a happy child into a murderous thug. Bull Drummond refers to him derisively as Cowboy Bob.

Other cops present share Hurley's sympathy. Some have brothers or sons who are gangsters. Or locked up. Or dead.

Drummond tells his men the Mayor wants results or heads will roll! He says bring me some gang bangers! Charge them with anything! Just lock them up! He tells O'Reilly and Cowboy Bob to bring him the Duke and his pussy ass partners, Shaka Zulu and Mad Dog.

SCENE III

The Headquarters of the Gang Intelligence Unit.

Stevie Wonder's *You Haven't Done Nothin* plays. O'Reilly and Cowboy Bob have collared Devon and Shaka and Mad Dog. O'Reilly taunts Shaka.

Maybe you'd like this nightstick up your black ass, Zulu man, he says. It's long and hard and would feel right at home.

How you get your kicks when you're not freaking off with your lame-ass Uncle Tom partner there, O'Reilly? Shaka says.

We jack up niggers and spics, that's how we get our kicks in Chicago—boy!

Shaka Zulu laughs.

Y'ain't gonna get a rise out of me with that boy crap, O'Reilly. I been hearing that shit all my life. What else you be doin for kicks?

Be banging your momma. Be banging your sister. Be banging your babies, too! Their tight little booties! Umm, umm, umm!

O'Reilly delivers these words with such vehemence that Cowboy Bob is startled.

Come on, O'Reilly, he says. You're going too far now.

Shaka Zula goes after O'Reilly. Devon and Mad Dog hold him back. Bull Drummond enters the room.

Recess is over, boys and girls, he says. We're not here to jack up anybody. We're here to make peace. O'Reilly, you and Cowboy Bob go do some paperwork. Me and this posse of posers got some talking to do.

O'Reilly and Cowboy Bob exit the scene. Bull Drummond tells the Duke and Shaka Zulu and Mad Dog that some very naïve politicians in Washington and Chicago have a proposition to make.

I think they're wasting their time and the taxpayers' money, he says. But you punks better take their deal or we will lock you up and throw away the key!

He opens the door. Two men enter: Jesse Jackson of The Rainbow Coalition and Theodore Baker with the Office of Economic Opportunity. They propose to grant $900,000.00 to The Nation to open a job training program and train black youth. Devon will receive a salary of $30,000.00 per year, Zulu and Mad Dog will each receive $20,000.00. In return, they will shut down The Nation, cease and desist all criminal activity, and recruit their members and the members of rival gangs into the training program.

The Duke says he'll think about it. Shaka says, We ain't thinking about a motherfuckin thing. The Duke turns on Shaka. I'm Chief of The Chosen Folk Nation, nigger, he says, and you ain't Shaka of shit! So don't be telling me what we be thinking about! Drummond says, All right, kids, kiss and make up. Y'all got a decision to make.

Jackson gives his business card to the Duke. He says, Do the right thing, Devon.

SCENE IV

Visiting room of the State Penitentiary.

Stevie Wonder's *Nothing's Too Good For My Baby* plays. Devon visits his big brother Deontay, founder of The Chosen Folk Nation. Devon tells him about the deal. Deontay encourages him to take it. Says it's time to get his life right. Says the Nation ain't what it used to be. There's no more justice. No more love.

We didn't start out as a gang, Devon, Deontay says. We stood for the community. We gave back to the people like Robin Hood—now you just robbin the hood! Extorting the mom and pop shops you supposed to protect. Y'all just the Black Mafia now, Devon, no better than Al Capone's gang.

Goddamn right, Deontay, Devon says proudly. If that Guinea Whop Capone was alive today, he'd be shakin and we'd be takin!

Deontay hangs his head in despair.

You going for the okeedoke, Devon, he says, and it's breakin my heart. Chosen Folk used to be a Nation of the people. Now it's a Nation of the Damned! Boy, don't you get it? You done opened the gates of hell!

After a moment of strained silence. Deontay says, You still looking out for my little girl?

What you think, Deontay? Aisha taken care of real nice! Be stayin with a friend of mine down the block from Cabrini Green. Get walked to school every day. Tomorrow I'll walk that little girl to school my own self. Make sure she know she be taken care of.

SCENE V

Devon's apartment.

Stevie Wonder's *He's A Misstra Know-it-all* plays. Devon has been up all night doing cocaine with a lady friend. He calls the woman who watches over Aisha and says he has business. She'll have to walk Aisha to school herself. The woman screams back: She's dead, Devon! She's dead!

What?

Aisha is dead! It's all on the news. She went to visit a friend at Cabrini Green last night and was hit by a stray bullet. Don't you watch the television, Devon?

Devon drops the phone. He holds his head between his hands. He sinks to his knees. He delivers an impassioned soliloquy—To Be or Not to Be a Gangster. He takes a business card out of his coat pocket and dials the phone.

Put me through to Jesse Jackson, he says—and I don't mean tomorrow!

SCENE VI

Headquarters of The Chosen Folk Nation.

We hear Stevie Wonder's *A Place in the Sun*. Shaka Zulu and Mad Dog express their condolences to Devon. Mad Dog says: Yeah, we real sorry about your little girl, dog.

Devon struggles to contain his emotions. He pitches taking the deal.

Mad Dog says, For thirty grand a year? We makin that much on a Saturday night! Why you wanna be a house nigger for chump change?

It ain't about the money, Devon says. We can make a difference. We can make a wrong thing right.

Fuck a whole lot of making a wrong thing right, Devon, Mad Dog says. If it ain't about the money, it ain't about shit!

Shaka Zulu, who has been sitting quietly, gets up and walks behind the couch where the Duke sits.

Yeah, Devon, he says, we real sorry about your little girl—but that don't stop me from snuffing your sorry ass!

He slips a garrote around Devon's neck Mafia style.

You think we don't know you already made that deal? he says.

Devon clutches at the garrote.

And don't you never ever disrespect me in front of the man, nigger! Shaka Zulu says.

He tightens the garrote.

Who the Chief of The Chosen Folk now, chump? he says.

Devon struggles till he is still.

Mad Dog, put a bullet in this punk, Shaka Zulu says.

He already dead, Shaka, Mad Dog says.

He ain't dead enough for me! Want him more dead! Pop a cap on his ass!

Mad Dog pulls his pistol and unloads it into the body of the already dead Devon.

There is diabolical laughter. Shaka and Mad Dog become immobile. The rest of the cast comes on stage and becomes immobile, too. As the lights dim and the curtain comes down, we hear Stevie Wonder singing *Heaven Help Us All.*

THE RESURRECTION OF DANTÉ

IT'S A POWERFUL PIECE, ABDUL, I said. It jumped off the page and held me till the curtain came down.

We sat at a table by the oval track in a patch of sunlight created by a rift in the dense cloud cover above. Abdul's smile said he was pleased to be praised.

Tell me more, he said.

Stevie Wonder's lyrics made the story come alive, I said. I'll never hear him the same way again. When he sings *Heaven Help Us All* as the final curtain comes down, I got chills. I loved the Hamlet-like soliloquy of Devon when he learns Aisha is dead. We feel his grief and despair. And I like the irony of Devon being garroted mafia style, after the way he had trashed Capone. I like how the demise of Devon was foreshadowed in the first scene, how tragedy seemed inevitable, yet we hold out hope for a happy ending, which I'm glad we didn't get. It would have seemed sappy. That said, I'm a little confused about the message, Abdul. It seems ambiguous. If Devon was killed because he wanted to take the deal and do the right thing, won't the audience think he was a sucker for trying? Won't the final scene justify their commitment to money, murder and mayhem?

Many will feel that way, Dean, but a few others will understand that he was not killed by a corrupt society or a racist white cop but by his own people who, if they don't get their lives right, are doomed to dwell for all time in The Nation of the Damned. The message is for those who get it, and we hope they spread the word. But give me your thoughts on O'Reilly.

I think he's one dimensional, I said. He needs a human side. He's a malignant spirit all right, but like Genghis Khan or Attila the Hun, he probably loves his wife and children.

Abdul frowned.

He's there to fan the flames of hatred and bigotry, Dean. How would you make him more human without detracting from his role?

I'd have his fellow officers show a certain affection for him, Abdul. Make him an Italian Archie Bunker with a dark side. His name should be Danté Allegro, not O'Reilly. An Irish cop is a cliché. In the second scene, before the Captain enters the room, have there be an exchange amongst the assembled officers. Someone says, Come on, Allegro, everyone knows a whop ain't white! Allegro retorts that Sicilians ain't white, but his people are from Bergamo in Northern Italy, where Italians are white. His brother cops chant, Whoppo, Dago, Danté Allegro! I think this bit of levity will add dimension to his bigotry during his confrontation with Shaka Zulu in scene three.

We can do that, Dean. Why the name Danté Allegro?

In memory of a friend who was burned in a fire, I said.

Consider it done, he said. What else?

The line We jack up niggers and spics, that's how we get our kicks in Chicago? Great line. Lyrical. I would introduce it in scene two. The Captain tells Allegro and Cowboy Bob to bring him the Duke and his pussy ass partners. He exits, leaving Allegro and Cowboy Bob alone. Allegro bobs his head and sings that line absently, without ill will, reflecting something innocent about his bigotry. Cowboy Bob says, Allegro, don't be singing that racist bullshit around me!

He asks Allegro why he is so prejudiced. Allegro says he doesn't need a reason. It's just how he is. Cowboy Bob says gang bangers are victims as much as the people they prey upon. Allegro thinks this is stupid. Cowboy Bob says Danté is stupid. Some repartee along these lines, Abdul.

Very good, Dean, Abdul said, but it will be on you to transform a lovable Italian Archie Bunker into a full-blown bigot in Scene Three so that Shaka Zulu gets convincingly angry and the audience with him. Your fellow players have no problem expressing rage. They've been eating at that table for a long time. But you have some work to do. I want you to probe your memories for any experience that might cause you to feel and behave the way Danté does. We want complete emotional identification with the part. We don't want you pretending to be a racist. We want you to be one.

I see. A *Get in Touch with my Inner Bigot* sort of thing.

If you will.

I'll see what I can dig up.

You'll be surprised.

By the way, how does Major Drumm feel about being lampooned as Bull Dog Drummond?

He's such a bonehead, he's too unaware to have noticed.

But the similarity in names, I said. He couldn't have failed to notice that.

I changed the name after he approved the script.

He won't be happy.

He needs a mirror held up so he knows who he is.

He won't like what he sees. How about Shaka's gun in the final scene. How do we do that?

He'll reach under his coat and point his finger. The sound of the shots are recorded, courtesy of Bill Dobratz. As is the voice of the girl on the phone who screams Aisha's dead, Devon! Don't you watch television?

Whose voice is it?

Maria's.

You know Maria?

Let's say we're acquainted.

You dog, Abdul.

Let's walk, Dean, he said. I need to stretch my legs.

We walked counter-clockwise around the oval track. From the other direction came Choo Choo Rodriguez, with his hands in his pockets and his chin on his chest.

Choo Choo, I said. Que pasa, amigo!

Choo Choo looked up. He seemed to struggle to remember where he was.

Aiee! Downtown Brown! My cellie in the hole!

Choo Choo, this is Abdul. Abdul, this is Choo Choo Rodriguez.

I know who Choo Choo Rodriguez is, Abdul said. He's that famous Puerto Rican funny man we've been hearing all about. John Leguizamo ain't got nothing on you, Choo Choo!

You a funny man, too, Abdul. But Leguizamo is Colombian, man.

Choo Choo, I said, you're not looking too funny today. Where's your smile?

The Latin Kings didn't like our commercial, amigo. They say I make Puerto Ricans look like payasos estupidas, stupid clowns. I tell them to lighten up, we got to have un poco ligueza, a little levity. We're only on this planet for a short time. They say be careful it's not too short, amigo.

They'll get over it, Choo Choo, I said. Walk with us. We'll cheer you up.

No, man. I'm not in the mood. I'll see you around.

Choo Choo walked away. I watched him go. Abdul and I resumed our stroll. At the top of the track a huddle of inmates stopped speaking and watched as we approached.

There's Nathan, I said. I'll bet one of the others is Lonnie.

The tall brother with the goatee and the cornrows, Abdul said.

Come with me, Abdul, I said. I want to have a word with him.

We approached the group. Nathan stiffened and took his hands out of his pockets.

What it be like, Abdul? Lonnie said.

Slow motion, Lonnie, Abdul said. What's up with you?

Ain't nothin poppin, Ride. Is that your road doggie?

He's nobody's road doggie, Lonnie.

Nathan glared at me.

What the fuck you want, Newsboy?

I ignored him. I looked at Lonnie.

You must be Lonnie, I said.

Lonnie looked down at me.

Yeah?

I want to apologize, Lonnie. I didn't mean for things to come down the way they did.

How come they did, then?

Abdul is doing a play, I said, and I'm in it and we needed to kick it about my part, so I took the cell, but I didn't think about how if I got it someone else wouldn't. Sometimes I'm stupid that way. But I want to make it right.

How you gonna make it right?

I'll give up the cell after the play and you can have it. You're still number one on the list for African American. Till then we'll say it's yours but I'm paying you rent.

Keep talking.

A brick of squares a month. Plus a brick when I leave, right after the play. Three bricks. What do you say?

I say a brick up front, a brick a month, and a brick when you leave. Four bricks.

All right. But you know this means you're my landlord. If there's a problem with the plumbing you've got to fix it.

Lonnie said nothing.

Just bullshitting you, Lonnie, I said. I'll give a brick to Nathan Wednesday when I make store. Is that cool?

It's cool.

I nodded toward Nathan.

This man has your back, Lonnie, I said.

He's alright, Lonnie said.

I thought he was going to jack me up right there when he saw me in your cell, I said.

Stan the Man saved you an ass whuppin all right, Nathan said.

So, Lonnie, I said ... we're good?

We're good.

Check out Abdul's play, Lonnie. It's deep. You'll dig it.

We'll be there.

Abdul and I rounded the top of the track and started down the other side.

Well done, Dean, he said. I'm impressed.

It's not a good time to have an enemy in the house, I said.

It's never a good time, Abdul said.

Tell me something, Abdul. You know Lonnie. You must have known I'd be taking his cell.

Yes.

Yet you persuaded me to move.

It was to my advantage. And yours.

But you would have foreseen the outcome.

Yes.

And you didn't care?

It was on you to foresee the outcome and to care or not. I opened a door. You went through it. But you've made amends and the Universe smiles. Now we move on. I'll tweak *The Nation of the Damned* and give you the revised script tomorrow. Search your soul for the dark side of Danté Allegro. Our first rehearsal is Thursday. Bring us your very best bigot!

I walked silently beside Abdul and wondered what I might discover when I sifted through the soil of my memories.

A RIVER OF POISON, A RESERVOIR OF RAGE

A TRULY MAMBY PAMBY PERFORMANCE, DEAN! Abdul told me at a table in the dayroom after our first rehearsal. A less daunting Danté Allegro I cannot imagine!

I had met my fellow Players of Conviction that night and there could not have been a more gracious group of thespian gang bangers. I knew Reggie Brown, and recognized most of the others from the yard or the gym where, playing hoops or pumping iron or just standing around, they could be fierce and intimidating, but this night they made me feel welcome and part of a noble endeavor.

Following introductions, we played a game of Charades. The large and powerful inmate who played Bull Drummond correctly guessed that Abdul was miming Stevie Wonder's *I Just Called To Say I Love You*.

We rehearsed Scene One, the gathering of The Chosen Folk Nation. I observed that the players were intimately familiar with their roles, having lived them in the real world. In Scene Two, as Danté, I was comfortable engaging in repartee with my fellow officers—the requisite sarcasm came naturally—but in scene three, following the heated exchange between Reggie Brown as Shaka Zulu, and me as Allegro, Brown scowled.

Come on, Davis! he shouted. Give me something I can use! Don't be grinnin like a fool when you tellin me you gonna fuck my momma! Say it like you mean it! Make me mad!

It came from your head, not your heart, Abdul said now. Tell me what you found when you searched your memory for an experience upon which to base your bigotry.

I remembered back to my childhood, Abdul, I said. I was born in East Oakland in a neighborhood half black and half white and rapidly losing its white half. My father worked on the docks. By the time I was six years old and entered first grade, we were the last white family on the block. All my friends were black. I didn't know the difference. My first crush was on the little girl who sat in front of me in school, Natasha. She had a creamy beige complexion and dark eyes and would let me run my fingers through her long shiny hair. But she wouldn't give me her phone number. Said her momma would be mad if a boy called.

My best friends were Tyrone and Oscar. They lived in the adjoining half of our duplex. The older brother, Tyrone, was skinny and always smirking. Oscar was pudgy with fat round cheeks. We had pea shooter wars in the alley behind our house and played marbles in the park a block away. I had a huge collection of marbles, which I kept in a Folgers Coffee can. I had opals and glimmers and bloods and rubies. I had swirlies and tigers and jumbos and peewees, and the biggest damn selection of steelies on the block. One day Tyrone stole one of my steelies. He'd knocked one of my peewees out of the ring with his shooter and when he went to claim it, he palmed a steely. I said, Tyrone, I saw that. Give me back my steelie. He said, I didn't take no damn steelie! Did, too, I said, and we rolled around in the dirt punching each other till he gave me back my steelie. After that we were friends again. The next year my father, who had become an insurance salesman, and made a ton of money selling policies to his fellow dockworkers, moved us all to Sausalito in Marin County where now all my friends were white. But I've never forgotten Tyrone and Oscar. And Natasha, too.

Abdul scrunched his face in disbelief.

That's it, Dean? he said. That's all you've got to base your hatred of African Americans on—six-year-old Natasha wouldn't give you her phone number, and Tyrone stole your steelie but he gave it back?

I shrugged.

I'm afraid so, I said.

And in all your dealing days, you didn't do business with African Americans?

Only Demetrius, my distributor in Oakland. He was honest, forthright and fair. He never burned me.

Abdul shook his head.

This will never do, he said.

Sorry, Abdul, I said. I can't express feelings I haven't had.

But you can, Dean, he said. And you will!

His tone was ominous. I remained silent.

Are you familiar with the Akashic Records?

No, I said. Do they do the Motown sound?

He ignored my humor.

They're considered The Mind of God, Dean, known to every major religion throughout history. They're called by Tibetan Buddhists Atman, and by Christian mystics The Book of Life, which determines who gets into heaven and who doesn't. They make possible all manner of paranormal phenomenon: telepathy, clairvoyance, prognostication, past life regression, channeling—and a good theatrical performance. They're the repository of every thought, word, deed and emotion ever produced by conscious beings from the beginning to the end of time, and it's there you will find the acrimony you so sorely lack. You can be certain that if you have not personally had an experience which aroused animosity toward people of color, those emotions are stored in the Akashic Records, and you can access them and make them your own, and use them to inform your portrayal of Danté Allegro.

Interesting, I said. How do I do that?

You create a state of mind which opens a channel to the Records. This can be done with Yoga, deep sleep, sleep deprivation, extreme fatigue, self-flagellation and psychedelic drugs. But there's no time to learn yoga, and we're not going to ask you to spank your own behind or get you stoned. We'll just ask you to imagine an event which would cause you to genuinely dislike colored folks. To despise them. Imagine this event intensely, Dean. Play it in slow motion. Infuse it with sensory details: hear it, see it, smell it, feel it. Make it real. Doing so will cause the appropriate emotions to flow from the Records to your personal psyche, which will allow you to portray Danté Allegro convincingly, not in the pussyfooting fashion we saw tonight before Shaka Zulu put your ass in check.

Damn, Abdul! You're making me feel bad! All right, what sort of event do I need to imagine?

I suggest you imagine that your lovely wife Lucy is raped by a posse of black gangsters and disfigured. Or better yet, Lola blossoms into a beautiful young lady who is brutally raped by that posse and is traumatized for life. You fill in the details.

What? You want me to imagine a bunch of gang bangers raping my grown-up baby girl so I can learn to hate black people?

Yes.

That is warped, Abdul. Weird beyond words.

It will have the effect we are looking for.

But is hating black people an effect I'm looking for?

If it serves the purpose.

I don't know, Abdul. Is it permanent?

It can be nullified.

How?

By reversing the process. You'll figure it out.

All right, I said. I'm in. I'll imagine a horrid scene that will make me hate all you motherfuckers—but I won't like it!

You're not supposed to like it, Dean. Next rehearsal is Tuesday night. Bring us the beast!

I SAT CROSS-LEGGED ON MY BUNK with my back against the wall. I closed my eyes and fell into a dream:

Daddy, where are we?

Chicago, baby.

I know that ... but this neighborhood!

She looked nervously out the car window at the fierce and terrible faces of black men stamping their feet and warming their hands over fires set in trash cans; at men huddled in doorways of liquor stores drinking out of brown paper bags; at the blowzy and bedraggled women on street corners opening their coats for passing cars; saw a drunken man kick a drunken woman, who fell and lay sobbing and cursing on the sidewalk; saw four youths punching another who cowered against a graffiti-stained wall.

I took a wrong turn, I said.

No kidding, Daddy! We're in the ghetto!

It's no worse than East Oakland.

It's ten times worse!

We'll find the hotel.

I hope it's not on this side of town.

You could have gone to UCLA, I said. Or UCSF. Or St. Mary's in Moraga. They all wanted you.

I turned to face her. I put my hand on her shoulder and admired her pristine profile in the glow of the dashboard lights.

My brilliant, beautiful baby, I said.

Oh, daddy, she said, putting her hand on mine. Just get us out of here.

I supported Lola's choice of Northwestern against the wishes of my wife, Lucy, not only because it had the program she wanted, but because there was history and culture in Chicago not to be found on the West Coast. She would become a more enlightened young woman for the experience. Sophisticated and urbane. Perhaps she'd find her true love. And I had some history here myself, having spent five years in Lime Ridge State Penitentiary almost twenty years ago. Of course that was down south, not on the Mean Streets of the Windy City, but when visiting Lola I would get to know these streets a little. Maybe I'd run into an old pal from Lime Ridge: Abdul, Choo Choo, Mother Goose, Stan the Man. We would kick it about back in the day. Would we even recognize one another? It was so long ago it seemed like a dream.

We turned a corner onto a street darker than the last. At the end of the block a gathering of black youth loitered under a street light.

I'll get directions, I said.

Daddy, don't stop.

I know what I'm doing.

Oh, God.

You stay in the car.

She slid down in her seat.

I parked near the curb and got out. The gang of youth stopped talking as I approached.

Yo! I said with a friendly smile.

They looked me up and down. They looked at my car.

Pops, you on the wrong side of town, one of them said.

Yeah, I'm lost, I said. I zigged when I should of zagged. I'm looking for the Hilton. Can you help me out, Brother?

Ain't this a bitch! Ol boy think he my brother!

There was laughter from the crowd. They gathered around me.

Very nice, one of them said, fingering the lapel of my black leather trench coat.

I pushed his hand away.

Gimmee the coat, bitch! he said.

Whaat?

The coat, bitch! Give it up!

I don't think so! I said.

I stepped back and bumped into the man behind me. He shoved me forward.

A tall slim youth in dreadlocks slid his fingertips along the shiny hood of my rented car.

Nice ride, he said.

It's a Lincoln Continental, I said lamely.

Gimme the keys, motherfucker!

I wondered with a sudden sick feeling if I lacked the words and the presence of mind to keep a bad situation from getting worse. Twenty years ago in the gym or on the yard of Lime Ridge, it would have been different with only myself to look out for, but today ...

Lola stepped out of the car.

Daddy, she said in a frightened voice, are you alright?

Lola, get back in the car.

Lookee here now, one of the crowd said. Check out the bitch! Ol boy here a player! Come here, girl.

Lola, get back in the car, I said.

You come when I call, bitch!

Lola stepped forward meekly. One of the crowd put his hand on her arm and turned her around. Goddamn, he said. That's some sweet ass booty!

She's my daughter! I exclaimed.

You pimping your own baby girl, pops?

Now listen, guys, we don't—

Shut the fuck up, old man, said the one who had summoned Lola. He brought his fist around in a wide arc to my temple. My knees buckled but I didn't go down.

If you touch her, I said, my voice trembling with fear and humiliation, I'll—

You'll do what? Beat us up, old man?

There was more laughter.

From the back of the pack came a commanding voice.

The bitch is mine!

A figure stepped forward. The young gangsters stepped aside. He was old and hard and scowling and scarred. He stopped in front of me. His gaze was contemptuous. That scar, from his temple to the corner of his lip! Where had I seen it before? Like a string of knots beneath the skin. Could it be?

Botha! I said, a sudden faint hope stirring that our time together long ago constituted some kind of bond that would now save me.

How you know my name, motherfucker? he said.

I'm Davis, Botha. You remember. We did time together in Lime Ridge. North One. A long time ago.

The old gangster squinted.

Davis … Davis … .I remember your lame ass now. Danté Allegro, the wannabe cop. You get your kicks jacking up niggers and spics! You gonna jack me up now? Because here I am, motherfucker!

He back-handed me hard. I saw stars against a field of red. I felt the flesh of my lip split. Tasted the warm salt of my own blood. I blinked away the tears.

Y'all take care of this lightweight, Botha said to the group. I got me some business to do.

He looked at Lola. Lola back away.

Botha … don't, I stammered.

Someone punched me in the rib cage. The blows came down. When I regained consciousness, I was on my back. Cold rain spattered my face. I rolled onto my side, felt the cartilage of my cracked ribs tear. I was missing a tooth, and my coat and my wallet and my car … and I was alone.

Lola?

I struggled up and saw her on the far side of the street, sitting on the sidewalk, leaning against a wall, her legs spread wide.

Lola?

I hobbled across. I sank down beside her. Rivulets of blood coursed from her loins, mixed with the rain, and meandered across the pavement to the curb. Her face was battered, her hair hung limply, her lips were parted in a silent scream. I waved my hand in front of her eyes. Lola? Lola? She did not respond. Oh, baby, I said, pulling her head to my chest. I wailed to the night sky: Botha, you motherfucker! I will kill you! I will kill you all!

WE SAT IN THE DAYROOM DRINKING COFFEE from quart-sized plastic cups.

Tell me about it, Dean, Abdul said.

It was ugly, Abdul, I said. And melodramatic as hell. I used every cliché in the book to demonize African Americans, especially that of violating our women.

How did it make you feel?

Like I hate you, Abdul. You and all of your people!

I smiled and put my hand on his shoulder.

Not really, Abdul, I said. I don't hate anyone. But I'll say this: the darkest, vilest, most insidious emotions poured into me from the Akashic Records. They flowed through my veins like a river of poison and I now have one huge reservoir of rage to draw upon when I do Danté Allegro in scene three—Shaka, get your black ass back!

Abdul returned the smile.

That's what we're talking about, Dean!

And indeed, when I next rehearsed scene three with Reggie Brown, he took a step back and opened his eyes wide.

Goddamn, boy! he said. Where did that come from?

WHITE DEVILS

A DULL HALF MOON HUNG IN THE SKY like the failing eye of a dying cat. Inmates under guard streamed to the gym after the evening meal from housing units in all corners of the camp. Abdul and I strolled to the gym unescorted, a privilege of our honor dorm status, after having spent the day with our fellow Players of Conviction preparing the stage for the evening's performance. Bill Dobratz had contributed his handyman skills to rig the lighting and the sound system. Warden Wainwright had dropped by periodically to coordinate the preparations and remind us that he was the Director of Events.

A cold breeze blew across the compound. I felt its icy fingers on my face, a greeting from a distant place. I was calm and detached. I had done all I could to prepare. I had poured myself into my role. There was nothing left but for the night to unfold.

Inmates filled the bleachers on the side of the gym facing the stage, rowdy in anticipation of a good show. Few white inmates were among them. My fellow players and I took seats in the first row for the presentation of the Reverend Tipton Lee Brown, out of St. Louis, Missouri, who had marched with Martin Luther King Jr. and was now the pastor of a congregation that included Booker T. Williams. The Reverend Brown would chronicle the history of the Civil Rights Movement, laud its victories and address the challenges to come.

I noticed the beefed up security on opposite sides of the bleachers and on either side of the exit door, a dozen or more green-uniformed officers, Major Drumm among them, who often spoke into his hand-held radio.

Warden Wainwright stood by the locker room door alongside a slight, trim black man in sharply creased black slacks, a grey wide-lapelled herringbone jacket, a pale blue shirt, blue bow tie, matching handkerchief in his breast pocket, and steel-rimmed glasses. He stood still as a sentinel, listening and nodding as the Warden spoke, but not meeting his gaze. The Warden left his side and walked to the podium on the stage. He blew into the microphone. He rubbed his hands together.

Thank you all for being here, he said. We hope you enjoy the show as much as we have enjoyed putting it together. We commence the evening with a presentation by a dynamic speaker, and conclude with our resident theatre group, The Players of Conviction, performing the original drama *The Nation of the Damned.*

The Warden hesitated. He affected an air of chagrin.

I was prepared to present to you the renowned Reverend Tipton Lee Brown of St. Louis, Missouri, he said. The Reverend Brown is a colleague of Martin Luther King Jr. and would have spoken to you, from decades of personal experience, about the history and accomplishments of the Civil Rights movement. Unfortunately, the Reverend has been called away and regrets he cannot be here with you.

There were scattered boos from the audience. Wainwright held up a hand and smiled, rather smugly, I thought.

However, he said, we have a worthy replacement who, I have it on the best authority, is himself a dynamic speaker with an enlightened point of view on issues of justice, equality and civil rights. Gentlemen, allow me to present the Reverend Dr. Gideon Demarcus Love!

There was light applause and a few shouts of recognition.

You go, Gideon!

You The Man!

Abdul laughed.

We are about to have us some fun, he said.

You know this guy? I said.

I do, he said, and I know his message and I can promise you the Warden does not or the good Reverend Dr. Love would not be here!

The Warden walked away from the podium. The slight, dapper Reverend walked toward it. They met in the middle and again the Warden spoke briefly and again the man nodded but did not meet the Warden's gaze. He went to the podium and put the palms of his hands flat upon it and stared down between them and gathered himself. The overhead lights reflected off the lenses of his glasses and off his high, broad forehead.

He raised his eyes and scanned the audience slowly. They grew quiet under his gaze. He spread his hands and spoke in a booming voice that belied his slight stature.

My brothers! My friends! My people! On behalf of the Lord God Almighty, by whatever name you know him and love him—Allah, Jehovah, Shakti or Jah—I greet you and bless you and bestow upon you his peace and his power!

Amen, Brother! came a shout from the audience.

The Reverend put his hand over his heart.

Today my heart is in turmoil, he said. My heart is in tears. I look upon you, the most beautiful, the most intelligent of God's Chosen People, and I ask: Why oh why are your black asses locked up in the white man's jail?

A ripple went through the crowd.

Tell it like it is, Gideon!

He's wasting no time, Abdul said.

The Reverend continued.

You might say it's because you committed a crime and now you're doing the time, that's just how it goes, but I say no! It's because the white man is evil! Oh, yes, evil in his stinking flesh, evil in his blood, evil in the marrow of his bones, evil behind his lying eyes. He is the devil himself and he is afraid of you!

Major Drumm stiffened. He spoke into his radio.

The Reverend pointed his finger at the audience.

Yes, afraid you're going to take back what he has been taking from you. At the dawn of civilization, while your ancestors anointed their beautiful black skin with frankincense and myrrh, and adorned their magnificent black bodies with silk and satin, gold, silver and jewels, and flavored their food with spices from all corners of the globe, and built mighty cities to the greater glory of God, and taught poetry and mathematics and astronomy to their beautiful black children, the white man crawled on his hands and knees on the floors of the caves of Europe, all hairy and smelly, grunting and beating his children, dragging his women by their straggly hair, eating raw meat with his yellow teeth and sleeping in the dirt with his filthy dogs!

The Reverend paused. There was knowing laughter and murmurs of bitter assent from the audience. He continued.

Now the man locking you up in his filthy jails where he can keep you in check. Crackers get nervous when you are free to move about. When you are free to be organized. The El Rukins, The Black Gangster Disciples, The Nation of Islam, The Black Panthers—whoever is organized has the power to knock the devil off his throne and he can't be having that. No sir! He takes the smartest of our people and locks you up where he can keep you in check. He lets you have your liquor and your dope and your homosexuals and you go for it. You go for the okeedoke. Happy as pigs in shit! So happy he has to build more prisons. Contracts them out to corporations. Puts them on the stock market. Prisons are the most thriving industry in America! The farmers sell their land and get rich. Contractors build the prisons and get rich. Local boys whose coal mines and factories are shut down are given uniforms and a paycheck for keeping you in line. And judges and prosecutors get kickbacks from the prison corporations for finding you guilty. The 13th Amendment abolished slavery, my brothers, but if you're charged with a crime you're a slave all over again. The man can get thirty-five, forty years out of each one of you, more than he got out of a cotton picking negro two hundred years ago! You know what I'm talking about.

The Reverend took the blue handkerchief out of his breast pocket and dabbed at his sweating forehead. He dabbed at his lips. He lowered his voice.

My brothers, by what devious means does the white man turn you into his puppet? He starts by dumbing you down. Used to be that a public High School taught Latin, biology, chemistry, physics. It had laboratories. Music programs. Libraries. Counselors. Now all the money gone from public schools. The budget been cut. Reappropriated to the agenda of the rich white masters. Schools in the ghetto nothing but training camps for criminals and convicts. Instead of counselors, now they have security guards!

Reverend Love stepped back from the podium. His smile was ironic.

But that's all right, he said. Still have football. Still have basketball. Brother, you move that ball real good, you might get a scholarship to a real school where they don't care if you stay stupid as a monkey, because you're bringing them honor and glory and alumni dollars! And if you're real good, you go to the NFL or the NBA, where the White Devil gets rich off the sweat of the new slave generation! But how many of you don't make it to the NFL or the NBA? The rest of you are shooting hoops in the prison gym, pumping iron on the yard. Pumping homosexuals, too. Happy as pigs in shit, while your woman is on the street humping for scratch to feed your babies who sit at home alone watching television, getting more dumbed down by idiot sitcoms that show grinning stereotyped negroes who want what the white people have but ain't never going to get because there ain't no jobs for them when they grow up except hustling in the hood. Move over, Brother, make room for your baby boy, come to do time with his daddy—if he ain't already killed by some cracker ass cop who shoots first and ask questions later. Why ain't that man charged with murder? Why ain't he locked up alongside of you? Why don't they fry his ass in the electric chair or fill his veins with poison till he dies a miserable death?

The Reverend became quiet. The question hung in the air. The audience responded.

That's right! Why don't he?

Put his ass in my cell.

The Reverend spoke low and close to the microphone.

Now let me ask you this: Why are you all making the man's job easy? Yes, you! Let me give you some numbers. There were 746 homicides in Chicago last year. One every eleven hours and forty-six minutes. The majority of those homicides were black men killing black men. 112 of those victims were youth between eleven and twenty years old. Fifty-six percent of them murders were done with guns. Now where do you get them guns? You buy them from the gun dealer. And from where does the gun dealer get them guns? From Uncle Sam! That's right. Trace it up the line, you'll find the man is feeding those guns into the black community so you all can kill each other and make his job easy. Don't be played for a sucker!

Now let's talk about dope. Where does all that crack cocaine come from? I know you don't drive down to Bogota over the weekend.

No, that cocaine is delivered by the CIA, who buys it from South American gangsters with taxpayer dollars, then funnels it to the ghetto to finance their dirty war against brown people who are fighting and dying for Democracy in their own country. Then you all kill each other in your crazy-ass dope-fried crack-fueled drug wars or get shot dead by the police or locked up in the white man's jail.

Oh, yes, the White Devil is the Master of Trickery. The CIA, the FBI, the Gang Intelligent Unit of the Chicago PD, they infiltrate the black community every which way. Through the front door and the back door. Through the walls and the windows. They infiltrate the gangs, the mosques, the Nation of Islam, the Black Panthers. Wherever you have a leader who wants to organize his people and lead them out of 400 years of slavery, that's where you find the sneaky spy, sowing seeds of discontent so you can't get organized and knock the White Devil off his throne of evil. I don't mean white spy, either. He looks like you, he talks like you, he smiles like you. He gives you high fives, eats your chicken, licks his fingers, says, Be down, Brother! One love! He talks the talk, but all the time he is recording your conversation and taking your picture, sending them back to his boss, the tricky White Devil.

Oh, yes, he has us right where he wants us—divided. And when someone comes along with the courage and the wisdom to unite us, that nigger got to go! Malcolm X, Marcus Garvey, Huey Newton, Eldridge Cleaver, and lately the gifted brother Mumia Abul Jamal, these Brothers tell it like it is and The Man can't be having that. No sir! You know what I'm talking about.

The Reverend put his left hand in his jacket pocket and adjusted his glasses with his right hand. He chuckled.

Let me tell you the most devious trickery of all, he said. I thought I'd seen everything. Used to be if a negro even winked at a white woman, the man would string his ass up. Now he be giving them away. Look at all the bling-ass hip-hopping rap stars off to Las Vegas with white women on their arms! Ain't they the cat's meow! Forgetting what they left behind in Brooklyn. The Bronx. Compton. The South Side of Chicago. Now why would a black man proud of his own race want to get next to the daughter of the White Devil who lynched his father and raped his mother and put his women in the kitchens of their women? My Brothers, the White Devil tricking you! Twisting your minds with a little white pussy! And you be slobbering to get you some, while your beautiful black sisters, Laquita and Ranisha and Rihanni and Shacora, can't find a decent black brother to lie down with. Be home alone feeding your babies with breast milk tainted with crack cocaine, or on the street being pimped by you for money you spend on the white man's daughter! Ain't this sick? Brothers, leave them she-devil bitches alone! They the White Devil's trick! You know what I'm talking about.

The Reverend sighed.

How about them black athletes? he said. Making millions of dollars a year endorsing products that make you kill your own brother for a pair of tennis shoes. Living in neighborhoods you can't afford. Sending their kids to the white man's schools, while yours learn crime in the ghetto. Black politicians, too, in the pockets of The Man. Saying, I got your back, when behind closed doors they're saying: I got mine! And while I'm at it, the Baptist Preacher don't get no pass. Telling you, Be nice to your Uncle Charlie! Don't be tearing up the street! Don't be stealing back the chicken he stole from you! If The Man takes your pants, give him your shirt! Turn the other cheek! We shall overcome! Oh, yeah, the White Devil love Dr. Martin Luther King. Give him his own day. Ain't that sweeter than sweet potato pie? But you won't be seeing no Malcolm X Day. No Louis Farrakhan Day. No Marcus Garvey Day. No Eldridge Cleaver Day. No Mumia Abul Jamal day. No Gideon Demarcus Love Day. No sir, cause real live niggers don't get their own day. The Reverend Love ain't lying.

Brothers, let us now talk about badges and bullets. Boy, oh boy, do I get riled up when I see a black man dressed in blue! These Uncle Tom's trading black power for blue power because they want to be on the side that's winning. Brothers, there won't be a badge big enough to hide behind when the house comes down. Don't shoot me, I'm one of you all! will be their pitiful cry … but they should have thought of that when they put on that uniform. Take it off, I say. And take off that green uniform, too! And that brown uniform! And that white uniform! Why you be killing brown and yellow folks on the far side of the world when your own people getting shot down in the streets of America? For democracy? Listen to me: the people of Asia, South America, Africa and the Middle East aren't begging Uncle Sam to bring them democracy at the point of a gun. What did Mohammed Ali say? Ain't no Viet Cong called me nigger! They don't lynch me. Don't rape and kill my mother and father. How can I shoot them poor people? I'm not gonna help nobody get something the Negros don't have. If I'm going to die I'll die right here fighting you!

The Brave Fighting Men and Women of the Armed Forces of the United States of America my black ass! You're nothing but a pawn in the white man's game. You come back from the war, ain't nothing waiting but more guns pointed at your nappy head! Better you come back dead. You will have made the Ultimate Sacrifice for the Greater Honor and Glory of the White Devil and he will declare you a hero and declare your grieving mammies and pappies and wives and children a Gold Star Family! That's right. They will get their very own flag, with a Gold Star and a Certificate of Appreciation, in exchange for your dead black ass. Now isn't that special!

No sir, I better not catch you fighting for the white man. You tell Cracker Doodle Dandy Uncle Sam to go back to hell where he came from! It's time to fight for your own Sovereign Nation, one with its own Ministers—of Agriculture, Education, Information, Defense, Commerce, Culture, Science and Technology. And lastly, Spirituality, that we may come to know our true nature and our divine destiny, amen.

Shouts of Amen came from the audience.

Now let's talk about the R word, the Reverend said. You know what I'm talking about—reparations! Cash money! If each of fifty million African Americans was granted a mere one thousand dollars, a pittance to pay for the labor and the lost lives of our people, that's fifty billion dollars! With fifty billion dollars, and land of our own, and a vision of our Divine Destiny, we would be free of the White Devil at last! And where would we build our Sovereign Nation?

He leaned forward and spoke in a hushed and reverent tone.

Afreeka! It is our ancestral home. The good people of that great continent will welcome us with open arms! So, prepare yourself, my Brothers, for the day when you leave this stinking hell hole. Do not fight amongst yourselves. Do not do drugs, drink hooch or freak off with homosexuals. And most of all—educate yourself. Take advantage of the vocational programs here in Lime Ridge. Bring a skill back to the world, that you might contribute to the building of your own Sovereign Nation.

The Reverend paused. He looked toward the side of the gym.

I see that the Warden is pointing at his watch, he said. Telling me my time is up. But I say the white man's time is up! Him and all the Negro sycophants eating crumbs from his table. They will fall as we will rise.

He looked back at the audience. He put his hands out palms up.

I want you all to stand, he said. That's right, stand up now.

The bleachers clattered as the audience rose to its feet.

Now put your left fist in the air and repeat after me, Raise the black man up!

Raise the black man up!

Say it louder.

Raise the black man up!

Very good. Now put your right fist in the air and shout, Put the white man down!

Put the white man down!

The audience shouted with a single voice. I felt their pent up bitterness like steam in a teapot. I wondered if the lid would blow. I saw the Major talk into his radio. Saw a half dozen more green-uniformed guards enter through a side door and fan out along the wall. A window above the locker room slid open and a guard inside pumped a shotgun and rested its stock on his thigh.

The reverend put his hands out, palms down.

Very good, he said. Have a seat. I just wanted to wake you up. The white man wants you asleep in the dream he has wove for you for half a thousand years, while he's been robbing you of your power to think for your self. I hope I have given you something to think about. Thank you for your attention, my brothers.

He adjusted his glasses.

Though I have not read the script of tonight's production, he said, I'm sure it will be entertaining and instructive. I applaud the playwright and his theatre company for their commitment to the cause. I regret I cannot stay. I have a midnight flight back to Chicago, and a meeting tomorrow with some very important people. But when you hit those bricks, my brothers, come see me, The Reverend Gideon Demarcus Love. I won't be hard to find. Bring your newly acquired skills, and your love of freedom and justice, and there will be a place for you in our new United Nation of the Chosen People.

He held his right fist in the air and shouted, One love!

One love, Gideon!

You The Man!

He left the podium and passed the Warden without exchanging glances. The Major and two officers escorted him out of the gym.

Abdul chuckled.

I think the good Reverend Demarcus Love has done warmed up our audience, he said.

THE PLAYERS OF CONVICTION went behind the backdrop constructed of two-by-fours draped in white sheets stitched together by the tailor Marvelous Marvin Mayo, and illustrated as the headquarters of The Chosen Folk Nation, by Frankie Mother Goose Waters. The lights dimmed. The players of Scene One took the stage. Stevie Wonder's *Village Ghetto Land* played. The audience became attentive as the officers of The Chosen Folk Nation discussed strategies for winning the drug war and solidifying their position of dominance in the city.

In the second scene there was scattered laughter when Allegro's fellow officers chanted, Whoppo, Dago, Danté Allegro. And there were shouts of, Jack up *this*, motherfucker! when Danté crooned the lines, We jack up niggers and spics, that's how we get our kicks in Chicago.

In scene three the audience became hostile when Allegro told Shaka

Zulu he'd be banging his momma and his sisters and his babies, too.
Angry shouts rang out.

Kill that honkie motherfucker!

Kill that racist pig!

Kill that grease ball baby raper!

I was gratified. I'd become one with my character. I had my howls
of execration.

In the final scene, as the Duke made his pitch for acceptance of the
offer by Jesse Jackson, conflicting opinions were voiced.

Take the deal! Take the man's money!

Fuck that chump change! Get your life right, brother!

Likewise at the conclusion of the final scene, the garroting of the
Duke by Shaka Zulu.

Snuff his pussy ass, Shaka!

Don't do it Shaka! The White Devil done poisoned your mind!

But, as Mad Dog emptied his gun into the already dead body of the
Duke, the audience became still, perhaps because the callousness of
the deed reminded them of what they had been witness to in the real
world. And as the lights dimmed, and Shaka and Mad Dog became
immobile, and the lyrics of Stevie Wonder's *Heaven Help Us All* filled
the auditorium, and the curtain came down, there was not a sound in
the house ... until the curtain was raised and the players one by one
came out on stage and bowed, and the audience stood and applauded.
And the applause for Danté Allegro was as steady and robust as that
for any of his fellow players.

THAT NIGHT I SAT ON MY BUNK with my back to the wall. I
closed my eyes and rewound the tape of the rape of Lola to the moment I exited the car on the corner of a street darker than the last and
imagined now a different conclusion.

At the end of the block a gathering of young black men loitered
under a street light.

I'll get directions, I said.

Daddy, don't stop.

I know what I'm doing.

Oh, God.

You stay in the car.

She slid down in her seat.

I parked near the curb and got out. The gang of youth stopped talking as I approached. The smell of reefer was in the air. A bottle was being passed from hand to hand.

Yo! I said with a friendly smile.

They looked me up and down. They looked at my car. Pops, you on the wrong side of town, one of them said.

Yeah, I'm lost, I said. I zigged when I should of zagged. I'm looking for the Hilton. Can you help me out?

They gathered around me. A stocky young man in a black knit cap and a faded army fatigue jacket fingered the lapel of my black leather trench coat. Nice, he said. Where you cop your threads, old man?

A leather store in San Francisco, I said. And I'm not so old. Do I look old to you? Come on!

The young man laughed. You old, he said, and you a long way from home.

Just passing through, I said. I'm looking for the Hilton.

A tall slim youth in dreadlocks slid his fingers along the fender of my long white car. Nice ride, he said.

It's a Lincoln Continental, I said.

I can see that, the youth said. He bent down and looked through the window.

Hey, there's a bitch inside, he said.

That's my daughter, I said. We're going to the—

I know where you going, pops, the youth said. Don't have to say it again! He knocked on the window and made a rolling motion with his hand.

Lola rolled the window down and stuck her head out. She looked at me. Daddy, she said in a timid voice, are you alright?

I'm fine, Lola, stay in the car.

Lookee here now, the tall youth said. A fine bitch! Ol' boy a player! Come on out here, girl. Let's have a look at you.

Lola, stay in the car, I said.

The youth turned on me.

Someone talking to you, motherfucker?

Overhead, thunder rumbled and a flash of lighting lit the walls of the building across the street. I wondered with a sudden sick feeling if I lacked the words and the presence of mind to keep a bad situation from getting worse. Twenty years ago in the gym or on the yard of Lime Ridge, it would have been different, with only myself to look out for then, but today ...

From the back of the pack came a commanding voice.

Leave the old boy and the baby girl be, Shaka!

The tall youth straightened. I was just messing with the man, he said. Wasn't hurting nobody.

A figure stepped forward. The young gangsters parted to let him pass. He was older than they, and hard and scowling and scarred. He stepped to the window of the car.

Roll the window up, girl, he said.

He stepped in front of me and looked down without smiling. I looked up at his face, dark as buffalo hide. That scar, from his temple to the corner of his lips, like a string of knots beneath the skin— could it be?

Botha! I said.

How you know my name, motherfucker?

I'm Davis. Remember? We did time together in Lime Ridge. North One. A long time ago.

The old gangster squinted. Davis ... Davis ... .Oh, yeah, I remember your lame ass now. Downtown Brown. The reporter. Or was it Danté Allegro, the racist white cop? Whoppo, Dago, Danté Allegro! Who you jacking up these days, Danté?

Not jacking up anybody, Botha, I said, a faint hope stirring that our history together was a bond that would defuse the current situation.

This cracker a cop, Botha? Shaka said.

No, he's alright, Botha said. He just don't know who he is. Davis, why you bring your little girl to this side of town at this time of day, fool? You think you're on a cruise ship?

Cruising to the Hilton, I said. Taking my daughter to school tomorrow. But we're lost.

The man smoking a joint stepped forward and extended it to me.

Be down, he said.

I hadn't smoked in years. I looked back at my car, at Lola behind the window. I took the joint and turned away from the car and took a big hit, then another.

Right on, Brother, I said.

The man with the bottle handed it to me. I took a healthy swig and felt the cheap vodka burn my throat and my stomach and bring tears to my eyes. I smiled.

The Hilton's across town, Botha said. You got to make three left turns and four right turns and go through half a dozen lights, and your lame ass will be lost again before you get there, Davis, so you better let me show you the way.

All right, I said.

You pay my cab fare back, Botha said.

It's a deal, I said.

I had a few more hits off the joint, and off the bottle.

Cool, I said to my new friends.

I opened the right rear door of my rented Lincoln Continental and told Lola to get in the back. Botha got in the passenger seat. I drove across town. The sky opened and the rains came down. The red and the green and the yellow of traffic lights reflected off the glistening windshield. The wipers slapped rhythmically while Botha told me lefts and rights till we got to the Hilton.

I invited him into the lounge for a nightcap and to kick it about back in the day. He declined. He had to get back to his crew. I hailed a cab. Peace, brother, he said, as the cab pulled away. My head was in a good place, my faith in humanity restored.

POSTPARTUM FUNK
AND THE FUTURE OF MANKIND

ABDUL, WHAT DID MAJOR DRUMM SAY about being lampooned as Captain Drummond? Did he read you the riot act?

Abdul had brewed herb tea in the hot pot in his cell. He and I sat in the dayroom sipping, and discussing the White Devil speech and *The Nation of the Damned*. On the far side of the room, the elderly porter chain-smoked cigarettes and dealt cards to himself and an imaginary opponent. The television mounted high on the far wall played a sitcom with the sound turned off. The guard in the control room leaned back in his swivel chair reading a paperback book, his lips moving. From somewhere down B Wing the clarion notes of a jazz piano tune drifted.

Two days had passed since the night of the play, after which Abdul had suggested we wait before discussing it. I had agreed, having much to reflect upon.

The Major thanked me, Abdul said. The bonehead thought I was giving him a shout out, giving him his props. He said the Captain was the only character in the play who had any sense.

That's too funny, I said. You held up a mirror and the man liked what he saw.

Self-love, Abdul said. The most enduring kind.

Speaking of love, Abdul, I can't help but wonder what joker recommended to Warden Wainwright that the Reverend Love replace the Reverend Brown? Any ideas?

It wasn't me, Abdul said.

But you knew the Reverend …

We were recruited into the Nation of Islam at the same time. I rejected their dogma and went my way. Gideon was dismissed. He gave the Nation a bad name. He wouldn't stay on message.

But some of his message mirrors your own.

Yes, that the black community must do for itself and not be the dupe of the white man. But that community won't be in Africa, Dean.

Africa is not interested in sharing its wealth with fifty million African American immigrants, and the U.S. Government isn't going to come up off fifty billion dollars. How many African Americans want to go to Africa, anyway? We'll take our equality right here in the good old USA. Gideon doesn't have a plan. He likes to hear himself talk. He says to look him up, he won't be hard to find, but what you'll find is that he has no organization and no cause except his own big head. When he speaks of politicians and preachers who talk out the sides of their mouths, he forgets to put himself on the list. He signs off with One Love—but where is the love?

So you didn't recommend him to Wainwright?

Abdul hesitated.

No, he said, but Wainwright came to me and asked if I knew him and I said only that I heard he was a dynamic speaker on issues of race.

And you let him hire the man?

It was his choice to make.

But you concealed what you knew.

Yes.

Why?

To warm up the crowd. The Reverend has a way of waking your ass up if you're susceptible to his message.

I wondered if Abdul would have risked the Warden's confidence merely to warm up the crowd for his play. I was sure there was a deeper reason for concealing his familiarity with the Reverend. He seemed to sense my thoughts.

And to hasten the inevitable, Dean, he added. Good and evil pulse through the Universe in waves. A dark wave is welling, swollen with fury and hatred. The sooner it crests, the sooner we will have an era of peace and love, however brief. Gideon was sent to help bring the house down.

I appreciated Abdul's metaphors but longed for something more concrete.

And what can we expect to see when the wave crashes and the house comes down? I said.

Abdul's eyes became opaque, as though he were looking inward.

An increase in crime and violence on the street, he said. A growing prison population. The transfer of unruly inmates from maximum security prisons in the North to medium security prisons like Lime Ridge in the South. An emphasis on punishment and deprivation, and the elimination of rehabilitation programs. Distrust and hostility among inmates, and between inmates and the Administration. A day of reckoning, of fire and smoke and bloodshed, and the settling of old scores.

That sounds grim, Abdul. How about on the other side of these walls?

Perpetual warfare predicated on lies. Economic disparity and the demise of the middle class. Teeming homelessness and rampant unemployment. Disregard for civil liberties, loss of privacy, technology in the hands of tyrants being used against the masses, the extinction of species, the destruction of the atmosphere, and more dumb sitcoms.

Damn, Abdul! That's a freight train full of catastrophe. We might be better off locked up! Do you see anything good happening in our lifetime?

I see a black President.

Whoa! Terrific! And that will make things better?

Worse. There will be a White Backlash. The Radical Right will elect a man who embodies all the hatred and bigotry that yet dwells in the heart of America, who is truly the White Devil Gideon speaks of.

That's bad.

No, that's good. The dark wave will have crested and crashed.

After which we will have Peace and Love?

By and by. The White Devil and his cohorts will be loath to let go of their power, but the people will prevail. But how about yourself, Dean. How do you feel?

About … ?

Racism. Bigotry. The oppression of African Americans. Have these last few weeks altered your point of view?

I considered how best to reply. I wanted to be honest.

They've made me aware that it will never be my problem in the same way that it's your problem, Abdul. I can be sympathetic. I can be encouraging. I can be angry. I can be appalled. I can be of service to others if called upon. But I go to sleep white and I wake up white. I'm free to come and go. Free to think about anything or nothing at all. I guess that's White Privilege and I can't take it off like a pair of pants. My burden is to be the best Dean Davis I can at any given moment and the next moment will take care of itself. And if I behave badly, which I have and will again, I will try to learn from my mistakes and move on.

Abdul looked away, then back at me. He smiled thinly.

No one could ask for more than that, Dean, he said.

But I wondered if he found my answer wanting.

THE NEXT MORNING I VACATED my borrowed cell and packed my canvas cart. I went round to Nathan's to pay my respects and the last of my rent. He lay on his bunk reading *Ebony Magazine*.

Yo, Nathan!

He looked up. I tossed him a brick of squares. He dropped the magazine and caught the brick.

I'm all paid up, Nathan, I said. I'm out of here today and Lonnie's in. Tell him thanks for the loan.

Nathan reached over and put the brick on the cardboard box next to his bunk that served as a night table.

All right, he said.

How did you like the play, Nathan?

Made me think about shit I ain't thought about for a long time.

How about that speech?

Nathan looked around at his cell.

Don't guess I'll be going to Africa anytime soon, he said.

I went by the house of Stan the Man. He was sleeping with the pillow over his head. He'd been up half the night frying bacon and scrambling eggs and whipping up bull dick gravy for twelve hundred men. I would catch him on the yard. We would run the track together and kick it about The Sweet Science. I would ask if there was news about his son, Rashan.

I went by the house of Abdul. I peered through the window. He sat in deep meditation, his long legs wrapped in a full lotus, his hands loose on his knees, palms up, his lids heavy behind which he dwelt in a sanctum sanctorum to which I did not have the credentials to enter. It was just as well. When the curtain came down on *The Nation of the Damned* it seemed to me that a curtain came down on our relationship as I knew it. Abdul went into a kind of post-partum funk, a limbo mode, to await an evolving future. Last night's conversation had a certain conclusiveness about it. When I bade him good night, there was in his response a tone of disregard. He once told me, When you are gone, you will have never been. I accepted that if Abdul were to have an inner circle, I would not be in it. But I would always treasure the privilege of having known the man.

THE GREAT SAN FRANCISCO
CHRONICLE RIOT

SWING LOW, SWEET CHARIOT

NORTH ONE WAS NOT THE HOUSE it was when I left it two months ago. I could feel it in the air. I pushed my cart to the door of 12B, Buster's old cell. Pauly the Paperboy came down the corridor wrapped in a towel, trailing wet footprints on the concrete floor.

Double D, you moving back in? What's up?

I got homesick. Where's Buster?

They cut him loose. His Petition for Post Conviction Relief came through.

No way! After all this time? Incredible!

Yeah, well ...

What?

The fucker's dead, man.

What!?

His old man shot him in the head. He hadn't been home a week. Woody the Screw brought the news.

I struggled to comprehend. I looked down the corridor at nothing.

I know, man, Pauly said. There weren't a whole lot of spooks I gave a flying fuck about.

Who else is gone? I said.

Old Man Mosley.

They let him out?

They carried him out.

THE BAD NEWS DRAINED ME of any enthusiasm for putting my seventy-five square feet of living space in order one last time. I removed my books and papers and personal effects from the white canvas cart and stacked them wherever I could. I closed my door and lay on my bunk. Soon I drifted like smoke into a subterranean chamber of sleep filled with the voices of The Ghosts of North One Past: Old Man Mosley's mournful voice singing *Swing Low Sweet Chariot* through the common wall of our adjoining cells; his crusty belligerent voice declaring, I ain't paying no goddamned million dollars for no goddamned chicken shack! Get my own motherfucking chicken shack! Buster's booming voice lamenting: That bitch, Belinda, flapping her nasty pussy lips for my goddamned cousin in the back seat of my Eldorado while she sposa be home taking care of my kids!

FOR THE SECOND TIME SINCE I'D ARRIVED in Lime Ridge, Botha came round to my house. I waited for him to speak.

You're all right, Davis, he said. Just keep doing what you're doing. It ain't about you and me. It never was.

He walked away. I was stunned. I wondered what had prompted this unlikely pronouncement. Did something seen or heard the night of the play account for the man's capitulation? Or had my casting of him as the Good Samaritan during the deprogramming of the Rape Of Lola been stored in the Akashic Records, then conducted ethereally to his subconscious mind, there to awaken a dormant wellspring of goodwill? I felt vindicated yet profoundly sad. Botha had been secure in his identity as an uncompromised straight-up gangster who killed motherfuckers who got in his business, but with this seeming admission that his thug life had been a waste, what did he have now? What was an old gangster like him to do? How would he get his groove back? What statement could he make?

HORDES OF THE UNRULY

MEANWHILE ON THE STREETS OF CHICAGO shots rang out and the death toll rose. The public and the press decried the lack of police protection. Cops in leather coats and checkered hats pulled their pistols and swung their billy clubs with abandon. Somber judges in regal robes rapped their gavels resoundingly. Cook County Jail and maximum security penitentiaries filled to capacity, and hordes of the unruly descended from the North.

All of the South House and half of the East were now double-bunked. Fights broke out in dayrooms and in the gym, solitary confinement was standing room only, and lock-downs and shake-downs were commonplace.

The chow hall, too, was a hotbed of hostility. Fish lines were longer and more frequent, and the banter between newly arrived prisoners and current residents was loud and aggressive as alliances were renewed, meetings on the yard or in the gym arranged, and insults and threats between old rivals exchanged. The guard-staff doubled in numbers and they patrolled the aisles with heightened vigilance.

I observed these deteriorating conditions from a distance. I was in them but not of them. I had no ties to the new arrivals, no friendships to restore, no score to settle, no unpaid debts for which to be held accountable. Why then, I wondered, was one particular African American inmate in the fish line, his head a mess of dreadlocks like the serpents of Medusa, pointing his finger at me and grinning like a fool?

I WALKED THE YARD ALONE. The last snow of the winter of '88 had melted, and dandelions, like curious children, poked their yellow heads above the tufts of new green grass. The sky was the purest, palest blue, the breeze a kiss from a baby's lips. I closed my eyes and inhaled the scent of a brand new day, but I wasn't fooled by the tranquility of nature this morning. All around the track inmates huddled in small groups, talking furtively and eyeing other groups with suspicion and malice. From loudspeakers in the watchtowers blared the frequent command to Break it up! Only three inmates to a group at one time! Break it up! Then groups would disperse, only to reform elsewhere on the yard. I thought, To hell with these jokers and their petty intrigues. Their business was not my business; I was only passing through.

I rounded the bottom of the track and started up the other side. I noticed a group of three black inmates eyeing me closely. I recognized the one with a head full of dreadlocks as the one who had grinned and pointed his finger at me in the chow hall.

Yo, white boy, he said. Come here.

I stood my ground.

Come here, man, I just want to kick it a minute.

I walked to the group and looked closely at the dreadlocked inmate.

Do I know you? I said.

Know me and owe me, homey!

What I owe you, Rasta Mon?

Owe me eleven roses.

It all came back in a flash: Cornelius Corn Dog Watson! The real live nigger led away in handcuffs almost five years ago, who said he'd be back to make the joint jump, and here he was—and with a brand new head of hair!

I recalled my confusion when Corn Dog had demanded a dozen red roses, which hadn't been the deal at all.

I don't owe you shit, Corn Dog, I said. We're all squared up.

I don't think so, white boy. We ain't squared up till I get paid.

Done been paid, Corn Dog. This a brand new day.

The day I jack you up, I don't get my roses.

We can go right now if you want, I said, guessing Corn Dog would back off, having been expelled from Lime Ridge once already for making his move too soon.

One of Corn Dog's partners punched him on the arm.

Damn, Corn Dog. This cracker calling you out. You better put his ass in check!

Corn Dog shrugged.

I'll deal with this lightweight when the time come, he said.

You'll know where to find me, I said. I won't be faraway.

Corn Dog nodded toward the track.

Go ahead on, man. We'll meet again.

I rounded the top of the track. The sun was warm on my neck and shoulders. I marveled at the shapes of the clouds gathering over the

tree line that bordered the Mississippi River west of Lime Ridge, beyond which, two thousand miles and four months away, was home.

MORNING YARD WAS BEST FOR RUNNING on hot summer
days. The sun was low, the heat not yet risen from the earth like a
belch from hell, and there were fewer thugs present to rile things up.

I felt the steady beat of my heart. Twenty-five pounds lighter than
when I arrived, and thousands of running miles later, I felt I could
go on forever, that I could sprint from the south side of the track to
the north, and leap over the razor wire fence in a single bound, hit
the ground running and not stop till I had passed Kansas City and
Denver and Reno and Oakland, and crossed the Bay Bridge and the
Golden Gate Bridge and pulled up in front of Lucy's apartment in
Sausalito, my running shoes still smoking.

I reflected on recent events: the disbanding of the Honor Dorm,
its residents divested of privileges and scattered to houses throughout the camp; the transfer of Warden Wainwright to a Minimum
Security Facility further South; and the cancellation of The Players of
Conviction, the Jaycees, SEIU's Bachelor's Degree program, and the
prison's boxing team. Nostradamus had nothing on Abdul's predilec-
tion for prophecy.

Footsteps fell in alongside me.

Stan!

What's up, Flea Weight?

Everything's good, I said. Sorry about your team, though. That's
tough.

There's worse things to lose, Stan said bitterly.

He handed me a piece of newsprint. I stopped running and regarded
a grainy photo of two black youth sprawled on the sidewalk, one
face down, the other doing a death stare into the camera. Two cops
stood over them, looking bored. The caption said the victims were
suspected gang members killed by unknown assailants in the early
morning hours.

The one in front with his eyes open, that's my boy, Rashan, Stan
said. His momma, the bitch, she don't even put a fucking note with

the picture, just sticks it in the mail. The bitch!

He ran off down the track alone, leaving me holding the news.

I WAS ESCORTED TO THE OFFICE of a middle-aged white-haired woman with a kind face, wearing a long black skirt, a white cotton blouse and a necklace of black beads.

Please sit down, Dean, she said.

The guard remained beside the door. I sat. I didn't like that the woman had called me Dean, nor the note of condolence in her voice, which augured ominous news.

You've had a death in the family, she said.

I caught my breath. I quickly tallied my family members: Lucy, Lola, my mother, my brother and Wally.

Who? I said.

You're father-in-law, she said.

Wally! I said.

I'm so sorry, she said.

How? When?

We know only that your wife called this morning. Would you like to call her now? I can step out of the office.

No, I said. I mean yes. I mean … I'll need a moment.

I'm very sorry, she said.

There will be a funeral, I said. She'll need me there.

The woman's face told me I wouldn't be there.

Inmates are only allowed to attend the funerals of immediate family members, she said: Mother, father, brother, sister, wife or child. I'm sorry.

But she has no one else …

I'm sorry.

I wished the woman would stop saying she was sorry. The words were no consolation. I wondered what words I might use to console Lucy. I wondered, too, if I would ever forgive myself for the relief I felt when informed of which family member had passed.

For wishing Wally dead.

I'll make that call now, I said.

PITTSBURGH WAS KNOWN for the Steel Curtain, Denver the Orange Crush. The Broncos defense changed from a 4-3 alignment to a 3-4 alignment in 1976. Dubbed the Orange Crush by sportswriter Woody Paige because of the team's orange uniforms, and its intensity and teamwork on the field, it became one of the dominant defenses of its era. The Broncos won the AFC Championship and played in the Super Bowl in 1987, the year before Lime Ridge State Penitentiary formed its own anti-riot defensive unit. Dressed in polyester orange jumpsuits, combat boots, fiberglass shields and helmets, and wielding bone-busting hardwood batons, they were drilled daily on the yard throughout the summer and into the Fall of '88 by the fanatical Major Drumm, and became known as The Orange Crush by inmates who eyed them warily.

Sergeant Woody Buffett, a popular guard on the day shift in North One, and a member of The Orange Crush, expressed his feelings to me in a moment of candor.

Our guys are very emotional, Davis, he said. We train hard and we train for each other. It's very exciting to be a part of this special team and we look forward to the day we put our training into play and our lives on the line. We hope you guys don't disappoint.

A HOUSING UNIT ON A HOT AUGUST NIGHT simmered like the hold of a steamer up the Amazon. Constructed of cinder blocks, it soaked up the sun all day, then released its heat and humidity upon its hapless residents till long after sundown. With no air conditioning and little ventilation and one hundred men milling about, the walls of the cells seemed to perspire.

Pauly paid me a visit dressed in a threadbare towel tied around his waist and a pair of flip-flops. Fresh from the shower, his long hair hung limply past his shoulders. He gave me a friendly rap to the chest with his knuckles.

Damn, Double D, he said, you're getting short, aren't you, bro?

Sixty-four days and a wake-up, Pauly. Not that I'm keeping track.

I know you're going to hit those bricks in a minute and make up for lost time!

Do my best, I said.

I sensed that in spite of the cordial banter, Pauly was a man on a mission. I cut to the chase.

What's up, Pauly?

The boss needs a favor before you go.

I didn't know I had a boss, I said, though I had no doubt who Pauly referred to.

Ten shanks, Pauly said. You've got the steel and the grinders and the opportunity. You know Bobo?

I do.

He's in the bakery next to the welding shop. When he goes out the back door for a smoke, you go out and have one with him. Pass him two shanks a day for a week, then you'll be square with the man.

Not going to happen, Pauly.

Why not?

I don't smoke.

That's the wrong answer.

It's the only answer I've got.

That's too bad, Double D, but I'll pass it along.

I WAS SORRY TO SEE ODUM AGAIN, but with the recidivism rate hovering at sixty percent, I was not surprised. I'd last seen him a year ago walking the track alone. It was one of the few times I had seen him not in the company of a pack of his fellow xenophobes and I ventured to say hello.

Billy, how've you been?

Ain't how I've been, Bud. It's how I'm gonna be!

How's that, Billy?

I'm fixin to pull up. Y'ain't gonna see my white ass again, Davis. Tomorrow it's gonna be Jack Daniels straight up and a Pabst Blue Ribbon behind it, by God!

You sure know your liquor, Billy, I said.

My liquor and my women. Yessiree, Bob!

Now here he was back and signed up for welding.

Welcome to the program, Billy, I said.

Thanks, Bud, he said. I'm gonna get it right this time. I figure if I can learn me a skill, I might could find a gal to make babies with and buy ourselves a lil ol farmhouse high on a hill.

That would be nice, Odum, I said. I'm here for you. If there's anything I can do, just ask.

Thanks, Davis. You're all right by me.

Odum didn't do well in the classroom, where he had no interest in welding theory, but he applied himself in the shop, especially to the grinder and the scrap metal bin. Soon he was seen slipping out the back door to have a smoke with Bobo next door. Two weeks after he enrolled, Odum quit the program.

PAULY'S SMILE SEEMED GENUINE. We hadn't spoken since I had refused his request for shanks.

Double D, he said. Are you still getting that San Francisco paper?

I am, I said. I have a dozen of them under my bunk right now. Unread and rolled-up tight.

Give them to me, Double D. The boys would like to read them.

I hesitated. I was loath to part with my papers for sentimental reasons. I no longer read them, but my subscription had outlived Wally and they seemed like a gift from beyond the grave. I had a hunch why they were wanted now, and it wasn't for the Pink Pages or the Far Side cartoons. But that was not my business and I was sure Wally would understand.

All right, I said.

I retrieved them from under my bunk and stacked them into Pauly's arms like firewood. Perhaps I had paid my debt to Herr Mann.

THE JOINT JUMPS

ON THE MORNING OF MY FORTIETH BIRTHDAY, two weeks before my scheduled release, I did one thousand push-ups on the cold concrete floor of my cell, fifty every fifteen minutes for five hours. I could not have done this when I came to Lime Ridge five years ago, but I was not the same person I was then. Having arrived a proud but diminished outlaw loath to let go of my glory days, but yearning for a new and better self, I had assumed a series of identities, donning and discarding them like suits of clothes: Flea Weight. Double D. Dean the Destroyer. Daddy Dean. Downtown Brown. Danté Allegro. I had taken the best of each of these alter egos and incorporated them into a new self which I would take out into The Real World and begin a new life.

While I was doing my time on one side of the wall, Lucy had been doing hers on the other side, and we had grown apart. It was time to grow together again. Going forward, I would be Dean Davis, husband, father, brother and son. And if that wasn't enough, a teller of tales. A resuscitator of the living dead. A rat scouring the cellars of the souls of the damned, nibbling at the crumbs of their despair.

Or not. Time would tell.

That evening I ran the track alone. A jagged cloud, like a piece broken off from an iceberg, drifted across an otherwise empty sky. The yard was crowded. On the north side, Major Drumm, his bwana helmet perched on his head like a giant walnut shell, walked the track flanked by two Lieutenants. In the center of the yard, Abdul sat in a yoga pose, still as a statue. I sprinted the last of twenty laps, then stopped on the south side of the track to catch my breath. I saw Abdul lean forward, put his forearms on the ground, cup his hands together, put his head into the cup of his hands, and rise slowly into a perfect headstand. As if on cue, the crowd on the north side erupted into frantic activity. Figures ran to and fro, shouting and swinging. Major Drumm went down beneath a mob. Shots were fired. Tear gas canisters burst with a popping sound, and toxic fumes wafted across the lawn. From between two housing units, the Orange Crush emerged four abreast, batons at the ready, their boots thumping the ground in unison. Loudspeakers crackled orders to lay face down on the ground with arms outstretched.

I felt the first blow beneath my left shoulder blade, dull yet piercing, a second blow above the first, and a third to the right of my spine. I arched my back and fell to my knees, then slumped forward. A figure ran past. I did not see who.

When carried across the yard on a stretcher a long while later, my vision dimming, I observed Abdul yet standing on his head, straight as the axis round which the wheel of the Universe spun.

I ROSE THROUGH THE RARIFIED AIR of anesthesia like a hot air balloon through layers of cloud. I had a fading memory of frolicking with Miranda in some faraway place. I blinked away the bright light. A woman in starched white linen stood like an apparition.

Doctor, she said, your patient is awake.

My wounds were not life-threatening, I was informed by the slim, bespectacled young MD who had patched me up. No vital organs pierced. But I'd lain on the yard a long time and lost a lot of blood, and there had been some anxious moments.

Someone was looking out for you, Davis, the Doctor said.

Will there be scars? I said.

Yes, there will be.

Good.

How so?

Souvenirs, I said. Proof that it hasn't all been a dream.

I WAS KEPT IN THE COUNTY HOSPITAL under guard for three days, then transferred to the infirmary of Lime Ridge State Penitentiary. My torso was taped, my arm immobilized in a sling. I spent the next four days convalescing and getting the lowdown: three guards and a dozen inmates suffered an assortment of bone breaks and punctures. Otto Mann took a shank to the larynx. He wouldn't be singing Das Deutschlandlied any time soon. Berserker took a baton to his tibia. He'd be laid up for a while, but would live to rage again. The Valkyrie would have to wait. Another dozen inmates were overcome by smoke inhalation, having foolishly set their mattresses afire in the mostly unventilated housing units. And there were three fatalities: Botha, of a bullet through the heart moments after swinging a twenty-five pound bar like a baseball bat into the base of the skull of Major Drumm, nearly taking his head off; the Major, who was probably dead before he hit the ground; and, of multiple stab wounds, Choo Choo Rodriguez, El Muchacho Loco, who would not in this lifetime become the Oldest Puerto Rican on the Planet.

The riot made national news.

I called Lucy.

No, baby, I'm fine, I assured her. It was just a minor scuffle. Well, yes, three deaths ... but out of twelve hundred men? No, really, I'm fine. No, I did not set my mattress on fire. I will see you in a week! I can't believe I will see you in a week!

I had made light of events for Lucy's sake, but I grieved for the loss of Botha and Choo Choo. I would carry their memories to the grave.

I had mixed emotions about the demise of Major Drumm.

I WAS CALLED BEFORE A COMMITTEE of four Department of Corrections officials in a bright bare room. They sat on folding chairs behind two folding tables. I was directed to a chair facing them by an unsmiling woman in a pantsuit and glasses. Her hair was short and brushed back severely. She seemed vaguely familiar. She had a file before her. She slid her glasses down the bridge of her nose and regarded me without expression.

Do you know why you are here, Mr. Davis? she said.

I had seen that gesture and heard that voice before—Judy Blue Eyes! I knew better than to greet her like an old friend. This was serious business.

No, I said. I don't.

We are conducting an inquiry into the circumstances leading up to the recent disturbance here at Lime Ridge. We would like to ask you a few questions.

I refrained from saying Twenty is the limit. I had nothing left to prove.

Whatever I can do to help, I said.

Thank you, Mr. Davis.

She pushed her glasses back in place. She opened a file and perused a page. She fixed her blue eyes on me.

Within a month of incarceration, she said, you refused a work assignment and were sent to solitary confinement. Is that correct?

Yes, I said. There were extenuating circumstances, but that is factually correct.

You were reprimanded for conducting unauthorized interviews with fellow inmates regarding gang business and homosexual activity. Is that correct?

Academic research for a professor, I said. When informed that the interviews were inappropriate I stopped.

The late Major Drumm characterized you as cunning, calculating and conspiratorial. Would do you make of that?

I'm sure he had his reasons, I said. He seemed a very thorough and conscientious man.

Judy noted my file.

You have been observed in conversation with many of the principals in last week's riot, she said. Would you care to comment on that?

There aren't many inmates I haven't had a conversation with in the last five years.

Was the subject of any of these conversations the riot or events leading up to it?

No. It was none of my business.

Are you aware that the shanks used in the riot were made in the welding shop of which you are Inmate Assistant Foreman?

No, I am not.

And you have no knowledge of how those weapons might have gotten from the shop into the hands of the inmates involved in the riot?

That is correct. There are many students in the program who have access to materials and tools.

Are you aware that many of the white combatants in the riot had wrapped their torsos in the *San Francisco Chronicle* for protection against stabbing?

No, I am not.

But you are the only inmate in Lime Ridge to have ever had a subscription to the *San Francisco Chronicle*. How did they get into the hands of other inmates?

When I finished reading them I put them out in the dayroom. They quickly disappeared.

And you have no knowledge into whose hands they disappeared?

That is correct.

Judy turned to her fellow Committee members.

Does anyone have additional questions? No? Very well. I would like to acknowledge that Mr. Davis has been commended by the former Warden of Programs, Wesley Wainwright, as an exemplary inmate who strove to be an inspiration to his fellows; that his Civilian Supervisor Booker T Williams regards him as a model inmate and a conscientious assistant, and that he was the first inmate to graduate from Southeastern Illinois University's Bachelors Degree Program.

I share that honor with Randy Bone, I said.

She put her hands together on the table.

You'll be notified of our findings in five to ten days, Mr. Davis.

But I'm scheduled to be released in a week! I said. What if—

Your release may be delayed until a finding is made. If the Committee determines that you had a role in the riot, your release will be delayed by however many days of good time are taken from you.

The maximum of which is … ?

An amount equal to the time you have served.

I winced.

Do I have a right to an attorney?

This is not a Court of Law, Mr. Davis.

I said nothing.

We'll be in touch, she said.

I stood. I felt light-headed.

Thank you for your time and consideration, Ms. Sorenson, I said.

You're welcome, Mr. Davis.

She closed my file.

I was escorted back to the infirmary by a slouching guard with red hair and a handlebar mustache. The skies were an angry grey, behind which a silvery light struggled to shine.

LEAVING THE MONASTERY

I CALLED LUCY AND TOLD HER there was a bureaucratic blunder and my release might be delayed a few days. But not to worry. They would get it straight. Only don't fly out to meet me at the gate, I said. Save the airfare. The State will give me a Grey Hound Bus ticket home. I can watch the countryside roll by. I'll call the day they cut me loose and tell you when I arrive.

She protested, but I insisted, though a Greyhound Bus ride sitting up was the last way I wanted to spend my first three days a free man. Assuming I would be one.

FOUR DAYS BEFORE MY SCHEDULED release, I was given the choice of waiting in Protective Custody or returning to North One. I chose North One. I had nothing to fear. Whoever had done the hacking had gotten their pound of flesh.

North One felt like a ghost town and me a ghost in it. A diminishing presence. Abdul's words echoed: When you are gone, you will have never been.

Pauly the Paperboy was in Solitary Confinement awaiting transfer to a max joint. I fancied he stopped a shank with a Far Side cartoon. I would remember him fondly. Extra, extra, read all about it! I want some pussy and I'm going to shout it! A defiant refrain, it would echo down the corridor of my memory long after I left Lime Ridge.

Botha's absence was palpable, like a howling wind that suddenly ceased. I went to the house of Mother Goose. She wore a blue ribbon around her neck.

Sorry about Botha, Frankie, I said. He was a good man.

Mother Goose released a deep quivering sigh.

Maria has not come out of her house since they shot him, she said. I bring her food every day.

Give her my best, Frankie.

I will, she said.

She looked at my sling.

Who did this to you, Dean, Honey?

Don't know, I said. And don't care.

Because I didn't.

FORTY-EIGHT HOURS BEFORE MY scheduled release I was called to the Control Room and given an envelope with my name on it. I extracted the folded letter inside, on Official Department of Corrections letterhead.

> *Mr. Davis,*
> *It is the finding of this Committee that you bear no culpability in the events leading up to the recent riot. You will be released as scheduled.*
> *Judy Sorenson LCSW*

Below, handwritten, was added:

> *Pack your bags, Dean. You're going home.*

I breathed a sigh of relief. I hadn't realized I'd been holding my breath for five days. I would call Lucy the morning of the day I walked through those gates. I would tell her when to expect me, and would use that big old lumbering Greyhound Bus as a kind of decompression chamber to ease my passage back to the real world.

TWENTY FOUR HOURS BEFORE MY RELEASE I gave Wilbur my electric typewriter and my books, all but *The Science of Mind*, which I would keep for myself, and *The Prophecies of Nostradamus*, which I gave to Rusty Bone.

Tell our stories, Double D, Wilbur said. Don't let us be forgotten! We're dying in here!

We shall see what we shall see, Wilbur, I said. But you keep writing yours. I loved them. They took me away when I needed to be somewhere else.

To Willis I gave my Hot Pot, my cassette player and cassettes, my electric fan and my television. I put my remaining stash of whams and zooms on a table in the dayroom. I kept for myself my journal, my gold medal, my denim jacket hooked up real tough by Marvelous Marvin Mayo, my drawing of North One 11A, my small-speck-of-a-bird bookmark, and my picture frame fashioned of cigarette package paper by Cornelius Corn Dog Watson.

For Rusty the Drummer I agreed to go by the Mitchell Brothers' O'Farrell St. Theatre in San Francisco and inquire after his wife Beatrice, stage name Honey Bee.

She's a stripper there, Rusty said. Or was. She took my money but doesn't take my calls. I just want her to know that I love her and miss her and when I'm out of here, we'll be together again. Back to the island. Just like old times. Talk to Artie. Artie Mitchell. He'll know where to find her.

I sent a kite to my old boss:

> *Booker T,*
> *Thanks for the coffee and the conversation. May the blues*
> *never die.*
> *Your friend, Dean*

Regretfully, I did not have the opportunity to say goodbye to Stan the Man. I would never forget him, nor his admonition to Raise that baby up right, Flea Weight. You only get one time around. Abdul and I would meet again if he so chose … and it would be as if no time had passed at all.

That same day in the mail I received from Brodie a poem on a page torn from a book:

> *LEAVING THE MONASTERY EARLY*
> *IN THE MORNING*
> *In bed, asleep, I dream*
> *I am a butterfly.*
> *A crowing cock wakes me*
> *Like a blow.*
> *The sun rises*
> *Between foggy mountains.*
> *Mist hides the distant crags.*
> *My long retreat is over.*
> *My worries begin again.*
> *Laughing monks are gathering*

Branches of peach blossoms
For a farewell present.
But no stirrup cup will sustain
Me on my journey back
Into a world of troubles.
                              - Lu Yu

ON THE MORNING OF MY RELEASE I was summoned to the infirmary. My sling was removed. My stitches would dissolve in time.

I called Lucy. I got her answering machine. I could not leave a message. I would call her from a payphone at the bus station and tell her they got the date straight, and I would arrive at the station on Folsom Street in San Francisco at ten o'clock Monday morning.

I went from office to office till I got ever closer to the bright light of day and the blue skies of freedom. At each stop along the way the personnel processing my release seemed to share my feelings, a mix of joy and trepidation. Some said, Good luck out there, Mr. Davis.

In the far wall of the final foyer, a threshold upon the real world, the morning sun shone through glass doors that opened onto a parking lot. To the right of the door, from a bench reserved for visitors, rose a woman and a child. They stood and faced me, hand in hand, backlit by the bright light, seeming to have materialized from another time and place.

Lola, say hello to your daddy, the woman said.

My little girl stepped back behind her mother's leg.

Go on, Lola, Lucy said, say hi to your daddy.

Lola stepped forward timidly and stopped in front of me.

Hi, daddy, she said.

Hi, Lola, I said.

I knelt on one knee and held out my arms.

Lola retreated to her mother's leg.

She's shy, Lucy said.

I stood.

How did you know? I said.

I called every day, she said. Did you think I'd let you ride a Greyhound bus sitting up the first three days of your freedom? I don't think so!

She stepped forward into my arms and we embraced for the first time in a very long time.

LA PETITE MAISON REDUX

THE SPINES OF THE OLD BOOKS on the shelves around the room glowed warmly in the light of the fire. I ordered the catch of the day with mango salsa, asparagus spears and a crisp Chardonnay. Lucy ordered crab salad with herb vinaigrette and a bottle of mineral water—her condition precluded drinking alcohol—and for Lola three-cheese macaroni and chocolate milk.

Michael, the waiter, brought Lola crayons and a placemat to draw on. She drew intently, pressing hard and pursing her lips. She looked up at me.

Daddy, she said, why do we always set a place for Poppa when we come here? He's in heaven!

The food is better here, I said. What are you drawing?

A pig! she said.

She turned the mat for me to see.

That's good, Lola, I said. It has a curly tail. But it only has one eye. Why does it only have one eye?

She frowned.

I don't know, daddy, she said.

Give it another eye, I said.

Okay, Daddy, she said.

She drew another eye.

That's better, I said. Now the pig is happy.

How was the writing today? Lucy said.

Good. *Making, making, someday made.* Do you remember the first time you came to visit and they turned you away because I was in the hole?

How could I forget?

I finished the story of that incident. It's called *Slaughter House Jive*. Would you like to read it?

If you want me to.

I do, I said. I'll print it for you tomorrow.

All right, she said. How was the visit with your Mother?

She's in high spirits. She's weaving a blanket for the white stallion she plans to ride from Bucharest, Romania, to her ancestral village outside Calcutta, India, to rendezvous with her long lost relatives. She invited me to ride along. I declined, citing Lola's Gymboree schedule.

I'm sorry ...

Don't be. She might be the happiest person I know.

Present company excluded, Lucy said.

She reached across the table and slid her fingertips up my forearm to my bicep and squeezed.

Hey, no touching above the elbow, I said.

She slipped off her sandal and slid her toe up my pant leg.

Or beneath the table, I said.

She put her hand on her abdomen.

Ouch! she said. I think the little man is awake.

Can I feel? Lola said.

Lucy took Lola's hand and held it where Bertie kicked.

Lola smiled.

He's trying to fly, she said. But he's trapped in your belly!

BACK AT THE COTTAGE WE PUT LOLA to bed beneath the painting of Mother Goose. I tucked her in. She lay on her back twirling a lock of hair around her finger.

I'm glad you're home, Daddy, she said.

I'm glad I'm home, too, Baby.

But you look funny, Daddy.

Why do I look funny?

I don't know. You just do.

She turned on her side. She put her little hands together as though in prayer and slid them under her cheek. Her eyes closed and her lips parted like the beak of a little bird.

Good night, Lola, I whispered.

Kids say the darnedest things, Lucy said.

I went downstairs. I built a fire. I put a CD in the player. Johnny Mathis promised: Until the twelfth of never, I'll still be loving you.

Dance with me, Lucy, I said.

We moved slowly in the glow of the fire.

I'm glad you're home, too, she said.

I'm glad to be here, I said.

Come to bed, she said.

Soon, I said.

I SAT AT THE BAR AND POURED a snifter of brandy. The fire sputtered and popped. Shadows danced on the walls like playful spirits. I smiled. Lucy had surprised me all right. She might have gotten her secret-keeping skills from Wilbur. En route from the airport the day of my return she had said, Before we go home I want to show you something.

All right, I said.

But you have to wear this, she said.

She put a blindfold over my eyes. She drove to the cottage. She pulled the blindfold off.

Welcome home, she said.

Month's earlier it had been the first anniversary of Wally's birthday since he had passed away, and Lucy's heart ached. The cottage was the last place we had all been together. In a sentimental mood, she took Lola and drove to see it. An old woman tended flowers out front. Lucy sat in her car and watched and thought how that could have been her one day. The old woman approached.

Can I help you, dear? she said.

Lucy told her she used to live there, and her daughter was born there, and they had loved the house but had had to move. The old woman smiled.

Why, dear, it's for sale, she said. I bought it five years ago and it's been lovely, but now I'm too old to live alone. I'll be spending my last days with my children. It goes on the market tomorrow.

I wasted no time, Lucy told me. It was our house and no one else was getting it! Between Dad's life insurance and the remains of his retirement, she said, there was more than enough for the down payment. I decided to surprise you.

You've done that, I said. What was the old woman's name?

Miranda, she said.

Of course, I said.

I rolled a joint and stepped outside. A breeze soft as a fairy's breath brushed my cheek. I took a bountiful hit off the joint and held it till a space opened in my head. I gazed skyward: a blue cloud draped the upper half of the moon like the lid of a winking eye.

I know you're up there, I said. Good looking out, girl.

I stepped to the edge of the deck and relieved myself into the bushes. I liked to piss outside, the old penis pent up in the pants all day.

It felt like freedom.

THE END

ABOUT THE AUTHOR

EA LUETKEMEYER'S short fiction has appeared in *Sou'wester, Opium Magazine, Del Sol Review, Commonthought, Perversion Magazine, The Ilanot Review*, and the anthology *Stories That Must Be Told*. He is the author of the novel *Inside the Mind of Martin Mueller*, the memoir *The Book of Chuck: A Memorial Compilation of Poetry and Prose*, and is knee-deep in his next novel, *The Outlaw Ethan James*.

He has been a martial artist, a long distance runner, an outlaw, a fugitive, a husband and father, and sometimes a fool. In the eighties, he spent four years in a state penitentiary for possession of marijuana, an experience he embraces and which informs much of his work and his worldview.

His stories are not for everyone. The good guys don't always win, and the bad guys don't always lose. The language is explicit, the situations dicey, the characters debased, and the reader will be taken to places best visited on the page.

He lives and writes between the San Francisco Bay Area and Southern Oregon and favors the trite but true adage that bad roads lead to good stories.

In 2015 he was awarded an MFA in Creative writing from Lesley University, Cambridge, MA.

His website is **www.ealuetkemeyer.com**

www.ingramcontent.com/pod-product-compliance
Lightning Source LLC
Chambersburg PA
CBHW070047120726
47909CB00002B/311

* 9 780578 581224 *